"Pure Heart Guide"
(Lev Antas Shuesa)

Book 1

"TWIN LAKES"

Author:
STEPHEN HULS

First Edition 2015

Twin Lakes
Pure Heart Guide
(Book 1)

© 2014. All Rights are reserved by the Author Stephen T. Huls, no copies can be created in part of full in any format of print, electronic, audio, film, or future technology of any kind, with out the written permission from the author.

Print ISBN: 978-1-66784-1-489

eBook ISBN: 978-1-66784-1-496

CONTENTS

Introduction 1
A Letter Found 5
Prologue 7
1. Family Gathering 19
2. Box of Mystery 44
3. Twin Lakes 59
4. Curiosity of Boys 74
5. Exploring the Cave 98
6. Search and Rescue 120
7. Lev Antas Shuesa 131
8. Harvester 148
9. Truths Learned 166
10. Intruders 191
11. Cave Fight 206
12. A Mother's Rage 223
13. Lab Rat 242
14. Moving the Dead 258
15. Uncle Travis 273
16. Adair's Homestead 285
17. Council of Spirit Owl 289
18. Searchers Assemble 297

19. Warriors come to Beaver 301
20. Missing team and questions 305
21. Final Gathering Before Entering The Darkness .. 317
22. The Search Begins 330
23. Missing Memories 346
24. The Prisoner 350
25. New Specie's 367
26. Another Failure 379
27. Searchers Discovered 384
28. Mistrust and Assumptions 391
29. Eeeleesssoe Speaks 401
30. Master Keronkenken 406
31. The Watcher 422
32. Getting Close 434
33. Prisoner Rescue 443
34. Rumblings of War 457

INTRODUCTION

I find in life many people have similar idea's or dream's that are never acted upon due to self-doubt, fear, life getting in the way, many reasons, then people you share your idea with may tell you it is not possible for you to achieve that dream or goal, you do not have the education, the skills, the money, etc. They knowingly or unknowingly steal your dream.

Life is full of challenges in our daily living we tend to focus so much upon survival our family and other responsibilities its normal to subdue our personal creativities.

However when we take a moment for peace and quiet we can listen to the distant suggestions placed upon our minds and then work to achieve that which may seem out of reach.

When we choose a thought or idea and plant it in our heart and soul as we would a seed in a garden. Then we must take the time to nourish it and care for it so it has the opportunity to grow and become what it is meant to be.

That is how this book series has come to be. There was a lingering thought back in the spring of 2006 about this story. It would come and go teasing my mind and my dreams; I could see the story come alive before my eyes from time to time. So I finally began writing it down. I will share some background to help put this into perspective.

Life is what it is; everyone has different trials and experiences. It has been said that we shall never be given anything we cannot overcome, with Gods assistance. This thought has helped our family during the last 31 years to keep going. I share this to say, you can overcome whatever is placed before you, keep walking one step at a time, leaning upon others as needed to survive life's challenges. Even though life is full of distractions you can slowly achieve your dreams.

Life is a journey full of trials and miracles, light and darkness and lots of gray areas that we need to all journeys through, I hope in the telling of this story it can help others to deal with the issues of life, and walk towards the path of light and truth, and in helping others as best one can.

Nothing ventured nothing gained, it is said everyone has at least one story in them, but it is up to us to share it. I am sharing one of mine here. I hope you enjoy it; I do like the writing when time permits, after this one is published I shall work on book 2 a lot is written in my mind already.

Someday I shall finish the whole 5 book series at least for my children and friends to enjoy; I hope others on Earth may enjoy it as well. Anything is possible if you never quit, you may not be as good as others, however the prize goes to those who have the courage and tenacity to never ever quit. The parable of the race between the rabbit and the tortoise, remember the tortoise wins because it never quit when all odds were against it, and it won in the end.

You see the real story is not that which I have written; it is a joint experience between what the words are on paper and what you have created them to be in your mind. Together the writer and the reader create the true life of a story; I hope it is a good one for you.

—S.T. Huls

"We often search for things in life,
Yet seldom do we find,
Those things in life that really matter,
Until we take the time"

S.T.Huls

A LETTER FOUND

"It's dated June 12 of 1918 so this is old. 'To whoever is most unfortunate to find this letter and this place, I would suggest you leave as fast as you can and get off this evil mountain and never, never come back. It is cursed."

"Great, a cursed cave now. Sounds weird Sis." Levi said.

"Just hold on and let me read this ok, it's kind of interesting don't you think? A mystery maybe."

"I am Frederick the son of Norman Adare the miner who lived here but has now long since vanished and we have not been able to locate him. My older brother Alex has gone for help but he has been gone quite a long time and I fear he may not have made it to Beaver for help. This is a cursed place for bad things have happened to anyone who has been foolish enough to stay here too long.

"The Ute speak of a great evil in these mountains and that it should be avoided. They warned us not to mine, hunt, or travel here and that the evil spirits of the underworld roam these lands and will take anyone who is foolish enough to travel here down into their spirit realms and they are never heard from or seen again.

"We did not believe in their foolish stories about spirits, ghosts or their demons and the like for they are just uneducated Indians after all full of dumb myths. That is what we thought at first but now I am not so sure. Dad is gone and I have abandoned working the mine and barricaded myself here in this cave for safety. Strange things have come in the night; they are quiet and have carried off the mules and supplies. Now I remain alone. I am running out of provisions and do not know how much longer I can stay, I do know that whatever creature or demon is outside. I can hear it scrapping and clawing at the door and pushing on it during the night trying to open it to get to me. They leave a three toed large print, larger than that of a grizzly bear, I do not know what it could be. I do know this: I seem to be a prisoner now and if I venture out by day I am not able to get very far for the demons seem to come in the dusk and I must flee back to this cave for safety, I do not think I can travel to Beaver to escape, as in the open at night they would catch me. It's over a day's hike back to Beaver so for now it's safer in the cave I hope Alex will come back soon with help I think it's the only way I will survive. Alex, if you read this I am leaving the extra gun in case you need it. If you do not find me then I have either made my escape and will find you in Beaver or the demons have taken me. You are warned! Leave and never return. There is some strange evil here. A dark magic. I hear something,

"Alex there is a strange humming sound behind the back wall. Its glowing white hot like when the black smith melts iron. I cannot leave, I am trapped, for the demons are back at the door again. Know this, not sure how much time I have so I must end this letter. Tell the family I love them. I must go; I hear them. The demons they are coming."

PROLOGUE

"Levi is it much further?" Sariah asked

"Just be patient it's just around the corner in the rock face, you will see it in a minute so just relax."

Sariah and Levi soon entered the clearing and she was able to see the old door on the other side of the clearing and it was indeed in the mountain face. Interesting she thought not exactly what one would expect to find way out here.

"So I take it this door leads into the cave you spoke of then?"

"Yep sis you're right so you wanna go in, we left the door open a little as it was a real bugger to open the first time."

"Sure since you left the door open might as well go take a look" she said as she pulled out a hand crank flash light, she liked using it because she never had to worry about batteries just crank it a while and you had light.

She walked into the room and shines her light around to see what was there. She saw the desk and other items lying around she noted it was a very dusty and musty place.

"Hey sis this is cool come look at the wall over here this is the writing we found"

"That is interesting so do you think its Indian writing or what did Ben think about it."

"Ben is not sure what it is, that's why he took all those pictures and was in such a hurry to get back to camp, he wants to put it on the lap top and get a better look."

"So how far back does this cave go anyway?"

"We don't know really never took the time to go look, Ben and Tarton had to be so bossy and we had to leave and they wanted more flash lights before they would go looking deeper, I think they were just being chickens if you ask me." Levi said hoping she wanted to look deeper into the cave.

"Well let's go look around for ourselves then and see if we can find any good stuff." She said and started slowly walking deeper into the cave.

Levi agreed and followed her looking around where ever she shone her light hopping to glimpse some old treasure or old relic.

"Hey look over here at this little box, shine your light back over here." He said excitedly.

As Sariah moved closer with her light Levi could see better and the small box was now in front of him at his feet. He bent down and noticed it was wrapped up in an old cloth so he began carefully unwrapping it. It revealed an old wooden box, looked like it was made of scrap wood full of character, it had a piece of leather tacked down in the place of a hinge on top of the box, and there was a strange bluish stone with some carving on it in the center along the edge of the lid. He opened the lid and inside was what looked to be an old hand gun and some ammunition, a big knife, and letters. This was a really cool find he thought.

"Levi let me see that it might be loaded."

"Awe sis you have to spoil the moment don't you, ok." He handed the box with the gun to her.

Sariah picked up the gun it looked like a .45 caliber and as she turned it over sure enough it was a Browning 1911 and as she thought it was loaded. She took out the magazine and made sure there was not any ammo in the chamber. It reminded her of some of the hand guns she saw in her grandpa's old collection.

"It's a good thing we found this; the older boys would have fought over who got to keep it. Do you think Dad will let me keep it after all I did find it right?" Levi asked.

"Well you did find it so maybe he will, but he may make you put it in the collection in the gun room until you are older. We will have to smooth talk him some but don't worry about that now. Let's see what else is in here."

She had noticed there were some letters and a couple of 1890 liberty silver dollars that were really nice. She showed them to Levi then picked up a letter from the old wood box the gun had been in. She picked up the big knife and looked it over.

"This is cool, it's a U.S. knife from 1917 so this is old stuff, I wonder who could have left a gun in a box and these letters and stuff and never came back for them? Let's take a look and see if we can find any clues in the letters as to who was here and when." She said as walked back to the desk and placed the box on the top and handed Levi the light then she carefully opened a letter.

"It's dated June 12 of 1918 so this is old. 'To whoever is most unfortunate to find this letter and this place, I would suggest you leave as fast as you can and get off this evil mountain and never, never come back. It is cursed."

"Great, a cursed cave now. Sounds weird Sis." Levi said.

"Just hold on and let me read this ok, it's kind of interesting don't you think? A mystery maybe."

"I am Frederick the son of Norman Adare the miner who lived here but has now long since vanished and we have not been able to locate him. My older brother Alex has gone for help but he has been gone quite a long time and I fear he may not have made it to Beaver for help. This is a cursed place for bad things have happened to anyone who has been foolish enough to stay here too long.

"The Ute speak of a great evil in these mountains and that it should be avoided. They warned us not to mine, hunt, or travel here and that the evil spirits of the underworld roam these lands and will take anyone who is foolish enough to travel here down into their spirit realms and they are never heard from or seen again.

"We did not believe in their foolish stories about spirits, ghosts or their demons and the like for they are just uneducated Indians after all full of dumb myths. That is what we thought at first but now I am not so sure. Dad is gone and I have abandoned working the mine and barricaded myself here in this cave for safety. Strange things have come in the night; they are quiet and have carried off the mules and supplies. Now I remain alone. I am running out of provisions and do not know how much longer I can stay, I do know that whatever creature or demon is outside. I can hear it scrapping and clawing at the door and pushing on it during the night trying to open it to get to me. They leave a three toed large print, larger than that of a grizzly bear, I do not know what it could be. I do know this: I seem to be a prisoner now and if I venture out by day I am not able to get very far for the demons seem to come in the dusk and I must flee back to this cave for safety, I do not think I can travel to Beaver to escape, as in the open at night they would catch me. It's over a day's hike back to Beaver so for now it's safer in the cave. I hope Alex will come back soon with help I think it's the only way I will survive. Alex, if you read this I am leaving the extra gun in case you need it. If you do not find me then I have either made my escape and will find you in Beaver or the demons have taken me. You are warned! Leave and never return. There is some strange evil here. A dark magic. I hear something,

"Alex there is a strange humming sound behind the back wall. Its glowing white hot like when the black smith melts iron. I cannot leave; I am trapped, for the demons are back at the door again. Know this, not sure how much time I have so I must end this letter. Tell the family I love them. I must go; I hear them. The demons they are coming."

"It just ends, that's weird"

"Yep, sounds like a bad movie sis, so you think someone came up here and planted the letters just to spook us?"

"Well knowing the boys anything is possible, I just don't know when they both could have got together to set this whole thing up... they could be messing with us"

"Well sounds like a weird prank lets go see how far back this cave goes maybe there is some cool stuff we could find back there."

"Sounds like a plan lets go take a peak."

Suddenly they hear great booming sounds and the crackles of lightning reverberating off the walls of the cave room Sariah and Levi both jump at the sound.

"Well that's that then, a mountain thunderstorm is here, may as well stay put and stay dry Levi, so now we have some time to really explore this place." Sariah said.

"Yep I sure don't want to get all soaked walking back to camp, let's get to looking and see what else we can find then." Levi said excitedly.

"Then let's get started "Sariah said as she put the letter back in the box with the gun and closed the lid to keep it safe, then pointed her light towards the darkest parts of the cave room.

* * * * *

Deep inside the bowels of the mountain we find a race that time has all but forgotten; in a room we would call a security station. We find a member of the Teesa Clan monitoring his station.

For the second time the illumination dot on his console glowed again, this was to the older seldom used entrance on the mountain. No one had used it in a very long time, one signal could be a malfunction or the odd encounter by an outer crust creature tripping the alarm, however several such alarms in so short a time and then followed by the motion sensor devices placed farther in from the entrance states there must be something wrong, an intruder must be present and should be challenged.

Pushing the com button on his console he notified his superior.

"Sleesesa clan Tessa to Security Head Quarters" Sleesesa calmly said.

"SHQ here what's your problem Sleesesa?"

Sleesesa disliked discussions with these primitive weak creatures and having to speak through their translators was demeaning and some day they will have to put them in their right order of place in the cosmos. Beneath his race as it was in the beginning; however they had their useful purposes such as times like this.

"You have a possible intruder in section 39 of Tushar tunnel, you will dispatch your team to investigate and detain any outer crust dwellers if found, is that understood."

"Sleesesa, your message is received will search and detain as needed." was the response.

Working with this clan less outer crusters was demoralizing to say the least, he wondered if they were even up to such a simple task without help. He returned to monitoring the area.

At Security Head Quarters in the Teesa grid the head of security, Chief sent for his teams.

"Sir reporting as ordered what is our mission?"

"Sergeant Smith, you and your team are to go to the Tushar tunnel section 39 to see what the problem is, we have an intruder censor alert, check out the area if you find any intruders they are to be detained and brought here is that understood?"

"Yes sir"

"Good you know how touchy these Nemekans are they always assume the worst. So be safe."

"Understood." Sergeant Smith said then turning to his team, "Let's move out".

The Sergeant had been on duty for eight years now in the black opps dealing with the inner Earth cultures and races. Since his recruitment he had seen a lot of strange things and all though he did not agree with everything going on down here, he understood it was for the long term good of his country. Now it was time to keep himself and his four man team safe as usual.

"Well men lets go intruder alert so let's gear up and take tube 68 to the area it should be about 20 minutes so let's get moving." Sgt. Smith said they all went to gear up and headed for the tubes at a trot.

Sgt. Smith (as he was called here, no one used their real names openly down here all need to know stuff it was on the coded computer ID's that everyone had to wear.) One thing the Nemekans were good at was hi-tech stuff, and the tubes he had to admit were a neat smooth ride. One such tube ran coast to coast and only took a few hours to travel between them. All he knew was it had something to do with super magnetics.

His team stepped into the egg shaped vehicle used in the tubes and pushed the needed symbols on the console and away they went at high speed. Soon they were miles away from the security base and nearing their destination. As they approached the disembarkment location the vehicle made its slow relaxing stop, it was amazing how it could slow down without jarring one around from the high speed it traveled at.

"Let's go earn our pay, should be about 15 minutes and we should be at the location let's move".

They all started their jog up the tunnel it was easy going as it was illuminated with the soft green glow that the Nemekans preferred as they did not like the yellow/white lights we used at all.

Soon they reached Tushar entrance 39 and when all had a moment to calm their breathing they then silently took up their positions and ever so slowly and quietly moved towards the entrance that led to the exterior door of the mountain.

* * * * *

Back in the cave we find Sariah and Levi slowly walking deeper into the cave.

"This must be the back of the cave that guy was talking about in the letter, just look at the hole in the wall here." He said.

"It could be, let's get closer, see here it does look like the rock was melted at some time, and see how smooth it is like a lava tube, interesting." She said.

Sariah took a really good look at the opening that seemed almost completely cylindrical like, with uniformity to the edges and it was melted very smooth not like if one used dynamite to blast open the hole. But it was about nine feet high and maybe twelve feet wide. Compared to the back wall itself that must be sixteen feet wide or better, so this unusual opening must have been man made somehow. But if it went back to the times of the note, that would not make sense.

"Levi you know that if the letter we found is true, then this hole was made way back in the early 1900's, and I don't think I know what could have carved it out today let alone back then. You know what Levi this is starting to get a little spooky, it just does not make any sense you know?"

"Sis, I think your right, maybe we should go get Dad and let them look at this and the other stuff we found as well, it is getting a little scary back here." He said a sign of worry in his voice.

"I think your right, hey wait a minute do you see that strange greenish light inside the hole?" Sariah asked curiosity overcoming her feelings of fear for a moment.

"Kind of, turn off your light and let's see if we can get a better look at it." He suggested.

Sariah turned off her light and sure enough the glow was a lot brighter.

"Cool, this is kind of like in the movies when there was a deep ocean or cave creature that gave off light, I wonder what is creating it?" He said.

"Well I guess all your TV & movie watching is paying off a little bit then, your right about the possible cause of the light, let's go see what is creating it and then we can take it back to camp, that would really one up Ben and Tarton."

"Sounds good, but it is really spooky ya know, maybe we should go get that old gun just in case some booger man is back there, what do you think?" He commented.

"Oh come on it is an old gun and may not even work; besides there are no booger anything in this cave, unless you've been picking your nose again, so don't get all scared on me."

"Ok, ok, ok, let's go then sis, keep your light on so we don't get lost or fall into a deep hole, or trip on a boulder." He said nervously.

"Right but this does look pretty straight, more of a tunnel than a cave see here what ever made this must have been really hot, looks more like it was melted like those lava tubes ya know, but it should make it a lot easier for walking as the floor looks pretty smooth." Sariah said as she entered the tube.

* * * * *

Almost to the opening Sergeant Smith could hear noises, and see the beam of a flash light piercing the darkness near the tunnel entrance as well as the light from the open outer door to the surface, so someone was here and needed to be dealt with. From what he could make out it was only a couple people that was good and would make his job easier.

Using hand signals he directed his team into their positions along the walls where they would stay deathly quiet and still until his order was given to move.

He brought up his stun device the Nemekans had developed it was harmless for the most part but very effective and gave one a huge head ache when you woke up. He aimed it towards the un suspecting people, he wished they had not discovered the tunnel, but that was not his problem, orders were orders and these poor saps where just in the wrong place at the wrong time.

"Sariah?" Levi asked in a more shaky voice.

"What now?" Sariah responded.

"I am getting a bad feeling now, you know like maybe we should just go back and get out of here."

"Your letting your imagination get the best of you, caves are just spooky is all, there is nothing to worry about in here." She said getting a little irritated with him.

"Are you sure? You're not just saying that are you?"

"Look, we are getting closer to the green glow, just a few more minutes and we should be able to see what's causing it, then we can go back to camp when the rain has stopped, I promise." She said trying to calm her little brother down, this was interesting to her, an adventure of sorts and he was breaking the mood of the whole experience with his whining.

"Ok, if you promise, hey look at that there are some rocks in the tunnel, turn your light back over this way I thought I saw a funny looking rock." He said as he stared at a place along the wall it was dark but he could make out what was a really weird shaped rock.

"Let's have a look at your rock so exactly where is it then." She said glad his attention was distracted for a moment he just might start having fun again. She shines her light around at Levi and he points along the wall she follows his gesture with her beam of light some yards down the tunnel.

"See there is your rock." Sariah said as she shines the light on what looked like a rock, but suddenly as her eyes focused better in light from her flashlight the rock looked more and more like it could be a man crouched along the wall. That doesn't make any sense, and then she saw it move.

"It's not a rock it's... Run! Levi Ru...." she was not able to finish as her chest exploded with pain, felt like getting kicked by a horse and she felt herself go numb as she was falling to the floor dropping her light, as the sensations of unconsciousness began to overtake her the last thing she saw was Levi also laying on the ground in the beam of her light, then a pair of boots, military style boots then the shadow of darkness enveloped her and all was black.

CHAPTER 1

Family Gathering

In a perfectly normal little town in the central mountains of Utah we find an older pioneer home built in the 1890's like others in the area built of wood, stone and brick by those who braved these wild mountain lands long ago. We find a pretty normal family of six consisting of two parents and four children which is not unusual in Utah. The home for its age is in good shape and over the many years through repairs, remodels as needed the 3 room brick home had evolved into a 6 bedroom 3 bath home. With plenty of extra rooms for the family, when they come to visit during the holiday times.

The homestead is located along the Beaver River near the mouth of Beaver canyon along state highway 153. It contains 100 acres of land along the river, and is irrigated during the summer. With cotton woods, pines and willow's growing there, some well over 100 years old providing shade and homes for the wild and domestic animal life that abounds in the area.

Black Angus cows and a mixture of horses and goats are walking in the fields grazing on the long lush field grass that is available. Some of the animals are resting in the shade from the summer's heat provided by the older ancient trees. And as one looks around you will see the rolling hills climb quickly and steeply into the mountains above the homestead, some of these mountain peaks reaching over 12,000 feet in elevation. Like ancient sentinels protecting as it were the valley from the world without, giving a sense of peace and security to those who have dwelt here for over 140 years. And longer for those of the ancient races who once walked these lands over the thousands of years these mountains existence. If the mountains could only talk what great tales they could tell about the happenings throughout their time.

Now we find the Adair family, James the father had become wealthy due to the enormous demands for the Beaver area pure spring water which they bottled and started selling, Not long ago the city received national status for the cleanest and best tasting water in all of the USA, this helped his fledgling business to grow and become one of the most successful natural water bottling companies in the western part of America. James often thought on that who would have thought 20 years ago anyone would actually buy bottled water. Now with his thriving company James is able to find the time to explore the country around him a lot easier, the Tushar & Kimberly ranges were only a few that made up the Beaver Mountain range and there were plenty of wild area's still left to explore. He had spent many years with his wife and his four children taking day hikes and longer hikes when time permitted some lasting several weeks at a time. Since they had the option of walking the non-motorized trails where seldom did they see any others, during their hikes they had experienced both the beauty and ruggedness of the wilder places of the central Utah Mountains. It had been his wife Katasha's idea years ago to start breeding goats for the purpose of pack animals, to use for the longer hikes in conjunction with the pack horses or even without them as they could access some of the more rugged slender trails where horses were not able to go due to their size. She having grown up for part of her life in the Pacific North West where it was more common to use pack goats for hikes as they are easier to manage on the trails than llamas, mules, or horses and did not need special feed as they eat just about anything and do not spook easy. However James still liked using the pack horses for the heavier gear a good base camp needs in the mountains.

We find Katasha planning yet another annual family gathering, this time the whole clan was coming back home with their families for the two week visit for their summer vacation. What a reunion this will be she thought, Now what is left in the planning, food enough for the Adair Clan and room to bed them all down, she was grateful that there was enough room for some campers, and tents as well in order to fit the whole family during these visits at home. But this time they were going to be camping somewhere in the Tushar mountains, using a large base camp and then doing day hikes enjoying the outdoors the family just loved these visits.

She was grateful that James sisters Mary and Martha were excellent cooks it was a great help during these get together's. Katasha liked to cook but Mary was a wonderful baker of sweets and all the kids and some of the adults drooled over her concoctions, which seldom made it more than a few hours after their completion.

She thought a moment, I had best call Mary and see what their arrival plans are. She picked up the cordless phone and dialed her number.

"Hello Mary, I was wondering what day you're going to be coming over for sure?"

"Hey Kat, (an abbreviation of her name her kids had given Katasha when they were really young and were not able to say her full name, and it stuck) we should be there by Thursday that way we can help get things packed up and ready for the hike and other activities. If that's alright with you?"

"Sure fine with me, have you heard anymore about how Martha's doing? Last I heard she was going into the hospital again for premature labor. Do you know if they were able to figure out the cause of it this time?"

"No, I haven't yet, will need to give her a buzz today and get the updates, I hope all is well she so looks forward to these trips to the homestead. And traveling from Manti to Provo a few extra times each month can sure cut into the gas budget. I know she is back home and resting, hope she is not stuck on complete bed rest again, remember when she had Drake she was down almost 3 months straight in order to not have him too premature, and Walter was about 1 month preemie if I remember right ?".

Yes Walter was 1 month early I hope she really is ok, it is really hard on her when she has to stay down drives her nutty, and the rest of her family as well, I thought Tom was going to go nuts trying to run the house all by himself, Men they think they have it so hard going to work all the time, they hardly ever realize what we do all day, kids off to school, house work, and all the extra's, and in my case farm chores as well. So that must have been a real eye opener for him."

"Yes it sure was" (she smiled to herself she realized she was pacing her house again it was a bad habit she had when on the phone), "Hey Kat I need to be going, I have to pick up Natasha and Thor from school today, have a bunch of errands to run with them, Will chat with you later ".

"That's ok with me chat later then, looks like the weather is going to be good for the vacation, so Love you all and be seeing you soon, bye now".

"Bye Kat".

Katasha looks out the window at the mountains she always did find a peace and security feeling being so close to the mountains. Now it was time to check in with Martha and her family. She called Martha's home. The phone rang until the machine answered. "Hey Martha, this is Katasha, was just calling to see how things are going with you and the baby, sorry to have missed you will try again later, Have a great day, bye".

She always disliked talking to answering machines, but they do have their purpose. Well better get the kids to go do the outside chores before dark as they had other things needing to be done as well. She went into the living room where she found Joseph, age 11 playing his x box and Sariah age 17 with her nose in yet another book laying on the couch she was always reading something which in today's world may seem unusual for a teenager. She loves to read and research all kinds of history type stuff along with her entertainment reading.

"Hey you too it's time for you to take a break and to go out and feed the critters."

Joseph acted almost like he didn't really hear his moms request; after all he was in the midst of a great battle saving the world once again from Evil. But he did respond.

"Oh mom, can't it wait, I am really ... wait... (he had to focus on the fight in the game) can't Sariah and Levi do it, it's their turn and I am busy..."

"Joseph, it's all your turns, now push the pause or save, whatever you do to stop the game and get moving! Levi is already outside working."

Joseph glared at his mom, talk about bad timing, he paused the game right in the middle of a tactical emergency, chores he was getting tired of doing all these chores. But he knew better than to argue with mom last time it did not turn out too good for him.

Katasha looked down on Sariah." Now Sariah it is ok to put the book down for a moment and go help Joseph with the chores, it will go quicker with both of you."

"Ok mom" she said a little reluctantly she was just getting into the book it was just getting interesting for a history type book, it was written by one of her ancestors named James Adair on the Native American Indians and his thoughts on their origins and interactions with the early Europeans during the mid to late 1700's.

She was learning a lot. But she knew the chores needed doing, and the book would not be going anywhere.

Katasha turned and left the room knowing they would take care of the chores, and she heard their conversation some.

Joseph asked Sariah "Why does mom always have to interrupt my game at the wrong time!" He grumbled a little bit as he put on the farm work boots by the back door.

"Joseph just calm down its part of having the animal's right? They need to be feed just as we do so stop the whining and let's go get them done!"

"All right"

As they shut the door and headed out to barn and corrals, Joseph remembered the head aches his dad caused him the last time he argued with his mother.

Katasha just smiled as the kids left the house, Sariah is a good daughter and does her best to help around the place as well as teach her younger brother that life does exist outside his game worlds. After all the last time Joseph put up a defiant argument with her about having to leave his game to do something and when he started getting mouthy James over heard it and promptly turned off the power to the family room thus effectively removing the excuse not to do his chores. She chuckles at the thought of Joseph's reaction to the sudden loss of electricity which shut down his game before he could save it, James had given him a grin and told him it's an automatic reaction for getting mouthy with his mother, and promised it would happen as often as needed until the lesson was learned. After all life is not about entertainment games, there is reality outside of the gaming worlds.

Well better get some dinner going while there out doing the chores, she looks in the cupboards and chose a simple yet filling dish, macaroni and cheese with old sausages sliced and mixed in. The kids just loved it. Not to fancy tonight just simple and quick. As she begins to prepare dinner the phone rings, she walks over to pick up the phone. "Hello?"

"Katasha this is Martha, how is your day going? Mine is doing better I got your message thought it would be best to call and let you know we are still planning on coming down for the family get together. The boys are just a little excited about it, they have been packed now for 3 days, and I keep reminding them they have to wait a few more days. Now don't worry about me and the baby we are both fine and resting I will be coming as well and may just need to rest on your nice fluffy couches and take advantage of your hot tub when time permits. "

"Ok Martha, if you're not able to go with us you can stay at the homestead and take care of things." She laughed lightly as they both knew she liked to hot tub.

"After all someone has to manage the fort while everyone is off gallivanting around the wilds of Utah for days or weeks, I may surprise you though, I just might feel good enough to go on this hike if it's not too hard of one. Or maybe I could ride a horse while you all walk. Time will tell".

"Well I am glad you're doing better we heard you had a scare a few days back and was just wondered how your holding up?"

"Oh? Is Mary telling stories about me again? You know she is always blowing things way out of proportion, anyway so don't worry about me."

"Now Martha we all know that you wouldn't tell us the exact truth of your health if we tried to force it out of you, so maybe that's why she worries so much".

"Come on now you know me, if it was really a problem I would let you all know right? Anyway, do your men folk down there have some good hikes planned? The boys really need a good work out and it does ware them down and when young boys are tired and fed they behave better."

"Of course they do and they plan these things out for weeks, James and Ben burn the candles at both ends just to think up stuff to ware out your boys." Katasha replied as she laughed a little.

"You win well I need to be going now but will update you on the baby and myself as needed, so no more worries right."

"Alright, I promise no worries as long as you keep us up to date".

"Ok, I promise well gotta run talk later say hello to everyone for us".

"I shall and dido's on your end have a great week" Katasha replied then hung up the phone and went to finish dinner.

* * * * *

We find James driving home after visiting with the city and county officials again; they wanted to go over some concerns about the water resources and his bottled water company's needs verses the needs of the valley and some future planning, same usual stuff, however some legitimate concerns pop up now and then. I wonder if we could pipe the water directly from the Shelly Baldy area, that's where the really good water comes from, oh well enough about work. Time to focus on the upcoming reunion. Ben has really been excited about this next week's activities as Martha's boys are getting older now and can go on the longer treks, the goats really come in handy with the younger packers, letting them see the neat things farther into the back country. Better call Ben and see how he is coming along. James reaches for his cell phone and hits the buttons for Ben's number and sends the call.

"Hi Dad what do you need" Ben said as he answered his phone he knew it was his dad by the specifically chosen tune for him.

"What are you up to?" James asked his eldest son.

"Well I have been working and will be home soon, what can I do for you?"

"Well how are the plans for the hike going? Was just thinking about all your cousins, are you going to have enough to keep them all busy and of course ware them out for their parents? (James couldn't help but chuckle) You know that worn out boys usually stay out of trouble right?" James replies.

"Dad you know darn well that even worn out boys can find ways into mischief. Not that we ever got into any of course, so don't worry I have been talking with Peter and Tarton and we have loads of fun planned out, see you tonight at dinner, better run for now."

"Ok Ben we will talk later then, see ya bye." James hung up his cell phone and laid it on the console he always drove better when not talking on the phone. It tended to cause a distraction which usually was not a good thing. He smiled to himself thinking about Ben, he has grown up into a good young man; he was always athletic and has chosen the construction trades as a possible carrier move over working in the family business. I have to respect that although construction was a dog eat dog business, feast or famine. But his wanting to make a stake of his own without relying on the family business was a good thing he did have a strong heart for going his own way. Since he came back last year from his mission to New Mexico area he has been actively searching for a career, through trial and error looking for his niche in life.

He is a fun loving kid, and loves the outdoors, if the dry walling does not work out for him, he just might open a goat packing exploration hiking company and take the city dwellers out so see our back country. Now that may not be a bad thought however we shall see what he chooses in time, no need to push him. And he and Tarton where always the schemers and their pal Peter may as well be family for how close they are in thoughts and actions. We were always pulling those three out of trouble with their mothers over the years.

James pulls off highway 153 at his turn and starts down the long driveway to their home. He has been blessed as he reflects on his life; his Father in Heaven has greatly blessed his life with his wonderful wife and kids, and his successful company. Now it is good to have a place for the whole family to gather and spend time together and to get to know each other letting the children grow and learn and build strong bonds that should last a life time and beyond. His grandfather always taught him in his youth "Now James we see in life that whatever our Heavenly Father blesses you with be it your skills, talents, income your everything that you should always remember to use it to help and bless the lives of others around you, after all we are all his children no matter what nation, kindred or tongue that We are all God's children, like one big family as such we are not always happy one with each other but family never the less. So we who know must help and bless each other as best we can. You see James; wealth does not always come in the form of money, gold or silver the riches of the Earth. True wealth is through service to ones fellow beings, thus the world is improved on, the riches of the Earth can bless and corrupt based on one's own values. The riches of Heaven will never corrupt, so seek that which will bless the lives of others and you shall be made truly rich in your life here on Earth and in your life to come. You see James no one remembers how many toys, or how much cash is in the bank or what political power or how much success in business you had in life, or how much cash, gold, jewels are in the bank. Those who are truly wealthy are remembered by their deeds in life, by how many they blessed during their sojourn on this Earth. Always remember this." He would always have such thoughts to pass on to us grandkids; Grandpa Jan's was a good ole Adair and a fine story teller at that.

James pulled up to his house and turned off his truck then got out shutting his door as he looked over the homestead memories flooded through his mind of all the good times had by the generations past and present and hopes many in the future as well to come on this place.

He is happy to see Joseph and Sariah both finishing up the evening chores, it was a good learning experience for them both, however each learns at different paces, Joseph would rather play than work sometimes, good boy though, they will appreciate the lessons learned now later on in life, as we all do after our childhood that is. Well best go in and get cleaned up for dinner. James walks into the house.

After dinner James entered the library room to relax he was wondering what was keeping Ben, usually he calls if he is going to be late or miss dinner, oh well he is a young man now and should not worry. I will have to ask him when he gets home if it's at a decent hour. James sat down in his large leather chair which he liked to use when reading, he picked up the book on the table next to the chair he had been working on reading and reached over and turned on the cd player to relax and meditate on life listening to some native American flute music which was very peaceful and good for the soul, as it allows one to think. He opened the book to where he had left off and began to read.

* * * * *

Ben was driving his truck along the dirt road that was the back way to his parents' home, he noticed off in the distance the little farm of old Fairsong Tree Talker, he had been a longtime friend of the Adair's and I think he knew my great granddad he was very old and at times strange but he was a good soul and was a very good story teller. Ben felt the odd impression that he should stop by and check on the old man for a minute and see how he was getting along, so having gotten used to following impressions given to him he made the turn onto the dirt road that lead down to the old cabin Fairsong lived in.

As he pulled up into the drive area Ben shut off the truck and got out, then walked up on to the old wooden porch listening to it creek and moan a little as he stepped onto the old grey wood. He reached out to knock on the door when suddenly it was jerked open and he saw Fairsong looking at him with a little smile and a twinkle in his eye.

He opened the door fully and said, "I was wondering when you were going to stop by youngster." And motioned Ben to come in. Ben did so entering the small front room and sat in the seat Fairsong pointed to, it was a little surreal as it was almost like Fairsong was expecting him to stop by, kind of weird. Fairsong took a seat directly opposite of him in an old wooden rocking chair that he had made many years ago, he was always making things if he needed something he is very handy and skilled but that was just how he was.

Fairsong looked intently at the young Ben Adair no longer a boy it had been a while since he had seen him and he was becoming a fine young lad, tall in stature, broad in the shoulders and had strong features, Yes indeed a fine lad and with it he noted that he had finally come to a good level of spiritual awareness as his essence was visible for him to see finally that was good. A very hard quality to find in today's children, yes rare indeed. Hmm he thinks to himself then a thin smile cross's his worn face.

Ben just maybe the one and the time is about right he may be the one that we have been waiting for all these many years. One can only hope and never truly be sure but he just might be. Most of the kids today don't or won't listen to their elders, parents and show little respect for anyone let alone their histories. I shall see if he truly is prepared for what will need to be shared with him and if he is ready, truly ready then the way will be made known and the path will be re-opened in time.

The thin smile returned as he looked intensely at young Adair then he spoke.

"Well young Adair, you find yourself in my humble home once again, it has been such a long time since our last meeting here. I must assume you have learned much in your travels these past years, if I recall you should be about 23 years now. And that is a good age for I sense you have learned some wisdom in these last few years and even as young as you are, however there is much you still need to learn, to study and to know the ways of your fathers who have gone before you and the ancient ones. We have spoken in times past of your family's history, your family's journey into this place and how they once had to live to survive here not too long ago." Fairsong paused a moment then continued.

"Now it is time to ask yourself young Ben these questions, how shall you live? What will you give the world? What of your Faith, your Family and what will you do with your life? These are not as easily answered questions as one might think, not a matter of a job or schooling or of worldly success in their sense of definition. Have you taken thought of what you could become some day? During your sojourn on this Earth? Have you discovered what this life's existence truly is about my young Adair?

It is much more than even you at such a young age can truly fathom however let us see where your next step in your journey shall begin. Now what say you my young Ben Adair what shall you become, you may speak now what think you?" He ended and waited for his response.

Ben had learned long ago it was unwise to interrupt Fairsong when he was speaking, but now he was not sure what to say, he had just dropped in to see how the old guy was doing and now he starts drilling me with all these questions he had not been ready for them, but he should have known better as Fairsong was always doing things like this. Ok think and focus what is he expecting me to say, he is just sitting there with that little grin of his like the cat waiting to pounce on the prey, Now what do I want to do in life but not a job that does not make much sense so then what is he getting at, Ben thought a minute on it.

"Well I am not sure what you're getting at but let's have a try at it, What should I do with my life outside of a career let's see what is left someday I would hope to find a wife and raise a family but that comes back to needing a good job to support the family's needs. So I do need to focus on a career in order to follow that pathway. Unless there are other paths that you see that I am missing, help me out a little here Fairsong because I am not sure I am following you 100 % tonight, so specifically what is it you're getting at" He stated and waited for a hopeful response that would help him define what Fairsong was needing so he could leave and get home for dinner.

Fairsong just sighed then gave Ben a smile and again the twinkle in the eye, "Ben my young friend you have much to learn but that is ok you are just starting your life's journey and sometimes to look to the future one must start in the past to find the proper direction and learning."

Ben sat there somewhat confused, not what he expected ok, back to more riddles, Fairsong did like riddles or doing things in a roundabout fashion like you're supposed to be able to read his mind or something. "It's been a long day and I am missing dinner so can we get on with it. Please, There is something you're trying to tell me however it seems to be going over my head right now so just go ahead and spit it out for me" Ben said a little impatiently.

Fairsong's smile faded then and he looked and Ben wondering if now really was the time for this boy, everything did seem to be in place however he was still a little impatient, the boy still did have much to learn.

"Ben, do you know of how our two families became intertwined over the years?"

"Dad said you and grandpa served in the World War II together and that's where you met and that later you came and settled in our little valley and that you have been like a family member since that time. So why ask me this now you have known me most of my life or all of it right?"

Fairsong sat in thought looking at Ben still, interesting he thought neither Hyrum or James have chosen to give any further details to this younger generations of Adair's it would seem, interesting indeed as busy as the world was becoming one should always have time to teach the youth of their own past.

"Ben there seems to be much that you may not have been informed about but no matter we shall remedy that shortly. I must take some time to fill in the blanks so where to begin, you are at the age of life that leads to many paths, each of which will lead to the start of a most interesting journey, and each one will affect everything about you and those around you for the rest of your and their life time. So the key to life is in choosing which of the many paths you could follow and which one you will choose to follow that you feel is right, at least for the moment."

"In order for you to choose a path one must know at least a little of what each path offers and where it may lead. You have explored some paths already in your young life, and some have brought you some wisdom and blessings and growth while others the lessons are the results of unwise choices. You see Ben the Great Creator has blessed us of the human race with the freedom to choose our own paths, no matter the results for good or ill, he will allow us this freedom, it is inherent in all sentient beings throughout all time and space to have this freedom. As we refer to him as our Father it is because he truly treats us as his children and guiding us, teaching us in his ways and how to avoid the bad choices in life even though we are at times too arrogant to listen for we think we know more than he at times, so he lets us learn by our success's and mistakes so Ben do you understand what I am sharing with you now?" Fairsong waited quietly.

Ben thought a moment, "Yes I understand it is like what they taught us in Sunday school at church from the Bible stories right? So this is not too new to me just the same ole story." He replied.

"Awe so I see, so you think in order to learn something it must be new and up to date then? Most true and good wisdom comes from the ancients days long past and passed down from the parents to the children for thus it has always been and shall always be in the future to come so do not become bored with repetitions in learning you must seek the wisdom found in the lessons and see the knowledge of the ancients to understand where your path may lead you in this life and your future."

"Well I didn't mean to sound bored, go on."

"You see to find your place in life one must know their Creator, from what I have seen over your life you have learned to communicate somewhat with your Father in Heaven the Creator and you know how to pray and ask for guidance and understand how the answers come and directions you should follow, is this not so?"

"Yes, I have learned these things however I am sometimes unsure of the answers, if they come from my own mind or if it is a true answer to my prayers."

"This you will learn and re-learn over time as you continue to grow and mature in spiritual matters, you see if your mind is open to explore other regions of the mind you will be able to think beyond the normal teachings of the schools of man and you will be able to have an open mind to new idea's no matter how foolish or strange they may seem at the time," Fairsong replied.

"Well I do consider myself somewhat of an open minded person so what are you getting at?"

"First I must know that what I share will not fall upon barren earth, dry and desolate. You know that a seed must be planted in fertile earth in order to explore the potential and growth and maturity of the seed turning into what it has the potential to become. So I shall assume you understand this thought, now we shall move on and see where the path takes us. Ben your grandfather Hyrum and my paths crossed during the wars and we became what some say fox hole buddies, We were lucky enough to have survived those awful conflicts however sometimes the good people of the earth need to unite against that which is evil in order to protect the weak and helpless from being enslaved or slaughtered by the evil ones of Earth. You're Grandfather and I did our duty to the best we could do at the time war is a sad and awful part of life and I hope you never have to see one for yourself. I grew to care for Hyrum and was intrigued by his stories of the mountains of Utah and where he grew up so naturally I followed him to his mountains and eventually choose to stay in the valley."

"Ben it is getting late and I should rest now we shall continue this at another time if you will promise to come back soon there is more I would share with you." Fairsong said.

"Sure I would like that and I should be going home," Ben goes to stand up and Fairsong stops him with a wave of his hand.

"Wait Ben just a moment there is something Hyrum wanted me to give to one of his posterity when I felt the time was right he gave strict instructions that I would have to wait and pick who to give it to according to what choices the one has made in their life. He said also that I would know by the spirit when the time was right and to whom to give his box too. I sense that the Creator has chosen you to have the box so sit and let me go get it for you." Fairsong got up and left the room, he hobbled into the back room looking for the box he had been keeping for a very long time, ah there it was, and he picked it up and carried it out to Ben.

"Ben this belonged to your grandfather Hyrum Adair, inside is something he wanted to share but only to one whom was open minded enough to appreciate it and not scoff or quickly pass it off as nothing. So before you make any choices in the matter look at what is inside study on it then if you have any question's I will be here to help you with them, at least for a short time longer." Fairsong said then looked at Ben and studied his reactions.

Ben took the box which was a wooden box about 35 inches long and 18 inches wide and about 20 inches tall it did seem old and had an old key lock on it and of course it was locked. The box did not seem too heavy for its size.

"I will take this home and look it over then."

"Ben here is the key to the lock, please wait to open it until after you get home and do it in private."

"I promise and thanks, (Ben took the envelope that felt like it had a key in it) I will get back to you after I look things over and if I have any questions I will come back and ask them." -

"Night then Ben, take good care of it for I have been its caretaker for a very long time and it is full of memories but you will discover that, so till next we meet farewell."

"Night and take care." Ben said as he picked up the box and carried it out to his truck and places it on the passenger's seat, and then he drove home wondering what was in the box and what this was all about, many questions and not a lot of answers."

As Ben drove into the drive way he realized he had missed dinner once again, he carried the box up to his room and put it in his closet for the time being, then went down to the kitchen to find something to eat.

"Well you missed dinner again, what was it this time?" Katasha asked her son with a smile

"I stopped in to see old Fairsong and well you know it is hard to get away after he starts talking, is Dad around?"

"I understand, and yes your Dad is in the library, I think he is reading, which means he has most likely fallen asleep."

Ben nodded and put the left over's from dinner in the microwave to warm them up.

"Just need to talk with him for a bit, after I finish dinner."

"Oh? What about? "

"Nothing really just wanted to clarify some of Fairsong's stories again, no big deal" Ben said as he quickly ate his warmed up dinner and drank down a glass of milk.

"Well you two have a fun talk then, I am going to make sure everyone is settled into their rooms and get ready for bed myself, it is going to be a long day tomorrow." Katasha said and left the room.

"Night Mom." Ben replied, and then he put his dishes in the sink and went to the library to find his Dad.

Ben smiled as he saw his father asleep on the couch, he should know better than to try and read a heavy book while listening to that flute music of his, almost always puts him to sleep, well Ben chuckles quietly time to wake him up so he can go sleep in his own bed, Hmm how to wake him up this time, last time he wiggled a feather under his nose that was always good entertainment, well for me anyways however the side effects could be almost dangerous depending on Dad's mood when he awoke. He did take a good joke however he was able to dish it out as well and usually got even at Ben's expense. Ok I will be nice tonight and it will be safer for me in the long run.

Ben walked over and gently shook his father's arm to wake him up.

"Dad are you awake? Hey Dad wake up, (he pauses a moment) Hello in there it's life calling wake up ya old fart" Ben said as his dad's eyes snapped open in a sleepy eyed glare at him that made him back up a little.

James rolled over and sat up looking at Ben then realization kicks in, "Oh uh ok well Ben what do you need"

"Well you awake yet Dad" Ben said with a smirk on his face.

"I am now, you pesky kid why would you wake up your old dad when he is sleeping, and why did you miss dinner again?" James responds as he stretches out then folds his arms waiting for Ben's explanations.

Ben took a seat in the chair across from the couch, "Sorry Dad I should have called to let you know I might be late again. Anyway too late for that now, and I spoke with mom and she is ok."

"Well good then, so what is so important you have to wake me up."

"The reason I was late was I felt the need to stop by old Fairsong's place just for a few minutes of course, or I thought anyway, I forgot one never has a short visit there he sure can talk a lot for someone who was born a few hundred years ago." Ben laughs slightly

James smiled, anyone who thought they could just stop in for only a minute with Fairsong Tree Talker did not know him very well, that ancient of days sure can tell a yarn and since he lives all alone out in his little cabin he does get lonely for company so if you stop by your fair game.

"Ben first off, Fairsong Tree Talker is an old man however I think he is only in his 90's, however he is full of wisdom and you need to remember that, second your right he can talk a long time. So what did he have to say tonight then?"

"Dad exactly how long has our family known him? Sometimes he seems to know more about our family than we do our selves."

"Let me see, your Grandpa knew him back in the old days, like really old days, I think they served in the 2nd World War together or something and after the war he just followed Grandpa home to our little town, and eventually he retired here, not exactly sure where he is originally from though, never gave that much thought."

"Well I felt that I needed to stop in and check on him and he seemed in good spirits, acted almost like he was expecting me to drop by. He came to the door just before I had time to knock, and opened it up and then he just smiled at me and says 'I was wondering when you were going to stop by youngster' then asked me to come in and sit down. So I did just that, then he just stared at me a while not saying a word, then he spoke about a lot of things some were a little confusing, however he seems to be a little strange at times. Anyway we had a talk then I left and now here I am. Feels like bedtime."

"Well that's Fairsong for you; why don't you get some sleep and we can talk about it later, I am still tired as well, so go to bed and we shall discus it when we are more awake good night Ben." James said as he lay back down on the couch.

"Sounds good night dad" Ben goes up to his room.

Ben laid in bed reflecting on what Fairsong had told him during their little visit and what could be in the box. He fell asleep and had some strange and unusual dreams.

Ben awoke much later than usual it seems like those weird dreams kept him up all night, even though he was asleep. Well better take a look at what was in the box, as his curiosity was peaking. Let's see for starters he needed the key and Fairsong had stated it was in the envelope he had given him, so where was it, he looked around the room until he remembered it was under his jacket on the desk. He held the old tattered envelope and slowly opened it up and looked inside to find an old key and a letter.

The letter said: "To whom it may concern, since your reading this letter that means I did not live long enough to talk with you in person so I surely do hope you're a relative if not just as well, there is a reason your reading this then. Remember you must keep an open mind as you learn of what is to be found in the lessons of the past, what we have learned and what you may learn in your time, and how it could change your world for the better. I have entrusted this task to my good friend Fairsong Tree Talker, one whom I have trusted over the years. I think he shall live long past my passing from this Earthly realm, thus in this envelope I have put a key, and the key goes to the box that should be in front of you at this time. If you should choose to open the box, realize that you will be held accountable before your creator for the care and wellbeing of its contents. Thus you can use the items found there in or relock the box and return it to the care of Fairsong Tree Talker as its care taker once again, The choice is yours, I hope you can choose wisely.

Signed, Hyrum Adair.

That's a little ominous sounding letter from old Grandpa Hyrum, interesting but oh well Ben thought to himself. Now where is the key, he looked at the envelope and turned it upside down over his hand and old iron key fell into his hand. Ben placed the key into the lock on the old box and attempts to turn it, but it did not budge. It must be frozen shut or dirty due to old age, ok if you want to act like that I shall fix you right up. Ben goes to his closet and gets a can of WD 40 spray, great for this type of job. He sprayed the lock and the hinges also just in case they need some help as well. Then he lets it sit for a few minutes then retries to open the lock, then wiggles it a little until it moves and finally turns and unlocks. Ben slowly opens the lid of the box the old iron hinges protest a little making a slight squeaking sound.

Ben peered into the open box and gasped in amazement, what he saw almost took his breath away. This was not what he was expecting to find, yet then what does one ever expect to find in an old wood box kept by and even older old guy, definitely not this. Ben thinks a moment catches his breath and realizes the reason why Hyrum said what he had in the letter. Suddenly there was a loud knocking at his door or rather a loud pounding by his younger brother.

"Hey Ben, you Up Yet? Ben Hey you UP? "Came from the other side of the door that could only be Joseph again.

"Yeah I am awake Joseph, now give me a minute and I will be right out." He yelled back through the door. Guess this will have to wait, Ben closes the box lid then relocks it then looks for a place to hide it, after looking and thinking it over he puts it in his closet and covers it with some blankets.

"We gotta get going, Dad says your helping Levi and me with the chores today so get the lead out, I want to get them done so get moving I ain't got all day you know." Joseph yelled back through the door.

"Hey just let me get my shoes on I'll meet you at the barn."

"Ok, but you better hurry cause I got important stuff to do ya know"

Important stuff yeah right what could be important for an 11 year old brat, computer games most likely.

"Joseph just put a sock in it or you'll be doing the chores all by yourself." Ben said as he opened the door and smiled at his little brother then followed him down stairs and outside to do the chores.

CHAPTER 2

Box of Mystery

It had been a very busy day as usual when preparing all the animals and supplies needed for the reunion hike this year. Ben sat in his room thinking of all the places they had gone in the past and was wondering about a different place for the whole family to visit this year. He had been given the job of finding the location and of course there were many places that he liked that were large enough for the base camp they would need for the group. There was the Blue Lake area under the Baldy's and there was Twin Lakes not much of a difference in the length of the hike in, However Blue Lake was a harder hike out, and with Aunt Martha in her condition he had to consider her needs, as he was looking over the maps he felt his thoughts being drawn back to the mysterious box Fairsong had given him. Since he really had not had the time to give its contents a good look over, now with the house quiet and most everyone was busy in the last minute preparations, now was as good as time as any to revisit the mysteries of the box.

Just as he was about to stand up to get the box, he felt a strong feeling or impression come over him that Twin Lakes was the correct place to go this year.

With that question now answered in his mind he crossed the short distance to his closet and opened the door and began digging through the blankets where he had hidden the box. Picking it up he took it to his bed and set it down. Then for the second time he opens the box and gazes at its contents. Once again his breath is taken away at the strangeness of what was in the box. Amazing just amazing was all he could think there were several strange objects, some wrapped in bundles covered by a type of cloth he was unfamiliar with that had some unusual markings woven into them. He emptied the box one item at a time and placed them upon his bed.

He then looked at each item one at a time. The first was a round shaped crystal ball with what looked to be fine silver decoration on the outside of it, it reminded him of a kind of compass device. It had some strange style of lettering on the inner surface on a circular track like one might find on a ships compass or an Armillary device. Only this was in an unfamiliar language, also there were several inner circular tracts one horizontal and the other vertical; there were several pointers like small arrows inside the center of the device. At the center was a solid looking small ball that these pointers were attached to somehow or maybe actually floating around the ball somehow. Really strange but interesting he thought, it seems to be all floating in a clear liquid and there was the strange writing on the base of the device as well. Ben wondered if this were some type of old compass device, possibly from the south pacific used during world war II. Maybe Grandpa brought it home as a war souvenir.

Ben placed it down and picked up another item that he felt could be another souvenir as well. It looked to be like a large knife or dagger or maybe even a short sword, he wondered if it was Japanese? It was elegant but simple in design for a weapon and was about 34 inches in total length, the blade was about 22 inches long and thin at the hilt then widened towards the middle and sloped to a point with a slight opening in the blade at the tip like a tuning fork, the metal was of a dark grey and he was not sure what type of metal was used to create it. However it was light weight and showed no signs of rust. The hilt was wrapped in black leather it was some type of snake skin, at the hilt end was what looked like four large fangs or teeth of some creature. So this must be an old dragon oriental style sword of some type, thus Japanese or Asian they did like dramatic looking swords with dragons on them. Kind of a cool sword he thought and he placed in down on the bed by the other items.

The next item turned out to be some scrolls and charts with the same strange writing on them, the maps were very strange old looking and unusual. He set them aside to look over later. Then there was what looked to be a long crystal of about 12 inches in length and 3 inches in diameter at the base up to about 1 inch at the tip. It was a flawless looking crystal and was set into a silver handle that was about 7 inches in length, again with some strange symbols, but a little different writing style than the other items. As he held it in his left hand it looked like you could twist the lower part of the handle so that the symbols would line up. So he turned the handle so they did line up to see what if anything would happen and it started to glow and light up like a glow stick only more powerful.

I wonder if there is an instruction manual that could explain how to work these things, but like normal he did not find any instruction booklets.

There was a small package that as he unwrapped it revealed a large ring, and I mean large, Ben could put two of his fingers in the ring and still have a little room to wiggle. Either it belonged to some giant or it was an ornamental ring. He noticed it had some kind of a family crest on it and looked like it could be made of gold with the crest inset in a green jade stone. Beautiful and it did look ancient like something one would find in a museum. So the bigger question besides what is all this stuff would be why Grandpa Hyrum did have all this stuff and where did he get it. He thought to himself about the fact Fairsong had it in an old wooden box instead of some big museum somewhere displayed for the whole world to enjoy.

The next item he unwrapped was a necklace made of a strong thick looking silver chain with a medallion that had a clear stone of about 2 inches in diameter for its center, again with the strange runes or crest on it similar to the design on the large ring.

The last object was heavier and almost intimidating as Ben unwrapped it he realized in shock and to his surprise that he was looking at the mummified remains of some type of skull or rather head. Now this was getting stranger by the moment it looked like something you might see from a freaky side show or spook alley. He could assume it would be a prop or something of the like, because it looked like a skull with the skin still on it but only dried and leathered or mummified so it must be old. However the stranger thing about it was that its features had more of a reptile look to it than humans and it was larger than a human head with a more oval looking shape to it. The color was dark, almost black with large eye sockets and a small double slit opening for the nose area. The mouth was closed shut and frozen by time and not able to open. It had to be a prop for some type of show that's the only thing that could make sense of the whole thing; no way could this be real. Just unbelievable is what it was he was having a hard time getting his mind wrapped around this discovery.

He just took some time and studied the items now laying on his bed and he wished he could speak with Grandpa Hyrum Adair because he was building up a long list of questions concerning the box's contents now, and not able to make much sense of it.

He started putting all the item's back into the box and he realized that old Fairsong might just have some answers for his questions, because as caretaker of the box he just might know a lot about its contents. Ben closed and locked the box and returned it to his closet he decided that Fairsong Tree Talker was most definitely due another visit.

Ben realized that with the reunion starting his questions would have to wait at least a week as he would not have the available free time to visit him. As for now he had to focus on the family gathering and his responsibilities there. Yes he thought Twin Lakes would be the spot and all could make the hike in pretty easily, even Aunt Martha in her condition should do well. Ben heard a vehicle enter the drive way the family was coming back from their shopping.

So he went down to meet them and notify them of the chosen location of the main camp and then he would go out to the barn and make sure everything was ready and packed up in the right saddle bags that the horses and goats would take for the hike. The rest could wait until the family arrived. He liked helping to teach the younger kids how to pack their individual goat packs and make sure the weight was even and matched for each goat. It was good to give them some responsibility as well for their individual pack goat during the hike, good training for the kids and the goats.

* * * * *

Martha was glad when Tom finally pulled into her brothers drive way, even though Manti was only about 2 hours away it was usually not an easy drive for the boys, after about the first hour they would start picking on each other which leads to them fighting. So the last 30 minutes had been truly a headache for her. Now that they were here they could get out and burn off their excess energy and maybe their Uncle James would even have some left over farm chores for them to do.

Martha opened her door on the van and got out, her boys were immediately out and running for the playground equipment James had installed in the back yard.

"Lance, Walter and Drake!" She yelled at her boys. They all stopped and turned around to look at her hoping she would let them play for a while.

"Yes mom" Lance asked.

"You three remember to behave and see if your Uncle James needs any help with the chores before you go play."

"Oh Mom, do we have to?" Walter replied

"Yes you do, after you help get things ready for the camp, and our things are packed as well then you should still have time to play, so don't run off there is plenty to do."

"Ok mom we won't we just need to have a little fun before we have to work" Lance said

"Alright just make sure you help out." Martha told her boy's as she watched them take off around the corner of the barn.

Martha walked towards the main house she had better go say hi to her brother James and Katasha to make sure they know that her family was finally here. She walked over to the porch and went up the few stairs, a little slower than the last time she had visited. Either the stairs were getting taller or she was feeling more pregnant. She smiled to herself knowing that it was her being 8 months along that was the real reason that she had a harder time going up the stairs at times. Once she got to the front door she lifted the large iron door knocker and let it fall several times creating a loud clang every time it struck, she remembered when James had bought it, and he claimed it was the perfect fit for the old house. When there was no immediate response she just turned the knob and entered the old home of her childhood.

"Hello, Kat you home?" Martha called out as she went over to the living room couch and sat down.

Katasha walked into the living room and looked down on Martha

"Hi Martha we are glad you're here I could suggest you go ahead and make yourself right at home but I can see you have already done that." She said smiling at her sister in law.

"Yep after being forced to walk all the way up those steep stairs I am so glad that James thought about putting this nice soft couch so close to the front door so people can recover from the stairs, maybe he should take some of his free time and just build me a ramp to walk up, would be easier." Martha said smiling.

"And it is good to see you too Katasha. I do think this will be our last baby, I am getting more worn down with each one and one forgets all the stuff you have to go through just to have another child, then as they grow into teenagers you wonder some days why you ever wanted to have kids at all." Martha added as she stretched out onto the couch letting her body be enveloped by the soft couch.

"Now Martha you know better" She smiled knowingly at her for she more than understood the nature of her comments.

"So I take that it was another tough drive with the boy's then." She added sympathetically.

"Yes it was I don't know why they have to fight once they get inside the car, sure would be nice if someone invented a remote control so you could just push the pause or mute button, maybe a sleep button, sure would make traveling with kids a lot more, hmm civilized. The boys sure do know how to push everyone's buttons, oh well; maybe someday they will learn to get along. Or is that too much to ask?" Martha said in a tired voice.

Katasha thought a moment she completely understood where Martha was coming from and thought it best to change the subject to a better topic.

"Martha could I get you a drink of juice or water?"

"That would be great thanks, if you have any orange juice with ice, lots of ice would be perfect".

"Orange juice it is then and we have plenty of crushed ice." Katasha said as she turned to leave the room to get Martha her drink, she paused and asked another question.

"So where are Tom and the boy's you didn't leave them outside all by themselves again did you?"

"Now why would I do a thing like that Kat"? She answered smiling "Tom is taking our stuff to the staging area for the repacking and the boys were going to burn off some energy then hopefully help in the repacking or any chores that need doing. So where are we going to go this year Kat? Or is it a last moment surprise again?"

Katasha came back into the room and handed the large glass of orange juice full of crushed ice to Martha. "We are letting Ben decide this year and he is going to take us into the Twin Lakes area, he felt in your condition it would be one of the easier places to go and since we can drive into the trail head it would be only about a 2 hour walk for you unless you prefer to ride a horse of course.(She giggled) so do you think you can handle that after all once your there you're going to have several days to rest up before you would have to walk or ride out."

Martha drank some juice and got a mouth full of crushed ice to chew on as she thought over the Twin Lakes idea. They were right it would be one of the easier places Ben could come up with but still it was up hill in some spots she was sure, almost everything out here was up or down hill.

"Well I guess it could be worse, it could be back to Blue Lake or the meadow area on the south eastern side of Shelly Baldy again. Sure why not I think I can handle it and if something happens you can always have someone carry me out." Martha said. I must be nuts thinking of this trip in my condition however wouldn't want to spoil it for everyone. Kat was right once there she would have several days to recover and it would be a quiet peaceful place to be.

" Now Martha we already have it all planned out we are taking the goats as usual but just for you we will be taking some horses this time, and if there is a problem we can always radio for the search and rescue chopper to fly in and rescue you if need be." Katasha laughed.

"Well don't you think I can make it? I don't think you do. Now listen up Kat we Adair's are of good stock you know and I'll just show you all, I won't be needing a helicopter so Bah! I will keep up with the rest of you as well and maybe not even use a horse and it may just be the rest of you slowing me down." Martha said as she grinned right back at Kat.

"Calm down gal I didn't mean to get you all riled up, so drink your juice and get some rest I will go out and see about helping them get your things repacked and the rest of the family should be getting here soon." Katasha said as she walked towards the door.

"I will just sit here and relax all wrapped up around these pillows and your soft couch at least until lunch time and let you all do the work today." Martha said as she lay back down and stretched out again on the couch letting her body sink into its comfortable softness and all the pillows as well. A little nap was always good for the soul she thought.

* * * * *

Ben was overlooking the preparations of the repacking as the goat packs each had to be as evenly balanced as well as individually weighed and matched for each goat's body mass and ability as a packer. With the other kids helping with the smaller stuff it was going along ok, and it did help keep them out of mischief they would be done in a bit with this part

"So Uncle Tom can I ask you to help me with the horse pack's once we finish with the goat packs? We are going to use them this trip to carry the larger tents and heavier gear and that saves the goats from needing to carry extra stuff, it should make things a little bit easier for Aunt Martha, anyway you older folks do need your creature comforts when camping I am told." Ben laughed.

"Ben you had best mind your words as your still a youngster, and some day you might be allowed to grow older and wiser, you see we don't need you to spoil us however the canvas tent will come in handy I suspect in case of poor weather and with group meetings. Now quit your teasing and let's get these packs loaded up and into the truck then." Tom said thinking Old eh, well I will just have to show this kid who is old later when we start the hiking, I bet he wears out long before this old bear does. I will make sure of that, darn kids now days don't have enough respect for their elders.

Tom and Ben finished what packing they could do and loaded all the packs into the truck. Leaving some out for the other family members to put their stuff into once they arrived, they had some regular human style back packs that where to be used as well the ones ready to go were also loaded up.

"That's about all we can do for now, let's go get some lunch and a break before the others get here." Ben said to Tom and the boy's.

The boys darted for the house at the sound of food.

"Well Ben where are you taking us this year?" Tom asked

"We are going to Twin Lakes, should be ok for Aunt Martha" Ben replied as they started walking towards the kitchen door of the house.

"If you think it will be easy on her then it must be, I trust your and James' thinking on these camping trips. You can fill me in as we eat lunch then."

James looked out the door when the 4 door super cab truck pulled into his yard, finally the Barrett's where here; he felt he had been waiting all day for them to finally show. James walked out the door to meet them.

"Hey Olaf and Mary so nice you could join us today, your drive go ok?" James asked with a twinkle in his eye, he did always like to razz Olaf some.

"Yep the drive went just fine James" Olaf responded as he jumped out of his truck.

"We got a late start you see Natasha here had to put her pretty face on or something just in case she ran into some of them rare good looking Cowboys or Bears or maybe even a teen age Bigfoot, You know she always trying to impress the teenage wild life." Olaf stated and laughed as he did.

Natasha was now 16 and allowed to start dating and she was always worried about her appearance in public and you never know who one might meet, she would always say to him.

Natasha heard her dad's remarks and shot him a piercing glare.

"DAD! You stop it right now! I don't need any more lectures about boys again. Some people just like to look like normal human beings and I don't want to grow up looking like a lost redneck that just came off the mountain like some of you guys do." Natasha said, her Dad irritated her all the time about this topic and some day's it just made her mad at him.

Tarton now 20 years old had gotten out of the back seat and could not help but laugh at his little sister once again, and at his Dad's humor about Natasha needing to look pretty all the time.

"Now Natie why don't you just calm down and don't be insulting the family men folk just because were normal folk, not everyone has to live in front of a mirror just in case they run into some cute little boy" Tarton laughed again.

Now Natasha with her young woman's pride, being stepped on by these men, well she had had just about enough of their teasing and she figured it was about time to at least teach Tarton another lesson.

"Tarton I'm a going to kick your butt!" and she slammed her truck door and started running after Tarton with the intention of planting her boot on his butt as hard as she could.

Now Tarton knowing his sister he saw this coming, after all he usually did go fishing with good bait and he had set the hook well once again. So now he ran full tilt to the closest haystack and jumped up several bales and continued to climb till he was on top of the bales only then did he pause and turned down to look upon his now angry sister who was trying to figure out how to climb up after him without getting dirty.

"Now Natie just calm down little sister, you know I was just funning ya a little that was all, so I am sorry ok?" Tarton said from his safe position high above his sister, still grinning.

"Sorry, Sorry! I tell you what Tarton you're gonna be sorry later if you don't come down here right now and face me, and I mean right now! Tarton Barrett! If I wasn't in my good clothes I'd come right up there and shove you off into the manure pile on the other side, I WILL get you either now or sometime when your least expecting it so you'd better come down right now and take your medicine"

Tarton just smiled down at his sister, "Natie poor little Natie, so worried about messing up your good clothes you never know there might just be some cute young cowboy neighbor just waiting for you inside Uncle James house right now for you to impress and you wouldn't want to get all sweaty and dirty or mess up your make up, so maybe you'd just be better off to let it go, calm down and go cool off in the house for now." He said in a very teasing voice.

Natasha turns about 4 different shades of red some darker shades than she already had turned if that were possible she just glared up at her brother menacingly.

"Just remember Tarton you have to sleep sometime." With that Natasha turned and stomped off into her Uncle's house. Thinking to herself just you wait you big chicken, she will play nice for now to make the adults happy but sometime on this trip she would find some way to get even with her loud mouthed brother.

Tarton took a breath of clean free air, and only after Natasha had disappeared into the house did he begin his climb down to the ground.

Uncle James had stood on the porch about ready to burst from laughter but refrained, no use adding insult to injury these two were always going at it and seemed like they were not happy unless they were fighting over something, kids sure could be silly he thought.

"Tarton you leave her alone and let her cool off we have a long few days ahead and you two need to be able to get along during the hike if that's even possible." James said.

"Well ok Uncle, I promise it's just some days it's so easy to pick on her. I will try to be nice during this visit. I promise."

"Well Olaf, looks like life is about as normal as usual with your kids, so where is little Thor did he fall asleep again or what?" James asked.

"Yep he did, he should be waking up, and not sure how anyone could sleep with all the bickering these older two can get into during the 3 hour drive it takes to get here. Hey Thor come on out and say hi to your uncle and cousins."

Thor now age 14 crawled out of the back seat and rubbed his eyes, he realized they were at Uncle James home now, and as a surviving veteran of his siblings disputes he now removed the ear phone buds he usually wore during such trips music was much better than those two always going at it.

"Hello Uncle James" Thor said as he got out of the truck.

"Thor I see you brought ear phones this time, great idea a sure sign of intelligence and a good way to survive trips with your sister and brother I would think there may be some hope for you yet as you show some common sense." James said smiling at his nephew.

"Well it is the only way to get any rest with those two stuck in a truck for hours on end."

"Well all you Barrett's had best come on in and get some grub, lunch has been ready for a while now and if you don't hurry there won't be anything left for you," James told them then added. "Olaf let's get your things repacked into the packs and loaded up in the truck and as soon as you have gotten something to eat and a few moments of rest we will think about when to head out."

"Sounds good to me let's get it done then."

Olaf and James got the work done then headed in to the main house for a little rest.

CHAPTER 3

Twin Lakes

With everything packed up in the several trucks and the livestock trailers finally loaded with the goats and horses. The families also loaded into the 4x4 suburban and trucks that would transport them to the trail head since most normal street vehicles would have a hard time going where they needed to go. So the 4x4's were always kept around for the adventure trips. It only took a little over a half hour going east up state road 153 before they came to the turn to the North that lead to Big John's Flat, they turned onto it and traveled a short distance before turning again to the east onto a dirt road that led to Round Flats from there they followed a jeep trail road it was slow going due to the ruts cut into it by the many 4x4er's who loved to tear up the roads when muddy. This was the reason they needed to use 4x4's in order to get to the trail head and pulling trailers just made it go a little slower avoiding the ruts, tree limbs, rocks, boulders and other normal woodland debris.

After a slow and bumpy 20 minutes they finally came to the open meadow that sat beside Merchant Creek. There we parked the vehicles and began unloading the pack animals and gear then put the packs on the goats and horses and got everyone lined up and ready for the trail.

They let the younger members of the expedition have at least one goat to help pack their gear and this not only helped the kids with a lighter load for the hike it also gave them some responsibility for the goat that was helping them as well. The teenagers and adults carried their own large back packs and the younger kids each had a day pack with some snacks and water to drink during the hike. Now all the older members of the family would take turns teaching the youth how to work with the horses and goats on the trail, thus enabling each generation to pass on the knowledge to the next generation on how to hike with animals.

With everyone finally ready to start the hike to Twin Lakes James asked the family to gather around for a brief chat before they left.

"I am glad to see that everyone was able to come this year it has been difficult for some we know and I hope that Martha can do well on this hike or riding the extra mule if she needs. I expect Martha to let us know if she needs a break and we will take one. The same goes for you younger kids this is not a race but to get there in a goodly way, so if you need a break let us know also.

Now I expect the older kids to assist the younger kids and keep an eye out for them during this whole trip as we don't want anyone getting lost. Now no wandering off alone always have a buddy with you just in case and always let the parents know where you're going, that includes answering natures call. Keep in mind that you're in the wilderness now so common sense is a must, so beware we may run into a bear or even a mountain lion so be aware of your surroundings. No running on the trail it spook's the horses and goats not to mention makes parents worry as well and keep an eye out for snakes but don't forget that this is a fun hike as well. Now as head of this little expedition I think it only best to ask the oldest one here to ask our Heavenly Father in prayer for a safe journey and that of course would be you Olaf." James said.

"Oldest eh? Only got you by a year or so James, you old fart so watch it." Olaf answered back.

This brought chuckles from the families as there was always a little jesting between these two older men concerning age even though there were both about the same age.

"All you kids let us bow our heads while the prayer is said." Olaf commented with a smile.

Everyone bowed their heads, some fidgeting to be on the trail shuffled their feet.

"Our dear Father in Heaven we thank you for our health and for allowing us all to be here as family once more and we ask your blessings to protect us and our animals from harm during this expedition to Twin Lakes. Help us to use the knowledge and wisdom you have given us to help each other on this hike and to learn from each other and that we can all get along. And bless Martha that she will be strong enough to manage well during our trip. Let us have good weather as well. We thank you for all you have blessed us with and ask these to assist with these small things in the name your son Jesus Christ Amen."

Olaf said reverently.

"Ben you and Tarton start out on point" He said.

"The rest of us shall follow your lead just remember don't get us lost and don't run off and leave us behind." James added.

Ben and Tarton just grinned at each other then at the group.

"Does anyone have a map or compass? And where is that trail anyway? Tarton said humorously.

"Let's get going" Ben said as he took the lead up the trail.

They crossed the wood pole fence line that the forest service had in place to prevent motorized vehicles from entering this part of the forest they even had a sign posted stating 'No motorized vehicles beyond this point and what you pack in you pack out that could be why it was such a nice quiet secluded area to hike in.

Ben and Tarton led the group up into the upper meadow then followed the trail through the tree's to the east it was a short uphill hike and then was easier hiking after that. They did make sure everyone stayed in line of sight of each other and it did make for a stretched out little caravan. 16 people and a couple of pack horses and 1 nice ole mule for Martha to ride and 12 pack goats. All where excited to be on the trail they did like getting out and going anywhere as long as it was off the ranch. The people mixed in with the pack animals some single file others side by side the whole caravan stretched out about 100 yards in length. They followed an old jeep trail that was used way back in the old logging or mining days and only the forest service was still allowed to use them every now and then for their needs.

Finally they entered a higher meadow with slow rolling hills surrounded by the Aspen and Pine forests. In the last hour and a half they slowly climbed about 1000 feet in elevation. As they came around and old growth dead fall log Ben saw one of his favorite sites on this trail. There was an old Aspen tree that years ago had obviously been struck by lightning and when it hit the tree it severed the main part of the tree about 4 feet up and the burned part of the old tree about 20 feet of it was laying on the ground where it fell that day now just an old weathered log. However over the years the roots had given new life to the tree which continued to grow from the spot where the lightning had cut the tree and this new growth was over 30 feet tall and very healthy and strong. It was a very interesting picture and made one think that even after the harsh times this Aspen had gone through surviving near death by the lightning now renewed with life, so are our lives from near death trails, a new life tends to spring forth as we all struggle throughout our lives if we but only persist and never give up no matter the trials. This tree could teach a lot he thought.

Up here they were close to 10,000 feet in elevation and the air was clean and almost crisp, it had become a partly overcast day so the blue sky was covered with the white billowy clouds that provided some shade for the expedition and with the slight breeze Ben doubted anyone would get over heated on this trip. As Ben looked back along the caravanning trail of family and animals he noted that all seemed to be doing just fine, however soon he would stop and let everyone catch up for a breather and to count heads.

Ben crested the next hill and stopped this meadow was big enough for the group to take break in, and he did notice some elk grazing in the distance and beyond them a few deer. It was a wonderful view and you could see the Twin Lakes not far from his vantage point at least as a crow flies. Now Twin Lakes was actually 2 small lakes around 2 to 3 acres each almost perfectly round basins with a small little pond off to the south west of them, The main 2 lakes were connected with a small stream about 4 feet wide and roughly 25 yards long and if you were to be able to look down on them from above it would resemble an old pair of spectacles.

"Well Tarton have you ever seen such a nice looking peaceful view in your whole life?" Ben asked.

"Actually as wonderful as this view is I would have to say yes, I have seen better views, you see Ben if you go walking by BYU campus in the summer there is a lot of great natural scenery there that I personally find more beautiful." He replied and smiled at Ben.

"OK, ok I have to say you got me there; however you know I was meaning nature's natural beauty. Not a bunch of college girls you nut, you always have girls on the brain don't ya just bringing it up almost spoiled the view just now."

"Nothing wrong with girls Ben, and as for nature's beauty well I would have to admit there just happens to be a lot of natural beauties on campus and with the Provo Mountains for the back drop, well what better natural beauty could one ask for? Oh and you can actually talk with them too Ben, you know conversation with a girl has never killed anyone that I know of, you might just need to try it someday." Tarton said in a humorous tone.

"Tarton I am sure you're right, well maybe… however out here in nature as one overlooks the beauty of creation, its quiet peaceful and a most spiritual feeling a place to reflect on things. No need to have to try an impress some college girl, and out here there is no drama. Just the animals, trees, grass, water, clouds you know just everything in life. And if you take the time to quiet your mind Tarton you can hear nature talking to you."

"Ben now you're going weird on me again, so now nature talks to you so does that mean your hearing voices too? You really need to get out into my world more often, you know civilization can be fun also Ben and no matter how much you like those tree's you can't dance with a tree." Tarton said.

"I really don't care for the city life you know that. Someday when the time is right I might look around, but why spoil all this fun with a girl? All she'd want is for me to spend my money on her and then it's do this or do that, can we go here or there, oh and then your life is so messed up because some skirt is controlling your every move. I have seen that too often and you city folks can just keep all that drama I don't need it. This country boy don't need no gal pulling his strings. I like being a free man." Ben replied as he looked over the trail watching the last few stragglers come into the rest area.

"There they come now we will let them all take a little rest before we go down into Twin Lakes, So try and enjoy the view and peace and quiet with no more talk of gals, its spoiling the moment for me ok." Ben said.

"Sure Ben no problem but one of these days some gal is going to come along and you'll be like a bear to honey, just stuck no matter how many times you get stung you're going to go back for more hoping for the sweet taste of honey. I just hope to be there when you fall cause you're gonna fall hard cousin. And it will be proof to all that modern day miracles still happen." Tarton says as he slaps Ben on the shoulder. Then he walked off a little way so as not to further impede on Ben's Zen moment with the mountains. He smiled to himself as he thought it over someday Ben you'll wake up out of your dreamy world down here in the back woods of Utah and realize there is plenty of life outside of this little box canyon world you live in. Some days I just don't get where he is coming from, but I do like him even though he can be very strange at times. Tarton thought to himself.

Once everyone had reached the top of the hill overlooking the area of Twin Lakes, they all spread out and took some time for a little breather enjoying the view of the country side.

After about 30 minutes or so, they began the final walk down the hill into the meadow where there was an opening in the tree line that took them to the lakes, it only took another 35 minutes to arrive at the lake and they went down the 20 foot sloped hill into the main grassy meadow area of the lake's.

Tarton looked at the area they were to camp in he saw the old fire pit with logs around it for benches to sit on to the south east about 100 yards was the lake and it was about 2 acres in size but not too deep in the middle as he could see the bottom when he was on the ridge line. To the west of the lake and there was short and tall grasses of various types, that was another reason he figured Ben picked this area, plenty of good feed and water for the animals. There was a small creek feeding the lake from the north western side and then sure enough there was a little creek connecting both circular lakes. There were blue spruce, pines; some fir trees and some aspens spread throughout the area, the meadow area must have been about 4 acres worth of space. He did notice that there was what looked to be an old mine entrance on the south east side of the main lake and that it was caved in or blocked but must have been a working mine a long time ago. On the other side of that he noticed you could walk up the embankment and look out over the valley and see the whole south western area where Beaver must be far in the distance. And also to the south east there were some old ski runs cut into the tree lines, on those hills he realized they must now be around 10,000 feet in elevation. He remembered Ben talking about the only civilization you might come in contact out here were the daily fly over's of the commercial airplanes but he usually never met anyone on the trails we had just come in on. So it should be a nice quiet camp, he noticed that Uncle James was calling for everyone to gather around him so he walked over and joined the rest of the group to see what was up.

James had called everyone over and when they were all gathered he began his usual camp speech.

"Now that we are all here together I would like to point out some things. This is my safety speech adults so keep an eye out for your own kids and everyone else's as well. No one is to go out of camp alone and kids always let someone know where you are going so the buddy system is still in place. It is a lovely place and peaceful however remember you are now on the wilderness food chain you know the circle of life, so pay attention and remain on the top end of it and not the dinner end, there are bear and lions out here.

Now kids you see the old mine over there keep in mind it is OFF limits so just leave it alone and to keep this short just use common sense and you all should be just fine. Enjoy your stay but for now we need to get camp set up and the animals looked after and ready for the night.

Everyone just nodded their approval and a few of the boys looked depressed about not being able to explore the mine but what could anyone really say James was right to be cautious and had to remind everyone of the potential dangers of the wilds.

"Alright boys let's put the cabin tent here in the open where the ground is more level the rest of you pick a spot to set up your tents remember the only open fire will be at the big fire pit." James directed.

Everyone went to setting up camp and it took a couple hours before it was all done, the boys had put the animals over on the south side of the lake and had rubbed and brushed them down and put them on a picket rope line for the evening. Once camp was finally set up they noticed that Thomas had brought two portable latrine tents for those who wanted to have a little sense of the civilized world, he brought them mainly for Martha but the rest of the women thought it was a great idea as well. However James did make sure they were put a little ways downwind from the camp.

"Everyone it's time to relax and have a little dinner, we are going to eat light tonight so make your selves some sandwiches or something simple" Katasha told everyone.

Katasha walked over to Martha to see how she was doing.

"So Martha, how are you holding up?"

Martha was sitting on a large folding chair she looked up at Katasha and sighed.

"Well I am here, sure is good to be off the mule, but it was nice to not have to walk all that way." She stated tiredly.

"So would you like a snack then and you can just sit back and relax all you want, Mary and I can look after the boys so you won't need to stress about them. They need to run I am sure." Katasha told her.

"Kat thanks, but I see Tom has our tent up, I think I may just go lay down on the air mattress and take a nap if that's ok with you."

"Sounds like a great idea, you go to your tent and I'll bring you something to snack on then." Katasha said she then turned and went to find Martha a snack.

Martha slowly got up and walked over to their tent and slowly got down on the large air mattress Tom had brought for her. With the sun on the tent walls, the slight breeze and the rustling of the leaves she was glad she came and also glad she was now laying down finally. She was almost having second thoughts about joining them on this hike as far along as she was, but she just had to come, she loved being with the family and hoped not to be a burden to any of them during this trip. She could handle it as long as she took it easy the next few days. She lay on her back looking up at the top of the tent and watched the shadowy silhouettes of the tree leaves and branches dance in a rhythmic wave on the tents ceiling she was not sure when she fell asleep however it was a good long nap.

Katasha ducked through the door of the Martha's tent and realized quickly that she had gone to sleep. Well best not bother her she does need her rest. So she quietly left the tent to go and check on the boys to be sure they were behaving.

Levi, Lance, Thor and Joseph were over by the lake having a contest on who could skip their rock the best.

"Hey Levi I was thinking you and Joseph ever do any exploring around here?" Lance asked.

"Sure we have some, so what you thinking up now Lance? You know that the old mine there is off limits and the parents won't let us go off very far from camp, so that about kills any fun." Levi responded.

"I know that but Thor and I don't get the chance to do a lot of real fun exploring so any caves or other cool places we can look at?" Lance asked with a hopeful tone in his voice.

Joseph thought about it a moment then said "Well now that I think about it there are some places not too far from here, there is kind of an interesting rock face like a little cliff, but has a lot of hand holds we could climb it and look around and see if we can find any arrow heads, you know stuff like that."

"Yep that could be fun." Levi thought, I had forgotten about that area and he is right not too far so the parents wouldn't miss us at all. And they never said we couldn't do any climbing right?

Lance and Thor looked at their cousins and in unison said "Let's get going then, sounds like fun."

With that the boy's headed off towards the eastern side of the lake and past the old mine up the hill and into the tree line there was a slight trail or foot path probably made by the deer that they followed that would lead them to the cliff face. After walking about a half hour Levi started scanning the area in front of them.

"Well if I remember right it should be around here somewhere so keep a look out." Levi said.

Thor looked at Levi "So you are sure you know where you're going or are you just making this up as we go along?" Thor stated.

"Just calm down Thor and wait a minute, it looks like things grew a lot since we last came here see all the growth over that rock wall over there I think that might be the place."

Levi looked over the rock face that stood before him it may be the right spot or not either way it would be fun to climb, however it did look a little different than when he last came there so maybe he wasn't remembering exactly right.

"Guy's let's start clearing some of these bushes away from the wall so we can get some better areas to climb on. "

They all started looking around and clearing some of the lower bushes out of the way so they could be closer to the rock face. As they did Lance bent over and picked up what he thought were strange looking rocks and he held them up for Levi and the other to look at.

"Hey look what I found, Levi is this an arrow head?" Lance asked hopefully.

Levi looked at it and yep it was, "Yes it sure is an arrow head, where did you find it? There could be more of them lying around or maybe even some old pots or other Indian tools." Levi told them.

With that they all started looking along the base of the rock face and the search for arrow heads or anything that would be a cool find for a kid. After a good hour had passed by Thor had found another arrow head but no one else had any luck. However Joseph was still determined to find something to take home, so he moved some bush branches farther to the left of where they had been searching and to his surprise he found something very interesting.

"Hey Thor come take a look at this." Joseph asked.

Thor joined Joseph and as he got close Joseph pointed through the trees.

"There is something in there, it looked like wood and maybe some metal on it can you help me move some of this stuff so we can get a better look at what it is?" he asked Thor.

"Start pulling these bushes out of the way and I will try to bend some of these little trees so we can get a better look." Thor told him.

"Ok" Joseph replied as they went to work.

As Thor tried to clear away what he could with his hands he found himself looking between some small aspen saplings crowded together in a shaded area of the rock wall under a small overhang maybe about 10 to 12 feet above him, as he looks closer he sees what looks like a rusty old door hinge so he continued pulling back some more of the saplings in order to reach out to where he could touch and feel the old hinge.

"Joseph you're right there is something here, Hey guys I found something come take a look."

The others all came over anxious to see what he had found.

"Look here, it's an old door hinge I think, but it is hard to get at with all these little trees in the way help me pull up some of them and clear out some of the bush so we can see exactly what it is."

"Sure we will help with that."

They started pulling up the younger trees that were in the way and then stood back to get a better look at what they had found. They realized with amazement they were looking at an old door but still from its age it still looked pretty solid. There was a huge ring style door handle or door puller more like it, the door itself was huge and very much larger than the boys.

"Wow! "exclaimed Thor, "Now that's a door, it must be 8 or 9 feet tall and I'd say 5 to 6 feet wide I bet my dad could get his 4 wheelers through that door way with no problems at all."

"Can we get a closer look?" Asked Joseph and Lance, as they said this they both let go of the trees they were holding which let them spring back into place just about hitting both Levi and Thor in the face as they leaped back out of the way just in time to miss the oncoming tree's.

"Hey watch it that about hit me" Thor stated.

"Sorry we didn't mean for that to happen we just got excited is all" Lance commented.

Levi stood back and got a better view of the new situation and he thought for a moment, 'You know what we need guys is an axe or saw to trim these trees out of the way so we can get at the door easier and see if we can open it to see what is inside it."

"Well where are we going to get and axe around here we are way out in the mountains "Asked Thor.

"You have been in the big city for too long, my Dad never comes out on these big camps without at least one axe, usually he has a few of them on hand so let's go and see what he's got he won't miss one of them I am sure." said Levi.

"Sounds like a good idea lets go see about that axe and maybe a shovel or saw or some other tools just in case we need them to help open the door." Thor added.

So they all headed back to camp with their new secret, after all if they told others now it might ruin their fair chance at opening the door first and seeing what was inside. So as they walked down the trail they wondered out loud what could be behind the mystery door.

CHAPTER 4

Curiosity of Boys

Sariah and Natasha had finished helping the adults in setting up camp and then took care of the horses and goats making sure they had access to water and grass by high line picketing them over by the smaller of the lakes.

They were now resting with their feet soaking in the cool water of the smaller lake enjoying the warmth of the sun upon their faces.

"So Natasha, how has your summer been?"

"Just fine, it is nice to be out of the big city for a while, it is so refreshing here in the mountains with the clean air and just everything about it is peaceful, its good to rest and enjoy nature."

"Good to hear and thanks for helping me with the animals the boys were supposed to help but they snuck off as soon as it even looked like there were chores to do but nothing new there."

"Yep boys will be boys but there will be plenty for them to do when they get back from where ever they went. They have been gone a while do you think their ok?"

"I am sure they are fine, Levi knows the area pretty well and the others should be fine with him. Looks like the kitchen tent is ready lets go see if we can be of any help and then everyone can get some rest after dinner."

"Sounds good the sooner everyone is fed then the whole family can get some rest, I like that idea."

They stood up and started walking over to the cabin style tent that was to serve as the kitchen during the trip.

"Hey Natasha look over there, they must have a radar for food or smelled it cause here comes the wandering brats now." Sariah laughs then yells out to the boys as they emerge from the tree line on the other side of the main lake.

"Levi, where have you all been? Natasha was getting all worried about you boys, thought a skunk got ya or something." Sariah said.

Natasha smirked at Levi and the other boys. "Hope you have not been getting into trouble again and even if you all end up lost just means more grub and peace for the rest of us." She teased.

Thor glared at his sister, "Naty you had best be nice or maybe you'll wake up tomorrow with a cute little skunk in your tent." He threatened with a smile.

"Skunk? Really? Now if I remember correctly wasn't it not just a year or two ago when you boys came into the camp smelling like skunk because you had the bright idea of trying to catch and tame one? And if I recall all you got for your troubles was a very, very, smelly present from the skunk. Also you were all banished to the other end of the camp ground too, so let's not have any idle threats or pranks this year ok, I don't think your clothes can handle it, I know my nose can't." Natasha said with a smile.

Levi sheepishly smiled at the memory, they had actually been trying to catch a skunk that day to put into the girls tent and it did not go as planned.

"Well girls I think we learned our lesson on that one, what is there to eat we're hungry." Levi stated.

They all walked over to the dinning tent and found out that tonight dinner would be whatever type of sandwich they could make with a drink and some chips and some salad.

They sat around wherever they could and ate; Tom looked over at the boys and just had to ask them the question.

"So where have you boys been this afternoon? I did notice you all disappeared instead of helping your sisters with the animals so when everyone is done eating you boys get to put everything away and take care of the trash, remember we don't want the critters getting the food or the trash tonight." He said and smiled at the boys.

The boys didn't complain much it could have been worse, after they had cleaned up the area everyone went to their tents and all went to sleep about dark or soon after as it had been a tiring day for most of the hikers.

* * * * *

It was a chilly mountain morning as usual at this elevation, as the sun peaked over the distant horizon the dew start to retreat and melt away as the warmth of the rays of the dawning light touches them, and a slight mist rising from the meadow and lakes as a new day begins. A few curious deer came to drink cautious of the intruders at their watering hole, they melded into the forest before the camp arose.

There is a stirring amongst the younger boys tents as they awoke anxious for the day to begin as a few of them had had a sleep deprived night in the excitement of their discoveries the day before.

Thor looked over to where Lance and Levi were sleeping and sees them stir in their sleeping bags so he decides to wake'm up as he had not slept well anyway that night.

"Hey Levi, Lance you dudes awake yet?" he asked.

"Yeah I am, had a hard time sleeping last night I think I must have tossed and turned all night kept having dreams about the door we found yesterday sure would be neat to see what was behind it." Levi answered. Wiping the sleep from his eyes and sitting up.

"So you ready for another look today then?" Thor asked hopping for a yes.

"Sure am but we had best get moving before all the grown-ups wake up and wreck our day with chores or something." Levi responded.

"Do you think we had best get Ben or Tarton to help us clear the big stuff off the wall and door area?" Thor asked.

Levi looks down and thinks for a moment he really didn't need the older boys telling them what to do however it would be easier. And it would help keep the parents from worrying about them so much if they were helping.

"Do you think we really need their help then?" Levi asked

"Well I think Ben would be all for it and Tarton might as well I think we could use their bigger muscles to help get the bigger stuff out of the way and in case the door doesn't open, it could be stuck as old as it is. And if they are with us they can't tell the parents what we are up to. So let's go see if they wanna come if not it's their loss right. Lance you go wake them up we need to go find some tools that can help us today." Thor commented

"Right so let's go wake'm up then." Lance says as he pulls on his hiking boots then crawls out of the tent and stretches in the morning sun then he is off to wake up Ben and Tarton. He finds Tarton still in his sleeping bag and he was still sleeping so he was forced to wake him up.

"HEY! Tarton! Are YOU AWAKE?" he said in a loud voice but not loud enough to wake the other campers in the area.

Tarton stirs in his sleeping bag and thinks now who in their right mind would wake him up so early when he was camping at that moment he heard the sound once more.

"HEY! Tarton! Are YOU AWAKE! Come on dude wake up sleepy head." Lance repeated.

"Oh it's you, so what is so important that you have to wake me up so early kid? And this better be good or you just might find yourself taking a morning swim." He said groggy still.

"Good you are awake." Lance said with a smile glad he was making progress.

"I am now since you woke me up you nut now what is it."

"Well ok you see Thor, Levi said we should ask you and Ben for your help."

"Help? Yeah I'll help you right into the lake if this is not really worth waking me up" Tarton was getting a little perturbed.

"Man you sure do wake up grouchy so look here, yesterday we were exploring and found this strange old door in the wall of the rock not too far from here, and we could not get it open, actually there are some tree's and stuff in the way and we figured since your bigger you could help us move the stuff and get the door open and see what is inside, that is unless you're just a wimp and need your beauty sleep." Lance stated hopefully.

"Wimp I'll show you wimp by tossing your little hide into the lake just for waking me up for nothing."

Tarton moves as if to get up and grab Lance to fulfill his threat about the lake and that sends Lance back out of the tent and almost running to find Ben.

Tarton laid back down and tried to return to his sleepy dreams but to no avail. What Lance said was interesting and if there was a mystery here it could prove to be entertaining at the least. And since he also like to explore it started his mind moving, well better get up and go help the little kids so they don't hurt themselves or something. He got up and dressed then heads out of the tent. Then looks around for Ben if I am going to be stuck helping these kids then he may as well come along and help baby sit, also and he knew this would peak Ben's curiosity as well, so where was that early bird he was always up early. He starts looking for Ben.

Meanwhile Levi and Thor had been digging through the expeditions gear looking for anything that could help clear the area to the door. They had found an axe, shovel, pick axe plus some rope and a few other things they felt might be useful.

Lance sees them and walks over to them and their growing pile of tools.

"Well Thor, your brother sure does wake up grumpy in the morning, I told him what we were going to do and I am not sure he will help he told me he was going to throw me into the lake so I got out of there right quick."

Thor just looked at Lance and shook his head "Throw you into the lake eh, well maybe not a bad idea, so is he going to help or not then?"

"Not sure, I did see him go looking for Ben and why does everyone want to toss me into the lake now, that's not a very nice idea." He said if they wanted to toss him in the cold lake then he would make sure at least one of them would go in with him.

Levi grins "Well Ben never was one to sleep in when out in the mountains he is usually awake just before sun up, it's always been that way and he usually goes off on walks but Tarton should be able to find him."

"So where does that leave us then just waiting on them? Cause I don't like the idea of wasting a good morning sitting here in camp doing nothing." Thor blurted out impatiently.

"No need to worry while we wait we can get something to eat, I know they have some cereal and they put the milk in the stream bed to keep it cold last night, so Lance go over and get the milk and we will go find the cereal and we will meet you at the kitchen tent then. We can at least get a good breakfast in while we wait on those two." Levi said.

The three all looked at each other nodding agreeing to the idea, when Thor had to add his two bits

"Well great idea we will need some energy to work today, and we will also need to make sure we take plenty of water and maybe some snack foods just in case it takes a while."

So they did as suggested and ate breakfast then got some water and snacks ready, then sat down waiting for Ben and Tarton to show up.

Meanwhile Tarton had found Ben walking along the ridge line south west of the lakes.

"Morning Ben looks like you are up early as usual." He said.

"Of course you know I just cannot sleep in when we are in God's country. So why are you up so early you normally like to sleep in as long as possible when camping?" Ben grins at his cousin.

"Well let's just say I was rudely awakened by Lance, Thor, and Levi." Tarton replied.

"Really that's too funny and so what are the three amigo's up to this early then?"

"Well Lance mentioned something about finding a door in a rock wall or something yesterday and they are needing to use an axe or other tools to clear the brush or trees that were in the way in order to see about opening the door, and they want our help to open the door.

Now I am not fully sure what they are talking about, but it probably would be a good idea to go with them to find out what is actually going on and to watch out for them as well."

"Your right about that, a door in the mountain sounds like a good story, I wonder if they got too much sun on the brain yesterday, however if there is one sounds like a recipe for trouble with those boys" Ben said as he looks out over the valley below and thinks on it, a door in the rock interesting but I have been all over this area for years and never have seen a door in a mountain wall, well better go baby sit them at least to keep them out of trouble.

"Well lets go get a bite to eat and then go along with those boys no telling what they actually found, could be an old mine and we need to keep them safe at least." Ben said.

So they went back to camp, as they entered it they noticed the boys all gathered around the fire pit and with them a pile of tools and other things.

"Now Lance I hope you're going to carry your own stuff, we are not here to be your pack mules" Tarton jested.

"Don't worry about that we can carry our own stuff" Lance said.

"Good, Now let's see all we have to do is just baby sit all of you then the rest of the day, but before we go Tarton and I need to eat and get our stuff together so don't go anywhere got it." Ben stated.

"Baby sit? Who you calling a baby Ben?" Thor retorted starting to get fired up over the comment.

"You just calm down there or you won't be going anywhere and you start whining you may just wake up the whole camp then your day will be over before it begins" Ben replied.

They agreed to calm down and finish getting everything done so they could start their expedition.

After everyone was done eating and preparing for the day hike, Ben thought since everyone else was still sleeping he would leave a note with his sister, he didn't really want to wake her but it was best just to make sure his Dad got the note.

Ben walked over to her tent and peaked in, sure enough there she was sleeping nice and sound, So he holds out the stick he found just for this purpose and pokes his sister with it.

"Sariah, Sariah? Time to wake up." He pokes her again a little harder this time.

"Hey, who is that, what? Hey stop hitting me with that stick" She said as she rolled over sleepily rubbing her eyes as she could focus she saw Ben staring at her.

"So what's the matter now did I over sleep or what?" She asked in a tired voice.

"Nope, nothings the matter just wanted to make sure this note gets to mom or dad ok, so they know were the boys and I will be."

"So where you going then?" She asked as she yawns.

"Just for a little walk with the boys, they found something they wanted to show Tarton and me so we think it best to go with them and keep them out of trouble, so here is the note if there are any questions." He handed her the note.

"But who's going to keep you older two out of trouble then?" She asked.

"You're tired just hush now and go back to sleep see you in a few hours or so." He said as he backed out of the tent door.

"Ok whatever." She said and turns back over and got back to her comfortable spot of ground and drifted back into her sleep filled dreams.

Ben looks at the motley group of young boys and folds his arms across his chest then asks.

"What are you up too and where are we going this morning?"

Levi gives a brief description of what they found yesterday and their plan of attack.

"Well that sounds like a little adventure then since there are three of you one can carry the shovel, one the pick axe, and one the axe, Tarton and me will carry some extra water and your lunch so if you each have your water bladders full then let's get going." Ben said.

Levi smiles "Ok follow me you guys you won't be disappointed were gonna have some fun" and with that he takes off leading the little group up the trail.

It was not that long a hike from camp and that was a little bit of a surprise to Ben as he thought he had been all over this area over the years and he had to wonder how he could have missed this place.

"So Levi where is this door you keep telling us about anyway?" Tarton asked.

"It's over there behind these trees and bushes, that's why we had to bring the tools to help clear the area in order to get at the door."

Sure enough there was an old door behind several trees in the wall this just might be worth the hike Tarton thought. I best help them clear it with the axe it would be faster after all.

Tarton put down his water and day pack that held the lunches.

"So let me have a try with the axe it will speed things up a bit in clearing all this stuff out of our way."

Thor handed him the axe and then stepped back out of his way and watched him go to work, better him than me, good thing he thought of bringing them along.

"Here goes nothing" Tarton said as he started hacking and chopping at the trees and heavy brush in front of him. In not too short a time he had cut through the small trees as the largest was only 6 inches thick.

"There you go now let's clear the area, Levi use your pick axe to clear the smaller stuff out of the way and Lance use the shovel and help him. And we shall see what we have after we get it all cleared which shouldn't take too long." Tarton said.

Ben stood watching the boys and Tarton work clearing the brush and trees it took about an hour before they had cleared the area completely in front of the door area, the only thing remaining were the few stumps which Tarton cut down to grown level after the brush was cleared enough for him to see what he was doing.

Ben just had to make the comment he had been holding for all this time as he watched them. "You know guys you do really good work, I could watch good workers all day long and never get tired at all, maybe after this trip you can clean up around the farm." He said as he smiled.

Tarton replied back "Of course you could Ben, we wouldn't want you to break a sweat today now would we you might break a nail or something" He said and they all had a good laugh.

"Now let's take a look at this old door and see what it's all about." Ben said as he stood up and walked over to it.

* * * * *

Natasha left her tent and walks over to Sariah's tent and as she did she looked around and noticed all the boys were not around. She wondered where they all could have gone off to this early in the morning most likely trouble again.

Poking her head into Sariah's tent she sees her still sleeping. "Hey Sariah, Hello sleepy head, time to wake up!" She said in a loud voice.

Sariah stirs and then turns over and looked at Natasha with still sleepy eyes. "Ok, ok so what do you want Nat everyone seems to want to wake me up this morning just as I drift back to my dreams, so what do you need?"

Natasha looked at her and asks "Have you seen the boys this morning? I can't seem to find them anywhere?"

"Well Ben did wake me a while ago, or I think it was him. He said something about him and Tarton were going to go look at something the other younger boys found yesterday or something." She replied now sitting up looking at Natasha.

"Really, so what did they find? And do you know where they went? And why is it they never invite us to go along on stuff like this? Just like a bunch of boys never letting us in on the fun stuff." She replied.

"Sorry Nat they didn't say, just that we were not to worry and to let the parents know they went for a walk if anyone asked, wish I could help more but, Oh wait Ben did give me a note guess it would be ok for us to read it." She said as she hands the note to Nat.

Natasha read the short note. "Dad Tarton and I went with the boys to check on something they found yesterday mainly to keep them out of trouble, we will be back in a few hours so don't worry about us, and yes tell the moms they had some breakfast." It was signed by Ben.

"That's ok, guess we will have to grill them on what they did when they get back. You may as well lie back down and get some sleep if you can, not much else happening this morning." Natasha says.

"Rest are you kidding, I think me trying to get any real sleep today is pretty much shot, I may as well get up and do something since I am awake now. I'm going to go fix me something to eat and then I wonder if we can figure out where those boys went to and follow them to see what they are hiding that sound ok to you Nat?"

"Natasha brightened up "Sure sounds like something fun for us to do let's get moving I will meet you at the breakfast table." She backed out of the tent and walked over to find herself some breakfast.

As Sariah joined her they decided to cook some scrambled eggs then added a slice of cheese for a sandwich, it was filling and quick.

"So Nat where do you think our silly brothers have gone?"

"Not sure I did see them go off to the east side of the lake yesterday ,maybe we should walk over there and see if they left any trail to follow."

"Sounds like a plan grab some water bottles never know how far they went and we do need to stay hydrated at this altitude. It will help walk out the soreness from yesterday's hike in." Sariah agreed. And they went and retrieved the water and started off in search of the boys trail. Which they found pretty easily as it was very obvious by their tracks the direction of the trail.

"Well looks like they went this way it should not be too hard to find them as noisy as they can be." Natasha giggled as they followed the path left by the boy's.

* * * * *

Ben tried to open the door by just pulling on the large iron ring that acted as the door handle, but it would not budge. Then he put his foot up on the wall by the door and pulled hard on the ring as he pushed with his foot against the mountain. This time it did creek and groaned and it did finally move a few inches then stopped.

"Hey Tarton come and give a fellow a hand, when I pull this time use that branch as a lever and see if we can pry this thing open."

Tarton picked up one of the thicker tree limbs about 8 foot long and 4 inches thick and he placed it into the crack Ben had made and together they both grunted, pulled and worked the door open far enough for them to enter.

"Well that does it" Ben said and he slowly poked his head in then walked into a room, Followed by Tarton.

Ben stood in the door light allowing his eyes to become accustom to the darkness of the room, once he could see a little he walked forward a couple more feet exploring the floor for any obstacles or other potential problems like a hole in the floor.

Tarton looked at Ben and asked, "So can you see anything yet or is it too dark? Would you be needing a flash light?"

"I have a light" Ben said as he pulled one from a pocket and turned it on.

"Now let's see what there is to see." He began to search the darkness with the light.

As he did so he started making out the interior of the room they found it to be a good size room or actually a cave the ceiling must be around 14 feet high sloping downward as it went back into the darkness the room must have been at least 40 feet wide and they could not determine exactly how deep it was yet as it seemed to go on and on. However there were some items of interest they noticed near the entrance or door, there was an old wooden desk and some really old looking mine tools, rusty pick axe's shovels and lamps and a good assortment of old fashioned tools and old wood box's and other items. Also there were 3 old wood beds along the left wall and a few chairs.

"Tarton lets have a look over here at the desk maybe we can find out something about this place" Ben suggested.

Meanwhile outside the cave door Thor, Lance, Joseph & Levi stand impatiently waiting.

"Hey Thor why don't you go in and see what they're doing and if they found anything?" asked Levi.

"Well it is kinda dark in there, and a little spooky but I guess I can go ask them for you" He responded a little nervous as he did not really care for the dark.

Thor cautiously enters the room but made sure he stood in the sun lighted area by the door.

"So Ben, Tarton you guys find anything cool in here? The guys wanna know what you found?" He asked.

"Just be patient, you have to be careful in these old caves one never knows what you might stumble across, there could be a dead body or a bottomless pit to fall into or snakes or scary animals, then there are the spiders and spooks one really never knows until it's too late, so be a little more patient and invite the others to come on in if they want to, but make sure they stand by you for their safety of course." Tarton replied with a smile.

"You don't have to try and be so scary you nut" Thor said he was a little spooked already and Tarton knew that and he knew he was messing with him.

Thor backed up to the door and poked his head out the opening and called to the other boys. "Hey come on in but Tarton wants you to stay by the door area where the light is so we don't fall into a bottom less pit that's in the middle of the floor so be careful guys." He said with a slight smile.

The boys followed him into the cave room and stood by the door while their eyes grew accustom to the darker room. They watched as Ben and Tarton looked things over with the flash light.

"Thor I don't see a hole in the floor anywhere what's the big deal trying to scare us like that for anyway. Maybe you need your butt kicked for doing that." Levi said.

"Hey was just funning you so put a sock in it and calm down." Thor replied

Ben looked around at the boys, "Now no one is going to be doing any butt kicking so pipe down and let us have a look at this old desk maybe we can find out something about this place in it." He said as he looked at the desk he realized there were some old papers on the table some were very crumbly and tender to the touch as one of the corners had fallen to pieces when he attempted to pick it up.

"Tarton don't touch the papers I will take some photos of them with my camera and then we can read them later just in case they all fall apart on us. They may be worthless but never know it could say something about what happened here and who lived here stuff like that." Ben stated as he pulled out his camera then takes a deep breath and carefully blows across the top paper blowing most of the dust off as best he could then he took some pictures and then gently slid the top one aside to reveal the next paper and took a picture of that one he did this 4 times and then it was time to open the drawers to see what could be found there.

They opened up one revealing some mine weight scales and other instruments and items related to it. The next drawer contained some unusual items.

Ben pulled out what looked like an old animal skin rolled up and some kind of parchment tied together with a leather tie as he looked it over he placed it on top of the desk.

Meanwhile Tarton had been looking around the room and found some strange writing on the walls that made him wonder if it was some old Indian cave art or something like it.

"Hey Ben come over here with your light and have a look at this writing on the wall you know a little about this stuff don't you? Looks like whoever was mining here chose some old Indian cave to live in."

"Just a moment this is really interesting, come here and look at this, we will look at your writing in a minute. I need your help figuring this out." Ben said.

Tarton came over to where Ben was and between the light of the flash light and the camera ambient light they looked at the items on the desk.

"So what great mystery did you find?"

"Well let's all take a look, you boys can come on over here also, but just look and don't touch anything for now." Ben stated.

The boys all nodded in agreement and promised to look but not to touch and they all gathered around the desk area trying to get a good look at what was on the desk.

"Now boys it would seem that we have found some kind of old document inside this rolled up animal skin, as you see it is in relatively good shape, because the desk and the leather protected it some. I also found this map with it; now let's see what kind of history or story it may tell." Ben leans over to get a closer look at the documents.

The first paper looked like a miners deed of claim and then some other official type of stuff as well. "Well boys looks like just official stuff, will have to look at it in the day light to get a better idea of what it is."

"So Ben do you think any of this old stuff could be worth anything?" Levi said as he was looking in the larger desk drawer at the bottom he found a book so he pulled it out for a look. It was a leather covered bundle. He turned it over and then set it on the desk.

"One never can tell what any of this could be worth, most likely not much. Let's see what you found here Levi" Ben said as he picked up the bundle Levi had just put on the desk. He untied the leather strings that held it closed and it opened like a large envelope style pouch as he looked further he saw that it held a book like an old journal about 11 inches long by about 8 wide and about 1 ½ inches thick. Carefully opening the book so as not to damage it he slowly turned several of the pages and saw it looked like it was written in English and then some other strange writing as well, also there were some drawings and possible rough maps. Ben also noticed it had some of the unusual markings he saw on the wall on the cover as well and he felt it would be best to wait till they got out into the light to really explore this find. Closing the book he turned to Tarton.

"Well we will have to take this back to camp and give it a really good study in some good light, never know could be a really interesting story in here." Ben said.

"Now how about these writings on the wall Ben, what do you make of it?" Tarton asked.

Ben finally looked over at the walls that Tarton had been asking him to look at and he felt a strange sense of amazement and the tingly chill ran up his spine once again. They were pictograms and some other stranger writing he was not sure if they were old Native American in fact they started to remind him of style of old runes maybe a type of cuneiform, like he had found on some of the stuff in the box Fairsong had given him.

"Well guys I am not sure exactly what type of writing this is but I will take some pictures so I can study them more closely later"

"Finally the great know it all is stumped for once" Levi taunted his older brother as he chuckles.

"Well Levi learning is a process you know it would be good for you to embrace more of it as you grow older, now I am going to take my photos and then we can cross reference it with other styles of writing when we get home." Ben said, and took several pictures of the writings and of the surrounding areas of the room that were visible and some of the darker area's one never knows what you can find in the dark with a flash from a camera.

"I think we have enough stuff to look at for now so let's go back to base camp and get a better look at it in the day light."

Tarton looked a little bit discouraged as did Levi. "Go back right now? We have a whole cave to explore and we just got here and you want to leave already that's not fair" Levi whined.

"Ben is right, let's go and we can come back later with some good flash lights so we can do some serious exploring of the cave" Tarton said to the boys who were looking like their puppy had just been taken away.

"All right lets go then, but you promise we can come back right?" Levi said.

"I promise when I come back you can come."

The boys all nodded and agreed it would be cool to come back later. They all headed out of the cave and Tarton went to close the door but Ben stopped him. "Go ahead and just leave it open for now it was hard to open the first time, we will be back soon and I doubt anyone is going to bother it." Ben said.

"Fine with me would hate to fight that old door more than once in a day." Tarton replied to Ben.

Before leaving the area Ben turned to the group and said." Now I want you boys to promise us that you won't come up here or go into the cave without an adult, exploring is fun and exciting but it is also dangerous is that understood."

Levi looked around at all the boys nodded in agreement. "Ben you always spoil the fun you know that, Dad won't let us back into the cave he will give us his same old speech of this and that safety etc. which adds up to no fun for us." He said a little sadness in his voice.

"Don't worry about that I just need you to all promise ok, and I will deal with the Dads and Moms later, as long as your with me I will let you come back." Ben promised.

Once they all had agreed they picked up the tools they had brought with them and headed back down the trail towards base camp.

* * * * *

Natasha and Sariah had skirted the lake and found the trail and had hiked about a half mile from base camp when they could see the boys coming down the trail towards them. Sariah noticed the younger boys chatting excitedly between themselves and Ben and Tarton leading the way.

"So Tarton what's the big mystery and what have you been up to this morning?" Sariah called out to him when they were close enough for him to hear her.

"Well we found something kind of interesting, but we are not sure we want to tell you about it yet." Tarton said with a sly smile.

The younger boys all ran up and surrounded the girls showing their excitement and started talking. "Tarton you didn't find anything, it was us that found it and you would not even know about it if we had not told you about it." Levi said in a proud voice.

The other boys added their own statements that supported what Levi had said.

"Now everyone just calm down." Natasha stated. "We can't make any sense of what your all mumbling about so now start over, no actually be quiet like good little boys, Tarton, Ben what is it you all have found?"

Ben looked at Natasha and Sariah and just grinned from ear to ear, "Well we, that is all of us did find something quite interesting and we even took some pictures and we have some stuff we found with us, It would be better to look at them when we get back to camp."

"But in a nut shell there is an old cave room in the side of the mountain up there in the rock face, we think it was home to the miners who lived here way back in the old days. Also some Indian writing on a wall by the looks of it, but we are hoping to get a better look at what we found in camp, going to put the pictures on the lap top and get a closer look at them and ask the parents if they have any idea's what it all means."

"Then so if you have some artifacts lets seem right now then." Sariah stated.

"Yep have to be sure you're not just pulling a prank on us again." Natasha added.

Ben lifted the pack he had been carrying off his shoulders and let them have a look inside the pack. "Now there you go you can look but no touching and as for the photo's you'll have to wait till later in camp so we only have to tell the story once." Ben said.

Everyone nodded in agreement.

"Now just remember it was us that discovered the cave." Thor stated firmly as Lance, Joseph and Levi all nodded in agreement with what he had said.

"Don't worry boys you'll get your credit." Ben said smiling at them.

"All right then." Sariah said impatiently Tarton and Ben always did like having secrets and liked to keep them away from here. If they thought she would play along with their game and have to wait like they wanted, they had another thing coming. She was sure Levi would take her to get a quick look at this cave with or without Ben and Tarton.

"So Ben can we go see it too, like right now?" Natasha asked.

"Nat it can wait, I would really like to show everyone at camp first and then we can decide what to do from there."

"Then let's get moving so we can get back here quicker." Natasha replied.

Ben started leading the group back down the trail towards camp once more.

Sariah on the other hand had other ideas, she waited for most of the group to get in front of her and down the trail a bit and she motioned to Levi to wait a minute so they could talk.

"What do you want now?" Levi asked her.

"Levi would you like to show your favorite sister where this cave is? You do want to show me now don't you?"

"You're my only sister you know that, I could but Ben wants us all to go back right now and I did promise him after all. He promised we could all come back later."

"Levi do you really think the parents will let us kids go climbing around in some cave, and one with all this old stuff in it as well? They will say it's an archaeological find of the century or something and we will never be allowed to go back in."

Levi took a moment to think about it, he knew Sariah was right of course. And one more little look won't hurt anyone.

"Ok, ok it's not far from here and you're right, it may be the only time we can get a good look at it on our own. So let's get going quickly though so they won't miss us much." Levi replied.

"I knew you were a good little brother, you know they will be so busy in camp they won't miss us a bit so lead the way."

So as the rest of the group returned to camp in their hurry to share the discovery with the others they did not see Levi and Sariah sneak back up the trail towards the cave.

CHAPTER 5

Exploring the Cave

"Levi is it much further?" Sariah asked

"Just be patient it's just around the corner in the rock face, you will see it in a minute so just relax."

Sariah and Levi soon entered the clearing and she was able to see the old door on the other side of the clearing and it was indeed in the mountain face. Interesting she thought not exactly what one would expect to find way out here.

"So I take it this door leads into the cave you spoke of then?"

"Yep sis you're right so you wanna go in, we left the door open a little as it was a real bugger to open the first time."

"Sure since you left the door open might as well go take a look" she said as she pulled out a hand crank flash light, she liked using it because she never had to worry about batteries just crank it a while and you had light.

She walked into the room and shines her light around to see what was there. She saw the desk and other items lying around she noted it was a very dusty and musty place.

"Hey sis this is cool come look at the wall over here this is the writing we found"

"That is interesting so do you think its Indian writing or what did Ben think about it."

"Ben is not sure what it is, that's why he took all those pictures and was in such a hurry to get back to camp, he wants to put it on the lap top and get a better look."

"So how far back does this cave go anyway?"

"We don't know really never took the time to go look, Ben and Tarton had to be so bossy and we had to leave and they wanted more flash lights before they would go looking deeper, I think they were just being chickens if you ask me." Levi said hoping she wanted to look deeper into the cave.

"Well let's go look around for ourselves then and see if we can find any good stuff." She said and started slowly walking deeper into the cave.

Levi agreed and followed her looking around where ever she shone her light hopping to glimpse some old treasure or old relic.

"Hey look over here at this little box, shine your light back over here." He said excitedly.

As Sariah moved closer with her light Levi could see better and the small box was now in front of him at his feet. He bent down and noticed it was wrapped up in an old cloth so he began carefully unwrapping it. It revealed an old wooden box, looked like it was made of scrap wood full of character, it had a piece of leather tacked down in the place of a hinge on top of the box, and there was a strange bluish stone with some carving on it in the center along the edge of the lid. He opened the lid and inside was what looked to be an old hand gun and some ammunition, a big knife, and letters. This was a really cool find he thought.

"Levi let me see that it might be loaded."

"Awe sis you have to spoil the moment don't you, ok." He handed the box with the gun to her.

Sariah picked up the gun it looked like a .45 caliber and as she turned it over sure enough it was a Browning 1911 and as she thought it was loaded. She took out the magazine and made sure there was not any ammo in the chamber. It reminded her of some of the hand guns she saw in her grandpa's old collection.

"It's a good thing we found this; the older boys would have fought over who got to keep it. Do you think Dad will let me keep it after all I did find it right?" Levi asked.

"Well you did find it so maybe he will, but he may make you put it in the collection in the gun room until you are older. We will have to smooth talk him some but don't worry about that now. Let's see what else is in here."

She had noticed there were some letters and a couple of 1890 liberty silver dollars that were really nice. She showed them to Levi then picked up a letter from the old wood box the gun had been in. She picked up the big knife and looked it over.

"This is cool, it's a U.S. knife from 1917 so this is old stuff, I wonder who could have left a gun in a box and these letters and stuff and never came back for them? Let's take a look and see if we can find any clues in the letters as to who was here and when." She said as walked back to the desk and placed the box on the top and handed Levi the light then she carefully opened a letter.

"It's dated June 12 of 1918 so this is old. 'To whoever is most unfortunate to find this letter and this place, I would suggest you leave as fast as you can and get off this evil mountain and never, never come back. It is cursed."

"Great, a cursed cave now. Sounds weird Sis." Levi said.

"Just hold on and let me read this ok, it's kind of interesting don't you think? A mystery maybe."

"I am Frederick the son of Norman Adare the miner who lived here but has now long since vanished and we have not been able to locate him. My older brother Alex has gone for help but he has been gone quite a long time and I fear he may not have made it to Beaver for help. This is a cursed place for bad things have happened to anyone who has been foolish enough to stay here too long.

"The Ute speak of a great evil in these mountains and that it should be avoided. They warned us not to mine, hunt, or travel here and that the evil spirits of the underworld roam these lands and will take anyone who is foolish enough to travel here down into their spirit realms and they are never heard from or seen again.

"We did not believe in their foolish stories about spirits, ghosts or their demons and the like for they are just uneducated Indians after all full of dumb myths. That is what we thought at first but now I am not so sure. Dad is gone and I have abandoned working the mine and barricaded myself here in this cave for safety. Strange things have come in the night; they are quiet and have carried off the mules and supplies. Now I remain alone. I am running out of provisions and do not know how much longer I can stay, I do know that whatever creature or demon is outside. I can hear it scrapping and clawing at the door and pushing on it during the night trying to open it to get to me. They leave a three toed large print, larger than that of a grizzly bear, I do not know what it could be. I do know this: I seem to be a prisoner now and if I venture out by day I am not able to get very far for the demons seem to come in the dusk and I must flee back to this cave for safety, I do not think I can travel to Beaver to escape, as in the open at night they would catch me. It's over a day's hike back to Beaver so for now it's safer in the cave I hope Alex will come back soon with help I think it's the only way I will survive. Alex, if you read this I am leaving the extra gun in case you need it. If you do not find me then I have either made my escape and will find you in Beaver or the demons have taken me. You are warned! Leave and never return. There is some strange evil here. A dark magic. I hear something,

"Alex there is a strange humming sound behind the back wall. Its glowing white hot like when the black smith melts iron. I cannot leave; I am trapped, for the demons are back at the door again. Know this, not sure how much time I have so I must end this letter. Tell the family I love them. I must go; I hear them. The demons they are coming."

"It just ends, that's weird"

"Yep, sounds like a bad movie sis, so you think someone came up here and planted the letters just to spook us?"

"Well knowing the boys anything is possible, I just don't know when they both could have got together to set this whole thing up... they could be messing with us"

"Well sounds like a weird prank lets go see how far back this cave goes maybe there some cool stuff we could find back there."

"Sounds like a plan lets go take a peak."

Suddenly they hear great booming sounds and the crackles of lightning reverberating off the walls of the cave room Sariah and Levi both jump at the sound.

"Well that's that then, a mountain thunderstorm is here, may as well stay put and stay dry Levi, so now we have some time to really explore this place." Sariah said.

"Yep I sure don't want to get all soaked walking back to camp, let's get to looking and see what else we can find then." Levi said excitedly.

"Then let's get started "Sariah said as she put the letter back in the box with the gun and closed the lid to keep it safe, then pointed her light towards the darkest parts of the cave room.

* * * * *

Deep inside the bowels of the mountain we find a race that time has all but forgotten; in a room we would call a security station. We find a member of the Teesa Clan monitoring his station.

For the second time the illumination dot on his console glowed again, this was to the older seldom used entrance on the mountain. No one had used it in a very long time, one signal could be a malfunction or the odd encounter by an outer crust creature tripping the alarm, however several such alarms in so short a time and then followed by the motion sensor devices placed farther in from the entrance states there must be something wrong, an intruder must be present and should be challenged.

Pushing the com button on his console he notified his superior.

"Sleesesa clan Tessa to Security Head Quarters" Sleesesa calmly said.

"SHQ here what's your problem Sleesesa?"

Sleesesa disliked discussions with these primitive weak creatures and having to speak through their translators was demeaning and some day they will have to put them in their right order of place in the cosmos. Beneath his race as it was in the beginning; however they had their useful purposes such as times like this.

"You have a possible intruder in section 39 of Tushar tunnel, you will dispatch your team to investigate and detain any outer crust dwellers if found, is that understood."

"Sleesesa, your message is received will search and detain as needed." was the response.

Working with this clan less outer crusters was demoralizing to say the least, he wondered if they were even up to such a simple task without help. He returned to monitoring the area.

At Security Head Quarters in the Teesa grid the head of security, Chief sent for his teams.

"Sir reporting as ordered what is our mission?"

"Sergeant Smith, you and your team are to go to the Tushar tunnel section 39 to see what the problem is, we have an intruder censor alert, check out the area if you find any intruders they are to be detained and brought here is that understood?"

"Yes sir"

"Good you know how touchy these Nemekans are they always assume the worst. So be safe."

"Understood." Sergeant Smith said then turning to his team, "Let's move out".

The Sergeant had been on duty for eight years now in the black opps dealing with the inner Earth cultures and races. Since his recruitment he had seen a lot of strange things and all though he did not agree with everything going on down here, he understood it was for the long term good of his country. Now it was time to keep himself and his four man team safe as usual.

"Well men lets go intruder alert so let's gear up and take tube 68 to the area it should be about 20 minutes so let's get moving." Sgt. Smith said they all went to gear up and headed for the tubes at a trot.

Sgt. Smith (as he was called here, no one used their real names openly down here all need to know stuff it was on the coded computer ID's that everyone had to wear.) One thing the Nemekans were good at was hi-tech stuff, and the tubes he had to admit were a neat smooth ride. One such tube ran coast to coast and only took a few hours to travel between them. All he knew was it had something to do with super magnetics.

His team stepped into the egg shaped vehicle used in the tubes and pushed the needed symbols on the console and away they went at high speed. Soon they were miles away from the security base and nearing their destination. As they approached the disembarkment location the vehicle made its slow relaxing stop, it was amazing how it could slow down without jarring one around from the high speed it traveled at.

"Let's go earn our pay, should be about 15 minutes and we should be at the location let's move".

They all started their jog up the tunnel it was easy going as it was illuminated with the soft green glow that the Nemekans preferred as they did not like the yellow/white lights we used at all.

Soon they reached Tushar entrance 39 and when all had a moment to calm their breathing they then silently took up their positions and ever so slowly and quietly moved towards the entrance that led to the exterior door of the mountain.

* * * * *

Back in the cave we find Sariah and Levi slowly walking deeper into the cave.

"This must be the back of the cave that guy was talking about in the letter, just look at the hole in the wall here." He said.

"It could be, let's get closer, see here it does look like the rock was melted at some time, and see how smooth it is like a lava tube, interesting." She said.

Sariah took a really good look at the opening that seemed almost completely cylindrical like, with uniformity to the edges and it was melted very smooth not like if one used dynamite to blast open the hole. But it was about nine feet high and maybe twelve feet wide. Compared to the back wall itself that must be sixteen feet wide or better, so this unusual opening must have been man made somehow. But if it went back to the times of the note, that would not make sense.

"Levi you know that if the letter we found is true, then this hole was made way back in the early 1900's, and I don't think I know what could have carved it out today let alone back then. You know what Levi this is starting to get a little spooky, it just does not make any sense you know?"

"Sis, I think your right, maybe we should go get Dad and let them look at this and the other stuff we found as well, it is getting a little scary back here." He said a sign of worry in his voice.

"I think your right, hey wait a minute do you see that strange greenish light inside the hole?" Sariah asked curiosity overcoming her feelings of fear for a moment.

"Kind of, turn off your light and let's see if we can get a better look at it." He suggested.

Sariah turned off her light and sure enough the glow was a lot brighter.

"Cool, this is kind of like in the movies when there was a deep ocean or cave creature that gave off light, I wonder what is creating it?" He said.

"Well I guess all your TV & movie watching is paying off a little bit then, your right about the possible cause of the light, let's go see what is creating it and then we can take it back to camp, that would really one up Ben and Tarton."

"Sounds good, but it is really spooky ya know, maybe we should go get that old gun just in case some booger man is back there, what do you think?" He commented.

"Oh come on it is an old gun and may not even work; besides there are no booger anything in this cave, unless you've been picking your nose again, so don't get all scared on me."

"Ok, ok, ok, let's go then sis, keep your light on so we don't get lost or fall into a deep hole, or trip on a boulder." He said nervously.

"Right but this does look pretty straight, more of a tunnel than a cave see here what ever made this must have been really hot, looks more like it was melted like those lava tubes ya know, but it should make it a lot easier for walking as the floor looks pretty smooth." Sariah said as she entered the tube.

* * * * *

Almost to the opening Sergeant Smith could hear noises, and see the beam of a flash light piercing the darkness near the tunnel entrance as well as the light from the open outer door to the surface, so someone was here and needed to be dealt with. From what he could make out it was only a couple people that was good and would make his job easier.

Using hand signals he directed his team into their positions along the walls where they would stay deathly quiet and still until his order was given to move.

He brought up his stun device the Nemekans had developed it was harmless for the most part but very effective and gave one a huge head ache when you woke up. He aimed it towards the un expecting people, he wished they had not discovered the tunnel, but that was not his problem, orders were orders and these poor saps where just in the wrong place at the wrong time.

"Sariah?" Levi asked in a more shaky voice.

"What now?" Sariah responded.

"I am getting a bad feeling now, you know like maybe we should just go back and get out of here."

"Your letting your imagination get the best of you, caves are just spooky is all, there is nothing to worry about in here." She said getting a little irritated with him.

"Are you sure? You're not just saying that are you?"

"Look, we are getting closer to the green glow, just a few more minutes and we should be able to see what's causing it, then we can go back to camp when the rain has stopped, I promise." She said trying to calm her little brother down, this was interesting to her, an adventure of sorts and he was breaking the mood of the whole experience with his whining.

"Ok, if you promise, hey look at that there are some rocks in the tunnel, turn your light back over this way I thought I saw a funny looking rock." He said as he stared at a place along the wall it was dark but he could make out what was a really weird shaped rock.

"Let's have a look at your rock so exactly where is it then." She said glad his attention was distracted for a moment he just might start having fun again. She shines her light around at Levi and he points along the wall she follows his gesture with her beam of light some yards down the tunnel.

"See there is your rock." Sariah said as she shines the light on what looked like a rock, but suddenly as her eyes focused better in light from her flashlight the rock looked more and more like it could be a man crouched along the wall. That doesn't make any sense, and then she saw it move.

"It's not a rock it's... Run! Levi Ru...." she was not able to finish as her chest exploded with pain, felt like getting kicked by a horse and she felt herself go numb as she was falling to the floor dropping her light, as the sensations of unconsciousness began to overtake her the last thing she saw was Levi also laying on the ground in the beam of her light, then a pair of boots, military style boots then the shadow of darkness enveloped her and all was black.

* * * * *

"Tagem and bagem; let's get them out of here. You two carry them back, just a couple of kids so you can handle that, we will go see about re-sealing the outer entrance."

"Yes sir, we shall wait for you at the tubes." His number 2 man said.

They each picked up their limp package and proceeded back down the tunnel to the Tube station.

As Sergeant Smith and the rest of his team entered the room of the cave they noticed the old mining gear and other stuff, not really taking the time to look at any of it as they still had a job to do, so they went outside and took a look around, not seeing any signs of other interlopers.

"Men go back inside; I will hide the door and join you." Sergeant Smith said.

He pulled another crystal Nemekans device out and pointed it at the door area and the rock wall, turning the handle setting to the right mark, then pushed the button and in that moment the door disappeared visually from view, he then walked through the illusion he just created, turned around and adjusted the settings once more and hit the button, this solidified the illusion creating a hard surface to it, no one would ever know the door was there now. He did find some of the Nemekans tools very interesting and useful and this was one of them.

They then closed the wooden door.

"Well a job well done, let's go, we have a couple packages to deliver to the command center for processing." Sergeant Smith said.

And the team all headed back to the tunnel then quickly went to join the remainder of the team with their two packages; they all entered the tub vehicle and set the controls to return to the command center.

* * * * *

Tarton, Ben, Natasha and the others walk back into the camp area and as they did the younger boys scattered to go look for their parents and anyone else. So they can share their discoveries they had found.

"Hey, (Tarton yelled at them) have everyone meet at the big tent."

The boys nodded and scampered off.

Ben and Natasha entered the big tent with Tarton.

"You two clear the tables." Tarton asked.

In not too short a time a majority of the family had gathered most with puzzled looks on their faces.

"So Ben what are you all up to now?" James asked his son.

"We found some interesting things during our hike in an old cave, we want to show you and tell everyone about it."

"So where are Sariah and Levi? I haven't seen them, you lose them on your little expedition?"

James inquired.

"What? They were right behind us, Levi was dragging along, and he didn't want to come back so soon, so Sariah was walking with him. Those two I bet they are just fine and will come in soon." Natasha said.

"Now you boys have our attention so tell us what this is all about so I can go back to my afternoon nap" Said Martha.

With most of the family gathered around the tables as best they could Ben told the story.

"Well yesterday Levi, Thor, and Lance went off exploring like they do and found an unusual thing, in the side of the mountain not too far from here about 1/2 hour hike they found an old door. They could not open it, so they asked me and Tarton to help this morning with opening the door to see what was inside."

"As it turned out once we got the door area cleared and opened it turned out to be a cave, and it had been used as a home by the looks of it. Probably some old prospectors. So we looked around a little bit, and took some photo's, I thought we could use a lap top to enlarge them so we could see them better, there was some old looking writing on one of the walls." Ben continued.

Ben handed them his phone, and the adults passed it around looking at the picture.

"It is interesting, we would like to get a better look, and we will have to put them on the lap top for sure." James responded.

"We had planned on taking you up there but here take a look we brought some stuff we found in an old desk." Ben said as he places a bundle on the table and opens it up. And gently shows them the journal and some of the papers and his dad James, and Uncles Tom and Olaf all bent down for a closer look. The others gathered around behind them a little closer so they could see the items.

"James, what is it?" Katasha asked.

"Just give me a moment dear, at least let me look it over a minute."

"Looks like these papers are official mining stuff; however this book seems to be a journal." Olaf stated to group.

Tom, Olaf, James all got a pretty good look at the item's and Tom started reading parts of the journal.

"Yep definitely a journal, it's a history of what they were doing up here. However near the end there is some unusual writings or characters that I am not familiar with, can anyone else make any sense of this writing?" Tom asked.

James looks closer at the symbols on the cover of the journal then at the pages in the book.

"It does look strange, and yet somehow familiar, yet I am not sure why any of this would have a familiar look to me, I do not recall ever having seen this type of writing before." He stated puzzled.

Ben took a closer look at the book.

"You know Dad, now in the light it does look a little familiar let me think a moment, You know Dad it has some of the same look to it as some to the stuff I have seen over to Fairsong's' place, he does have some similar things, I wonder if he could tell us what it says." He said.

"You do have a point there Ben, guess it will have to wait though, meanwhile let's see what we can find out from the English writing." James said as he continued to read some of the journal.

"Mary, Martha come here this is amazing and almost unbelievable, if I did not have this in my hands right now I would have thought it impossible." James said surprised by what he was finding in the text.

"What is it you have found then, do tell?" Mary asked.

"Do you remember in our family history a man by the name of Norman Adare? He spelled it differently than we do today, but that was common back then. Well Norman and his son Frederick disappeared a long time ago in these mountains way back in the old mining days. No one could ever figure out what happened. Our family line comes through his son Alex, I barely remember much about it, but Alex never could fully explain what happened to his father and younger brother, we know they vanished, and eventually were thought of to be killed by either claim jumpers or rogue Indians."

"Well sisters, it seems we have a journal with a Norman and a Frederick Adare in it, and odds are they could very well be our long lost relatives, they do say that truth is sometimes stranger than fiction and so this must be one of those times. The papers put Norman Adare as the owner of the claim, so it could fit and that means it would be our Great, Great, Great Grandfather." James said in amazement as it began to sink in.

All of a sudden there was a huge booming sound that made most everyone jump, followed by some crackling and more thunder as lightning began crashing across the mountain tops, with the wind picking up then followed by a big southern Utah mountain rain storm.

"Great, just great, get everything gathered up and keep as much of the stuff dry as you can." Ben said.

"Well everyone better stay under cover until this thunder buster is done, should not take too long as they usually blow over quickly." Tom said.

"Natasha, Tarton and Ben go see to the animals and make sure they aren't spooked by the storm, we don't want to be chasing livestock all over these mountains this week." Katasha said.

The older kids ran out to see about calming the stock and making sure all was in good order. Some of the younger goats who were not used to the high mountain storms were pulling on their ropes frightened and scared near to death, ready to bolt if they could. After a while they were able to calm them down and protect the other gear that was uncovered from the wind and rain. As all in the camp waited out the storm they took some time reflect on what they had seen and learned so far.

"Hope Levi and Sariah are safe and out of the storm" Katasha commented worriedly.

"Mom, I think they should be just fine, they are smart enough to get to a dry area and wait out the storm, when it's all done I am sure they will be back to camp soon. If not we will go out looking for them." Ben said.

"They should still have been able to catch us even if they were dragging along before the storm hit, you don't think those two would have gone back to this cave on their own, do you?" Tarton asked.

"Well if they did there will be a discussion about that when they do get back to camp." James said.

"Ben how far away did you say this cave was again, I would bet those two may well have chosen to go back there to look it over, you know how they can be."

"Well it should only be about a thirty to forty minute walk to the place." Ben said looking at his Dad with a knowing look.

"You know Dad the more I think on it, the more I think you may just be right. They are probably sitting out this storm in the cave room all nice and cozy. Levi did want to stay longer and Sariah did want to go see it for herself in a bad way, so sounds like the makings of a problem with those two." Ben said, and started pacing in the big tent, fidgety about going out to find his siblings to make sure they were all right.

Martha looked the group over and turned to Mary and Katasha, "I really need to take a nap, and this fresh air is really talking me into a good long nap."

"Lance help your mother to her tent, here, take this umbrella." Tom told his son.

After Martha and Lance had left, Tom turned to James and Olaf.

"I am not sure about you guys, but I am feeling a little apprehensive concerning Sariah and Levi. As soon as this storm passes we should go along with Ben and Tarton to go find them." Tom said.

All the men agreed nodding their heads in agreement. They started making what preparations they could during the storm for their search.

It took almost one hour for the storm to subside, then the men with Ben and Tarton shouldered their packs and began the search for the kids, walking towards the location of the cave.

James turned to the group and said, "Time to get moving, Ben show us the way and mind your step as the ground is wet and slippery now. Let's all be safe."

"Ok old guys, follow us and no slipping we wouldn't want to have to call the life flight to haul your old bones out of here, now would we." Ben said with a laugh as he grinned at the older men.

"Mind your manners boy, or I shall have to put you in your place, again kid." Olaf said with a smile, he was the oldest and was use to the youngster's jabs over the age thing.

So off they went on their uneventful hike until they came to the little clearing where the door to the cave should have been.

Ben turned to the group and said, "This is the place now just over there in the mountain side is the door to the cave."

Tarton looked at Ben in amazement and shock." Ben, this is the right place, right? He said in a worried voice.

"Yes it is, there are the tree stumps we had to cut through, but where is the door? What in the world is going on here? The door should be right here." Ben said as he walked over to where the door should have been and slapped the rock face.

The door that not too long ago was there and a reality was now gone.

"Dad, seriously this is the place, the door is gone, I don't understand it, It should be right here." Ben stated again becoming really anxious and obviously confused.

"You two are certain this is the right place?" Olaf asked.

"Yes it is." Tarton replied also worried and confused about what happened.

Both Ben and Tarton began feeling the wall searching for any sign of the entrance.

"Maybe there was a rock slide with the storm then, could that be possible?" Tom asked.

"This wall face shows no signs of a rock slide." James responded now becoming worried himself.

"Something is not right here I can feel it, we need to look for Levi and Sariah so let's walk back to camp searching for any signs, tracks, etc. and see if we can find them, maybe they took another path back to camp and we just missed them." James said with his anxiety rising, where were his kids!

All the way back to camp they all yelled and called out their names but to no avail, neither did they see any foot prints in the wet ground nor any other sign of the two. As they entered the camp the women and the rest of the children came over to meet with them.

"Buy the look of it you did not find them." Katasha stated

"Maybe they will come in before dark, you know they do like to explore." Katasha said.

"Yes they do, however I don't feel right about this, we did not see any sign of a cave door or the kids, if they are not here soon we are going to strike camp and go get some more help to find them." James stated rather matter of factly.

James turned to Ben, "Ben you have about three hours till dusk so you can make it down the trail to the parking spot, I want you to take a truck and go call for help." He said.

"Ok Dad will do, on my way. I will try my cell phone along the way just in case I get a signal by chance that could speed up the SAR boys. If I do then I will wait for them and bring them up."

"Good thinking now get going, and no time to waste."

Ben was packed up with some food stuffs and water then he took off at a jog towards the trail head. He was stopped by Tarton and Olaf leading one of the horses.

Olaf looked a Ben, "Now Ben it will be quicker if you ride, don't you think?"

"Get on the horse and get going." Tarton said.

"Glad someone's thinking Thanks." Ben swung his leg up and over the old mare, she was a pretty good old paint and it would not be the first time for a quick ride on her. He just nods to Olaf and Tarton turns the horse and trots off down the trail.

"Ok gal let's get moving we have stuff to do."

James turned to the rest of the family, looking down for a moment to gather his thoughts, and then back up to face everyone.

"I need everyone's attention. We do not know exactly what has happened, however it looks like Sariah and Levi have gotten lost or worse. We should plan on this camp becoming the base camp for a search and rescue party. There is not enough time for all of us to pack up and get down the mountain before dark, so we will stay here and make preparations for the searchers who will be here in the morning. And the kids may just come walking into camp tonight. They may have just gotten lost."

Meanwhile Ben had reached the ridge line, the high point of the trail where it opens into a meadow, allowing for a good over view of the valleys to the south west, where Beaver City was located and should be within range of a cell tower. Ben pulled out his cell phone and dialed 911.

CHAPTER 6

Search and Rescue

The Beaver county 911 dispatcher had notified the Sheriff and SAR's unit as soon as the call came in about the two lost children in the Twin Lakes area of the Tushar's. As it is voluntary unit it would take a little time for all to assemble at the Sheriff's office.

Sheriff Noland Thompson was glad to see most had been able to answer their calls; He had a pretty good group of guys and with their skills and abilities were able to cover a good amount of ground.

He walked over to his deputy, Jordon Everson.

"Jordon, it looks like about everyone is here."

Jordon looked over those in the assembly room.

"Yes, and Bill called and says he will be on the way as soon as he gets his dogs loaded up."

"Good to hear, Bill and those dogs are about the best trackers I have ever seen."

"Any news from Ben Adair yet?" Asked the Sheriff.

"Dispatch says he is on the way down to meet with us, he should get here about the same time Bill and the few stragglers come in." Deputy Jordon answered.

"That will be good then. It will be dark by the time we get everyone laid out on what needs to be done. We may need to wait till dawn before fully deploying into the woods."

"It would be good to get to the main camp at Twin Lakes today if at all possible, so we can get a jump on the search tonight and hit it hard at first light." He added.

"I would have to agree, sounds like they got the afternoon storm front that hit the mountains today, it caused some flash flooding in a lot of the area's up there, may be best to let it calm down a bit, but we should be able to get to the staging area and then take it from there." Deputy Everson replied.

* * * * *

Ben had reached the valley floor, he felt it would be a good idea on his way into town to stop by Fairsong's place and ask him about the cave and the area, to see what if anything he may know about it. He may be of help. Ben pulled up to Fairsong's place. He ran up to the door and banged on it hard until finally Fairsong answered the door.

As Fairsong opened the door he saw young Ben and wondered why he was not with his family. Then he noticed he seemed somewhat distressed.

"So Ben how can I help out this afternoon, what's the matter?"

"We have had some problems up at camp, what can you tell me about the Twin Lakes area? You have been around those parts for a long time, and did you know about the cave up there? Also Sariah and Levi have gone missing." He stated and took a breath.

"Ben slow down, now let's see it's been a while since I have been up there, however I as yet do not ever remember seeing a cave. You say Sariah and Levi have gone missing? What has taken place."

So Ben had a seat and went over the events of the day as quickly as he could.

"So when we returned to the cave we were not able to find the door, we were in the right area but the door was gone, just disappeared. We don't understand it." He said showing his confused worry in his voice and body language.

"Indeed this is an intriguing tale, you don't think they would just wander off as they explored the area do you?"

"No they know better, something has happened, something is wrong all wrong, they are just gone."

"I see, a door that was and now is not, and your siblings are missing. Tell me again about what you discovered in the cave and about the wall writings, what did they look like?"

"Here I have some pictures of them on my cell phone, here take a look." Ben said as he looked up the pictures and then handed the phone to Fairsong so he could look at them.

Fairsong took a long good look and studied them a moment, he paused and nodded to himself, mumbling quietly.

"Well, what is it? Do you know what it says then? Have you seen it before, tell me."

"Ben you need to calm down, now listen, you remember the box I entrusted to you?"

"But what does the old box have to do with anything?" He was getting a little irritated he had no time for Fairsong's games or stories, he had to get going.

"The writing it contains looks like that of your pictures they seem to be similar, and they well could be related. I do believe that the key to finding that which you seek will be found in the items in the box I gave you. Bring the box to me and let's see if we can make sense out of it and I shall think on things."

"Tomorrow, we will be searching the mountains, I am on the way to meet the Sheriff and SAR team right now, and I have to show them where they disappeared so they can start the search, so I need to be going, so can you help me today or not? I don't have time to waste running around the valley?" He responded a little irritable.

"Go then and lead the men to their mission of searching for your family members. However I feel they will not find much of anything in their search. I sense that you may know this as well, for the key to discovering where your door went to, and what you will need to do in order to find it and your family is to return to me and bring the box. Then I may be able to assist you, think about it. Do you really feel they are just lost, wandering in the mountains, or still in the cave room you mentioned which is now hidden?"

"So what think you now? You need to make some choices, go and see your team and send them on their journey, but if you return I may be of help still if you so desire."

Ben just stared blankly at the wall over Fairsong's shoulder and thought; he can't be in two places so he decided to do both. He will take the SAR team to the site and let Dad and the others help them in their search, then he would come back and see if Fairsong could actually help him with that strange box, and if it was of any use. Maybe he was right what if there was a key to finding them, if so it was worth a shot.

"Here's the deal, I need to lead the SAR team to the right trail that will take them to my family's camp, then I shall return with the box and maybe you can see if you can help. That way everyone is helping and doing something at least."

"As you say so shall it be, be on your way now so you can return sooner, I shall ponder over what you have told me so far and see what I can make of it, be on your way now."

Ben walked back to the truck and got in, turned around and drove as fast as he could down the road that would lead him to the Sheriff's office.

As Ben drove off, Fairsong looked at the mountains to the east, and he thought about the situation, then slowly he shook his head, starring at the mountain peaks and commented to himself.

"So it begins, may this journey end better than the last, may the Creator of all, Bless the paths of Ben and his family and all who seek to help them, for they have yet to learn what shall await them in the near future. Oh Great Father of Creation help me lead young Ben in my old age, along his new path he must tread in a good way." Then Fairsong slowly turned and walked into his home.

As Ben drove into the Sheriff's office parking lot he noticed the members of the SAR team and others with trucks, ATV's, horse trailers and one truck with a box containing hunting dogs. All had come to aide in the search. Looks like we were going to have at least fifty people or more searching that will be a great help. Although he doubted that they would find them, as he did feel that the key to this mystery had something to do with the cave. But no one would understand his thoughts about that or believe him for that matter. So let them look, they may find some clues that could help in finding his brother and sister.

Ben got out of the truck and walked into the Sheriff's office. It was a hub of organized chaos; he asked one of the deputies for help.

"Where is Sheriff Thompson?.

"He is really busy right now, maybe I can help, what do you need?" responded the desk deputy.

"Well I am Ben Adair, I called in about my missing brother and sister, so I need to talk with him now and see how fast we can get into the mountains to begin our search?" He stated a little impatiently.

At that moment Sheriff Thompson came into the front office.

"So Ben, I would ask how you're doing but I know better, come show me where you are camped and the locations we will be searching on our wall maps in the SAR room. We still have a little more prep work to do before we can depart as a group." the Sheriff said.

"I'll show you, I don't like wasting time standing around." Ben said as they walked back into the SAR room and started looking at the maps.

"This is where we are camped at Twin Lakes, the kids found a cave entrance in this area about a twenty minute hike from the camp about here." Ben said pointing out the spots on the map.

"My sister and brother snuck back to the cave by themselves and we have not seen them since, we did go search for them ourselves but could not find them."

"So Ben you said they went to look at a cave they had found, so if you think they may be stuck inside the cave will we need to take some cave rescue gear as well, just in case we need it." Sheriff Thompson responded.

"Sheriff, this is going to sound very weird, we did find a cave and went inside, it looked like an old miners place but when we left for camp to tell out parents about what we found Sariah and Levi snuck back for a look, we assumed they were in the cave. But when we got back to the area of the cave the door or entrance was just gone, and I mean gone, we could not find it and we looked. We saw where we had cleared the underbrush and some trees to access the cave door, but the door has just vanished, we don't get it nor can I explain it without sounding crazy." He said showing his exhaustion.

"I see, Ben that is strange, could a slide have covered the entrance?" the Sheriff asked.

"The area did not look like a slide had happened, that's just it, and it is very weird."

"Is there a chance you could have been mistaken about the location of the cave?" Asked the Sheriff puzzled but knowing there had to be a simple answer to this.

"No way, we were at the right spot all right." He was starting to get the idea the Sheriff may be thinking he was just a little crazy.

"Look, we need to go look, and maybe we can find a trail or something we missed, I noticed you have some hunting dogs, and maybe they can turn up something we are missing. And yes go ahead and have some of your cave rescue team join us just in case we do find the door again."

"Ben you are tired and worried I can see that, so just calm down, now you have to admit the story of a disappearing door to a cave sounds just a little crazy. However we will look and you may have just missed the location in the emotional turmoil and stress in your initial efforts to find them. I will make sure we have some of our trained cavers ready to go with their gear. Who knows there could be another entrance to the cave as well, if it was a miners place they always had a second entrance, or air hole. We should be ready to go with in the hour. Get something to eat from the break room they have some food to grab before we get going. Then by the time you're done everyone should be here. And you can tell the group the location of the search. I have some more work to do before we leave, so go eat." The Sheriff said as he turned to continue his preparations.

"Thanks see you in a few then." Ben said as he turned down the hall to find some grub.

After he had some food he did feel a little better, it did give him some energy.

Sheriff Thompson mean while went back out to the SAR assembly area, he saw Deputy Everson across the large garage that served as the staging area.

"Jordon, I need you and Bill, Tony and the rest of the team leaders in the SAR room now, Ben is going to meet us there and fill us in where we need to start the search."

"Yes Sir, will get them for you Sheriff." Deputy Everson said as he turned to go get the guys.

Sheriff Thomson went to find Ben, and found him on the couch in the entry.

"Ben we are getting the team leaders together, so come with me and you can fill them in, one thing though, I suggest you don't say anything about the disappearing door. Just tell them the area to be searched and the possibility of a cave search as well."

"I understand you there, I don't fully understand it myself so I know you all wont." He said as he got up and followed the Sheriff to the SAR room.

When they had all gathered in the room, the Sheriff had Ben go over the locations again on the wall maps and the rest of the pertinent story. When he was done Sheriff Thompson looked the team over and said.

"Now men lets saddle up and get up there. Tony make sure your guys have all their gear and be ready for a long cave search if needed. Bill I hope your dogs are ready this sounds like we could be out there a few days, and the rain may have washed a lot of signs away."

Old Bill just took a good look at the Sheriff and said. "Now Noland, you should know better, you know darn well my boys can track just about anything, anywhere, anytime. I remember a couple years back you had a jail bird headed for the hills and them boys treed him like a scared cougar in less than a day, and if I remember correctly it was a rainy day as well. So don't you worry about them boys of mine, they are good to go." Bill said with a twinkle in the eye. He knew the dogs just lived for days like this.

"Ok Bill you're on, let's see how good they are today then. Let's get going." He said as he passed Bill and left the room.

Everyone loaded up their vehicles and the caravan began its journey led by the Sheriff who was following Ben's truck. Ben drove up to the meadow where the family had left their vehicles. With all the extra trucks, and a few horse trailers it was a hard squeeze to fit everyone in the remaining open areas of the little meadow, they actually had to remove some of the pole fencing to allow more room for all the search vehicles and trailers.

Upon arrival Ben went to check on the horse he had left by the creek. While the Sheriff organized everyone barking orders to his team until finally all were ready and lined up to go.

When everyone was ready the Sheriff had Ben came over and the team gathered around for a last minute talk.

"Now before we get moving, I don't need to remind everyone that Being Safe is the motto, and keep an eye out for signs as we go into Twin Lakes never know when we may find some. Now if all are ready let's get moving."

Ben knew they would get to the camp just fine without him, and the others could fill them in on the other details, so he felt the need to go back to Fairsong with that old box and see if he could really help like he said he could, if it were possible it was worth the try.

"Sheriff got a minute" Ben called out.

"What? We need to be going."

"You know where you're going, my family can fill you in and take you to where you need to start your searches, I need to go back down the mountain there is something else I need to look into that may be of help in our search."

"What do you mean, we could use you up there as well, every man counts."

Ben led him a little ways out of ear shot from the rest of the team.

"I told you the door disappeared right? Well I may have a person that might have a clue about finding the door, or some clue as to the crazy things going on up here. But I need to go ask him some questions and I will hurry back as soon as I can, so see you in camp."

"If you think it will help, who is this person anyways."

"Well don't worry about that it would just make this whole deal sound a little crazier is all."

"Then get out of here and hurry back the longer it takes to find them you know the elements of nature can have their way with folks in a hard way up here. So do what you feel you need to and we will see you at camp."

"Good luck and thanks for your help."

"Ben it's what we do, it's what we train for, see you when you get to camp then." He responded and went and got on his ATV and headed up the trail followed by the rest of the team on their ATV's followed by the mounted horse teams. Ben walked over and made sure his horse had some area to feed by the creek then hopped in to his truck and made his way out of the makeshift parking lot and back down the trails and finally the black top that led down to his house.

CHAPTER 7

Lev Antas Shuesa

Sariah slowly opened her eyes to the brightness of the light and blinked several time to focus her eyes. Her head pounded as if there were kettle drums being played during a thunderstorm inside a tin bucket and placed in her head. As she was finally able to bring her eyes into focus she took in her new surroundings. Where am I? Was the first thought, how did I get here? Was the second and where was Levi? She found herself all alone in a room.

She worried about where Levi could be, She was not sure where she was or what had even happened to them.

She tried to think through the pounding in her head, what had happened? They were in the back of the cave, and were walking towards the green glow in the tunnel when, what? Something had happened. The only thing she could clearly remember was seeing a shadow she had thought was a rock, it suddenly moved in the darkness it looked like a man, then she felt a jolt that shook her entire frame, like being shocked really bad, then she fell. She must have hit her head on the cave floor when she fell that would explain the head ache. Oh what else was there, think she told herself. Yes there was another thing, a pair of boots like the army guys wore and she vaguely remembered seeing

Levi, he was also laying on the ground just as she blacked out, then she awoke here in this room.

So what in the world was going on? She stood up and that was not a good idea as she felt like she was about to pass out again. So she sat back down, when her head cleared enough to stand again she slowly walked around her little room. It was bare and cold feeling, she went to the door and was not able to see any way to open it, she clenched her fist and pounded on it several times as hard as she could and then screamed! "Can anyone hear me? Help! Let me out of Here!"

She waited a moment and realized that was quite melodramatic, like you expect anyone to hear you, and if they did they would actually help you. Time to calm down take a few deep breaths, she walked back over to the corner and slumped down on the floor and put her head on her folded arms supported by her bent knee's and rested her aching head. Screaming really had been a poor choice as it did not help her headache at all.

She tried to pull her thoughts together on what had happened; it really did not make any sense, the only sounds she could hear were her own breathing. What she did know is that they were kidnapped, that meant they were in trouble, but why or who would do that. She was getting extremely worried and now scared. She sat and just stared at the wall wondering what was going to happen next.

After what seemed like hours of dozing off and on, pacing around the room and every now and then venting her frustration by yelling and pounding on the door which of course did nothing but hurt her head and her hand. She realized she had no idea how long she had been held prisoner in this room. Also she was getting thirsty and hungry.

How can you think of food at a time like this she told herself, were was Levi, and why had no one come to check in on her, someone had to have put me here, so I must be a prisoner and whoever was in charge had not even come to check in on her, were they going to let her starve to death now, she was getting angry at the whole idea. The Reality of not knowing even where she was or what was happening to her or to Levi and that the family would be looking for them and worried sick about their disappearance. This is not fair. The despair of the whole deal began to really get her down, and she sat down in her corner again and began to cry into her folded arms, this just is not fair, it's not right. She thought to herself.

She must have fallen asleep because the next thing she noticed was feeling a poking in her ribs that woke her up with a start. She opened her eyes and sat up with her back against the wall. Facing her standing in front of the door was a woman dressed in a blue jumpsuit; she slid a metal tray with some food on it across the floor towards her then backed away.

The woman had a no nonsense look about her. "Here eat something." She said in a cold stiff voice then turned around pointed her hand at the door and it opened and she walked out quickly with the door closing behind her.

Sariah sat there for a moment thinking, so here is some food, I hope it's not been laced with anything she thought and considered not eating it, but hunger and thirst won out and she ate the sandwich and the sliced apple and drank from the cup of water that came with it.

Not long after she was done the door opened and the same cold woman entered.

"Well looks like you're done." She picked up the tray and turned to leave again.

"Hey, who are you? And where am I? And what have you done to my brother Levi!" She demanded.

"Oh so the little girl has an attitude now does she, well as for your silly questions you don't need to worry, your nowhere, where your brother is should not be your concern anymore, you should be worried about your own future kid. Oh and don't worry or even try to consider some foolish escape idea, no one, and I mean no one ever leaves this place, ever, unless we allow it and that is rare. So get used to the idea of being here kid." She said in a harsh voice as cold as stone.

Sariah just sat stunned no one had ever talked to her like that before; she glared back at the woman.

"You better just let us go, and if you hurt my brother I will, well I am gonna..." She was not allowed to finish her petty threat.

"You will what?" The cold woman stated with a sneering grin.

"Your little threats are a waste of time kid, there is nothing you can do, your here now and we shall do whatever we want, whenever we want, to whom ever we want any time and there is nothing anyone can do to prevent that, and nothing you can do about it. Oh and no one will ever know where you are, or what is happening to you anyway, so get used to the idea, you're in our world now, there is no escape the sooner you come to grips with it the better for you." She stated as she glared coldly at her.

She pointed her hand at the door again, and as soon as it opened she turned and quickly went out, it again closed shut as soon as she was through it. She noticed the door had slid sideways from within the wall while it opened and closed, there were no hinges, no way she could tell to open the door.

Sariah again was left stunned and worried she curled up in a ball and a new stress and fear enveloped her and she began to cry again, she realized she was beginning to feel light headed, then her vision blurred and she felt herself passing out again. The last thing she felt this time was her head hitting the floor, again, great she thought as her head began to pound again as she passed into unconsciousness.

* * * * *

Ben was just pulling up to Fairsong's home, he had returned home and grabbed the box and hurriedly drove to Fairsong's in the hopes that the old guy could actually be of some help.

As he was about to knock on the door, Fairsong opened it. He looked Ben over and noticed the box.

"Well shall we see what there is to see then and maybe I can help you discover a key to unlocking the future to your next path in your journey of life." He said with a knowing smile, he opened the door and let Ben in and had him sit in his little living room, placing the box on a make shift coffee table in front of him.

"Go ahead and open the box I will be right with you." Fairsong said as he slipped out of the room into his little kitchen. He soon returned with a couple cups of his special tea. Handing a cup to Ben he said.

"Now drink this, it will help calm your nerves from the worry, and will help you focus on what the task is at hand, for now that is your box."

Ben took the cup it was warm and he took a sip of the tea it was a special blend of herbs the old guy grew himself, it was ok and it did have a calming effect on him, and yet he felt rejuvenated as well.

"I hope you can help as we don't have a lot of time, the search teams have already started looking, I told them I would meet them in camp tonight. My family will be wondering where I am and why I didn't return with the search teams. So this visit and the box had better have some good value to it. Or I am just wasting my time."

"Ben you're tired and stressed that is understandable; your time is not wasted if you learn from it, and find a way to help the ones you love right?"

"I guess you're right, now let's have a look and you can tell me what all this weird stuff is I hope."

Ben began placing each of the items from the box on the table.

As Fairsong looked at the items before him he looked at each one carefully and his thoughts were taken back many years, to a different time and to many different places, Hyrum my old friend he thought, I do miss you and our adventures, however I must wonder old friend why you kept all these things, I knew you liked memories but this is interesting, I wonder old friend if you truly had the gift as some thought after all. He thought to himself.

"Well it would seem your Grandfather Hyrum kept a lot of what you could say were old keep sakes or souvenirs. Now let me see here if I can remember what any of these items are and what we used them for, it has been a good while after all, a good long while since I have seen any of these items." He said somewhat lost in his thoughts.

"Just please tell me what you know and that some of this stuff is actually useful. And if any of it will help find my brother and sister?" He said, even with the calming tea he was still a little impatient and would like to be up searching with the others.

"I shall do the best I can; my mind is not as young as it once was my young friend."

Fairsong picked up one of the items it was like seeing and holding an old friend the item was familiar to him, very familiar as he was the one he remembered who had given it to Hyrum many years before. It is what Ben may call a compass, but his own people called it the Lev Antas Shuesa.

"This is what my people call 'Lev Antas Shuesa'. "Fairsong picked up the item and fully exposed it letting the cloth that covered it lay on the table.

"In your words you could call it a compass, in our words it means Pure Heart Guide it is the closest I can translate its meaning into English. We used this to guide our travels much like your compass only this works in a very unique and different way. It works by sensing one's pure intents of the heart, and then helps in guiding the one holding it.

It will guide you based on your pure desires, so if you seek to go somewhere or are looking for an item with a pure and righteous purpose or intent then it shall help you on your way." Fairsong said.

Ben Just looked at Fairsong and thought this old guy just fell out of the nutty tree hitting every branch on the way down.

"So are you telling me this is some sort of spiritualized compass?" Ben said skeptically.

"Ben you must realize that form this point on you must unlearn what you have learned in a lot of areas of your life, in order to learn what I must teach you, so that you can find your missing family members. So pay attention be careful not to ridicule that which you do not understand or comprehend, just have faith be quiet and listen with an open mind."

Fairsong took a moment and looked deep into Ben's eyes, searching for a moment then he spoke.

"Think of it as, let's see, remember the stories of your faith, there was a guide that led some of the old ones across the great waters to Ancient America, do they not tell of a similar device the one which father Lehi used? They called it the Liahona if I remember correctly. It too did work upon ones faith and diligence given it. The Lev Antas Shuesa is very similar in how it works, yet different as well." He added trying to help him understand.

"You see you're ready, whether you know it or not, your spirit is, so let your mind relax and allow your spirit to develop and to evolve in order for you to be more teachable. Do not complicate your soon to be new knowledge with the facts of your current learning; you must at times be as a little child so you can have the faith to learn new things." He paused to let that sink in.

Ben just stared at him with a more than little confused look, "I think I get it now just show me how it works so we can get moving."

"Just look here, (he turned the Lev Antas Shuesa over) see this bottom, you need to line up these words here and here, (he twisted the base until some of the words lined up.) Then you look deep within yourself, search your feelings and your desires and allow your mind to be still, like this, and then think of what it is you want or need the most in your search."

Ben watched then was amazed when the liquid filled sphere in the center all of a sudden began to glow, softly then brighter like a little internal light had been turned on, then the pointers on the exterior tracts began to move slowly and Fairsong handed it to Ben, as he did the glow faded and went out.

"You got me, where is the switch again? Does this thing need batteries or what? Is it solar? How is it powered?"

"It's as simple as I stated, you must remember to unlearn so you can learn, Hold it in your hand like this, relax and think in a good way search with a pure heart or desire and that is the way it works. It is powered by one's own personal spirit energy. The more you master yourself the better or more clear the Lev Antas Shuesa will become and the more accurate it shall be in leading you on your journey. There is a reason it was thus designed, only the pure in heart can successfully use this device."

Ben took it in hand, he held it and thought real hard about Sariah and Levi, and demanded to know where they were in his mind. Trying to will the device to work, he was getting very impatient and somewhat irritated after a while when nothing was happening.

"Look this is not working, there must be something wrong with it, can you make it work again? If you can." He said discouraged.

"You need to quiet your mind Ben, try slowly breathing in and out, relax your body and mind, become as one with the center of yourself and with the sphere, think through the sphere and picture in your mind's eye what it is that you seek, in this case your family members. Only then can it work, you must relax and remain calm." Fairsong said hoping Ben would figure it out soon.

Ben once again tried to relax his mind, which was not easy with all the stress he had been through lately. He pictured himself being in the celestial room, remembering all the white and peaceful feeling there, He felt his spirit float somewhat in this new found harmony he was finding, he saw the ball or the center of the sphere begin to glow ever so slightly at first but then it grew to a stronger light, not as bright as when Fairsong did it, but it was working now even if he was much slower.

"Now I think I got it." He said almost surprised it was working.

"Concentrate on your goal, search in your mind to know what direction to go in search for your siblings then." He said calmly.

Ben thought and concentrated on Sariah and Levi's faces, as he did he noticed the outer pointers on the ball start to move ever so slowly but they did move and adjust themselves and they were pointing towards the mountains, in the direction of the camp.

"Wow now that is interesting, even though I don't fully get it, seems like I can use it now." He said with hope in his voice.

Fairsong looked at Ben. "You see, once you learn to open your mind's spiritual eye more is possible than ever you can realize at this time, You have a strong spirit, some take a long time to learn what you have now discovered in a short few moments on how to use the Lev Antas Shuesa, do not take it for granted and take great care not to harm or loose this tool."

Fairsong gently took the device from Ben and placed it back on the table.

"Now what else did your Grandfather Hyrum have that may be of use to you." He said.

Ben picked up the short sword, and stated, "Well this may be of use, I guess we know what this is for anyways."

Fairsong snatched the blade from Ben's hands so fast he had to think and blink at what had just taken place. Wow that was fast for an old guy, how did he do that anyway.

"Hey what did you do that for?"

"Ben like all weapons of destruction they are not and I repeat not to be treated lightly, do you understand?" He said with firmness in his voice that brought Ben to full attention.

"Yes I do understand; go on, why did my Grandfather have this then?" He asked more soberly.

"This was a gift given to your grandfather a very long time ago, and with it comes great responsibility, if there comes a time in your travels where your need is greatest and you have to use this sword in defense it shall become more than it is now, and will help you in your quest."

"What do you mean then?"

"When the time comes you will understand, no need to explain at this time" He answered as he then picked up the large ring.

"Now do you see this ring? See the markings on it, it belonged to and old friend of the family a very long time ago. I gave this to Hyrum and now he has given it to you. If one day you ever meet the people who created it just show them the ring and they will assist you in your quest."

"Your buddies must have had pretty fat fingers then, see I can put two of mine in it and mine are size 15, so is that a real gem in it and is it real gold as well?"

"Yes it is, it's a pure emerald and it is gold, the crest on it is the family of an old friend, and is known among their people and there is no other value to the ring than that. Like the necklace that sits here on the table you need to take them both as you go in case you need their help. It may open doors where they seem shut, it will show you the way in darkness and be a light before you in your journey, it works in a similar way as the Lev Antas Shuesa, and may be the key you seek to begin your journey if your heart truly is pure enough."

"So you're saying it can find the door then, the one that disappeared?" Ben said hopefully, as his mind began to wonder and understand better what lay before him. These items seemed to be based on some unknown technology that they would work was all that mattered to him right now; he hoped they could help find his sister and brother.

"Ben if your heart is ready and pure, it may help you find and open your way." Fairsong stated with that same little all-knowing grin of his.

Ben started thinking, well that about wrap's it up then, it was getting late he must get going.

"I guess that is about everything, I need to be going soon."

"Ben you know, one that tends to rush off usually misses what is put right in front of them, take a look at this cloth covering and see what it has to share."

Ben looked and picked up the cloth that was on the table it was the one the compass had been wrapped in, now that he was taking his first real look at it, he realized it was a map, and on the map was the Twin Lakes area, and it showed the location of the cave room. So Grandpa had to have known about the cave then. He looked up at Fairsong in surprise.

"Yes he knew of it, in fact your family helped mine that area back then. "He replied.

"How come they never told us about it?"

"That is something only Hyrum could answer; let us not focus on the past but think to your future."

"Ok, then" Ben said as he reached in and picked up the mummified head looking thing.

As Ben brought it out of the box he noticed Fairsong had a very unusual reaction to it, out of his normal character, his reaction was not one of fear but more of anger. Ben had never seen the man with that type of fire in his eyes like what he saw now as he placed the head on the table.

"What's wrong, are you alright?"

"I am well enough, don't bother yourself with my reactions, I must apologize. Never mind please put it back in the box would you?" He said. His voice sounded shaken.

"What is it then, it looks like a movie prop to me." He asked with real curiosity wondering why it could affect him in such an emotional way.

"It is not a movie prop, but it is something I would really wish to leave in the past, however know this if you ever see a creature like this one know and trust to the swords blade, I would have preferred Hyrum had not kept the head, he should have left it were he found it. This is most troubling, most troubling indeed. But don't worry I doubt you will ever see another one in your life's journeys."

"Well then since you seem to know what it is then, tell me."

"It is a head, of an enemy of long ago, so please put it away and do not let it worry you anymore, this topic is done." He stated firmly as he reflected back on the time when Hyrum had picked up the head, why did you have to keep this head, you young fool, it was in poor taste however there must have been a reason.

Ben put it back into the box, and then he picked up the crystal stick thing from the table and asked.

"So what type of magic does this thing do then?"

"This is a weapon and you should not wave it around carelessly, it has several purposes, see here when you line up this set of runes it will power up." As Fairsong spoke he activated it, lighting the crystal part of it.

"Now you see if you turn it to this first rune it will act like a stunning device, it will render the person you use it on unconscious for a time, but unharmed except for the headache that accompanies it after one wakes up. Here at this second rune it will become deadly and this third and last rune well you should leave that one alone, as it will completely destroy what you use it on leaving no trace. So treat it as always dangerous, because it is."

Ben just looked everything over and had to wonder about it all, but he did not have much time to reflect on it as he did need to be going. He felt he just might be able to at least locate the door opening again, he was growing in hope again, it just may be possible.

"Thanks for your help it has been much more than I could ever have imagined, this stuff is just amazing and I did not know it even existed, where does it all come from anyway, and why wait until now to share it with me?"

Fairsong looked down and reflected on the past a moment before looking back at young Ben.

"Sometimes the past is best left undiscovered by the youth of the present, but in time I may speak of it more, but as for now do not worry yourself about it, what matters is that it is here and it may be of help to you in your search for your family. You need to go now, it is time, be swift in your search and be careful as well, there are strange forces in play. So may the Creator's Blessings be with you in your journey and safety and success be with you."

Ben had to agree it was time to go.

"When this is all done, I will return, and you will need to answer more questions?"

"Fair enough then."

Ben got up gathered the items together strung the ring on the necklace and put it around his neck. Then he put the other items in his waist pack, the sword he put in its sheath and the crystal weapon he noticed had a hole in the handle so he looped a piece of Para cord he had with him through it he could attach it to his belt later. The sword he would just carry for now but if needed it did have its own belt as well. He turned towards Fairsong.

"Is it ok to leave the box I do not have time to take it back home right now?"

"That would be ok with me, be on your way young Ben and good luck and remember what I told you." He said as he followed Ben out to his truck.

Ben waved good bye, wondering what kind of person Fairsong really was, very unusual and now even more mysterious than ever, he put the truck in gear and drove away headed for Twin Lakes and his journey to find his family.

After Ben had left, Fairsong went back into his home, he looked carefully and reflectively at the box upon his little table, he kneeled down and carefully pulled the head from its place and he spoke to no one in particular for he was alone.

"Well my Garsar friend I see Hyrum won your head, it is indeed a long time since we last met and may your posterity be no more successful than you, may they also leave their heads along the paths of Ben and his friends if they get in the way of his search this day." He said to himself.

He looked up towards the Heavens, "Oh Great Creator, please bless Ben, Sariah, Levi, and all others along this dangerous path which is before them now. Protect them from all the evils of the worlds and guide them in a good safe way, let them fulfill their paths in an enlightened and good way, and bless my family of old who I yet miss and if they come together in this journey may they be of good help to each other." He said reverently.

He bowed his head in thoughtful meditation and after a while he heard these thoughts in his old mind or were they more than thoughts, was it a message not of his own mind.

"Fairsong my good son, it is now time for you to return home, for your journey is not yet done, your path lies here now to help your young friend, Here lies your new mission your time above is about at an end, follow young Ben, for a guide you shall become and a teacher, go and return to the lands of your nativity. You are now blessed with the health of your race in their time." The voice trailed off and was gone.

Fairsong slowly opened his eyes, with a tear slowly rolling down his leather face; he slowly whipped it away and thankfully smiled. Finally he can return with honor to his home the place of his birth to be with his family once again after such a long absence.

As the voice spoke in his mind he felt the energies of his spirit become strong, stronger than he had felt in a very long time. He knew his path now lay in helping the Adair's in their distress.

He put the few items back into the box and locked it once more. Then put it back into its place once again in his home. Then he gathers all he will need as he prepares for his new journey, the journey that he has awaited many years, the one he felt would never be, now one who was old is now renewed, he starts feeling younger and stronger every minute as he gathers his things, the closer to being ready to depart the younger he felt, one of the last items he gathers he pulls out of its hiding place, it is a crystal clear globe about five inches in diameter with artistic gold engravings upon its surface from a box he had all but forgot about over the years. He reflected on the years he had been here and with humble relief realized he is finally to return home with honor, a smile of gratitude crossed his face as he turned the ball in his hand he stood in his door way and glanced in the mirror next to the door, yes indeed the Creator had blessed him and now it was time to go home, He walked out on the porch, closing his door behind him possibly for the last time.

Then he held up the crystal globe up towards the mountains watching the light refract in its sphere a moment, he thought of home, then took a deep breath letting it out slowly and looking deep into the sphere and into his heart he thinks of young Ben Adair as he gazes in to his now glowing white sphere, now a new journey is to begin.

CHAPTER 8

Harvester

Ben was driving around the last turn of the winding jeep trail to where the parking area was. As he drove the last few yards before the meadow, he noticed a single person standing there waiting. After parking his truck he went to see who the person was and what he was doing there.

The person had not moved, he just stood by the gate to the trail head, he was wearing what appeared to be a greenish cloak with the hood down that shadowed his face, and he was wearing a back pack and he carried a walking stick.

As Ben got close to him he said. "Can I help you?"

"Why yes you can, I think we can help each other." Said the cloaked figure.

Ben did not recognize him, he wondered who he was, it could be a late arrival of a member of the search team. However the voice sounded familiar, but different he could not place it.

"So what's your name." He said now standing only about 5 feet from the person.

"Well, you should know me by now, for you left my home not too long ago, and I have been chosen to assist you in your quest to find your family." As he spoke he took a hand and lifted the hood showing who he was. He gave him a smile and waited for Ben's next statement.

"Fairsong is that really you? (He nodded) it can't be you're a lot younger than when I left your house, it's not possible, who are you really? Fairsong is an old man; no way can he be you."

"Well here I am, and it is me, strange is it not how fate works at times, I have been blessed by the Creator to help you, he has granted me my youth in order to help you better. You now see me as I would have aged in the lands of my birth. For time runs differently there than here, at least for one's body, so let us be going now, show me the path and I shall follow you." He said, smiling, knowing Ben was really confused now, at least for the moment.

Ben was amazed then a little amused at himself, Fairsong no longer looked to be in his 90's but rather his mid to late 30's or there about, after all the other events of the day he was about ready to stop asking any more question and just take all the strange events as a new form of reality. Sure why not, sphere that glows magically that guides you, strange weapons and tools, now Fairsong has found a fountain of youth. Just assume you have gone completely nuts, and it all makes absolute sense, Ben told himself.

"With all that you have shown me today, do I even dare ask how you got here before I did. I don't see your old truck, and I know you didn't pass me on the road. So are you going to tell me how you did that little magic trick?"

"Yes you may ask, however since you are not yet able to fully understand the process and your mind is getting close to overloading, I think it best to wait until another time to explain as to how I arrived here. The important thing is I am here, so let's get moving." He said with a chuckle as he slapped Ben on the shoulder.

Ben realized that whatever was going on must be the Lord's way of helping him. It was the only way it even came close to making sense in his mind. He started to walk over to where the horse was tied up.

"Fairsong you win, I left a horse over here and I will need to ride him back to camp. It should be ok to ride double if that's ok with you, as it would be faster."

"Well you go ahead and ride the horse, I shall be fine following alongside, I have not felt this good in a very long time and I am quite enjoying it, so I will jog along with you."

Ben looked thoughtfully at Fairsong then shrugged his shoulders, by now he knew better than to ask any more dumb questions. So he mounted the horse and they started up the trail to the camp at a trot, then at a slow gallop when the trail would allow it. He noticed that Fairsong was doing just as he said, keeping up with the horse stride for stride and the amazing thing was he did not seem like he was even out of breath as they finally entered the base camp at Twin Lakes.

As they entered the camp Ben noticed the searchers were starting to come in for the evening. And they were gathering around the main tent, or what was now the command center. He noticed the SAR ham operator had all the antenna's and portable power up for radio communications with the group as well as the Sheriff's office in Beaver. It looked like the kitchen tent was being used as well by the teams; about everyone was gathered either there or at the command tent.

Ben left the horse with the others, and walked over to the command tent to see what news he could find out. As he walked through the door way he noticed his father James and Uncle Tom were with the Sheriff going over things.

"Dad so what's been going on? Have they had any luck yet?"

"Well good to see you finally made it back, so why didn't you come with the rest of the crew earlier? And no we have not found anything yet; we could have used you while it was still light out." James said looking unhappy with his son's choice not to get here sooner.

"Dad I had to make a stop and pick up some more help. Some very strange things have happened today and I am not sure I can explain it all to you. Maybe later I can tell you about it in private. But right now you need to meet an old family friend who has come to help you in our search." As Ben finished his sentence Fairsong entered the tent.

"Hello James my old friend, as Ben said I am here to help in the search for your lost children. Now how can I be of service?" Fairsong stated as he bowed his head ever so slightly out of respect to James.

James just stood there as did everyone else in the tent as silence fell over the group. James just stared in disbelief, and then he looked from Ben to Fairsong and back again. Almost speechless.

"So you are Fairsong the old man? but no your too young looking you've lost about 50 yrs. of age since we last met, so how can you be him then? Or are you one of his long lost kids? This does not make any sense." James stated a little confused if this were some game he was not up to it.

"Well James it is I, for there can only be one. To come on this quest a change had to be made and the blessings of the Creator have once again unfolded in my life, he has blessed me with a more youthful body in order to help your family once again. So do not be disturbed about my appearance, just count it a blessing and when time permits

I shall explain how I came to be as you see me now. But tell us how we can best help, for that is why we are here."

"I just have a hard time believing you're the same person at the moment, but you do sound like him. You can explain your fountain of youth pill later, now let's get down to business, and thanks for coming to help." James said still taken back by the experience.

"Some of the SAR team is still out; some will be going out taking infrared and night vision goggles and scopes to see if they can notice anything in the dusk and dark. Bill and his dogs are still out trying to cut trail, Olaf and Tarton are with him. The rest of the families are all here now and the girls have been helping making meals for the searchers. Your mom is pretty shaken up of course as are most of us. If we don't find something soon the stress is going to get a lot worse for all of us." James stated. As he sat down.

Ben looked at his Dad, and Uncle they did have the haggard stressed look. The Sheriff was marking the area's on the map where they had teams searching and where they had already searched today, and in the back ground he could hear the radio chatter from time to time as teams checked in.

"So Dad, have you been back up to the rock face? Did you find the door again?" Ben asked hopefully.

"Yes we have been all over that area, even with the hounds and the rest of us and no sign of the door you spoke of. You're sure it was there in the first place right? Cause it just doesn't make any sense it disappearing like that, maybe you got the location wrong." James asked.

"Dad it was there, you saw where we removed the trees and stuff, and it has to be there." He said in a sad voice. He knew it had to be there.

Sheriff Thompson spoke "Well we will send the boys with the night vision and IR scopes and see if they can notice anything unusual there tonight, If the rain caused a slide maybe we can find an opening or some type of heat signature, it's worth a try."

"Sounds like we have things to do, James takes Ben over to see his mom and you both take a break, we can handle it for tonight it has been a long day for all of us, you will need your strength for tomorrow." Tom stated.

James looked at Tom and he knew he needed some rest and with everyone else out searching he thought it was the best idea to gets some. He did need to go check in on his wife again. And get his batteries recharged for the morning. It's hard to search when your sleep walking. You tend to miss the obvious and get hurt. He knew that, but it was hard to stop knowing your kids are lost out there somewhere maybe hurt and scared just waiting for them to find them.

"I think your right, and Ben does need to check in with his mother." James said and walked out of the tent, as he passed Fairsong he looked at how young his friend looked once again and just shook his head.

"Fairsong I don't know what you did to yourself or how, but it is good to have you here to help. Dad always did speak highly of your skills and abilities when you served with him. Now come with Ben and me, his Mother has been worried about him as well, and she is dreadfully worried about Sariah and Levi, she has not had any real sleep or appetite since they disappeared." James stated and motioned them to follow him.

Fairsong nodded and replied "Yes it is good to be able to help you, I am glad that Ben came to get me, Now I am hungry after my little hike, so let's see to your family, I feel I may be able to help reassure Katasha some, then I must eat something and rest a little."

As James, Ben & Fairsong entered the kitchen tent they saw Katasha busy serving the search teams their meals. Mary and Martha where also helping.

Katasha looked over at James as he entered, the worry was written deeply in her face.

"Is there any news yet?" She asked him, as she took a moment from her work, she liked being busy as it kept her from over stressing, She hurried over to James and gave him a big hug, more for her own reassurance than anything else.

"Ben it's good to have you back finally" She said to her son.

After Katasha hugged James she suddenly felt light headed and literally fell back into his arms, he held her for a moment then placed her out at about arm's length to look into her worried eyes.

"You better take it easy for a while, and no dear we have not found anything yet. Some are still out and now we have a few more to help the search in the morning."

Katasha looked up into James eyes. "I am so worried about all that could have or is happening to them. None of this makes any sense just none at all." She was trying to fight back the rush of emotion that was over taking her now, she did not want to fall apart and start crying. She had too much to do. She noticed someone with Ben, who looked familiar but she was not sure who it was.

"Ben, who is your friend, I thought I knew all of them, you look familiar but can't remember your name at the moment." She said. To both of them.

Ben started to answer but was interrupted by Fairsong.

"Katasha, I am a younger version of the one you know as the old Fairsong, and we don't have time to explain the miracles of life that now have me in my current youthful state. But know this, the Creator has allowed me to be here, as you see me now in order to help find your lost children, so I am in your service." He said with a low bow showing her respect.

"You're Fairsong? This is really getting to be too much for me, so you're really Fairsong right?" She questioned in tired amazement.

"That is correct." He responded.

"We do need every person we can to help find the children, so thanks for coming." She said, wondering what magic could have happened to bring this amazing change to him, for he did look very young. But she needed to focus more about her children right now.

"Honey this is Fairsong, as my father would have known him, what has taken place or how no one can yet comprehend fully, but what I do know is that his being here will be a great blessing to us all."

"Well since we are going to be searching in the early morning, I will need to get some nourishment and then some rest as well, so if you two will excuse me I must go." Fairsong said. Bowing ever so slightly as he backed away, then he went to the table and made a very healthy meal. Then he found a chair along the wall of the tent, sat down and began to eat his meal. Soon he was lost in his own thoughts.

Ben looked at his mother. "Mom, so how are you really holding up?"

"I'm ok, just tired, stressed and worn down. Someone should have found something by now, anything." She replied.

"Mom I don't understand what is happening, but a lot of strange and amazing things have happened today. Fairsong I know will be able to help us figure out the problem in the morning. I will be taking him at sun up to the place where the door was, and see if he can help us there. When he is done eating I want to show him what we found and let him think on it." Ben told his mother with a mixture of sadness and hope in his voice.

"Ok, sounds like you two have some idea's that will help with this terrible puzzle, go now and get some food, you will need as much energy and strength as you can tomorrow."

"Mom, we will find them, I just feel it in my heart." He said and gave her a hug, then walked over to make a plate for himself.

James looked at his wife he shared the pain in his heart for their missing children; he reached down and took her by the hand.

"Kat, let's get some rest, you have done enough today and you really need some rest as well."

Katasha looked up and nodded her agreement, and he took her out of the tent and led her to her own tent so she could have a quiet place to relax and hopefully sleep for a good long time.

✱ ✱ ✱ ✱ ✱

"Is there progress with the new subject yet?" Sosaeen Garsar the second leader of the science group of level seven, Asked.

"Little, we have not been able to proceed as quickly as with past subjects of this same age group, It is unusual as his spirit seems quite strong for one so young," Answered lab tech. Elasseear Garsar.

"What seems to be the difficulty, is the youngling too much for your limited processing capability? You were informed that I need this one's essence; it feels strong and would be of much worth to me. I do not want your pitiful excuses this time, just do as you're told."

"We are doing our best, we must get around his mental walls, It is taking longer with this one, for as you have said it is stronger than most of the subjects brought to us." Replied Elasseear bowing his head ever so slightly, to show respect but yet not allowing himself to be totally exposed to the potential physical retaliation, Leader Sosaeen did have a reputation for this when he was displeased.

"I shall expect it soon, if not then you will be replaced by one who can be of better service, and you may be sent to the Tessa's for retraining." Sosaeen glared at this lab tech. Elasseear, he was capable but he had no patience, nor tolerance for weak excuses for not producing quick results. Weak links had to be removed for the Garsar to keep strong.

"It shall be done." He waited for 2nd Leader Sosaeen Garsar to leave the room before exhaling a low hiss of irritation, the last thing I would want would be to be demoted to such a low existence as to be with the Tessa.

Turning to his assistance he said in a guttural growling hiss, "If we fail 2nd leader Sosaeen I will not be the only one punished, I shall take you all with me do you understand!"

The others in the room all nodded and as a group bowed slightly and said, "Elasseear we shall not fail you or ourselves, let us see why this youngling is being so difficult, there is an easy answer, it just eludes us at the moment." said Lassoos.

They all turned to look into the room they had the human boy in, he was strapped to the table and still unconscious, those human soldiers were idiots, as they had used way too much stun force on this little one.

"Let's stimulate his brain to awaken him and in doing so that may help expedite the harvesting process." Elasseear said to his team.

"Lassoos awaken this one then, and allow a member of team 4 into the room to monitor the boy as he awakes for he shall then see one of his own kind and not be so confused, as a calmer mind is easier for the harvesting process." Elasseear told his assistant.

Lassoos wasted no time, he left the room walked across to the room where science team 4 was. He opened the door and announced.

"I need one of you to assist with a subject, to monitor him as we awaken him." Lassoos looked down on the smaller humans, even though they were weak and physically revolting creatures some did have strong minds for science and things that were of use to the collective, at least for the moment. He turned and walked back out the door not waiting for a response, and stood in the hall awaiting his helper.

The members of science team 4 looked at each other in agreement.

"Well looks like it's your turn George, the rest of us have other things to do, you know the procedures so just follow your orders and the rules of contact and you will do well. And remember do not address them unless they first speak to you." Science Team Leader Dr. Stanton said.

Even after all the years of working with the Nemekans he still thought they were an arrogant bunch of creatures, however they had much in the ways of science to share with us and the end results is what counted not what one does to get there.

"Yes sir, on my way." George a 3rd class tech said as he left the room to follow the Nemekans.

As soon as the human helper came out of his room Lassoos entered the room holding the subject without a word. The human just followed, like the sheep they were.

"You must watch the subject as we awaken him in order to start the harvesting process; you are to help him remain calm until it is over. This one is unusual; it has taken more effort than normal. Do you understand?" He told the helper.

"Yes I understand, proceed I am ready to assist." George replied.

Why is it these Nemekans had to drain the life force from these kids he did not fully understand, but orders where orders and it was not his business what they did with it, although he wondered at times. He went over to the table where the subject was bound and awaited his assignment as he looked down upon the helpless young boy.

The first thing Levi felt was a throbbing head ache, like when the mule kicked him in the head a few years ago. He slowly opened his eyes and the bright lights made them ache even worse. So he closed them then slowly blinked several times holding them half closed in order to ease the discomfort. He realized that he could not move, his arms, legs, and chest where all strapped down somehow, His head was also strapped to where he could not turn it, and it felt like he was on a cold metal table.

He started to panic, and fear began to engulf his senses like a tidal wave, what was going on, where was he, and why was he tied down? Where is Sariah?

He tried to scream but his throat was too dry and only a small croak came out and that hurt with the attempt.

"Anyone there?" he asked in a soft panicked dry voice.

"I am here." George answered as he moved over the boy so he could see him.

"Where am I?" He asked.

"You're in the Hospital?" He replied.

"What happened to me, where's my sister, and why am I tied down?"

"You are in the specialized trauma room for traffic accident victims, you were in a terrible car wreck and you're not to move that is why we used straps, we fear you may have some severe spinal cord damage. So do not move. As for your sister, I do not know about her as I am only assigned to you."

George answered, glowing within himself at how easy it was to create such a realistic story, how easily it was to fool this little boy.

"A Car Wreck? I don't remember being in a car, we were exploring a cave and then there was a light and well, then I woke up here." Levi said confused.

"Temporary amnesia is common when one has been in such a terrific accident, and you should feel lucky as you are the only one in the car to have survived the wreck. You have been in a comma for two weeks now, it may be difficult for you to understand right now I know, but we will help you in time to regain some of your memories." George was actually enjoying this game of setting the subject at ease before his essence would be taken. How simple it was to manipulate this type of person. Besides it helped break up the boredom of working down here.

"I was Not in a car wreck, where is my sister, and who are you and what are you really doing, I feel just fine, except that my head really hurts." Levi said, and he was starting to get scared again, this guy did not seem like any doctor or nurse he ever met before. And the room did not resemble any hospital ER or clinic room for that matter he had ever seen before. He knew he needed a drink because his throat was really hurting now with all this talking.

"Hey can I get a drink by throat really hurts?"

"Sure hold on a moment and I will be right back" He said as he walked to the other side of the room where he picked up a bottle of water off of the table, then he brought it back and held it to the boys lips so he could get a drink.

Slowly Levi drank a little at a time until he felt he had drunk enough water, it was nice and cool on his throat and it felt much better.

'Thanks, now tell me again what is going on, and where is my sister?" He asked again.

Why this little snot was just playing him for a drink, George thought.

"I do not know of any sister, your alone, everyone like I told you already, who was with you died in the car wreck." George said as he slowly walked around the table studying the boy.

"You see denial is normal in situations like yours, however you need to realize your family is all gone, and now you need to focus on yourself to recover."

"No! I remember exploring a cave, I remember that."

"That is normal, you see you remember a cave, your mind created this illusion to protect you in your comma state, now you have left the cave as you're getting better, and your mind realizes this and has allowed you to re-awaken once more."

"I just don't get it; it does not make any sense."

Meanwhile in the adjoining room we find the Nemekans preparing once again to harvest the boy's essence. Elasseear looked at Lassoos and snarled the command.

"Lower the cranial cap once again, and let us not have any errors this time, the subject seems calm and alert enough."

"It shall be done as you wish." Lassoos replied as he used the controls at his station to begin the harvesting procedure once more. He watched as the cranial cap was lowered towards the subjects head again, fully confident that it would work this time.

Levi noticed something being lowered from above towards his head, it was coming and would hit him soon and there was no way he could avoid it.

"Hey what's that thing for? You better stop it before it hits me."

"Don't worry, it is only a type of MRI scan, it will not hurt you it will come down gently just above your head and scan you close but without touching. We have to see why you have been in a comma so long, and if there are any other side effects now since you're awake." George told the boy.

Sounds like this guy is sticking to his story, well I really don't remember any car wreck, we were in the cave, but something happened now I am here, he wondered what was going on, this does not feel right at all.

As the device lowered and came closer to his head it lit up with a greenish blue glow, and with a kind of a sparkle in the center of it. This did not feel right at all, and he remembered seeing scans before and this was no MRI that he knew for sure.

"Hey can you stop and wait for my parents to come, I want to see my parents, they should be around here in the waiting room, so go get them." Levi asked.

"Remember when I told you everyone with you in the car died; your parents were also killed in the accident. I am sorry we have not been able to locate any next of kin at this time. We need to do this exam to be able to treat you so we can get you healthy faster." George was almost gloating with how simple it was to twist and keep the subject occupied, it would only be a few moments longer and his job would be done, and the Nemekans would have their little essence from this one and he could go finish his own projects.

Levi just laid there what else could he do, he knew this guy was full of lies, he knew there was no car wreck, and he was lying to him but why? What was this all about? Now he started getting really afraid as the light thing came closer and was almost close enough to touch now.

He remembered what he had learned in Sunday school about prayer when you're in a bad situation, and he figured this could be one of those situations. The only thing he could do was pray, and asks Jesus Christ to help him. So he began to pray silently in his mind, the closer the light came the harder he prayed, he felt really strange and knew he was in trouble, so he prayed with his whole heart and soul, he asked Jesus for protection, and for someone to help him, and to get him out of this place.

As he was praying he felt a deep warmth begin to fill his whole being he had felt the spirit before but nothing like this, this was really intense, it seemed to fill his whole body, and his fear subsided as he remembered how to calm his spirit as his dad had taught him.

As the device finally came into place the countenance of the subject changed, the monitors showed a different growth and change in the essence, it now filled the spectrum with unusual colors that led to a brilliant light then the monitor went blank.

In astonishment, Lassoos turned slowly to look at Elasseear.

"Tech Leader Elasseear, I am no longer reading the essence of the subject, something has gone wrong with our equipment, and it seems to have malfunctioned."

"What? That is not possible, what is the matter? What has happened?" Elasseear spoke.

"I am not fully aware of what has taken place, I have not witnessed such an event before, as the cranial cap came into place and we began energizing it for the harvesting process, there seemed to have been a power surge of energy from the subject and this enveloped and over powered the device now making it useless, it seems to be broken." Lassoos replied.

George stood above the boy, and he realized the boy was mumbling incoherently then he noticed that the device was no longer working. The lights that usually emanated from it were gone as if it had been turned off. What were these idiot Nemekans doing now, he had better things to do than sit here all day dealing with their problems wasting his time.

Elasseear thought a moment, Sosaeen had said this was an unusually strong subject and that would explain the possibility of what had just occurred. It was rare, very rare indeed for such a thing as this to happen, and yet it did happen.

"Tech Lassoos, do a complete check on all your equipment, I want a full diagnostic. I think I may have a reason why this has taken place, while you do this I will speak with 2nd Leader Sosaeen on this event."

"It shall be done my leader Elasseear, what of the human helper shall we send him back to his hole?"

"Tell him to leave and return to his duties, do not allow the subject to see our kind, yet. Is that understood, we may need to address this subject by other means, it is very unusual this one, the judgment of 2nd Leader Sosaeen will be known before we proceed further understood!" Elasseear hissed with firmness.

"As you command" Lassoos said, then he watched as Tech Leader Elasseear turned to leave the room. Then Lassoos keyed the intercom to the room.

"Tech your work is done for now, you may return to your duties."

George heard the intercom squawk the command to leave, so he did just that, he turned to leave the room.

"Hey, where are you going? You just can't leave me here?" Levi all but yelled at the guy who was walking out the door.

"Don't worry, you're in good hands, they will come and take care of you soon. That I promise so don't worry alright." George replied, with a smirk on his face as he shut the door to the room. Thinking that boy has no idea what's in store for him, Oh Well! Not any of his business, finally he could get back to his own list of duties he had to finish.

Levi heard the door close, then all was quiet, he noticed the lights from the scanner thing above his head had turned off, so they must be done doing whatever they did with it then. He still felt a nice warm glow all over his body. He had a feeling all would be ok in the future. Almost like he heard a distant voice, a calm soft voice say, "All is well we are here to help you, you will be fine, be at peace for we are with you little brother." He started feeling sleepy and slowly felt himself drift off into a soft warm place in a dream world.

CHAPTER 9

Truths Learned

Ben followed the small ball of light down the dark cavernous corridor; it illuminated the walls and ceilings of the strange passage in which he walked. As large as it was he could tell that the walls and ceilings looked as if they had been created by some type of machinery. The light extended several yards ahead of him, he felt like he had been following it for days and not getting anywhere. It only illuminated about 10 circular yards around him so it was hard to see everything he was passing in the dark.

In the distance he could hear a slight sound of movement, more like a whisper of a sound not yet fully aware of what it was. Suddenly he saw a dark shadow, no multiple shadow's, much larger in size than himself just beyond the circle of light, they were there, then gone again, like a dream not sure of what he was actually seeing, just the hint of shadows. Now he felt a wave of fear as he saw or rather felt the presence of more of these shadowy figures and a dread began to sweep over him as he began to start shaking, his hands where trembling slightly, he noticed he was carrying one of the strange devices or tools found in the old box Fairsong had given him, strange that he had no recollection of holding it until now.

He did not have much time to think about it, as the sudden whisper of movement of something large moving rapidly behind him, he then smelled the strong odor of snakes like when he found a large ball of rattle snakes once in a cave, where hundreds had balled up for the winter.

No sooner had that thought occurred to him, he turning rapidly to face what had created the sound, and felt the sudden rush of air caused by the movement, a small rock made a noise as it was disturbed from its location on the floor, as though it was kicked and then it bounced off a wall. As he circled his heart was pounding he could not see anything. Fear was beginning to grip his mind, then something grabbed his left arm with a powerfully strong grip, he felt like it would be broken just by the pressure of it. He dropped the device he carried from his hand as he turned to face a large black shadowy form, only this shadow had eyes that seem to glow with hate as they reflected the available light from the ball that lay now on the ground at his feet. He grimaced in pain, and fell to his knees as something struck him from behind and he felt himself go limp as he slumped to the floor, all went black and he remained motionless.

"Hey Ben! It's time to get up! Suns already up, so come on we have searching to do today,

Wake up Ben" Tarton said as he grabbed Ben by the arm and shook him several times to get him to wake up, this guy could really sleep when he wanted to.

Ben slowly opened his eyes, and blinked several times at the sun light streaming into his open tent door it hurt his sleepy eyes. Groggy and still tired Ben noticed it was Tarton who had grabbed his arm, figures that was why it was in his dream then.

"Tarton, let go of me, I am awake." Ben replied as he glared at Tarton.

"Easy there, we gotta get moving soon, day lights a burning and you sure do wake up grouchy"

Ben shook his head again and rubbed his eyes, waking up fully, He did need to get moving.

"It's all right, just had a really crazy dream and you interrupted it, so give me a few minutes to get ready and I will meet you in the cook tent, If you see Fairsong I would like to talk with him as well, now get out of here so I can get moving."

"Ok, ok, your acting like a spring bear who is starving, maybe some grub will help your mood." Tarton replied as he left the tent.

Ben lay back a moment, reflecting on his crazy dream a moment, well time to get moving he hoped Fairsong had some ideas and some answers this morning. Ben got dressed and left his tent, he took a moment to stretch his back and arms taking a deep breath of mountain air, and then he walked over to the cook tent.

Fairsong and Tarton were sitting in the cook tent on some camp chairs eating their breakfast and talking.

"Well young Tarton, even though it has been a while since I last saw you, you seem to have grown well and seem a little wiser now. So Ben told me about a cave that disappeared, can you tell me more about it then. "He asked.

"Well the kids found this door in the mountain, they came and got me and Ben to help clear the stuff in front of it and help them open the old wooden door. After we got the door open we went in and found an old miners cabin to put it simply. There were some strange Indian writings on the walls and some old furniture and stuff like that, looks like it could be 100 yrs. old, we took some photos and brought back to camp a few of the items we found in the desk so we could show them to the adults. The strange thing is after Levi and Sariah vanished, we went back to the cave looking for them and that door had just disappeared. We could see where we had cleared the area to open the door, so it has to be the right spot, just no door. You might think us all nuts, and I think some of the search team members do, but we just cannot explain it."

Fairsong had some more bites of his sausage while pondering over what Tarton had told him, there were ways to hide a door however the knowledge on how to do so would elude any of the people around this region. This was beginning to have a familiar ring as to the possibilities of why these younglings had disappeared, he had to ponder this some more, and he was not sure he liked what the reasons could possibly be for their absence. A few minutes later Ben came into the tent.

"Ben, good to see you this morning, I trust your sleep was not too unrest full. Tarton was just telling me about your last few days of adventure in this area, and we surely do have a mystery to solve. You will need some nourishment and then we shall begin the search." Fairsong said to Ben with a smile.

"Glad you're up to date, let me get something to eat, I have some questions for you." Ben stated as he went to the food table and then made himself a plate of food, then went back to sit with Tarton and Fairsong.

They ate quickly each lost in their own thoughts wondering what the near future would bring. When they had finished Fairsong glanced at Ben.

"Ben, go and get the items you brought and meet me outside near the fire pit, we shall learn more about them then."

"Ok" Ben said as he stood up to leave.

"What items are you talking about Ben?" Tarton inquired as he looked at them both.

"You will see soon, why don't you come with us and we can all learn together then, for you shall need to equally understand what is to be at hand to complete this search."

With that said they all left the tent, Ben went to get the items he had brought from the old box, and joined the others near the fire pit.

James, Thomas and Olaf had been looking over the valley to the south west edge of the lake, talking about the searches made and what they had to do today when they saw Tarton and Fairsong walking over to the fire pit, with Ben hurrying to his tent.

"Well looks like Ben's is up to something with Fairsong and Tarton lets go see what there up to." He said.

The three agreed and started walking to where the others stood. When they were almost at the fire pit, Ben joined them; he was carrying some unusual things. James noticed the sword Ben carried now and wondered out loud.

"Now Ben where did you get that?" pointing at the sword, "And why would you bring it out here?" James questioned him.

"Dad, just hang on and Fairsong and I will explain what we can about it and some other things as well that Grandpa left to us, or to me now and I really don't fully understand it all myself, so sit down and lets all listen to Fairsong, he told me some of these things may be useful in finding Sariah and Levi." He said as he sat down on the log bench around the fire pit.

"Then we shall all listen if it can be useful in finding them." James said and took a seat.

"The SAR teams will be going out again with the dogs to try and locate any sign soon. They are not used to failing in their searches and it bothers them they have not crossed a trail yet." James replied as the rest of the group all took up seats around the fire pit. Then they waited for Fairsong to speak.

"Well since the men of the family are all gathered now as it should be, Let us sit a while for I have some things to say and I feel we can begin the search anew this day in a good direction." Fairsong stated as he motioned to all with a sweep of his arm that they should remain seated.

"Ben come and stand with me a moment"

Ben stood up and went to where Fairsong was standing.

"James, and the rest of you men of Clan Adair look and learn this day, listen well for some will go on a journey with Ben so all should know and remember what is said so no one forgets."

They had all given Fairsong their attention, wondering what he was talking about.

"Ben, bring forth the Lev Antas Shuesa."

Ben produced the device from a heavy leather bag he was using to carry it with.

Curiously Olaf asked "So what is this then?"

"This is the Lev Antas Shuesa of course as I stated, you must listen and I shall explain what I can about its function. My people long ago created this tool for searching and looking for that which was good or needed at the time. It works based upon one's spirit energy. One of a blackened soul will not be able to use it for they would look for that which they should not. Only one of a white or pure heart with honest intent can use it."

Fairsong took the device from Ben, and again he turned it over and twisted the ring with the writing on it, then he looked into the center of it and closed his eyes with a calmness or peace about him.

The Lev Antas Shuesa slowly began to glow from the crystal at its center the light soon became very bright and the several pointers inside began to move, several of the other inner rings also with writing on them moved as well and all lined up with the pointers now floating over them.

"Well this is amazing" Said Thomas, and the others nodded their agreement.

"So what exactly is it used for then." Tarton asked.

"It is like a compass in many ways, however it shall lead you to what your heart seeks most as long as it is pure of intent. And it relates to your paths journey in life. I asked for where to go to find the door that leads to my old home, and thus it has answered." Fairsong answered, and as he did he handed the device to Ben, as he took it, it became lifeless again.

"Now Ben do like I showed you yesterday, think on where the door is that will lead you to those you have lost and it should lead you to it." He directed him.

Ben held the device, and again quieted his mind, finding a quiet peaceful place and thought on where the door that was now lost from view was. The Lev Antas Shuesa slowly lit up like a dull light, and then became about as bright as a 40 watt bulb, not even close to what had happened when Fairsong had used it.

"So, now what?" Ben asked.

"Just be patient, it takes a moment" Fairsong said. "See now, there it is working for you now."

Ben looked down as the pointers and inner rings began to move, they pointed towards where the door had been, and where now it was a solid wall of rock.

"We have been over there, and nothing was found, the door is gone. So is this thing not working right or what?" Ben stated.

"No nothing is wrong with the tool, it tells what is, what was, and where to go. So the door should still be there even if your eyes cannot see it." He stated with a little grin of knowing.

"So this can lead us to where Sariah and Levi are then, great let's get going then." James stated as he stood up.

"Wait a moment, there is more before you can go." Fairsong said looking firmly at James.

"Ok, but hurry it up they may need our help, and I don't like waiting we must be going like now." James glared back at Fairsong; he did not like waiting when hope was still there.

"Ben let me see the ring and necklace." Fairsong asked as he held out his hand to receive them.

Ben took off the necklace with the ring on it and handed them to Fairsong.

Fairsong turned to the others. Then holding up the necklace before them he pointed at the medallion on it.

"This James was given to your father Hyrum long ago from a friend during one of his journeys in his younger years. The ring also, now they shall if need be provide assistance or other forms of help during this journey you are about to take. These items were to be given to one of his lineage to whom I felt was ready and when the spirit spoke to me, and it was to Ben they are to be entrusted to now. Let me explain the other items you were about to ask about."

Fairsong points at the items as he speaks.

"The sword which Ben now holds is from a long lost friend of ours, mine and Hyrum's, the runes upon their blades tell of its name." Fairsong reached for the sword, and Ben handed it to him.

Fairsong pulled the blade from its sheath and held it in the air for a moment then sun light shown and reflected off it like a mirror, suddenly and without warning he swung the blade down upon the log he had been using as a bench which was about fourteen inches in diameter. As the blade touched the wood it sliced through it with surgical precision as though it were warm butter, with nearly no sound at all. There came a slight humming noise from the blade that was all. Fairsong stood back and held the weapon out so they could get a better look at it and the runes upon it. The log bench now lay in two pieces upon the ground.

All the men looked upon Fairsong with astonished faces and wonder at what they had just witnessed.

"Its name is Shoeeslah Nados; to you it would be Slayer of the Nemekans. It was created by a race of men who fight against the darkness of evil throughout the Earth. It stands for the good of all men and those who seek for the light and freedom. It is not to be treated lightly." Fairsong said as he looked at Ben in a stern teaching way.

"Ben your grandfather had use for this in our time, and he used it well. Let your spirit flow in times of need and its energy will come and flow through you and will help you fulfill your needs at the moment. Keep your heart pure at all times lest you waiver and fall."

"So do you really think it will come to fighting then, this is just supposed to be a rescue remember." Ben asked.

"One never knows what the future may hold young Ben. It is always best to be ready for whatever may unfold. And for now you have a door that has gone missing with the children, this is a mystery and shows evidence of more than just lost children in the woods."

Fairsong stood back and gathered all the men in his view.

"So ye men of the Adair's, as there are no more relevant questions I would suggest we go forward to where the door in the mountain shall be." He stated, and with that started to move towards were he had left his pack and things.

James looked after him, then said, "Fairsong, how do you know these things, and why did you not tell us about this stuff earlier, and where do you actually come from? There is much you still need to explain, like your youthful appearance now and more."

"James all will be answered in time, as for the why, I already covered that. Now we must be moving soon, we can talk along the way if you wish." He stated as he shouldered his pack and stood waiting for the others to prepare for their journey.

"Olaf, Tarton and Ben go get your things and let's get moving; Tarton let your mom know that we are going to look at the rock face where the door was supposed to be, and that we should be back in a few hours at the most." James said, he knew Mary would let Katasha know where they would be going, as he had allowed her to sleep longer this morning in order for her to deal better with the stress.

Tarton went to find his mother; he looked in their tent with no results so went to see if she was in the cook tent. He did find her there with Natasha having a lite breakfast.

"Mom, Dad, Uncle James, Ben and Fairsong are going to go look for that door again. Fairsong and Ben may have some tools that may help us find it. We will be back in a few hours, just wanted to let you know where we will be." Tarton said.

"Just don't get lost, and let us know as soon as you find anything, So that the whole crew can come to help search when you find the door again." Mary said tiredly.

"I wanna go to!" Natasha said with a hopeful look on her face.

"Not now, maybe if we find something." Tarton answered her.

Natasha looked disappointed and was about to say something when her mom said.

"Nat I could use you for a while with your Aunt Martha, she was having some trouble last night, so she may be starting some early contractions again. And if she goes into real labor I will need to have you here so you can go fetch Olaf if the need comes?" Mary said with a look like she really could use her help.

"Ok, I will help, but if they do find the door I do not want to be left out. I want to go searching too." Natasha stated pleadingly.

"We shall see about that when the times comes." Mary said.

"We need to be going, Fairsong seems to be in a hurry, bye mom, just let everyone know where we are."

Tarton turned and hurried out the door, he grabbed his day pack with some water and joined the others who were already at the trail head waiting for him.

"Well let's get moving then." Ben said as he turned and began leading the group up the trial to the area where the door was supposed to be.

* * * * *

Sariah slowly went in and out of semi consciousness, as she felt a light thumping sound every few minutes in conjunction with a swooshing constant noise, not loud just subtle and the feeling of motion but more of a glide than anything else.

As she stirred she felt the ties on her hands, legs, feet. She was bound again. She realized she was going somewhere but no idea where, nor who was doing this to her. She slowly opened her eyes and realized she was in a subway of some kind only strange looking; as she stirred there was a whisper from behind her.

"The package is waking up again, should we sedate her again?" the unseen voice asked another unseen person.

"No let her wake up, we can see what we have to deal with, with this one, May be interesting to see its reactions to what is happening." The other voice said, she could tell it was two males speaking.

Then she tried moving her head slightly and realized she could with only a little headache for the effort. As she thought she realized she must have been drugged again probably in the food she ate. She was being moved that was about all she knew for sure.

She noticed there were long thin windows along both sides of the car she was in, she would think of it as a subway car for now. As she looked around and her eyes adjusted to the lighting she noticed a guard in front of her, so there must be another behind her somewhere due to the direction of the voices she heard. She was lying in a cart of sorts, similar to a large laundry basket. Guess they did not want to carry her.

The guard in front of her was dressed in a black uniform with only a few insignia's on it. There was a patch on his left arm with some symbols and a possible name tag or something on the front. He wore a black beret with the same logo on it; he noticed her looking at him and took a step closer to look down on her.

"Well sleeping beauty you're awake, he grinned." His look gave her the creeps, and made her skin crawl.

"Where are you taking me, and who are you people?" She asked weakly.

"Well just full of questions now aren't you, you all ask the same things, predictable. As for the who, it does not matter we are just your escorts to your next destination. As to where and the why, we cannot and wouldn't tell you so don't waste time worrying about that. I would be more worried about the what may happen to you part." He sneered again and just crossed his arms in front of him.

His looks really made her skin crawl and how he talked made her a lot more scared than she hoped she showed.

"Well I guess that's about all we can help you with, not much of a help we know." The other guard said the one that she could not see yet.

"You may as well just relax; it will be a little while longer before we get to where we are going." The guard behind her said.

"Then you can't or won't help me then, so what did we do, and why am I being treated this way, I am not a criminal, your kidnapping you know that, and where is by brother?" She responded in the most helpless tone she could muster. Hoping for some sympathy help from at least one of the guards.

"Like we said, we are not here to help, just to deliver you from point A to point B, the rest well that's not up to us." Said the first guard the one she could see.

"Now don't get all upset and start bawling or screaming little girl or we will just put you out again." The guard behind her said.

"Well ok, but this is just un-American, and you two must be someone's lap dogs, if you won't help me then you're just poor excuses for men, More like puppets controlled by morons!" Sariah retorted in her frustration on her situation.

"Keep it up little gal and you'll be back sleeping the rest of the trip." The guard in front of her said coldly with a smirk.

Sariah thought it best to say awake, so she wiggled a little bit to get more comfortable as if that were even possible. And watched out the windows as they flew by to see if she could see anything, but the speed was to tremendously fast it made her eyes hurt. They were in a tunnel she could tell it was some sort of underground subway and every now and then she noticed a blue or green light flash by. She had lost all aspect of time; she did not even know what day it was. She turned her thoughts to Levi, what have they (whoever they were) done with him? Obviously they were separated and that made her upset. Who were these people? They were bad that seemed obvious. What they wanted with them was totally beyond her thinking. They had not done anything to deserve this.

After about what seemed like at least 20 to 40 minutes Sariah realized she was far away from anywhere she knew, just by the speed of the flashes of lights going by outside the window. She felt like they were slowing, yes it seemed they were and she could tell there was a slight change in the forward motion. But to where that was the question.

"So do I get to know where I am going at least?" She asked.

"Nope you don't, and that's orders, and since we are getting to where you're going I believe it is time for your lights to go out again." The guard she could see said as he nodded his head.

She felt a prick in her neck a second later from the guard she could not see.

"Hey that hurt! Why you din't haavveee tooooo dooo" Sariah felt herself fall into the void of blackness again.

* * * *

Ben led the group with Tarton and the rest right behind them as they hurried to the rock face where the door should be. As they walked up to the wall they spread out and waited for Ben and Fairsong to try any new ideas for finding the missing door.

Tarton said, "Well, just as we left it. You can see where we had to cut some of the brush and tree's to get access to the door, the rain has washed away all other evidence of the door being there."

Fairsong held up his hand in a gesture for silence, "Be still now and let me think on this mystery."

Everyone waited as Fairsong pondered in his mind for an answer. Some sat on the ground; others leaned up on the trees around the area and impatiently waited for him to come up with an answer.

"Ben, let us look closer at this wall, if you notice it seems solid and with no sign of ever having a door in it, correct." Fairsong said.

"Yes but we already know that."

"Well let us look a little closer then." He said as he pulled a device from his pack. It was a small crystal device about 3 inches long set in a silver handle with the same strange runes on it as the other things from the old box. He pointed it at the wall and pushed a little button on it.

The tool Fairsong was using emitted a faint humming sound, and then glowed white. Then as if from a mirage the wall became wavy and distorted then blurred and vanished, behind what was once solid looking rock was the door they had been looking for. Just as it had been a few days before. Only this time it was closed tight again.

James left the tree he was leaning against followed by Tom, they both approached the door.

"Now that was interesting, some type of holographic cloaking thing to hide the entrance of this door, as amazing as this is, it cannot be by chance, it has to be deliberately hidden for some reason. And that reason must be to hide the fact my children were here." James said flatly.

"You are correct, someone had to hide the door on purpose and this troubles me greatly, for the meaning may be clear all though the why yet remains a mystery. The only way to have done this is with a tool such as the one I just used to find it." Fairsong said somberly.

"Well let's get this door open again." Tom said as he went to open the door.

Together James and Tom got the door re-opened. Then James turned to Fairsong with a troubled look on his face.

"You said the door had to be hidden on purpose, that means trouble, my children are in trouble, and if they were kidnapped while in the cave room and then the door hidden to hide that fact, what dangers could they be in? You seem to know something about this stuff."

"Well, we know that is was hidden and this says something bad has taken place here, Exactly what we shall see in time, let us look into the room and see what clues are there. Then choose our course of action at that time. And we must not go off unprepared so let us look, learn, then plan what we need to do in order to find your children." Fairsong said to James and the others as he turned and entered the cave opening.

"We do need some lights to look around, Tarton break out those lights you have" Tom suggested.

Tarton dug into his pack and brought out several large light sticks he used when caving, snapped them shook them up and handed them out. They work pretty well and lasted a good while.

"Thanks, now let's see what is here." James stated, as he looked at the desk and its surroundings.

Tom and Tarton also helped James look for clues in the desk area. Meanwhile Ben motioned for Fairsong to join him at the wall where the writings were.

"What do you make of these writings Fairsong? Can you read them?" Ben asked.

Fairsong stood looking at the writings on the wall, and then he slowly shook and bowed his head slightly.

"Yes I can read what is here, it is a warning for all who enter to leave and never return or face death. It was written a very long time ago."

"Well you can read it then, do you know who wrote it, or who may have taken the kids?" Ben asked.

"The words are of an old race, almost older than the humans on this Earth but not quite." Fairsong responded. Then he motioned to the others.

"Everyone take a look at this wall, as you do I shall tell you some about this people who long ago wrote it, the telling is best done once we have no time for wasted efforts as we learn how to begin our search." Fairsong said to the group.

James nodded his head and they all gathered to where Ben and Fairsong were.

"Well explain then what you have found."

Ben looked at Fairsong. "Go ahead and fill us in about this writing, its meaning and whatever is important for us at the moment."

Fairsong ran his hand through his hair, and rubbed his chin. "Let's see, the easiest way is a very short version from the beginning. The old ones who wrote this did so as a warning to anyone who may by chance stumble upon their doorway that leads to their lands. These words are a warning as I told Ben, it says to leave and never return or face death. Those who wrote it did so for a reason, and will perform its warning if we continue. So to do so will be at great risk of life to those who are to go with Ben and me on this journey."

Ben glanced at Fairsong almost surprised then relaxed realizing deep down his future lay somewhere ahead of him and Fairsong was going to be part of that future now.

"What do you mean by continue, continue to where we are in a cave room, where are we going to go from here then." Tom asked.

"Awe yes, now Tom you must take care, for here is the answer you seek, Follow me." Fairsong turns and walks deeper into the back of the cave holding out his light stick. As he came to the back of the cave they were all able to make out a large hole, or entrance leading into a tunnel.

"Well would you look at that, it's a whole cave system not just a room after all." Tarton said stating the obvious. They all nodded in agreement.

"And if you have noticed the tunnel from this cave is not of nature's creation, a method was used to create such a smoothed surface almost polished there must have been some tremendous heat in the tools used to shape this surface and the tunnel." Tom commented curiously.

"I have read about tunnel boring machines on the internet that use some type of a heat process where as they bored it melts and re-cools the surface of the walls, thus eliminating the need to use concrete as a surfacing and support and cheaper in the long run." James mentioned. "But that was along the line of Sci Fi, and this looks like someone has actually done it." He added.

"Well would you look over there, down in the tunnel, it would seem that some type of natural glowing fungus or life form that is producing a type of light." Ben commented.

"Yes, there are life forms that can produce such a light, as in the oceans in the deep you will find that nature has found a way for light, like in these vast caves and caverns in the under worlds they have done this as well." Fairsong answered.

"Maybe that's where they went then, they found this and went to explore and probably have gotten themselves lost then." James said.

"Dad, look at this, it was on the desk and it has been opened I would bet by Sariah or Levi." Ben said as he showed the box to James.

James looked in the box and saw the old Browning .45 1911 with the ammunition clips and the letter which all looked like it had been recently handled.

"Well I wonder why someone would leave this gun here, Ben let's take a look at the note and see if we can learn anything from it."

Ben picked up the letter from the box and began to read it, James took the gun from the box and studied it a moment working the slide and chambered a round it seemed in good order for its age.

"Well as old as this gun is, it was well preserved looks like it would work just fine." James commented.

"Let me read this letter to you all as it does offer us some answers." Ben said moving his light wand to where he could get a better view of what it said.

"Well it was written according to the date in 1918." He started.

"Just read it out loud no paraphrasing ok, we don't have time for that." Tom said getting impatiently.

"Ok, ok just be patient it's dated June 12 of 1918 so this is old.

{To whoever is most unfortunate to find this letter and this place, I would suggest you leave as fast as you can and get off this evil mountain and never, never come back. It is cursed."

"I am Frederick the son of Norman Adare the miner who lived here but has now long since vanished and we have not been able to locate him. My older brother Alex has gone for help but he has been gone quite a long time and I fear he may not have made it to Beaver for help. This is a cursed place for bad things have happened to anyone who has been foolish enough to stay here too long.

"The Ute speak of a great evil in these mountains and that it should be avoided. They warned us not to mine, hunt, or travel here and that the evil spirits of the underworld roam these lands and will take anyone who is foolish enough to travel here down into their spirit realms and they are never heard from or seen again.

"We did not believe in their foolish stories about spirits, ghosts or their demons and the like for they are just uneducated Indians after all full of dumb myths. That is what we thought at first but now I am not so sure. Dad is gone and I have abandoned working the mine and barricaded myself here in this cave for safety. Strange things have come in the night; they are quiet and have carried off the mules and supplies. Now I remain alone. I am running out of provisions and do not know how much longer I can stay, I do know that whatever creature or demon is outside. I can hear it scrapping and clawing at the door and pushing on it during the night trying to open it to get to me. They leave a three toed large print, larger than that of a grizzly bear, I do not know what it could be. I do know this: I seem to be a prisoner now and if I venture out by day I am not able to get very far for the demons seem to come in the dusk and I must flee back to this cave for safety, I do not think I can travel to Beaver to escape, as in the open at night they would catch me. It's over a day's hike back to Beaver so for now it's safer in the cave I hope Alex will come back soon with help I think it's the only way I will survive. Alex, if you read this I am leaving the extra gun in case you need it. If you do not find me then I have either made my escape and will find you in Beaver or the demons have taken me. You are warned! Leave and never return. There is some strange evil here. A dark magic. I hear something,

"Alex there is a strange humming sound behind the back wall. Its glowing white hot like when the black smith melts iron. I cannot leave, I am trapped, for the demons are back at the door again. Know this, not sure how much time I have so I must end this letter. Tell the family I love them. I must go; I hear them. The demons they are coming.}that's all he said and the letter ends."

Ben handed the letter to his Dad; he glanced at it thoughtfully then put it back into the box.

"Sounds like this Frederick went to the back of the cave to deal with whatever was happening there and met his demise, now we know when this cave tunnel was made, that was a long time ago. Interesting."

"Ben it looks like this could be your lost Great Grand Uncle, your Great Grandfather Alex is the one mentioned in the letter, and he changed the spelling of Adare to Adair when your Grandfather was born. We often wondered why he changed the spelling, maybe this had something to do with it." James added.

"Well I would suggest we take a look deeper into this cave system, it would seem that the kids read this and they would have thought about exploring some at least. And if they were in here when the down pour happened, they would have waited out the storm, which would give them plenty of time to explore the area. Let's go back to the rear of the cave again and look for any sign that the kids went that way." Tom suggested.

"This would be a reasonable idea, and it very well may be that our journey could start along that path in the near future." Fairsong added then started walking to the rear of the cave where the tunnel opening was.

"Sounds just a little crazy to me, sorry guys, but the dude in the letter was speaking of magic, devils, monsters and demons, sounds to me like he must have been going crazy." Tarton stated as they all followed Fairsong back to the tunnel entry again.

"Tarton, in the old days things we take for granted today would seem magical, like these light sticks for example, or radio, TV, cell phones all new technology and everyday items for us, however to someone long ago would seem like magic. So it's as simple as that, as for the demons thing who really knows, the mountains can get one spooked at times, but you have to admit, some type of machine bored that tunnel, it's not natural at all, and it was mentioned in the letter." James replied.

"That makes sense." Tarton answered thoughtfully.

"Hey I just stumbled on this or actually my foot rolled over on it when I stepped on it." Tom said as he bent down to pick up something from the floor of the cave. As he stood up he held out several spent gun shells, and they looked like the old .45 cartridges that were in the box.

"Now that is interesting, and it looks like he must have shot at what ever created the tunnel or entered the cave, maybe his demons." James stated.

"Gentlemen, come now and look to where the cave extends on into the tunnel, we did not take the time to look when last we found this, see the floor, there are tracks in the dust, foot prints of your two children, and several others as well, adults by the size of them and they are boot prints." Fairsong stated as they all carefully gathered around his area to take a look.

"You see these smaller prints are most likely your children, these boots however have the look of adults. Let's go into the tunnel and see what else we may find to tell the tale of their disappearances." Fairsong said, and walked into the tunnel searching the floor for signs of disturbance.

"James, see here by this boulder there are tracks, it looks as if a man crouched here in wait for a little while, and then it looks as if there were a scuffle see here and there, the smaller prints, and it looks as if the children were subdued as there is the slight print of two bodies in the dirt floor." Fairsong said pointing out the spots as he spoke.

"And here James, it saddens me to tell, that the tracks of your children are no more, and yet the boot prints are leaving the area deeper into the tunnel, and two of them are much heavier, they must have carried your children with them." He said sadly.

"So they are kidnapped then, but that just does not make any sense, who could have known they were even here let alone want to take them? And who are they anyway?" James stated a little confused and dazed over the knowledge as it sank into his soul, his children were taken, but by whom and why, this realization was turning into anger now.

"Dad we need to go get some help from the others before we do anything, Fairsong and I will stay here at the entrance and you go get the rest of the SAR team, they have some caving equipment with them that will help us search this tunnel. Since this is a kidnapping the Sheriff should know of it as well and come out here don't you think? We could use some firearms as well. They will know what to do." Ben told his dad.

James looked at his eldest son realizing what he had said made sense they did need help.

"We will do just that, you two just be careful and don't also disappear on us, sit tight until we get back." James said as he headed towards the cave entrance door, and stepped into the day light which momentarily blinded him in his rush.

Everyone had followed James out of the cave knowing they had to act in a safe fast way as well as smart. Yet all felt they had to hurry this rescue mission.

"James, go and do as you must, you must hurry now and bring supplies for the journey for we know not how long it will take to locate your children." Fairsong stated.

"We shall do let's get moving now." Tom said as he hurried to the trail leading back to base camp.

James agreed and as he walked towards the trail he took the radio off his hip and called the home base camp and ordered that all SAR team searches be halted and for them to gather at the base camp as soon as possible.

After the group left the site, Fairsong and Ben went back into the cave to look for any more clues or signs that could help them in their search for the children.

CHAPTER 10

Intruders

Back in the realms of the mountain the lights had began flashing on Sleesesa Tessa's security panel. Location was again section 39, the old mountain entrance to this world. There seemed to be an abnormal amount of activity at this area.

It did not seem that the men had the ability to do their mission correctly or there would not be a new intruder now. It was amazing how inept their abilities were, it was a very simple task that they had once again failed at, one could not expect better from such primitive creatures, it would seem they would have to fix their failure once again. He once again must contact his superior and alert them to the inept ability of these men.

"Sleesesa to command." He waited only a moment.

"Ashecoosla at your service." Command center replied.

"Sleesesa monitor station, we have an intruder alert in sector 39 again."

"Ashecoosla confirms Sleesesa report sector 39 intruder alert, will deploy team." Ashecoosla of the command center stated.

"Sleesesa confirms you will send a team to investigate, let it be noted the last man team sent was inadequate as they failed in shielding the entry properly as new intruders have entered the entrance." Sleesesa snarled and hissed the last statement in discussed.

"I would agree, the man team was ineffective as younglings at such simple tasks, will advise a joint investigation this mission."

Ashecoosla was more understanding of the limitations of the outer crust dwellers and having to interact with such a under developed species was demeaning. However from time to time they did do well in their assignments. However this time they will be joined by a Nemekans who shall make sure the mission will be completed correctly, and as a teacher teaches a youngling he shall teach them once more how a Nemekans does the mission correctly.

Ashecoosla punched the button on his com system to alert the human leader of his area to report to him once again.

Major Jones was just finishing detailing the day's work to his Captains when the video com on his desk interrupted his meeting.

"Ashecoosla to Major Jones, it would seem we have more intruders in sector 39, your last mission seems to have been performed in a less than satisfactory way. We find a need to send a member of our team to assist you as you return to this sector in order to properly teach your men in the successful completion of their assignment, Send your team to the Tube departure area and one of our trainers will be there awaiting you. Make sure your team is willing to learn from our vast wisdom so that this matter can be concluded. That is all."Ashecoosla stated.

"Major Jones accepts your mission and your council and be rest assured it will be completed correctly this time. Major Jones out." He shut off is video com and cursed the day he took this assignment.

Working with these Nemekans was like hitting your head on a steel door some times, arrogant creatures that needed to be taught a lesson someday. But the pay was good. He decided to send the same team back if they messed up then they can clean it up and deal with having to work with the Nemekans.

Turning to the men in the room he barked. "Lt. Fred since your team messed up, I am sending your team back into area 39 to fix your own mess. You seem to have upset our Nemekans friends so you get a baby sitter to go back with you this time to wipe your little noses. So get it right this time! Is that understood?" He demanded glaring at Lt. Fred.

"Yes sir understood, Sir."

"Then you're dismissed." He snapped, dealing with the Nemekans sure was a pain in the butt most of the time, it was a hive hierarchy style leadership so crap always ran down hill. Kind of like the military. So they had better get it right this time or heads would roll.

He watched him leave the room.

As Lt. Fred entered the mess hall that served as a rest area during duty hours he began scouring the room for Sergeant Smith.

"Sergeant Smith!" He barked.

"Here Sir." He replied and hurried over to where Lt. Fred was, wondering what the problem was, he did not look happy at all.

"Sergeant your team had a simple mission in sector 39, you were to simply hide the entrance again from the surface population and it seems you were not capable of doing that correctly."

"Sir we did that as ordered." Sergeant Smith replied a little confused as they had performed well he thought on the last mission.

"Well it seems you messed it up, because you're now going back and this time a Nemekans is going with you to baby sit your sorry team so that you get it right this time. There are more intruders now at sector 39. So gear up and move out your baby sitter will meet you at the Tube station." Lt. Fred stated flatly.

"Lt. We did the job right the first time; we don't need any Neme baby sit'n us."

"Well Smith, that is not your choice now is it, it's already been made. Since there are more intruders it is obvious you made a mistake of some type. So be on your best behavior and learn how to do it the Neme way, and be nice to him or he just might rip your head off for fun. Got that." Lt. Fred stated firmly.

"Yes Sir, I understand, we are as good as gone." Sargent Smith replied as he went to gather his team and their gear.

Lt. Fred turned and left the room, he understood where the Sargent was coming from, these Neme's were a pain in the butt, and acted like they owned the whole world at times. I am sure the Sargent and his team did their job right the first time as they usually did, there must be another reason why the entrance was rediscovered by the surface population again, it was unusual, and puzzling at the same time. But Smith and his team could handle it.

Sargent Smith gathered his team and when they had all their gear and were ready to head out he spoke to them all.

"Men I will be blunt, we are getting the shaft from the top about whatever is happening back at sector 39, Sounds like we have new intruders there, so they are sending a Neme with us. So be nice to the thing as rules state. We resealed the entrance and we did it good, so someone found a way to reopen it and it seems no one knows how they did this. They just blame us for it. So our job is to deal with it just like last time. My bet is someone is missing the two kids we found, so be on your guard, They won't know about us so we should have the advantage if it's just some searchers looking for them, I doubt any will be armed but one never knows for sure, If this gets dicey and you have to shoot do so to eliminate all intruders. Understood?"

His team all nodded in agreement as they all headed down the hall towards the Tube station.

As they arrived they noticed their Neme waiting for them. When they approached him he turned to them and spoke through his translator, which was a small oval device all the Nemekans had placed on a short necklace on a thin chain hung around their neck it was a great techy tool for everyone.

"Sargent Smith, I am Seenswanee of Teesa, I am here to assist you on your mission this day. I shall observe you and your men and assist as needed." He greatly disliked the human creatures after all they were like the stinky surface scum off a shallow pond, but his leader had once again sent him to assist and to teach these ignorant beings what a youngling could easily do. He would be satisfied when this mission was complete and he no longer was needed to be around these lower life forms that were only a step above their obvious relations the monkey, who sometimes showed more intelligence.

"Seenswanee of the Teesa we accept your assistance for this mission and grant it an honor to ourselves to have a great Nemekans as yourself during our journey this day. Let us continue in the Tube car for our briefing as we do need to hurry." Sergeant Smith said in his best politically correct tone. As he motioned with his arm and all in the team boarded the Tube transportation car and embarked towards sector 39.

* * * * *

"Ben we have been through most of the items we can find here, not much to help us in our journey preparations; however there is something you can do. Bring out the Lev Antas Shuesa." Fairsong asked him.

Ben produced the item from his side pouch. "Ok, now what?"

"I would have thought you would have guessed by now, however let us begin, you need to think of your sister and brother, think of where to go in order to find them and let us see if you are ready to be guided by the Lev Antas Shuesa finally, now begin." Fairsong said in his teacher's voice.

Ben held the device in his left hand and thought deeply of his family as Fairsong had told him to do, trying to clear his mind of all else, he focused then on where they could be, or how he could find them. The device began to glow from within once more only brighter this time, he thought harder and with more earnest on where to go to find them and the device remained a solid constant glow. The pointer moved and arranged themselves pointing towards the back of the cave, to the tunnel.

"I would guess they are as you have said, somewhere down the tunnel, that is if this thing is working correctly."

"Ben do not distrust the Lev Antas Shuesa, it will never give you poor directions, although it may be faint at times, or not as clear as it works on your own spirituality and the care you give it."

"We do have a direction then as I suspected and feared, you may put that away for now for there is another item you are not aware of that will be of help to all of us who will join you on this journey." He said as he pulled out a crystal clear bottle from one of his pockets. It was small and had a twist top made of a crystal, this was filled with a bluish liquid. He held it up so Ben could see it better.

"So what is this then?" Ben asked the obvious question.

"It is called Shinearei a single drop in each eye helps one see in the darkness. In the caves and tunnels we will be journeying through there will be subdued lights like the ones you have seen in this tunnel, so this will be useful. In complete darkness it is of no worth, however we shall make use of the lights we take with us, and use this as well saving on the batteries for when they will be needed."

"Wow that sounds interesting, what other strange things do you have in your bag of tricks that you have never shared with us?"

"Ben these items have been held back from your world as they are not ready to use them in a good wise way, therefore I have not shared them. Some of them would have been used for war, or gaining advantages over each other and this was not the original purpose of most of these items. And they will not be made known in a large way to your world until there is a great need and the wisdom to use them."

"I think I can understand that, the others should be in camp by now getting reorganized for the search. So what do you suggest we do now? I see you have a sword, and since you have given me one and I do not know how to use one, and I must assume you do, could you give me some advice on how to use it?"

Fairsong thought on the idea for a few moments Ben had a good idea, as he did know very well how to use this weapon and Ben did need a few lessons, after all he will most likely come to a point where it could be beneficial. He did not have the proper amount of time to teach him much, but a few easy basics should do for now.

"Ben these are elegant weapons from a much older age, and are never to be used lightly. They will bring swift and sudden ends to those who will stand against one who wields it with faith and honor. Draw your weapon and we shall proceed with a few basic lessons as we have some time, however realize that learning to be a swordsman takes many years, and for some a lifetime." He said, as he drew his sword.

Ben nodded and also drew his sword; ready to learn whatever he could teach him in the short time they had available.

They spent the next hour dueling, Fairsong teaching him the basic blocks, parries and quick attacks then having him drill them many times each in order to get the feeling of the flow of the sword.

"Ben all though the technique is important and how much time you give to practice, your weapon will work best when you become one with its power, with its form as you become one unit, flowing in motion with the ease of the wind through the tree's. As you become a part of each other's energy you will be able to think and it shall react as your body does when you think it to act. So this is where you must set your goal to become as I have said. Then you will have entered the beginning phase of your learning."

"I will continue to work on it every day then and maybe someday I will become good at it."

Ben stated hopefully.

Ben wondered about what he had been told. "Sounds kind of mystical, becoming one with a weapon, not sure if I really understand that yet."

"As your faith grows so will your understanding of these tools. They were made long ago by some friends of mine and they know the Great Creator, and have used his wisdom provided to them to create many marvelous things. If we are all fortunate maybe in our journey we will come upon these peoples, if so it shall be a blessed day, so it is when anyone can spend some time with them and learn of their wisdom. They are as the ancients of your book, the Holy Bible, in many ways but enough of that for now, so let us prepare for your friends return and the beginning of our journey."

Ben and Fairsong took a rest from their activities and Ben sat down by the doorway at the mouth of the cave to ponder what he had learned. Meanwhile Fairsong went back into the cave to see what else could be discovered that could help, what they may have overlooked. As he looked around he noticed something that he had failed to see earlier. He felt a little disgusted with his old rusty senses; he should have looked for such devices at the beginning. He should have realized from the evidences shown in the disappearances of Frederick Adare and the quickness in which the children vanished as well. He should have realized that there would be monitoring devices in this place, he raised his sword to the top of the wall near the roof of the cave and using its edge plucked the metal device from the wall and caught it with his other hand as if fell.

He gave it a good looking over to verify his thoughts on what it was, a monitoring device for sure only much more modern than those he had seen long ago. What mattered now was that it had put them all in the same if not worse danger than what the children must have experienced. He shut off the device, then went through the rest of the cave room being very aware of what he was now seeking and found three other similar devices, he again shut them all off. Then he proceeded out of the cave and found Ben sitting and meditating on the day's events.

"We are in great danger." He said bluntly.

At this comment and with the tone of his voice, it brought Ben out of his thoughts and back into complete alertness at what Fairsong had just said.

"What exactly do you mean, Danger?" He asked.

"I have been away too long in my travels, it was my error not to have noticed them before and that will be my pain of failure to live with, however there were intruder monitoring devices in the cave and by the tunnel, that is how they knew the children were here, and they for sure know we also are hear." He said as he showed the devices to Ben.

"It is for sure that our presence here has been alerted to those who placed them there, I am also sure they will send someone to check out the intrusion again. And now the journey will begin sooner than I had thought, and we may have to deal with whomever is sent to find out what we are doing here." He said with a slight tiredness and sadness in his voice.

"What do you mean?" Ben asked somewhat nervous.

"You have over these last few years have grown into a good young man, growing in spiritual strength as well. However now you must be as one of the Sons of Helaman, you must pray for guidance and strength and for valor, for you will need them all before this day is done. You must prepare I fear for battle. For it comes soon."

"Battle? What do you mean, like war?" He said a little scared at the thought.

"The idea of having to defend one's family and one's self from those who wish to do you harm is not to be taken lightly, yes in your defense and to find your missing family you will have to fight, and if needed take the lives of others in your defense. We as warriors of light seek to protect and to defend the weak and helpless; however the enemies of light, the armies of darkness are many and rarely show any mercy. So let the spirit guide you in your fights, show mercy if possible, but remember it is better to send them home to their creator than to suffer yourself to make the trip.

Remember dwell not on those lives you may be forced to take in order to find your loved ones. For they will not lose a moments sleep if they take your life." He said with determination.

"I understand, I just hope I won't freeze up and fail you, so tell me what is needed to be done and I shall do what I can to assist."

Quietly he prayed in his heart, Lord help us this day, help me for if we are to find my sister and brother we will need to prevail in any fight we may have forced upon us. We would not, and do not seek to take anyone's lives, but if it is to be in our defense grant us victory so we can save our family, and succeed in our mission.

Ben turned to Fairsong and asked. "So how much time do we have before they arrive?"

"Unfortunately they should be here at any moment, based on the time we have spent after entering the cave again, and the time needed to prepare for an investigation party and it also depends on the type of transportation used and how far away from us they are, so let us prepare they will not expect us to know they are coming, so we will have the element of surprise to our advantage." Fairsong said as they re-entered the cave room.

"Now we cannot use our lights of any kind as it will betray our positions, However we shall leave the front door open and we shall now take advantage of the Shinearei drops, for we can hide motionless in the dark and let them pass between us, then we shall fall on them without modern weapons, swords are quieter than firearms, so only use the gun if needed."

"Ok I shall follow your lead."

"Very well, use your gun if needed, keep it loaded a round chambered and the safety off, our swords will be drawn and ready for action, pray and feel the strength of the Lord with you in spirit and let it help guide your actions in battle."

"Now let us position ourselves, and mind your fear, do not look directly at your target nor in its eyes as they will feel your presence before we strike. If there are any who come who are not human, fear not, they will sense it for they will smell it and you will be found out, so leave any of those to me. Is that understood then?"

"What do you mean Not Human?"

"There are many creatures of the Earth, you have never met or even thought about, there are races of men and creatures you cannot imagine and yet they are there. There may be some that come known as Nemekans, they are a race of reptiles and they are very large, do you remember the head in the box, well that was one Hyrum slew long ago. Leave them to me as I have said. There will be a group of men I am sure as they work in league with each other now." He said.

"I will do what I can." He stated flatly.

"It is time they should be here soon, and do not worry you will do just fine. Let's us go now and find our positions, remember to let them pass between us and they will be exposed to the light from the door way, and then we shall fall upon them from the rear. Here now use the Shinearei, one drop only in each eye; this will give us great advantage." Fairsong stated as he put a drop of Shinearei in each of Ben's eyes and then did the same with his own.

"There now you see better do you not?"

"Yes this is amazing, I see fine almost like daylight, this is really cool like night vision only more clear. Ben said surprised at how well this stuff worked. And it gave him a boost of confidence for the coming battle.

"Now breathe lightly, ever so softly as you will be crouched along the edge of the wall on the left, and I on the right of the tunnel opening. As they pass by us look to my signal and follow my lead and trust in your heart, have faith and all will be good in the end."

"Agreed." Ben said ever more nervously.

Then they proceeded to their positions as Fairsong directed, and then he motioned for quiet and to listen and then the waiting began.

Ben did so with a prayer in his head and heart to help the loud thumping of his heart, he was scared and nervous what if he messed up, what if he froze, what if he were killed. He hoped he could do well and survive what was to be his first battle of life and death; he had to survive to find his family. He saw Fairsong across the path, how quiet and relaxed he seemed like a cat just before it sees the mouse.

After what seemed like hours but actually was only about 20 minutes he noticed Fairsong tense up and become fully alert. He coiled like a spring like the wild lion who sees its prey just before the attack, This set the hairs on the back of Ben's neck and arms all strait up, he was very worried, but his fate lay in following what Fairsong had told him to do. He had to trust in him. Fairsong and God were his only help right now. All his own senses were very much alive now as he waited for the inevitable, the signal from Fairsong to begin the battle.

* * * * *

The Team had just about reached their objective in section 39; they could see the tunnel where it opened in to the cave leading to the outer entrance. To the door they knew they had re-sealed not long ago. Even in the soft lights along the walls they could see the light from the opened outer door show upon the wall of the tunnel.

Sargent Smith motioned for all stop, then he looked for a time into the cave and seeing no movement and hearing no sounds, he slowly preceded into the room, one by one his team members four in all, followed by the Nemekans in the rear. With no noise, and no reaction to their entering the cave they preceded towards the opened door, as they got closer they had to turn off their night vision devices as the room was becoming too bright due to the sun shining in the room.

Smith knew his men were behind him, and could now smell the Neme as it came into the cave room behind him, he always could tell the smell due to its snaky smell, they all found it very irritating. With all their tech one would have thought they could find a way to deal with their own stench much better.

As Sergeant Smith looked around he noticed the desk area had been searched through, and with the door still opened, he realized the intruders could be waiting outside. He noticed that the sensors he had placed on his last visit were gone. Someone had found them, Darn it, they must know we would come then, suddenly his whole body became motionless as it set in, this could be a setup, a trap. He turned to warn the team of this possibility and as he did so he saw out of the darkness a movement of incredible speed, some shadow that moved to attack the Nemekans, he shouted. "It's a TRAP!"

Ben watched Fairsong, totally alert now, he had heard what sounded like a round being chambered in a gun, then he heard the slight grate of boots on gravel. and he almost let out a gasp but was able to control it, as he watched as a man in dark clothing and military style equipment, wearing some type of night vision device slowly creep into the room. Then one by one he was followed by three more men, a total of four. Then a moment later he noticed a smell much like the stench of snakes, then about that time he saw an amazing thing, and he about came unglued by fear and a strong urge to run, this is what Fairsong must have called a Nemekans, for it was huge a good seven and a half feet tall and must be around four hundred and fifty pounds, and a very powerful and scary creature. He remembered to breathe lightly and turned his gaze away using his peripheral vision so as not draw any attention to him, Fairsong said to let him handle this creature, he would gladly do so. He watched what Fairsong was going to do.

Not moments after this creature had passed into the cave, Fairsong gave a nod of his head and then with amazing speed like an exploding tiger he attacked without ever a noise, slashing at the back of the Nemekans with his sword.

And then Ben heard the first man yell 'It's a Trap', as he took a deep breath and joined Fairsong in the work of death.

CHAPTER 11

Cave Fight

As the group entered base camp James went to the SAR command tent to look for the Sheriff. Tom and Tarton left to check on the women and to let them know what they had found out so far, also to see how Olaf and Mary were holding up.

As James walked into the command tent he found the Sheriff directing traffic on the SAR radio, dealing with updates and reports on the several different search groups.

"Noland we need to talk, we have found the cave entrance and have been able to re-open the door." James stated to the Sheriff and everyone else in the room.

Sheriff Thompson looked up at James with a stunned look. "You really have found the door? Where?" He asked.

"Right where it was supposed to have been, it was hidden by some kind of optical illusion. Fairsong had a way of removing the illusion and there it was, we went inside and well, we found some clues of what may have happened. So we need to re-group, and then start again this time searching the cave and the tunnel inside it. We need to get everyone here so we only have to explain it once or twice. We have left Fairsong and Ben at the cave in case the kids show up." James said excitedly, finally there was a more solid direction in which to focus the search, there was a glimmer of hope again.

"Calm down, so you say you found the door and have gone inside, now you want to call off all the other search teams so we can focus on the cave now, right?" He said.

"That's right, and have Bill bring his dogs there is a tunnel at the back and it looks as if the kids were taken deep inside the mountain, so they might be able to track their sent and speed up the search, or at least determine they did in fact go into the tunnel."

"James what do you mean by taken, are you saying they were kidnapped then? If so what makes you think so?" Sheriff Thompson asked.

"I will explain in a minute, meanwhile start getting all the searchers heading back to camp, we are wasting time. Ben said you brought some caving gear and a few of the team are cavers, so we may need to break that gear out as well." James replied.

Sheriff Thompson turned to the SAR radio controller. "George better recall all the teams then, and make sure they hurry." He said.

George did as ordered.

"It will take some time to get everyone back." Sheriff Thompson said.

"Sheriff, how many supplies do we have on hand? We should have a good amount for a search party, Fairsong said we could use up to a two week supply for those who are chosen to search the cave tunnel. Also he thinks the trip will be very dangerous for those who go

"Well, I will have Fred check our supplies and you check on yours, if we have a smaller group go search the cave tunnel then we could send the remainder home with a skeleton crew here at camp for communications and possible emergency."

"Well you heard the man Fred, go check our supplies, water, food anything light weight as it will be an unknown as to how long they maybe on the search." Sheriff Thompson said.

"On the way, will take some time, but I should have a good list by the time the rest arrive." Fred said.

The Sheriff looked at James thinking for a few moments then motioned for him to sit down at the table.

"James sit, we need to make some sense of what you're saying and then we will need to make plans." Sheriff Thompson said, then turning to another member of his SAR team he asked.

"Al, go get us some water and a sandwich would you please, may as well fuel up while we wait."

"On the way, be back in a few." Al said as he hurried out the door to complete his new task.

"Now tell me what's been going on up there at the cave James, and go slowly this time so I can make some better sense of it this time." Sheriff Thompson said. Then sat back and waited for him to begin.

"Like I said we went to the area, and somehow Fairsong found and opened the door, it would seem that he has an understanding of the technology that was used for the illusion of hiding the door. I know what it sounds like and if I had not witnessed it myself it would sound a bit nutty. Anyways we went in and looked around, it's like the kids said it was, some old miners cave home from way back in the early 1900's, based upon the things we have found in it. There were old books, maps, letters and such stuff.

"There was a letter we read that seems to have been written by a long disappeared relative of ours around that time, strange that. A Norman and Frederick Adare who vanished around 1918, they were gold miners and after they did disappeared, no one could figure out what exactly happened. My Great Grandpa was the brother to this Frederick, the letter stated he had gone for help, but that Norman had disappeared, also this Frederick was scared of some kind of demons or things, really weird stuff but you can read it for yourself if you need to, but by the letter he left he was definitely scared of something up there."

"That will be ok, when the time comes I would like to see everything you have found up there, continue." Sheriff Thompson replied.

"On the wall there were some strange and unusual writings and Fairsong could read them for us, now you know Fairsong, he is older than dirt itself, and a strange old guy at that. But he did read the old writings and this is what he said, that it was a strong warning to leave the cave and never return, that if you did not you might die. In the letter it did mention something about the back of the cave, there was a hole being dug or something at the back of the cave, so we went to look at it, we found some old gun shells and found a colt 45 1911 in a box that seems usable by its condition. The letter sounded like Frederick was in trouble, he cut short the letter and hid it and the box, then nothing else so whatever he was afraid of, may have done him in I suspect."

"We also found some tracks and markings on the ground, Fairsong said it was the kid's tracks and that it looked as if a struggle had taken place, some bigger foot prints, boots in the dirt floor and they lead back into the tunnel and disappeared. He said it looks as if the kids were kidnapped and carried off down the tunnel." James added.

"So James do you really trust Fairsong, it seems he may have something to do with this since he can read their writing, and knows how they hid the cave entrance and all. Do you think he could be a part of this? Or was he just lucky?"

"Look Noland we have been friends a long time, so has Fairsong to my family, I do trust his judgment even if he is somewhat of a old kooky guy at times, He does seem to be familiar with some things about this, but I know he is a true friend of our family. And with all this weird stuff happening up here how can anyone of us explain his younger looks now? We can't, he went from being like a 90+ year old to where he is in his prime, he is fitter than the both of us together, how can we explain that away? We can't. This whole thing is crazy if you ask me, but if he has an idea of where my children are I am going to follow his lead." James said becoming worn down and exhausted and yet still anxious and hopeful at the same time.

"Tell ya what we're going to do, were going to collect everyone and go see what you have found, look at the evidences, let Bill and his dogs try and find a trail, and then set up a game plan from there. We are just going to take it one step at a time. Now we will have about 1 hour before most of the teams make it back to camp, so let's go tell the women of these possible leads. We don't want to get their hopes up, but this is more than we have had so far, a possible direction in which to focus at least." Sheriff Thompson stated with a sigh, some of this was sounding farfetched and yet it was hard to explain some of the things he had already witnessed. He would see how this played out, and hoped it was a turn for the better as they had not been able to find any other clues, even the dogs had come up empty, which was unusual for them.

"Sounds good to me, let's go tell Katasha, she has a right to know what we have found so far, then the others, shall we go gather them up then." James stated as he got up and headed out the door with Sheriff Thompson on his heels.

They walked over to where the women were which happened to be in Martha's tent. They found Olaf there as well. They were worrying over Martha who had begun some contractions again due to all the stress.

"Olaf, how is Martha doing then?" James asked.

"She is having some contractions again, and this time I don't think these are the fake ones. If they keep up we will need to get her off this mountain fast." He said. Then he turned to the Sheriff.

"You have a helicopter don't you? If we needed to use it to get Martha down to the Beaver Hospital we could use it right?" He asked, concern showing in his voice.

"Yes I could have it on stand bye, I will go tell them to get on that for you, so you really think we will need to use it then?" Sheriff asked. Thinking what's next, this is really getting to be an all-out strange day, seems to be getting worse all the time.

"Yes, she has a history of early pregnancy and we argued about her coming up here on this trip, but she wanted to do it, and she is one of those stubborn Adair's after all, so here we are, and she may have done fine if all stress of the missing children had never taken place." He said tiredly.

"It's a done deal then I will get it on stand bye." He replied and hurried out of the tent to speak with the radio man again.

Katasha turned to James with a haggard worried face. "Have you found anything yet?"

James looked at his wife and was saddened by the stress and worry the last few days had put on her. "Yes I think we may have some leads finally. Fairsong has found the cave door opening right where the kids said it was." He walked over and gave her a hug and then sat her down then repeated the story as he had told it to Sheriff Thompson.

As he related the events at the cave James saw a glimmer of hope once again in Katasha's face and Mary's and Martha's as well, and he could tell that there could be an end to this story soon.

"Kat, if what Fairsong thinks has happened this is not yet over, we will need to keep searching to find who took our children and where they have been taken to. This could take a much longer time to find them, but in the end I have faith that Fairsong will help us in finding them. And with Bill's hounds we should be able to track them pretty fast I would think, cave or no cave they are good hounds." James smiled hopefully at this wife.

"I hope we can find them soon, I so miss them, and I am about to my breaking point, at least now we have a direction to search for them." Katasha replied.

At this time Sheriff Thompson poked his head back into the tent.

"James, Olaf most of the SAR team is back so we are going to feed them some grub then a little rest and we should have James fill them in on what you have found. Then we are all going to go up and see what is in this cave for ourselves. And hopefully find your children." He said with firm sound of resolve mixed with a hope for success in his tone. Then he ducked out and went to the assembly area the SAR team was gathering.

"Sounds like it's time to repeat this story again, catch you ladies later. Mary you just hang in there, Olaf lets go and you may be able to suggest some things to the group or add anything I may miss to the story." James said as he hugged his wife again patted Mary on the shoulder and left the tent to join the Sheriff at the assembly area. He was anxious to tell the story then get back to the cave as soon as possible to start the search.

After about another half hour the majority of the SAR team had arrived, even Bill and the hounds were back, after they had all gotten something to eat and were quiet for the most part all gathered around the Sheriff and James it was time to update them on the new happenings.

"Everyone listen up, James and his team found some things this morning and we are all going to go search in that area soon. He will fill you in now. So listen up, and no questions till he is done ok." The Sheriff said to them and then motioned for James to begin.

"Well I want to first thank everyone for all you have done so far in looking for my children, but now we have some new leads that most likely will shrink the search team some. We found the cave door entrance and there is a tunnel inside at the back, signs state the kids were in the cave, also some other signs of activities indicate that someone else was in the tunnel system and may have found and abducted my children, why?

We of course can't even guess, and by whom we don't have a clue. But that is what it is looking like and now we are going to put together a team to go search the tunnel system. So anyone with caving experience and who can go we would appreciate your help. However I must be upfront with you. There was a message left, it is a warning to stay out of the cave and tunnel or it could cost you your life.

Now we should take this serious as you think about joining this team. So only those who are willing and prepared to risk your all if needed, and knowing this upfront you will need to volunteer. I suggest single men only or those whose family are grown. If you have family and a job that you cannot leave for an undetermined amount of time then do not volunteer for this team if you have any reservations at all, your family comes first as it should be. My family and my self will look after our own and take the risks as needed to find my children.

So take some time to think this over. If you would like to go gather over at the command tent in one hour and we will go over the rest of the details at that time. Again thanks for your help and sacrifices being here away from your own families and work, now it seems most of you may be able to finally go home now."

James stated and then walked over to the command tent to wait and see who would be able to help further on this now dangerous journey they would have to endure.

Tom and Olaf had joined James in the tent with Tarton and the Sheriff; they sat around going over what they had seen in the cave sharing it with the Sheriff and Olaf.

"Well this is all interesting, and I hope it leads somewhere we have been all over these hills and nothing to show for it." Sheriff Thompson stated flatly.

"For now we shall see what is there when our new team gets together and we have a good look for ourselves at this cave and tunnel." Tom said, he was a little more comfortable knowing that the Sheriff's Helo was now on standby for Martha and Olaf, just in case and that help ease some of his tensions.

All of a sudden James came alert at the noise of what sounded like fire crackers, As James reacted to the noise so did Olaf and the Sheriff as they all left the command tent to see what the cause was.

"You know what that sounds like Sheriff." Olaf stated to the Sheriff as they listened.

"Yep possible gun fire, only subdued some." Sheriff Thompson replied, as he and the others in the camp who had also heard the noises stood to listen, wondering the cause of it.

James noticed most of the men around camp had also become quiet and were listening.

Again there was a brief flurry of popping sounds like fire crackers and it sounded a though it was coming from the location of the cave.

"Sheriff, I think it's coming from the cave area, we left Ben and Fairsong up there." James said becoming alarmed now.

"Men, anyone with a fire arm let's move out and now, sounds like trouble if you don't have a fire arm just stay put." The Sheriff ordered.

Everyone went into action, James and his family always traveled with some rifles and a few side arms when in the deep woods just in case of a rogue bear or mountain lion or worse, So James, Olaf, Tom and Tarton all got their weapons and Olaf grabbed his medical pack he always brought along. And they started up the trail with the Sheriff and Bill with his hounds, and seven others following them all moving as fast as they could.

James was almost running up the hill but it was too steep for one to do that, but he and the rest of the group were moving well and making good time, the gun fire had stopped, no other sounds came from the cave area, this made James worry terribly as Ben was there but he knew Fairsong and Ben were both armed but you never know what could have happened, he knew by his Dads stories about Fairsong when he was younger, he could deal with such things so he hoped and prayed both were ok.

Katasha watched from Martha's tent door as all the men ran up the hill, after a few minutes when no one came right back she decided she had to find out what was going on.

"Martha, I need to go and see what up, I don't like the sound of the men yelling and taking off like that so I will be back in a while, you going to be ok?"

"I will be just fine, you go see what all the noise and fuss is about so you can tell me, Natasha and Mary are here if I need any help, so get going so you can fill us in."

"See you later then." Katasha said as she bolted from the tent and went to find someone who could tell her what was going on. She saw a few men pointing towards the area the cave would be and talking excitedly amongst themselves. Someone mentioned gun shots, or fire crackers maybe, and that got her full attention. She went up to them and grabbed one of them by the arm.

"What is going on, and where is James and everyone else?" Katasha demanded.

"Mam, hold on there a moment, A few moments ago there was what could have been gun shots coming from up near that rock wall you all said the door was in. The Sheriff and your men folks all grabbed their guns and went off running up the hill to see what the matter was, the rest of us are to stay here and wait till they get back." The SAR member stated.

"What? Wait? I will not stay here and wait, my boy is up there and I am not going to sit by and wait another minute when two other of my children are missing and now a third maybe getting shot at. Which way did they go?"

"I would not advise it mam, the Sheriff said that no one..." He began and then was cut off in mid-sentence by her.

"I don't care what he said, just point me up the right trail or you'll have me to deal with first and then someone else will show me the way!" She demanded really getting herself worked up, between their worry and fear and now her anger; she needed to see what was happening up there.

"Mrs. Adair, Joeson was just telling you what he was told to do, calm down now; I've been up there so I'll take you to where they are." A young man named Bud with the SAR team said in a polite yet firm way.

"Good, let's get going then." Katasha said and allowed Bud to guide her to the cave area. On the way out of camp Katasha stopped by her tent for a moment and grabbed her own side arm just in case, her Baby Eagle .40 cal. and she knew very well how to use it. She strapped the gun belt to her waist and hurried out to follow Bud. They left at a fast pace moving up the trail as quickly as Katasha was able to move.

* * * * *

Deep underground beneath what surface dwellers called New Mexico we find the Nemekans thinking on what to do with this unique human boy.

Tech worker Lassoos had completed his diagnostic on his equipment and found that it had been completely shorted out, all the safety measures to prevent such an event had completely failed and the components were melted and fused together and therefore requiring it to be fully replaced. Now he must report this to Tech Leader Elasseear, as it was not due to the fault of his team workers or himself he could not foresee any negative reprisals at this time from the leadership as it was a mechanical failure of a unique form, beyond his knowledge at this time. Lassoos turned to enter the office of his leader confident with his report.

"Tech Leader Elasseear, Tech Lassoos with his analysis of the device as you commanded."

"Tech worker Lassoos explain what were your failures in the harvesting of the essence? Such a simple task to be performed, done so negligently is beyond comprehension." Tech Leader Elasseear hissed his response letting him know he was greatly displeased with his inability to perform what was an easy assignment.

"Great Leader, just before harvesting the essence there was an unknown surge of energy from an unknown and unforeseen place of origination. It has fused and melted the harvester's components and is now unusable. This was beyond anyone's control on our team, most honorable Leader, we noted in the report the energy source even though unknown and unexplainable to our unworthy minds did seem to come from within the human boy, as if by some supernatural method of defense. This is the only possible answer for us to give you most honorable leader at this time." Tech worker Lassoos slightly bowed his head keeping a wary eye on his leader in the case he made a move to retaliate in a negative way as a result of his unusual report as he handed the report to his leader, prepared to duck away if attacked.

Elasseear watched his worker flinch after he made his report, and well he should with such explanation of his team's failure's to complete the simple work given them. He thought a moment prior to responding, this truly was an unusual event however failure never can be acceptable, however he would allow a new harvesting device to be acquired and brought to their science work room to attempt the harvesting once more.

"Lassoos, your failure is plain before me, however I shall allow you one more opportunity to reevaluate your future by sending you another harvester, I will grant you a moment to repair and correct your failure. However if you fail me again then you will be dealt with as needed. Go move the human boy to a holding room until we can obtain the new harvester. Go now and do not fail me again." Elasseear stated flatly with a long threatening hiss hanging in the air to make sure Lassoos got the message clearly.

"Most honorable Leader Elasseear, I am grateful for you granting us yet another harvester to proceed and to complete your work as you so commanded." Tech Lassos again bowed slightly and slowly and cautiously backed out through the door way and headed back to the lab area. Grateful to be in one piece as Elasseear had a reputation of great anger upon those who did not complete their work as he desired.

Elasseear thought on Lassoos report, this is interesting as he looked over their details of the report its data he could clearly see that Lassoos and his team did what they could and truly was not at fault for the destruction of the harvesting device. However you can never let the mere worker class think they are even close to being on the same level of intelligence as he was, always keep them in fear and thus they will provide good work.

Thinking he mused to himself, this truly is a powerful and important essence, 2nd Leader Sosaeen would greatly benefit of such an essence, Maybe I ... he let his thoughts wonder at the thought. Do I dare use this human's essence for myself? Yes I could, I could report the malfunction and the death of this human boy as a result of the faulty device and the workers inept ability to realize the dangers in time resulting in the boy's death. As he thought on this he felt more empowered to the thought of using this powerful essence for his own needs, and the failure would be the workers of course thus they would be punished. This could improve his position amongst the clan leadership as well in the end. He hissed slightly almost a purring sound with the slight emotion he felt, yes this could be done. He must make his own report to 2nd Leader Sosaeen and he would suggest the punishment for the team's failures to him, leaving himself blameless of the failure. Yes this would be the way, it was time for him to design his own report now, as he plotted in his mind a thin almost smile crept across his mouth.

* * * * *

Levi awoke in a small room; he looked around to see where he was and noticed he had a toilet that was built into the wall and a sink, not much else. The floor was cold concrete as were the walls just a dull gray color. No windows and only a door that seemed to be some kind of sliding door as there were no hinges on it, and a key pad to the right side of the door.

He sat up and realized he was thirsty so he went and got a drink from the sink, he had to cup his hands together as there were no cups to use. Then he heard a slight sound coming from the door, he turned to look and watched as a tray of food slid through a slot that had opened at the bottom, as soon as it was in the room the slot closed again.

Levi thought on it, he was hungry and even though he was wary of the food, one never knew what they could do to it, but he was hungry and so he walked over and picked up the tray of food. There was a hardboiled egg, two pieces of toast and a sliced apple that was it no utensils. So he went over to his bed which was built into the wall and made of a solid piece of metal about three inches thick with a pad and a blanket and a small pillow. Like a prison cell. He sure was not in a hospital that was for sure. It looked more like a prison, and felt like it as well. That dude was lying there was no car wreck he was sure of that, I don't know what is going on here but must assume he had been kidnapped and Sariah as well, the how's and why's are just question's he could not get answer's to.

But now what to do, what could he do? He looked at his food and decided to pray over it just in case, He took the time to kneel on the cold floor bowed his head and folded his arms like mom had taught him to do. "Father in Heaven, please bless this food to nourish my body and do me good, bless that I can get out of this place and bless my sister where ever she is and protect us both, and let someone find us please, In the name of Jesus Christ, amen." He felt better after his prayer and sat on the bed again and ate his food.

He thought of the last time he was strapped onto the bed in that other room, they were doing or going to do something bad to him he felt that for sure, but something had happened to their machine and it must have broken, then he went to sleep again and he woke up here. He remembered being scared and praying and then the feeling of everything will be ok. He thought on that a while not fully understanding what it meant.

Maybe someone was looking for them already, he felt that he would be ok, and prayed in his mind again for safety for himself and for Sariah. Then put the tray down he started feeling tired again and laid down on the bed and was soon asleep once more lost to the world of dreams. And this time the dream world became alive within him and he dreamed for what seemed like a very long time, he dreamed of people, of strange creatures, of different worlds and of very strange things and as he dreamed he saw his family and angels and felt that his family was coming to look for him, very strange he thought and became lost in this dream world.

CHAPTER 12

A Mother's Rage

Ben looked around at the carnage of what their brief battle had produced upon the four men and what he assumed was a Nemekans.

He reflected on the moment and was amazed that he had not been hurt or worse in the fight.

He first remembered seeing Fairsong spring like a big cat upon the creature he called the Nemekans without a sound and exceedingly fast for any man, let alone one who only a day ago looked very aged. He had watched as Fairsong's sword had sliced the creature across the back, or actually through the back and the creature had fallen in two pieces and then his second took off its head, that part of the event only took less than two seconds.

Then the lead man had yelled "It's a trap!" and brought his gun to bear on Fairsong who rolled then leaped into the air slashing across the weapon cleaving it into two pieces as it fell to the floor with a clatter, the man looked astonished and fear blazed across his face about the time Fairsong relived his head from his shoulders effortlessly with a slash of his sword.

By then the other three men had opened fire with their guns shooting at any shadow or anything that moved. That gave Ben just enough time to seize the opportunity for they looked towards the open door where the sun light shown brightly which hid Bens movements a moment, and he could easily see his prey so the advantage was his. He used his sword to cut a man down, then turned and ran at the next man who turned quickly and fired a spray of bullets towards him, He leaped to the side as the bullets hit the cave wall and off down the tunnel, He recovered and leaped up and in one motion sliced off the arm holding the gun which fell to the floor, he then ended the man's life with the next stroke of his sword.

Ben turned to find Fairsong standing over the last man who was on the floor at his feet. Ben noticed a strange crystal tool in Fairsong's hand.

Fairsong looked over at him with the approval of a teacher. "Well done, your first battle of many I fear yet to come, you have done well as you're still alive."

"The first of many?" Ben answered. "That's enough for me."

"That is why you have been chosen, your lack of love for the battle is good, it is never good to take any life and yet we save all as we can." Fairsong stated and then he motioned to the man at his feet.

"See here, this man is not fallen, he is yet still alive and intact. The weapon we each have has many purposes you can kill with it or stun as well, as you see this man is stunned and when he awakes will have a tremendous head ache and then we can question him about what lies in our path before us, and to his knowledge of your missing family. It is always good to keep one enemy alive for questioning, much you can learn."

Ben took in the whole scene and then asked. "So this all happened so fast, was the creature you killed one of those Nemekans you spoke of then?"

"Yes it was, and sad it is that we find them working with men, this is sad indeed a great evil is taking place under the surface for sure, It has been a long while since the two races Nemekans and Men have worked together to do anything. This is a mystery and bodes bad feelings on what may have happened to your family. However when he awakes we shall question him and find the truth of the matter." He said flatly.

"Let us tie him up and make sure he is fully disarmed, go through all his clothing look for anything of value to find out who he is, and while you do that I shall deal with those now dead." Fairsong said with almost a hint of sadness in his voice.

"Will do." Ben said. And he bound the man both hand and feet so he could not move. Then he searched the man thoroughly for any weapons or clues as to who he could be.

Fairsong took the time to drag the bodies of the men out of the cave and laid them out against the mountain wall, the Nemekans as well, with all their body parts. The Nemekans he placed farther away from the men out of respect for the race.

"Ben bring out the prisoner and we shall question him in the light of day."

Ben dragged the still unconscious man out the door and propped him up by a large tree trunk.

"Double check his person and the dead men for any useful items in the light make sure you don't miss anything, I will deal with my Nemekans friend." He said as he turned to the creature.

They began their searches. Ben found several weapons on each man, the surviving weapons were two rifles and each had carried a .40 caliber side arm so that made four. They also each carried a crystal stun weapon and he placed them in a row away from the bodies. Then he looked at the uniform patches and insignias to see if he could tell who they worked for.

Meanwhile Fairsong was searching and disarming the remains of the Nemekans, he was a warrior he noticed of the Teesa class he could tell by the color and the outfit he wore. He removed his weapons belt, which contained a rectangle box that would face the front towards the enemies and when used it would either stun, or eliminate if not disintegrate the victim. He also took a few other items of interest. Then sizing up the young dead warrior he was glad he was able to dispatch him as quickly as he had, as it could have turned into a really hard scrape had he been forced into a face to face conflict with this one.

Fairsong kneeled down upon the earth and faced the eastern sky, and then he prayed. "Father of our spirits and creator of our clay forms, we thank thee for granting us victory this day against our new and old foes. We would not kill them if we were not forced to do so in our defense and that of our family and friends. Accept their spirits into whatever realms they may go to at this time, I thank you for young Bens ability to perform well in his first battle and grant us the power over our enemies in the times yet to come. We your humble servants thank you for your help, and ask to bless Bens family, young Levi and Sariah who are lost to the evils of the underworlds, let us have victory and bring them back safe to their family. This I ask as a humble servant my dear Father in the Heavens above. Amen." Fairsong closed his prayer and sat looking out over the horizon for a time.

* * * * *

As the men led by James came near to where the cave entrance would be, he signaled for all to stop.

"If you must catch your breath do so and we will go in quietly is that understood?"

"Sounds good to me, we do need to be quiet for we don't know what or who maybe there, and no one does any shooting unless I tell you to, everyone got that." Sheriff Thompson added.

The whole group of seven SAR members and Bill, James, Olaf, Tarton and Tom all took a moment to gain their breath and once it was normal again they all looked at the Sheriff and waited.

"Bill I want you to keep your hounds close but quiet."

"Sure thing." Bill answered as he bent down to pat his boys on the head and spoke with them telling them they needed to be quiet, and it seemed to those present that the dogs actually may have understood what Bill told them to do.

"Now the rest of us lets go in very quiet like, spread out and we will need to see what is going on before we commit to any action alright, so just follow my lead. James you and your kin will come with me, the rest fan out, now remember quiet like, let's go." Sheriff Thompson said as he started leading them the last 100 yards to the cave site.

As they walked through the tree line what they saw made them all stop with amazement and a little stunned. James took it all in and ran over to Ben.

"Are you all right? We heard gun shots and I thought the worse." James said and as he spoke he realized what the gun fire had been as he looked at the dead men on the ground, and then he noticed the creature also dead, what was that thing? Unreal he thought.

"Dad, we are fine, however there is more to this than we could have imagined, Fairsong has filled me in a little bit, but we are ok, however we do have a prisoner." Ben said as he pointed to the bound man by the tree.

"Fairsong kept one alive so that he could be questioned and maybe get some answers about where Sariah and Levi are. He is knocked out but should be waking up soon, and then we can question him."

"Sounds good, glad you're both in one piece the Sheriff and I will question this one." James said coldly.

The Sheriff and the rest of the men walked up to the carnage.

"Well it would seem that you two have everything under control, now I heard you mention this prisoner, how long till I can question him, and I will then take him down and lock him up." Sheriff Thompson said.

"So who can explain to me what on Earth that creature is?" Sheriff asked the question the rest of them had about the dead animal thing.

The rest of the team had all joined around the creature trying to figure out what it was. They all marveled at the size of the being and noted it was not in one piece. Bill even tried to get a close look with his hounds but they were not having any of it, and would not come within 50 feet of it, so he had to tie them up along the tree line so they wouldn't take off on him, they were really scared of the stench of that thing. Then he went up to see what it was.

"Well it would seem this would be a good time for me to explain some things to you men." Fairsong stated.

"Well I sure hope you can." Tom stated in wonder.

"There is much more to your world than many will ever admit or desire to know of, for most prefer to live in their little box's and wish not to learn or to expand their knowledge outside their comfortable little box's, you see even in your Holy Books does it not say the Creators creations are beyond the humans mind to comprehend? Indeed this is true, now you few here have been forced by life to leave your old box behind, it's time to begin your expansion into what others already know. The being that you see before you is a fully mature warrior class known as the Teesa of the Nemekans. The Nemekans have several clans or classes in their society; this one as I said is a Teesa or military clan. Now I see they have joined with the humans as these men are also soldiers of some type. This is a very bad thing and a great evil now lurks with in the Earth. A lot is still mystery however I have met and fought them many times, and also have befriended this kind before in my life's journeys. Those who seek to continue this journey will find many more soldiers and Nemekans along the way. So those who will journey with Ben and me will need to be made aware of the fact that some of us may not return home. That is a risk each one of you must consider." He explained to the stunned group of men.

At this moment Katasha emerged from the tree line moving quickly followed by Bud who was trying to keep up.

"What is going on and where is my Ben?" She yelled out in a loud voice to the group of men standing before her. She watched the men part and she saw Ben, but now she could see the dead humans and some animal thing as well. And that brought her to a full realization of the extent of the chaos of what had taken place here.

James turned to his wife. "Kat, what are you doing here, Ben is fine, you should not have come up here."

"Your darn right I had to come, I have two missing children and then Ben was in trouble and you think I would just sit around and wait to see what was going on? I am no longer waiting, so tell me exactly what's going on here." She demanded quite emotionally.

"Mom, I am ok and so is Fairsong, we have a lead on where the kids may have been taken, see we have a live prisoner, we had to kill the others as it was them or us, but I bet we can get this one talking soon." Ben said as he came over to his mother in an effort to calm her some.

Katasha finally took a good look at all the dead bodies; she gasp's and walks over to Fairsong grabbing him by the shoulders then demanded more about what is going on and what he knows about it.

"So What or who is this monster thing? And where are my kids, tell me they are ok, tell me where we can find them." She demanded of Fairsong as she fell to her knees and began to sob emotionally spent by all that had taken place as full weight of it finally hit her.

James came and knelt down beside her and put an arm around her while she sobbed and got control of herself once more. He looked up at Fairsong.

"Well tell us what is to be done, how or where we should look to find our children please."

Fairsong looked down on the couple with a sadden face.

"James, Katasha we will look for your little ones, and as the Great Spirit as our guide and the experiences we have from our own lives we shall find them, see there your young Ben has today become a man, he is a spiritual warrior as well as a physical warrior. Be proud for he did well in his first battle of what I suspect will be many before our journey is done. Katasha my little sister, the creature you see is a race known as Nemekans; it is a reptile race that can be much larger than the one you see now. They seek now for power over all the Earth, their leadership has been seduced by the dark forces of the universe, now they are in league with humans once more this is a very bad sign. Your children have stumbled upon this by accident, and they came and took them away to their inner worlds and did hide the door so that no one would find them. Now I have a key and have re-opened the door, they came to silence the new intruders, us, but we were the victor's this time. This gives us a small opening of time to now go and search. We shall find your children who are lost." Fairsong said as he also knelt and put a loving arm on James and Katasha's shoulders then he looked up to those present around them.

"Not all of you can come, but think carefully and look into your souls, if you feel your journey is to continue with us, then you're welcome to come on our journey. I would again suggest only single men or those whose families are grown, for the rest of you have responsibilities to your families first. It would be a shame to have them lose you if it comes to that. Our journey may be short but it also may be long as well." Fairsong looked sternly and very seriously at the gathered group of men.

"We must hurry now, you men take the dead and cover them with dirt for now, Sheriff you must stay behind to protect your town's people if the need arises. And watch our prisoner who should be awaking any moment now. Then the rest should strike camp and all go home. Take your families off these mountains for their safety. What we have done will not go unnoticed nor without reprisal in time. We do have some time, but we shall go and delay any action against this area. The Nemekans do not take kindly to the death of their kind. And the soldiers may want retribution as well for their fallen. So let us go and get ready for our journey then we shall begin." Fairsong stated soberly to everyone.

Katasha finally got herself together once more, and looked over at the live prisoner; this man had something to do with her kidnapped children. Her anger began to rise inside of her. She noticed he moved and that he opened his eyes, she stood and slowly began to walk towards this man, her anger turned to a motherly rage she had never felt before like a lioness who had witnessed her cubs demise she glared at the unsuspecting prey before her.

The soldier was groggy but was starting to regain his senses. He realized soon that he had been tied hand and foot and was not able to move. As he focused his eye's and tried to clear his head he realized he was outside and under a tree, then he saw the danger before him as he saw his fallen comrades even the Neme was dead, and fear began to grip him and he really started to get scared, and then he noticed a very emotional woman towering over him, he wondered who she was.

Katasha seeing that the man was now awake though groggy, her emotions got the better of her.

"James you'd best get a hold of Kat quick before she..." Sheriff Thompson warned but was too late.

The soldier realized his true danger when the woman above him suddenly lashed out at him with tremendous force she slapped him across his face nearly knocking him over sideways, definitely leaving a hand print with the force of it.

"Mom! Wait" Ben said as he hurried to her side.

"You tell me what you did to my kids, WHERE ARE MY CHILDREN YOU...YOU...DEVIL!!! Tell me or I will show you what pain is. You son of darkness and I will teach you what pain is for taking and harming my children!" Katasha stated as she grabbed him by both ears and began to twist them is such a way as it was quite possible she may rip them off his head.

It had been a very long time since the soldier had felt pain like that, but he had been through a lot in the past and this he knew would pass, he was sure of that and the others would stop this insane woman. He just grunted with the pain and remained silent.

"Kat, wait he will be questioned, let us do it." Sheriff Thompson said as he approached her with caution.

"Now I don't know who you are, nor do I really care at this point, however you have really made some mistakes of late, and kidnapping our kids is one of them, possibly your last. My wife you see is a nice enough lady however you have taken her cubs, now you must deal with the mother bear for if you do not answer her, you will then have to deal with me." James stated coldly looking hard into the soldier's eyes.

"Now tell me where my kids are." Katasha demanded again as she placed her knee on his tender parts and began applying her weight to the area, still gripping his ears.

"I cannot say anything, now get off me and let me go, I want a lawyer I request it, and You Sheriff have to comply with that, now get this crazy woman off me now!" The soldier yelled gritting his teeth against the pain. It actually enraged him as well as encouraged him in defiance against this crazy woman as he glared right back at her.

"You better let go of me or I will give you something you old witch!" He said to Katasha.

Katasha got right down into his face and screamed at him. "Where are my children?"

At that moment the soldier shook loose her hold on one of his ears and head butted her in the face breaking her nose, and he was pleased to see his work went well as blood flowed from her wound.

Katasha was surprised at how fast the man had attacked her, she let go and then moved a little ways off holding hands to her face livid in anger and pain. She was sure her nose was broken and maybe some loose teeth as well. As she looked back towards the man she caught the sight of James foot slamming into his face as a response to his attack on her ending his little grin.

Olaf was immediately at Katasha's side.

"Let me have a look at that, we need to stop the bleeding Kat." Olaf said in his doctor voice.

"Ok" she said still glaring at the man.

"Now you ignorant pile of horse dung, we shall have a little chat, you see that was my wife you just hit." James stated as he now grabbed the man by his throat and lifted him off the ground, his adrenaline was pumping and he was really enraged at this fool.

He lifted him up and shoved him against the tree a full 6 inches off the ground and held him there as his face began to turn a shade of blue, then he let him fall to the ground in a heap.

The soldier got his wind back and said." You fools, you are Nothing, Nothing! And your kids are as good as dead by now so go ahead just kill me and forget about ever seeing them again; others will come to avenge me you will see your all fools for messing with us!" The soldier croaked through his squished voice box.

James now picked the man off the ground and threw him across the clearing a good 15 feet and watched him bounce off the rock wall, then walked towards him.

Fairsong met James just before he got to the man. "James wait! Killing this fool is what he wants; this won't get us the answers we need! You need to back down and watch." He stated firmly.

At this Tom and Tarton both grabbed a hold on James arms and held him in place till he calmed down enough to see reason again.

Fairsong now looked at the soldier who was now lying upon his back, he glared down at him and studied him a moment before he spoke.

"Soldier you are in league with the Nemekans, your soul is now at stake, your life may end soon how do you wish to meet your maker, in a spirit of continued violence and evil of the soul or in one of a final deed of good will offering to help your spirit journey that is soon to come. Think well on it." Fairsong said as he looked the soldier in the eyes, looking deep into his soul.

Now the soldier looked at this man standing above him in shock, and wondered how he knew who the Neme's were how could that be possible, as for the rest it was a bunch of hogwash, he had rights here, and he knew it they wouldn't do much more harm to him the law was here, but if he told them anything he knew the next team sent would silence him for sure, if the Neme's didn't get him first.

"Why should I say anything either you or they will kill me for it." As he looked around at the group of men who had gathered around him all with anger filled faces.

"And you how do you know what a Neme is, who are you anyway." The soldier croaked, trying to show his toughness.

"Well think on this, I know of them because I have lived amongst them longer than you have breathed air little soldier, you see there, I am the one who slew the Teesa and most of your team. I am the one who will find the children and destroy any who get in the way. So tell me what we need to know or I shall start the questioning over, and this time I will do it as the Nemekans would do." Fairsong said in a conversational calm tone, with a hint of the promise threat.

"You're so full of it, you know nothing, you're grasping at straws, I won't tell you nothing!" Said the soldier. He gritted his teeth and glared defiantly at the group.

Fairsong just looked at his prey and a thin smile creped across his face.

"Well Ben, You see I warned this little soldier did I not?"

"Yes you have, fair warning. You see soldier boy, I am the brother of those you kidnapped and Fairsong here well you had better start singing to him what he needs to know or who knows what he will do with you." He replied.

"You don't scare me; none of you do, just kill me now and get it over with, or arrest me so the Sheriff can give me my phone call to my lawyer." The soldier arrogantly spat right back at them.

"Well I see that to talk nice is a waste of time. I have no more patients for you." Fairsong stated coldly yet calmly. He then reached into his pouch and took out a crystal like tool smaller than the one Ben had found in the box and different it was almost obsidian black in color.

"So little soldier do you know what this is then?" Fairsong asked the man calmly.

"Maybe I do, maybe I don't looks like a rock to me." the Soldier answered.

"Well maybe your right, maybe you're not, you see it befalls me to educate you in the use of this little device then. Now one last time, will you tell us how to find our lost children or not?" Fairsong requested firmly.

"Never! You can just go jump off a cliff, I am not speaking anymore to you, I demand my lawyer Sheriff!"

"Have it your way then for you have chosen foolishly and I am out of charity for you." Fairsong stated. and with that he twisted the crystal and as it turned it began to glow and the tip became white hot, then he pointed it at the foot of the man who looked at him once more and then he fired the weapon at his feet, a beam of light emerged from the device and starting at the soldiers feet Fairsong slowly and methodically began to inch its way up the soldiers legs.

The soldier screamed in pain he had never before felt it was like every neuron was on fire and about to explode!

"Are we ready to speak now, or shall you foolishly resist, remember this is a Nemekans device that I know you have heard of." Fairsong now passed the knees and was headed towards the belly button of the soldier.

This time the pain increased to the point of him wanting to pass out, and yet he did not. He knew how the weapon worked, it used the nervous system and it was like fire to every receptor in his body, and it was able to avoid putting one into unconsciousness and he knew that this could go on forever, he had seen this done once before. He knew he would break soon, everyone did. So why prolong it right? Your done and you know it he thought, they will never succeed they will never make it past the first check point before being killed. So he made his choice as the beam neared top of his thigh.

"Ok, ok "He screamed with the tears of pain upon his face. " I will talk, just turn it off, turn it off..." He pleaded.

Fairsong turned off the device; he hated the thing and only had it because the Nemekans he had just killed had carried it.

"Catch your breath, then tell us what we need to know, where the children may be, how to locate them and when you're through I shall end your life easily with a blow from this." Fairsong held up his sword so that the soldier could see.

The soldier again was in shock this time he was in awe for he had heard of such ancient weapons, they were legendary and the stories told amongst the men back at the base were amazing, never did he ever expect to see one. They had existed even before the Neme's, made long ago by some ancient race, who had once fought the Neme's into submission a long time ago. If this man had one that would mean he must be old or related to that ancient race, but he can't be old as he looked so young. He nodded and answered.

"You know I know of this weapon, not sure how you came by it, I will share what I know it will only lead to your deaths, so then you promise to kill me with that then, better you than the Neme's later on." The soldier commented. And he nodded to the guy with the sword.

"Very well it is agreed upon then." Fairsong said. "Now tell us what you know."

Everyone gathered around and listened as the soldier told of how to get into the tubes and where they had left the kids they had found in the cave. But that was about all he said, they could figure out the rest or die by the Base teams that would wipe them out.

"Are you sure that is all then?"

"That is all I know of we dropped them off and they were picked up by another team and taken further on." He said.

"Further on to where?" James asked.

"To the main base I suppose that's all I know." the soldier said once more.

"So now kill me as you promised, then you can go meet your own deaths." Sneered the Soldier.

"Fairsong a moment if I may." Sheriff Thompson requested.

"Be right with you Sheriff just one more moment." Fairsong replied.

As he looked down on the man he then motioned everyone to stand back then he lifted his sword and placed the blade at the throat of the soldier. Then raising it into the air he swung down hard and smoothly, unfortunately he missed somehow.

"There now you see I will not kill an unarmed man even if you deserve it, looks like I missed Sheriff, now here is your prisoner get him out of here before I change my mind and turn him into fish food."

"But you promised, you said you would kill me." the soldier stated mad now.

"Well let's see that would seem to be too good for you, if we don't succeed then maybe the Nemekans will find you out here and when they do they will surely kill you, even if it takes them a month or two to do so." Fairsong stated.

"You go get yourselves killed, do whatever." He said and then shut up and would not speak much after that. The thought of the Neme's taking out their anger on him was not a nice one at all.

"Let's finish covering up the rest for now, and get down to camp to sort this out and make a plan of attack. And we need to decide who is going. "James said, as he held Katasha who with Olaf's help had stopped her bleeding face.

"After we get things sorted I shall send a team up to pick up the bodies so we can try to identify them later in town. We will have to keep the Nemekans thing on ice till we figure out what to do with it." Sheriff Thompson stated.

They covered the dead with cut tree limbs and then they began the journey back to camp. The Sheriff taking his prisoner with Bill and the dog's right behind him to make sure the prisoner didn't accidently fall off a cliff. As the Sheriff started down the path he remembered he had turned off his two way radio when they got close to that cave area, so he turned it back on and sent a message to the SAR control center.

"Sheriff to base got a copy?"

"Base go for traffic." Was the response from Al at the base camp.

"Al this is the Sheriff, there was a fire fight up here we are bringing down a prisoner so find us a place to keep him for a while till we get him down to town. Also there are some dead men up here and another item I will have to tell you about in person that will need to be picked up later. We are on the trail heading back to camp now, eta 20 minutes. Copy?"

"Copy Sheriff, will make the arrangement you requested." Al replied.

"That sums it all up for now, will fill you in on the details when we get there." He replied.

"Let's keep moving along, they are expecting us now." The Sheriff said as he continued down the trail to base camp.

James helped Katasha walk back to the camp with the rest of the family members and those SAR members who had come along to help, each lost in their own thoughts as they were thinking about going on the mission or not, Some would but like Fairsong had said they had to stay and take care of their own family first. So they all had an individual choice to make and it would not be an easy one. However it would for some become a life changing one as they joined those on the underground journey of recovery.

CHAPTER 13

Lab Rat

Natasha was in the radio tent when the Sheriff called in his report; she was surprised about the news and ran out to tell her mom who was with Martha in her tent.

"Natasha what is the matter, what's wrong?" Mary asked her daughter.

"I was in the tent with the radio guy, and the Sheriff called in and said they were on the way back here, and that there are dead men by the cave and a prisoner." She blurted out...

Martha looked at the both of them and started to panic, what came out had gone very wrong, now she wondered who had been killed up there in the hills.

"Who is dead? What do you mean dead men Natasha? Did they say? Is anyone we know hurt and what about Tom and Tarton are they ok?" Martha said rapidly.

Mary had a very worried look, she knew Martha was really starting to stress out now, and that was not good in her current state.

"I don't know they did not say Aunt Martha, they gave no names but that they would be here in like 20 minutes and tell us what has happened."

"Now we really need to calm down being stress out and worrying about what maybe nothing won't help anyone now. They did say they had a prisoner, so if any of our family had been hurt I am sure he would have mentioned it, or requested a life flight helicopter right? And they didn't so everyone should be ok." Mary said trying to calm herself down by focusing on the others, this was already a tense situation; she quietly hoped and prayed everyone they knew was ok.

"Are you sure, maybe they just don't want to say anything?" Martha stated getting herself worked up.

"Let's not jump to conclusions, you need to remain calm Martha, they will be here soon and then we will have Olaf look you over again, I am worried about you starting some real labor now with all this added stress, so please try to relax, just take some deep breaths and try to slow down your heart rate. That's what you need to focus on; we don't need you going into full blown labor up here right?" Mary said as calmly as she could. Martha really needed to relax.

Mary looked over at Natasha and then back at Martha as she noticed her twinge in pain and then relax, Mary moved closer and put her hand on Martha's stomach, and felt the muscles contract again. This is not good, and is the wrong time and place for this to be happening on top of everything else.

"What are you thinking." Martha asked, as she began some labored breathing.

"I am thinking Natasha needs to go have that radio man call and tell Olaf to get here faster."

"Really?" Natasha said a little scared.

"Well do as I said, go have the call made and hurry."

Natasha left the tent, Mary took a deep breath and exhaled slowly, that should help some of the stress; this is not the right time or place for a baby birthing. Turning back to Martha she said. "Now you girl will need to relax, start some breathing we need to get you back to a slow rhythm and calm your whole body to a more relaxed state, you just might be starting for real, and we don't really want that now, so let's try to slow down."

In the radio tent Natasha was speaking with Al the radio operator. "We really need you to call and get Olaf here right now, Martha's not doing well and we need him and Tom here ASAP, we may have a baby on the way." Natasha said in an excited voice and a little out of breath.

"Will do, wait a moment and let's see what they say then." Al responded to her.

"Base to Sheriff Thompson, got a copy?" He began the call.

Sheriff Thompson keyed up his vest mic and answered "Go Al, what's up."

"We have a message for Olaf and Tom, they need to hurry back ahead of your group ASAP, sounds like we may be having a baby."

The Sheriff almost swore but he caught himself, that's all he needed after all the other stuff he had to deal with today, now this.

"Al copy will send them off down the trail to you should be able to get there in a few minutes." Sheriff replied.

"Roger out." Al replied then looked up at the teenager Natasha.

"Well they will be here very soon it sounds like so go tell your mother."

"Thanks." Natasha said and hurried back to the tent, feeling a little better.

The Sheriff stopped the procession and looked back at Olaf and Tom, who were near the end of his column, and yelled for them to come up to him. "Olaf, Tom get up here quick."

When they got up to him they asked, "So what's the problem." Olaf asked.

"Just got a call, sounds like Martha maybe having a baby soon; you two best beat it down to camp a.s.a.p. and see what you can do."

Tom just about fell over, he knew Martha was not doing very well and now his adrenalin started kicking in once more, as he stared running down the trail as fast as he could safely manage.

Olaf started after Tom. "Watch your step Tom or I'll have to carry you back if you twist your ankle, just be careful." Olaf yelled from behind Tom, hoping he would be smart enough to do so.

Back in Martha's tent, Natasha told her mom the message was sent and that they should be here pretty quickly. Mary looked worried, she hoped they got here soon she had about run out of things to do for Martha, just a few minutes went by before Tom then Olaf burst into the tent out of breath, and both took a moment to bring their breathing to a more normal rate.

"Martha, you ok, is the baby really coming now?"

"I think I am now that you're back safe, I maybe having some real contractions now, or that's what Mary thinks, Olaf needs to figure that out for us..." Martha said and was cut off as another contraction hit her hard and she had to focus on dealing with it.

"Yep looks like it" Olaf said with mixed emotions. "Mary, could you come here and talk with me a moment." Olaf said as he left the tent.

Mary joined him outside.

"So how is she really doing, and how long have these contractions been going on."

"I am really worried about her, she has been having these labor intensive contractions for about the last hour and now they are getting closer together about 20 minutes between them. I think if we can get a life flight up here she needs to get to the hospital in Beaver as soon as we can for her safety and the babies." She answered.

"If you think so then let's get it done. I know the Sheriff has a helo on standby so I will go call it in." Olaf said as he gave his wife a hug.

She liked his hugs they always seemed to calm her down when she was really starting to stress out, she was happy he was all right and back with her.

"You do that, I am not sure we should be waiting much longer, hope they can get here soon." Mary said, as she turned to go back into the tent, and Olaf headed for the radio tent.

As Olaf entered the tent Al looked up at him and nodded then said, "Let me guess you need the helo ASAP right?"

"You've hit that one square on the head Al how long you think their eta will be? She will need to go to Beaver Hospital. And make a call to them and let them know we have a baby on the way a few weeks early."

"Ok" Al said as he began his calls.

Olaf turned and left the tent for some fresh air and to calm down some, his adrenalin was running on high, and he needed to be calmer for taking care of Martha.

Al came and found him a few minutes later.

"Olaf, chopper is on the way eta 15 minutes and the hospital will be ready for Martha as well."

A wave of relief enveloped Olaf, some good news today that will help. He would bet Martha could wait at least one more hour or two before having the baby, which would be better so they should be safe.

"Great news thanks Al." Olaf said as he turned and headed for Martha's tent to tell them about it, and to do whatever he could to slow down the contractions, but that's like trying to stop a dam that's leaking with a shovel instead of a bull Dozier, almost impossible to prevent Mother Nature's course of action.

* * * * *

As the Sheriff and the rest of the men arrived back at the base camp.

Sheriff Thompson went over to where Bud and some others were holding the prisoner.

"Bud here's what we are going to do with our guest, you and a couple guys take him over to that large tree and tie him up good. Make sure he cannot move, or get out of his restraints. He is a very dangerous dude and is charged with kidnapping and attempted murder, so be careful."

The sheriff looked at the man, then read him his rights and placed him under official arrest then he told him. "You're going to go into my little jail as soon as we get off this mountain, and I plan on keeping you there until we find the kids, you don't deserve your rights as an American, since you so willingly steal them from others children. But we shall find out who you are, and what is going on eventually so you best think on talking to us, and telling us the truth for your sake. Oh if you do escape just remember Ole Bills hounds there, well they haven't had a good fugitive run in a while, so that would give them some short term fun, you see they like catching, treeing, and if you're lucky just eat your sorry excuse of a man for fun. Although, Bill prefers not to feed his boys junk food." Sheriff explained to the soldier the lay of the land.

"Right you are, now you just listen to the Sheriff and do as he says, Now we are gonna tie ya good, but if you give us any fuss there just might be some accidents here and there... along the way." Bud told the prisoner.

The soldier just glared at them, what a bunch of worthless men, he could take anyone of them if he was free and in good repair, they had just be careful, if they give him a good opening he would be gone, and he just might silence a few of these clowns along the way. He would have to wait and act the humble prisoner, but when and if the opportunity presents itself he planned on using it. Until then he would just play along.

The Sheriff looked over the camp and found Matt and his team and waved for them to come over to him.

"Matt, you and your boys take a few ATV's with trailers back up the trail to that cave clearing, you're to retrieve the 3 human bodies and one non-human creature that Fairsong calls a Nemekans. We threw a little dirt over them in their shallow graves to help with any critters bugging them, but I would like you to retrieve them and get them down to the coroner's office before noon tomorrow so you can put them on ice till we figure out what else to do with them. Now the creature I would like him preserved as best we can, I think we need to learn more about what makes that thing tick, and of course what stops the tick as well. And keep it all hush, hush, we don't need any media parade in town, so keep it quiet until I say different, you understand?"

"Yes sir we do, just as you say we don't know nothing. Be on our way as soon as we can." Matt replied.

"Good and be carefully when you're up there, never know if more will show up." Sheriff stated. He then walked over to Martha's tent to see how that problem was.

The medical helicopter landed in the meadow near the lake about 20 minutes after they got the call to fly; as they landed the EMT's on board jumped out and went to find their patient.

Olaf and Tom both heard the helo land. "Well it's about time." Tom stated worriedly, he was getting impatient and wanted to get Martha to a Hospital as soon as it was possible.

"I will go get them you stay here with Martha." Olaf stated as he left the tent to meet with the EMT's.

"Boy it sure is good to see you guys." Olaf said relieved.

"Well good we can help, now where is the patient?" Alvin one of the EMT's asked.

"Follow me she is over here in a tent." Olaf pointed then added. "It may be better to bring your stretcher, I am not sure she should be walking right now."

Alvin looked at Sally the other EMT, "Well go get the stretcher board then and I will meet you in the tent."

Sally turned to go get the stretcher and Olaf and Alvin hurried over to the tent.

"Tom we have a stretcher coming and will have her out of here soon. I assume you will be going with her right?" Olaf said as they entered the tent.

"You must be the father right, so we can take you with us if you want to go, so what's your name?" Alvin asked looking at the mother to be.

"I am Martha, and I think the baby's going to come soon."

About that time Sally and several others of the SAR team where at the tent door with the stretcher to help.

"So we ready to move her now?" Sally asked.

"Yep we are let's get her on the stretcher and in the chopper, the father Tom here is coming along with us but we need to be moving fast, so we can talk on the way." Alvin stated.

They quickly moved Martha from the cot to the stretcher and then strapped her in, four of the SAR team members picked her up and carried her to the waiting helicopter. After putting her on board, the EMT's followed and waited only a moment for Tom to get in.

Tom looked at Olaf. "What about my other kid's?"

"Don't worry about them, they will all be coming down to meet you soon, I think we are about to take anyone not needed here off the mountain, Now get going, and don't worry about us. You're having another baby." Olaf told him as he waved Tom off, and backed away to a safe distance from the helicopter.

Everyone else cleared the area as well, and the helicopter lifted up and swooped down the mountain headed for Beaver Hospital.

The Sheriff had watched Martha and Tom leaving, after they were gone he noticed Olaf coming over to him with a very stern look on his face.

"Sheriff now is the time to get all the kids and women off this mountain now, where they will be safe. Those soldiers may be missed and they may send someone to look for them soon. And I would prefer not to have the families up here if that happens."

"I agree, we will have the SAR teams mobilize and help your families pack up and head for home as soon you're ready to move out." Sheriff Thompson said with a grim look.

"Now the next phase who is going to go on the hunt for those kids, we need to choose volunteers as Fairsong stated, and his warnings are to be taken seriously. Then we need to plan and execute it as soon as possible." Olaf said in a firm resolute voice.

"Your right and we need to gear up as well, let's get moving then, lots to do." Sheriff Thompson stated as he called for all the SAR team members to gather around for a meeting.

Meanwhile Olaf went to gather up the families to let them know it was time to strike camp and get off the mountain.

After getting back into camp Ben saw everything in motion everyone running about getting ready to leave, so he went to find someplace where he could be alone, he had never taken a life before and it was starting to hit him hard.

He walked up the hill to the west of the camp over to the smaller of the twin lakes where there was a clearing under one of the tree's that allowed for a secluded area to think. The adrenalin had worn off now and he found himself reflecting on the fight. He had watched as Fairsong reacted with almost super human speed for a human, so cat like he killed the Nemekans before he knew what hit him, then he had dealt with the two men closest to him while I took the other two men's lives. I wonder who they were. Did they have families somewhere who would miss them? Did he just make someone a widow? Or some orphan's? Was he right in what he did? A lot of questions and some doubt were settling in on him now as well as guilt for the killing he had done. He sat down with his back to the large blue spruce and held his head in his hands that were propped up by his knees. Then he started to shake and the tears started flowing from his now swollen eyes. Why, why did they have to make us kill them, we did nothing to them, why did they have to seek our lives, if they had just left us alone none of this would have had to happen, why did they have to kidnap his family so many things hitting him all at once.

    Fairsong entered the camp and saw that all seemed to be in order, he saw Tom and Martha leave and noticed that Sheriff Thompson was doing what needed to be done, so he then looked for young Ben who had seemed to have disappeared. It was his first experience with battle and that was hard on anyone, let alone a young man of a soft heart. He had done well and reacted as one should during the heat of battle, and yet he felt sad at the same time for he knew like many others before, that once you have been in battle and taken life one can never go back, one cannot ever truly be the same being, and it changes one's soul. So he began a search of the area for Ben, his tent was empty as he visually searched the area he felt drawn to the smaller of the lakes, He walked over to it and there he found Ben under a tree and he realized this young man was indeed becoming a grown man now, for he felt sorrow for the dead, He just may be the one many have been waiting for, and as too many seek glory during and after battle the truest test of a warrior is one who does not delight in the death of others, no matter the need or reason. He walked over to Ben and knelt down by him.

    "Ben you will be alright, this shall pass. It is normal for one to feel such as this after the first battle or even after many. One will never forget however you must realize death is but another beginning of yet another journey for the souls of those whose lives are taken. Do not spend time dwelling on them, do not think about it, as a hunter must after he kills the bear, or big cat in defense thus we must take the lives of those who would take ours without any regret. Do you understand this Ben? You must move on, or it will sink your spirit into a great shadow of endless depression, and depression is a tool of the dark forces in the universe. It prevents the healing methods of the Light to enter and heal ones soul after events of terrible happenings. One must be able to open your heart and clear your mind in order to allow the forces of light in to help heal your soul.

Remember Ben, those we slew today would not have any such feeling of you or me if they had triumphed over us, and we were now separated from our mortal bodies, and became spirits. They would have rejoiced and never given us a thought beyond that of a bug they had squished under their boots." Fairsong said in a calm and soothing tone.

Ben was listening to Fairsong, he knew he was correct, and it did help him some. He would have to put it behind him so that he could continue and search for his family. He realized this and that this would be the start of something and in the future there may very well be more battles before this was over.

"Thanks, I will be ok, really. It was just getting to me that is all. Kinda all caught up with me all at one time. I will have to shake it off so that we can go find Sariah and Levi." Ben said trying to sound more cheerful than he was.

"Ben you feel sorrow for them, and that is alright, that means your human and a good man. And yes we will need to be going to prepare the long journey to find your sister and brother. I feel you're going to be strong enough to carry the burden needed during this long journey. The Father of all creation knows your heart, and will help you as you need it." Fairsong said as he stood once again and put a hand on Bens shoulder and gave him a little squeeze.

"Well we must be moving on now. Come when you're ready for I shall be waiting in camp." He said as he took one more look down on Ben.

Ben looked up into Fairsong's eyes and knew his resolve was firm and was glad he was here to help them.

"I will be there in a few minutes."

"Come when you're ready then we shall prepare." He stated and turned and headed back to camp. Yes indeed young Ben had become a man, he was strong and he may be the one, we shall see, for now only time will tell the tale.

* * * * *

Sariah felt her head ache again and was very dizzy as she tried to move and sit up. Once again she was in a room this one empty except for the toilet in the corner which seemed built into the wall, it was then she realized she was on some bed or rather a ledge also built into the wall. She noticed there was a slit at the bottom of the door large enough for a food tray.

This was getting old really fast she thought. If anyone else goes to knock her out again someone's going to lose some teeth the next time. This was really starting to tick her off to no end. This was no way to treat anyone.

Now she is in another room with concrete floor and walls, poor lighting and this was a smaller room only about 8 feet by 8 feet is all, more like a cell.

Again she wondered where Levi was, and what was going on. After about what she felt could have been 15 minutes or longer she was able to stand finally and leaning on the wall for balance went over and with what strength she had left she went over to the door and pounded on it with her fist, as the door was quite solid her pounding seemed more muffled for it made almost no sound at all.

So she tried yelling.

"Hey! Anyone there, Hey! Let me out of here!" She screamed as loud as she could and found that that was the wrong thing to do as she felt the light headache she had explode into a huge migraine that made her feel weak and very light headed again. And she had to go sit down on the bed before she fell down.

She had no idea of how much time had passed but it seemed like forever in her little prison room.

When the door suddenly slid open, to reveal several men standing in one piece jumpsuits that where blue with a white stripe on the sides of the arms. They looked at her without much emotion and entered the room.

"So are you going to tell me where I am, and what you think you're going to do with me? Who are you? And why am I here? Sariah asked as forcefully as she could muster with her head ache and dizziness.

"Actually we do not and will not answer these or any questions. You see life as you knew it is now over. Now you will remain with us the remainder of your pitiful little life. No matter how long or short that may be. It could be up to you." The man on her left stated rather factually with no hint or sense of feelings or emotions at all in his voice.

"So you kidnapped me then and my brother. Why? Why are we here and what do you mean the rest of my life?" Sariah asked them glaring as mean as she could muster.

"You see you're in a place where you will be used to benefit modern and future science, just think of yourself as a lab rat, that is about what you have now become. Your usefulness' and cooperation will depend on how long we will have use for you, in other words simply. You're like a candle when you're used up and no longer needed then you're done. So get used to the idea." The man on her right stated very coldly.

"Yes we have much experience with your type, now remember and know this for a fact, your family, and friends, everyone in your old life to them your missing and presumed dead. No one has ever left this place, ever." The third older man behind these two had stated arrogantly with a thin smile she notice he spoke in some kind of accent possibly German maybe, she wasn't sure but she did know she was in real danger now.

"So what's next then, what's going to happen now?" Sariah asked more subdued. She felt lost and rejected and like crying for a very long time. This can't be happening to me, to us, this is not right. She wished it was all just a bad dream that she could awake from, but she knew better, she knew this was reality, her new reality and she needed to figure out how to survive, and if given the chance to help Levi, if she could find him.

"Now that's better, we are here to determine what to do with you." The man with the German accent stated as he directed the other men to take up positions on either side of her.

"First we need to take some samples of your blood and DNA to see how you can best improve our needs in enhancing the human species. We need a base line of your current state to work off of." The man with the German accent said.

At this time they drew some blood and took some other samples, a skin biopsy, and some hair and then they backed away.

"We shall return in time and you will possibly be given some choices on what direction we shall take from there. You see we are equal opportunity scientists we give you equal opportunity on what we shall do to you next and about your future here, if we so choose." The man on the left stated and then they all left the room and the door again slid shut behind them, and once again the room was quiet and still.

She choose not to fight the inevitable and allowed them their samples, she was too tired and worn down to resist much anyways. Now she felt like a lab rat. She felt real fear once more in so short a time, time how much time had gone by since they were taken, a day, a week, a month? She had no way of knowing. She could not let fear grip her and take over; she had to remain calm in order to figure out how to get away from these creeps, and to find Levi. her heart sank as she felt that this is how her life and his were to possibly end as some victims to a crazy evil scientist who had no human feelings left what so ever, that was obvious they were cold and without caring. This was not fair, this is not what life was to be about, she had her dreams she wanted to fulfill at this point realizing she was in fact a prisoner to a group of evil men, she started coming apart and started sobbing and shaking almost uncontrollably, she curled up on the bed and eventually cried herself into a deep sleep, full of nightmares and demons, would she ever find peace again in this life.

CHAPTER 14

Moving the Dead

Matt led Albarsta, Julio, Joe, up the trail towards the cave. It was not too bad of a trip, most of the trail was wide enough for the 4-wheelers and since most of them were born to ride the mountain trails it was not much of a challenge and he felt would get there and back again in good time. Each of them had grown up in the mountains hunting and fishing and understood the outdoors well. All had been on body recoveries before and were used to the problems that had to be dealt with. The good thing was these were fresh bodies so they would not present too much of a problem.

Matt thought as he came into the clearing where the cave was and he saw the bodies covered by aspen branches. He drove over to the farthest one so as to give the rest of the guy's room to maneuver better, with their ATV's and trailers they did take up most of the area.

Matt turned off his ATV and looked over at the others. "Ok Albarsta you come with me, Julio and Joe you take care of the others. Let's not take too much time as I would like to get off this mountain before these stiffs start stinking too much." He said.

"You got that right Matt, sooner we get these bodies out of here the better." Albarsta replied.

"Well let's get it done." Joe said.

They loaded up Joe and Julio's trailers first and then Albarsta's and then finally last one was Matt's who got the strange creature. They put a tarp over each of them and bound them snug over the bodies and the trailers so there would be no losing a body on the way off the mountain.

"Well that wasn't too bad this time, Sure would have been better if they would have just shot these clowns instead of having to slice and dice them up like that, I think we got all the pieces right?" Matt said sourly.

"It's not good to speak ill of the dead even your enemies Matt, let us have some respect, we should have all their body parts, now it is time to leave this place, it feels uneasy here, bad spirits." Joe said uneasy.

Joe was never one to joke around much about death, he was Native American, and he could get all mystical on them sometimes when dealing with the dead or living for that matter.

"Take it easy there, I was just saying, now let's go, I agree it does not feel right here, could be that lizard thing, it's just not natural. And that lizard thing stinks." Matt replied.

"Yes it does, I bet it must weigh 400lbs or so when all together, it would be a nightmare to meet this guy in an alley, I must give that Fairsong dude and Ben some credit for taking out this thing." Albarsta commented.

"They called it a Nemekans, I have heard of such beings in the tales told by the ancient elders when I was a child back home. In their legends they speak of warriors fighting such things, other tribes also have such legends. In all my life I never would have thought to have seen one, as they were just tales, myths stories. Today I know better." Joe said as he looked at the body parts of the creature that were now in Matt's trailer. Something in the back of his mind was bothering him, some old story his uncle had told him. Yes the Sioux warriors had fought with these things in recent years out in the Dakotas or something. His uncle was Sioux who had married his Aunt who is Cherokee, and their legends and myths had mixed in his mind some as he tried to remember them. He wondered if now that the stories of his uncle were as true as the creature now dead before him.

He had pulled out his cell phone and took a few pictures of this creature so he could show his uncle. He then put his camera back in his vest and climbed upon his ATV. He was gaining new respect for the one they called Fairsong; he truly was a warrior of great worth to dispatch such a large creature as this and with a sword in the dark. Interesting he must find a moment to speak with him, for they say he was but an aged old man just days before and now some magic had changed him back to his prime once again, such magic could only come from the creator. Yes he must speak with him if time permits.

"Let's roll out of here and get off this mountain before the dead begin stinking to bad." Matt called out as he waved at Joe and Julio and Albarsta, he then turned and headed off down the trail towards base camp.

The rest of the recovery team followed, each lost in their own thoughts of the day's events and the questions and mysteries they each now had. For most their paradigms had been changed this day.

Sheriff Thompson was pleased with the time it took to strike the majority of the camp. The Adair family had worked quickly as well and had all their pack animals organized and ready for the trip down to their vehicles.

The SAR group had most of their gear packed as well; they had left the tent being used for communications and command center as well as the cook tent up. As there would be some returning to the area in preparations for the search of the tunnels and would be needed.

Sheriff Thompson went over to Olaf and James who were standing by their families.

"James, is everyone accounted for then?"

"Yes they are, some are not happy to be going and would like to stay, however we will get them all down to the trucks and then off to home, then we can come back to begin the search once more." James stated as he looked over the gathered families again making a mental note to make sure everyone was there and no stragglers this time.

"Have you started making your list of who is going with your team yet?" Olaf asked the Sheriff.

"No, not yet, I want to get everyone down off the mountain then we can settle down and see what needs to happen from here on out." He answered.

"Fair enough" Olaf said, and he noticed Fairsong and Ben over by the command tent. They had chosen to stay behind and wait until the rest of the searchers returned for the next phase of the search.

"Well let's get moving, day lights a burning and we should be back to Beaver before dark." James commented.

" James you get your pack train headed down and we will follow you." Sheriff stated. As he nodded and motioned for the caravan of people and animals and machines to start down the trail.

Just before the last of the SAR team had headed out over the first hill above Twin Lakes the Sheriff who was at the rear heard Matt's team coming into the camp area behind him. So he called them on the radio.

"Matt, got a copy, this is the Sheriff?"

"Copy you Sheriff what's up?"

He noted that the majority of the camp was now gone, so must be ahead of them on the trail.

"Matt, we have everyone headed down in front of us right now, I need your team to take the old jeep trail so you don't spook the animals, and it will be fast for you with your cargo."

"Ok Sheriff sounds good, we will get them down to the funeral home and let him put them on ice, then the creature thing, what do you want done with it?" Matt asked.

"Take it to the station and pack it in the walk in freezer for now, and don't tell anyone about it, this has to be hushed for now. No need for any media frenzy. You boys be careful." "Were moving out, see you in town." Matt answered as he waved for his team to follow him; he headed for the jeep trail to the south west of the lakes. And they began their return as quickly as the trail would allow them.

Sheriff Thompson watched them head off, then he turned back to his own trail to follow the rest of the caravan down to the vehicles then to Beaver. He needed some time to think rationally about what to do with the Nemekans thing. He could contact the Feds but he needed to get a better idea on who the soldiers were linked to first. If they were actual military that could cause some complications he would prefer to avoid at this time. If not then that could opened up a whole other can of worms. He felt that they were most likely some type of secret ops group. So he must play his cards carefully in order to keep his town safe and those already involved. He would do some ID checks; run their prints and the new DNA tester to see what turns up. That should give him some direction to work with.

But first things first get the civilians off the mountain back to town and make sure no one lingers behind. Once everyone is taken care of they will need to choose volunteers for the next phase of the search. Who knows what they may run into, but it looks to be a dangerous venture at the least. And he would not be able to join them, as he had to find out who, or what these soldiers where first. And then he had to deal with the Nemekans thing as well. What a mess this could turn into he thought as he refocused on driving down the trail. He needed some more time to sort things out. In the distance he could hear Matt's team pass ahead of them on the jeep trail they took, that was good. They would be in town long before they were.

What was going on here anyways, this was crazy if he had not seen it for himself he would question the whole story. So how do you explain this to anyone? It was turning into some sort of bad sci-fi movie. He knew it could not be kept quiet for long as people talk and the media will always show up. Great he thought one more thing to worry about. He had a lot to figure out in the next 12 hours.

After watching everyone that was going down the mountain leave, Ben turned to find Fairsong who was sitting alone down by the lakes edge looking to the east in profound thought. He walked down to see what was on his mind and what they needed to do next.

Ben approached Fairsong as quietly as he could so as not to disturb him, he seemed to be either thinking or relaxing. But as he got about 8 feet from him he spoke.

"Are you feeling better now?" He asked in a quiet voice.

"Yes I feel somewhat better now."

"That is well, you know that this journey will take some time, and will take you into places and to worlds that you have never even considered before, nor imagined. You must be able to accept what you see, and prepare your mind for new and incredible things, and yet do not let these new things distract you in your mission to find your lost loved ones, for distractions could cost one dearly. Do you understand?" He said still looking across the lake and over the valley below towards the eastern horizon.

"Yes I think I do, however there is a lot you have not told any of us yet, now that we are alone could you fill me in on how you know and what you know and this time explain in some detail. It will be very helpful to understand fully what we are up against if we are to have any hope of finding Sariah and Levi. Will you tell me now?" Ben asked respectfully and yet firm in his request to know more, for the one thing he had learned over his short life is that information can make all the difference in the world.

Fairsong sat and pondered Bens' request a moment or two, and then he spoke again still looking over the lake as if searching for something in the distance.

"Ben I cannot tell you all I know, however I can share with you that which will be needed for this journey. Your right that knowledge is good; knowing what you may be walking into is also a wise thing. For to jump off a cliff before looking to see if there is a safe place to land is not wise at all. So let us look before we jump shall we." He replied. Then he turned to Ben.

"Are you ready to listen then, and accept what I shall share with you of these things and accept them as the truth they are?"

"Yes I am ready to listen and to accept them as the new reality of our journey." Ben responded. He then sat down beside Fairsong.

"Very well then, since we have some time I shall tell you what you need to know for now." Then Fairsong began telling young Ben many things that were indeed fascinating and almost unbelievable as he spent the next few hours sharing and also answering some of Ben's questions as best he could concerning his old world from whence he came.

Fairsong looked at Ben and realized he was full at the moment from all the new information he had shared. The rest could wait until the need arises to share it.

"Let us see how your brother and sister are doing, if their health is in a good way, shall we?" He said in a whimsical tone.

"How do you expect to do that trick, we don't even know where they are?" He said realizing as he said it, that Fairsong had to have a way to do so or he would not have even mentioned it.

"Remember the tool you have, it does many things, remember it is a guide and yet it does so much more than you realize. Now bring out the Lev Antas Shuesa and hold it in your hands once again and I shall teach you this thing." He said as he looked at Ben's puzzled look.

Ben took out the Lev Antas Shuesa and held it with both his hands, he knew better now than to ask dumb questions, and so he waited for instructions, this was going to be interesting for sure.

"You need to activate it as you did before, you may begin." He directed him.

"All right then" Ben stated as he focused once again on the tool and began to see or actually feel the soft glow and the brightness as it grew but not nearly as bright as when Fairsong had used the device, but it was a good light he thought.

"Now you must focus on your sister Sariah and use your love from within your heart for her and focus on her own life's beat, seek to know if she is yet still upon this physical plain of existence."

Ben started thinking of Sariah's face, and with all the desires of his heart and love he felt towards her he sought with his spirit to know if she was yet alive. As he did this he felt the presence of the spirit, his hair on his arms stood on end and goose bumps came all over his body, as he looked into the device it did glow stronger now, and became very white producing a glow that radiated like a little white sun in his hands. Then in the middle of the little light he saw his sister, it was a clear picture of her and he could tell she was in some kind of concrete room, she was sleeping but she was alive.

"I see her! She is there and she is alive. She seems ok but looks like she is in a prison room, she is a prisoner, will this tell us where she is then?" He asked anxiously.

"Very well, now you know she is well for the moment. Next search for your brother in the same manor and I will answer your question after." Fairsong directed. Ben's ability to use the Lev Antas Shuesa was improving quickly, he is indeed learning and he saw the growing power of the internal spark and it is indeed quite possible that Ben could very well be the right one, the time was correct he and chosen well from the clan Adair. He was pleased to have lived long enough to see this day and be a part of this new journey. "Thank you Creator for blessing my humble life to live and to be found worthy of this day to be a guide for young Ben and may I do well in your eyes on this journey." Fairsong gave thanks in his minds thoughts.

Ben turned his own thoughts to search for Levi, and the glow did not diminish, soon he found his brother also in a prison like cell, but he felt that it was not in the same area as Sariah and that they were separated by some distance. However he was yet alive and seemed ok for the moment.

"I do see Levi, he is well and also a prisoner. But it feels like he is in another place separate from Sariah." "Very well, now you know of their good health now let us put the Lev Antas Shuesa away for now." Fairsong quietly said.

"But when do we go find them, we need to get going now, I don't want to wait." Ben said with a tone of urgency in his voice and impatience.

"You must be patient; they will be kept safe for they have a purpose as well in this journey, as you do. The Creator will keep them safe, but I feel there are others who must also come and join us on this journey in order for it to be successful. Soon they will arrive here at this place and then we shall begin the journey. Those who the Creator has prepared and will bless us with their skills as we search for your loved ones we must wait for. And live or die our life's purpose will be fulfilled in this journey for each will have a part to play in it."

"We wait then. I have been thinking about the cave, and the dead men, will they not be missed? Won't they send another group to investigate the missing men? I am sure they will be missed by now." Ben stated a little worry showing in his voice.

"You are correct, they will indeed send another team eventually to investigate the overdue team. This is something I should have remembered to do at the time we were at the entrance. We must return there now with haste for I must hide the entrance and what we have done." He commented realizing in all the commotion at the time how foolish he had been not to realize what should have been done at the time. He was slipping some in his old age, however if they hurried back to the entrance of the cave there should still be time to do what was needed.

Fairsong stood up and began walking towards the trail at a fast pace.

Ben also stood up and followed, but he took a moment to stop in at the command tent to let them know where they were going.

"Hey we need to go check on the cave a moment, Fairsong and I should be back before dark." He said to the radio controller and he noticed a few of the SAR team who had also remained in camp were there as well.

"Thanks for the check in, just be sure your back before dark, we don't want to have to come searching for you two." Lewis one of the team members spoke.

"No problem gotta go thanks." He said and hurried to catch up to Fairsong.

As Ben caught up to him Fairsong turned and said.

"We must hurry it was foolish of me not to have done this earlier, must be age, I shall work not to be so incompetent in the future."

"Well let's go then, do you know... "Ben stopped himself before asking the obvious dumb question, again.

"Let's get there and I figure you know what to do."

"Yes I do, but talking will just slow us down." Fairsong said. As his fast walk turned into a jog then soon was running up the trail moving like a deer.

Ben was having a hard time keeping up with him, but was able to keep him in sight barely. By the time he came to the cave door opening Ben was worn out and breathing hard. But he noticed that Fairsong who had beaten him there by a few minutes did not seem tired at all, not even breathing hard. Just amazing he thought, whatever miracle had happened to him to make him young again was some neat thing that was for sure.

"We must go in now, so catch your breath and I will go ahead of you, come when your breathing has calmed." He said with a twinkle in his eyes as he turned and entered the cave.

Fairsong went directly to the rear of the cave and into the tunnel area, as he looked he turned on his illumination device to look for any signs of the fight that had taken place earlier. As he looked at the floor he could see the foot prints in the soft layer of dirt of the men and the Nemekans these he had to erase. Then he took out the crystal wand device and set it for the correct setting then waved it over the dirt and watched as the vibrations it produced settled the dirt back down smooth with no signs of them within 40 yards of the tunnel entrance to the cave. That should do. Then he walked back into the cave and turned around to seal the wall leading to the tunnel.

Ben had now joined him at the back of the cave about the time Fairsong emerged from the tunnel.

"So what now, how do we hide this door then?"

Fairsong just smiled and turned around and looked at Ben.

"Well you must watch and learn, as they had hidden the outer door entrance so now shall we hide this one."

Ben just stood there and watched as the entrance disappeared and looked as if there had never been an opening at the rear of the cave, some type of hologram he supposed only this one you could feel as if it were solid. These devices were just amazing technology he thought to himself.

"There now if they send others they will only find that the tunnel will continue and I can hope they will feel lost as to where this entrance once existed. Now let us go back to camp and rest. For tomorrow your training will resume and you have much to learn in so short a time, and much to prepare for while we await the others who are to come and join us for the journey." Fairsong stated matter of factly and he passed Ben and left the cave room.

Ben followed thinking about what tomorrow would bring. He knew that Fairsong was done for now and would tell him in the morning. So he did not ask him questions about what may happen the next day for training. And they walked back to camp.

* * * * *

Ashecoosla pushed the com system button to contact the human leader of security in their area, Major Jones once again. He did not like the idea of working with these weaklings, so small of frame and inept in most every way. But they had to work with them.

"Ashecoosla to Major Jones we require your update." He said into his video monitor.

Major Jones here, what do you need Ashecoosla this time?" He was not as formal as needed this time, he was irritated and these Neme's with their sense of superiority and a great lack of respect for him and his men. This was about the team he sent to sector 39 he was sure because they were a few minutes over due.

"Major, we need a report on the team you sent to sector 39, they are overdue, I expect you to find out why they have yet to return and report. It would seem your team may not have been capable of carrying out this simple mission as we thought they could. Learn of their overdue status and report to me immediately is that understood Major Jones." Ashecoosla stated forcibly one had to put fear into these humans and treat them as younglings as well, since they show a great lack of respect for those superior to them, you must remind them of their place.

"Agree they are overdue, I have dispatched a team to investigate and shall let you know the reasons upon their return, that is all for now. Out." Major Jones stated firmly as he turned off the video com before the Neme could respond. Being rude on purpose.

Major Jones then pushed the com device for the men's barracks.

"Attention I need Lt. Fred in my office immediately!" Then he waited for Lt. Fred to arrive.

What now was the thought going through his head as he entered Major Jones's office.

"Reporting as ordered Sir, What do you need?"

"Well it would seem that your team led by Sargent Smith has gotten themselves lost, and needs to be found as they are overdue and the Neme's are crying about it. So send another team to go hold their hands and get them back here ASAP is that understood!" Major Jones barked.

"Yes sir, understood, consider it done." Lt. Fred responded. He was going to chew some butt for causing us all this headache with the Neme's, He turned and left the office.

Major Jones watched Lt. Fred leave, there would be discipline in his command and he would have them do extra details upon their return for this headache he would see personally to that.

Lt. Fred entered the duty room, "Sargent Atherby!" He barked. As all heads came fully alert and turned to him to see what all the fuss was about.

"Yes, Lt. What's up?"

"You assemble a four man team and go look for Sargent Smith who seems to have forgotten to report in on time and now the Neme's are all fired up about it, You go find him and then get him back here so I can kick his butt for a while, they went to sector 39 to check on an intruder alert there." Lt. Fred said.

"Will do" Sargent Atherby stated as he turned to pick out the three others of his team. They soon left after they had geared up for the tubes and sector 39.

CHAPTER 15

Uncle Travis

Matt and his team were able to get off the mountain before the rest of the group. They took the bodies to the local mortician's office and put them in cold storage. Then they took the creature over to the SAR building and put the thing in the walk in freezer and locked the door for safe keeping. He was glad that the coroner did not ask too many questions, and accepted the fact that Sheriff Thompson would fill him in later. And he was fine with that.

So what to do now he thought. He gathered Joe, Julio, and Albarsta together to speak with them.

"Well that's about if for tonight guys, Thanks for the good work today. Let's meet here tomorrow at 10 am and we will see what's to happen next. There is a need to go find where the kids are inside that mountain, if you're interested in going as Fairsong stated it will be dangerous, and could be a long trip. So think it over and let us know tomorrow."

"Ok, boss" Said Joe. "Be seeing you in the morning then. The rest of you get some sleep you look terrible." Joe said to them as he headed out the door to his truck. Once in his truck he dialed a phone number he had not used since Christmas, his uncle Travis Walking Thunder, who lived in North Dakota. He felt strongly he needed his advice on his next move.

"Well Matt, as much as I would like to go I can tell you right now my wife won't let me there is too much to do, gotta pay the bills so no time for me to help further on this one. So I wish everyone who goes good luck, but I need to take care of my own family right now. I hope you will all understand." Albarsta stated.

"No problem we understand and as Fairsong said, don't worry about it. Now go home be with your family and remember to keep quiet about the dead we found today, at least until the Sheriff gives the ok."

"No problem there, talk to you later then." Albarsta said as he headed out the door to his own car and off to home.

"So how about you Julio?"

Julio looked down at his feet a few moments thinking and he shifted uneasily.

"I will think on this tonight and will let you know tomorrow."

"That's fair enough, see you then. Go get some rest." Matt said as he slapped Julio on the back as they both headed out the door, Matt shut the door and made sure it was secure.

Each went to their homes that evening thinking on what will take place in the morning and if they wanted to be a part of it.

It was almost dark when the Sheriff and the others finally came into Beaver, they had left the Adair clan at their home, the SAR team members each went to their homes and the Sheriff went to the SAR building and checked in the deep freeze on the creature there, the

Nemekans seemed be in good order then. It was really amazing how quickly ones entire perspective on the universe can change.

Now what was he to do, he knew he would not be able to continue into the mountains with the next group of searchers to help explore the cave systems, he needed to stay here and direct things, as well as look for some answers, he needed to question his prisoner, and discover the identities of the dead men. His prisoner was in a room all by himself. He would start the questioning tomorrow. He could run their prints and see if anything showed up but then that could all wait till morning he was exhausted.

He left the office and headed home, he would have an early visit with Bill the town mortician in the morning and he needed a good acceptable story for the bodies there. Then he would meet the rest of the men around 10am as planned. And see who was going to go on the search mission.

As he pulled up into his driveway, he wondered what would happen to the searchers, would they be successful in finding the kids, or would they just become lost. Fairsong seemed confident he could find them, but who really knew for sure. He walked into the house and looked at his two little children who were already in their beds asleep. What would become of their world now with all this new information about Nemekans and who knew what all else. Paradigms surely were changing.

What would the knowledge of these inner world beings do to their future? His family had to be his priority, and the people of Beaver who relied on him. But would that change? Or has it already changed by the happenings of the last few days and where would it all end. Only time would tell. He closed their door and went in to check on his wife Karolynn.

Karolynn was just finishing up some baking she had been doing when she heard Nolan come in; she knew he would go check in on their kids as was his habit when he was worried about something. She turned and looked into his worn out face and eyes as he entered the kitchen.

"Is everything all right? Did you find the missing children?"

"No we have not found them yet, however there have been additional events that may change how we think about who we are, events may soon be out of my hands now, as far as the search goes. Others will need to continue the search in a place I won't be able to go. But we do have a better idea of where to start the new search." Nolan told his wife in a soft and worn out tired voice. He sat on a bar stool along the counter and put his head in hands. He felt drained.

Seeing the worry and tiredness in her husband and being somewhat confused by what he had said, she went around the counter and gave him a hug for a minute, and then she realized just how tense his whole body felt.

"Nolan tell me what happened, and why you said you can't keep searching for those children, you're not making much sense." She inquired worried about his behavior.

"You know of that old guy named Fairsong, he keeps to himself most of the time and is a friend to the Adair's?" Nolan asked as he was thinking about how to explain this so it sounded rational.

"Yes, I remember seeing him once or twice over the years, and have only heard rumors about him, but what does this have to do with the missing children, was he involved?" She asked not sure where he was going with this.

"Well old Fairsong now looks like he is in his prime of life, I mean younger than us in age. Also he and Ben had some kind of fight on the mountain today with some men whom we figure have had something to do with the kidnapping of the children that is what it now looks like happened. When we got to where they were there were three dead men, one live prisoner, and another body that Fairsong called a Nemekans, it is not human." He said wondering if she thought him going nuts on that last part.

"What do you mean by not human? Do you know who these men were they fought with? And what is a Nemekans, you're not making sense."

"Honey, all's I can say for now is that I have three dead men wearing some type of uniform, one prisoner at the jail who we will question and hope he can give us some answers. And then there is the Nemekans thing I had the boys put on ice till we figure out what to do with it. As for what it is, that's the question of the day for sure, it's about 7 feet tall, and looks more like a walking lizard, but we do know it was involved with the kidnapping of the children and it was a bad thing. Sounds like sci-fi however it is there, we can't explain it but it is there." He said shaking his head a little, thinking on how his paradigm had changed that day.

She stepped back from her husband a few steps at looked at him in disbelief.

"So you're telling me that there is some type of alien creature that was in a fight that happened today, and you have its body, this seems a bit too much. I find that hard to swallow, are you sure you're ok." She asked concerned. She knew Noland never was very good at making up stories, so there had to be some other explanation to this lizard man part of the story.

"Look dear I know it's hard to take in, and if I had not seen it myself I would not have believed it. Honestly, look here." He took out his cell phone and went through his pictures stopping at the one of the creature.

"Look here and see for yourself, you tell me what you think it is." He stated as he handed her the phone.

"Um all right, ok, uhm let's see, so this isn't some prank then right? So well then, Nope I can't say what it is, that is amazing and you have this thing in the freezer, looks like a good place for it, so you think this thing had something to do with the missing children then." She said handing the phone back to him, and then it hit her. This thing was huge and strong looking and very dangerous looking as well. She felt a tremor of fear run up her back.

"Yes we think this thing and the soldiers did have something to do with the kidnapping of the Adair children. Fairsong knew what this thing was, and sounded like he had fought them in his past or some type of interaction with them. He will be guiding the search into the cave system in a few days with others that have been invited to go with them. Tomorrow we will see who will help. However Fairsong said it will be very dangerous and I will need to stay here and look into the legal matters of what we now face. Also to find out who these men are. So that is what I will work on tomorrow." Noland looked a little more relieved, he usually never brought work home with him let alone share it with his wife. However this was an unusual case, and he would need her support and understanding on this one for sure.

"So if there are more of these things out there do you think they will come here? You did kill one of them, and the men with it, won't they now come looking for them? And if they do could it bring them here to Beaver? Are we going to be in danger now as well?"

"You know I am not sure, however I am staying here to work on the problems this case has developed, and we will deal with whatever happens, but I really doubt the county will see any trouble over this, it would seem that who or what ever these things are, they prefer to stay hidden from us. And have for who knows how many years. So you should not worry about that." Nolan stood up and put his hands on her shoulders, then looked down into her emerald green eyes that seem like two deep pools full of worry now; he bent down and kissed her on her forehead, and gave her a hug.

"Now don't you worry any dear? I need to go take a nice hot shower and some sleep as I think tomorrow shall be a very busy day. Just don't worry and please don't tell anyone about this yet. I need to figure out how to deal with this, people could think we are just losing our minds if the story got out." He said feeling more tired than he had in a long while.

"I won't be telling anyone about this, it seems too unbelievable. That I will leave up to you. So go wash off the mountain and get some sleep then you do look tired." She replied and gave him a big hug, then let him go and watched him head for their bedroom.

This realization once the public knows about it could change a lot of things, if what she was thinking was true, then they had some type of lizard people living under the mountains in their back yard, and that was disconcerting. It would be an amazing discovery and a lot of people would come searching the area to find out the truth for themselves, it would be like area 51, full of a lot of nuts. However it could be a boost to Beaver's economy as well. Great, just great then, they would think us as world class nuts as well. Then there is the dangers of these creatures, what would they do if a lot of people began to explore the area and found entrances to their world. What then? She went back to finish her baking and got lost in all of her what if thoughts of the repercussions of what Noland has just told her. She knew he was holding back on the whole story. He usually didn't bring work home with him, so she knew he was worried if he was telling her anything about this, and that worried her.

After his shower he felt a lot better physically he was worried though about what the future could bring. Just before he crawled into his bed, he did something he had not done in a long time. He knelt down on his knee's beside his bed, and bowed his head and said a prayer to his Heavenly Father for forgiveness of his faults, then asked him for help on this matter to guide him to make the right choices, to help those who would go on the rescue mission, to protect them and to help find the right people to go. Then for protection for his family, his town and his county. Then he laid in bed until his thoughts turned into his dreams, and his dreams were filled with strange places and even stranger things, then some fell deep into the darkness becoming nightmares.

* * * * *

It was late before Joe was able to get his Uncle Travis on the phone; he had been out talking with the old Elders who lived close to his home.

"Hello Uncle, this is Joe in Utah. I was wondering if you had a moment to talk, I really could use some good advice." Joe asked respectfully.

"Joe you know I have time for you, tell me what is troubling you tonight then. I have been thinking on you today I feel your about to make some important changes in your life that will affect your future soon." Travis responded. He knew that if his nephew were calling him this late at night and was asking him for his thoughts that there was a worry of some magnitude in his life.

"I am going to send you a few pictures I took from my cell phone today, and I would like you to look at them, wait just a moment." He said, and then he found the pictures he wanted and sent them to his uncles email address.

"You should have them in your email in box in a few minutes."

"All right then, let me go turn on the computer and see what you sent. It takes a minute to warm up. So what are you sending me then Joe, you in some kind of trouble?"

"No, no trouble, but I may actually be heading into some, that's why I need to talk with you." He stated.

"What do you mean then?" Travis asked curiously. As he waited for a response he saw his internet link slowly come up and connect, now let's see what he sent as he found his email, ok there we go, yep there are the emails from Joe now let's open up the attached photos and see what we have then.

"Well Uncle, we have been on a search for some missing children here in my county, we have run into some problems, the search will continue however it will take those who carry on the search to some unexpected places. We are going to have to go underground into some caves and tunnel systems in our area. The pictures I sent will help explain some, I remember you once told me a story when I was younger of some warriors of the Sioux who have fought from time to time a tribe of reptilian like humans, and that they lived in the Earth. I need to know more about those stories. Some of the men in the party had a fight and one of them killed the creature in the photo I sent." He stated wondering if the pictures had made it to his uncle.

As he listened to his nephew speak he was watching the pictures as they uploaded one at a time. As each one uploaded and opened one at a time the result was at first a shock of surprise, then he knew what it was, it was the old legends come to life, it was the times he remembered, the stories the Elders had spoken of so long ago. Even that night as he sat with the Elders, they had spoken of the coming times where they would once again have to do battle with such creatures again. He was surprised to see a photo of one from his nephew, and that it was indeed dead. For they have spoken of old about how hard they are to kill as they were great warriors all. These lizard beings. It left him quiet for a moment, and he forgot he was on the phone, lost in his thoughts.

"Uncle? Are you still there? Hello?" Joe asked since the phone had gone quiet on his uncles side, he did hear a slight gasp once, and then silence.

"Joe, I know of what you have sent. Are you prepared to know the truth of them? And are you prepared to fight such creatures?" Travis asked him.

"Yes, they have taken the children of a family in our county; the Great Spirit has told me to search for them, and to go where ever the path will lead me. I know my destiny now lies along this path, I have called to ask you about your thoughts on this."

"Very well then, only this night I was with the old ones, we spoke of these ancient stories, and they have spoken of their dreams and the future times, they have spoken truth, they have known that the time was soon at hand and that once again their young men would need to become young warriors once more to fight such creatures. You have been spoken to by the Great Spirit and to follow your path he has laid out this night. We here have spoken also of this, and so this is your journey to go on my nephew. I shall tell you what I know of these creatures. But know this, they are a mighty race, warriors all and they will not give up their lives easily. If your path leads you into their worlds you will need to rely on the Great Spirit to guide and protect you. Do you understand this Joe?"

"Yes Uncle I do understand" He replied.

Then for the next two hours his Uncle, Travis related all the known stories about these creatures and their weaker points and their strengths in battle and more. Finally Travis had ended.

"I am grateful uncle for your help." Joe humbly replied when his uncle had finished speaking.

"I am proud you have chosen to take this path, for to put your life behind the lives of children and to risk it in order to save theirs is a great honor to you, your family and your nation. You were named Joe Deer Runner after your father who was a brave warrior who gave his life in the war in far lands of Afghanistan, you know this. You carry his blood and you honor his memory as you seek to serve others. He did give his life as they went to the aid of his fellow warriors. You remember the story."

"Yes uncle I remember, and as my father honored us all so shall I try to do the same. If it will come to battle so be it. This search and finding of these children is our goal. If called upon to fight I hope to do so well. Thank you for your help, remember I shall be gone for some time, could be days, or weeks or longer we are not sure. Upon my return I shall contact you if not then someone else will tell you how I left this life if so needed." He said soberly, he remembered his father who was a great warrior and a good man, he did miss him and could only hope he had as much courage as his father did, for one did not know until put to the test of true battle.

"Joe, go with God then, and may the Creator of all bless you on your journey and keep you well in battle, remember life is but a moment in the long eternal aspect of our existence. Your path, your trail you take only one step at a time will be watched over by your father, and all your ancestors as well, they will help you as needed if you call upon their spirits to help guide your steps. You are a good nephew, and will be a good warrior. We are proud you are with our family. We shall have ceremony for your journey here, and ask for blessings to your success." Travis said with a tone of honor and pride in his voice, he knew this was to change many things in the time to come.

"I shall accept all your blessings uncle, and I shall ask the spirits to guide me in our journey and for help, I bid you farewell then Uncle, until we meet again." He replied, grateful he had called his uncle.

"Joe you may return home someday to share your journey with us around our winter fires, to be joined with the stories of the great warriors of old. Be well, good journey." Travis said in closing and he hung up the phone.

Travis knew that this was a good path for his nephew, he had chosen well. Now he had to let the Elders know that these creatures had again returned as they had spoken of, but that could wait till morning.

Joe had a peaceful but strong feeling in his heart as he hung up the phone from speaking with his uncle. He knew the path before him was as it should be. He knew this was where the Great Spirit wished him to be at this time. He only hoped and prayed in his heart that he was man enough to walk it with honor as his family and his ancestors would wish for him to do. Tomorrow was indeed a new day, and a new journey. He would need to pack well for it.

CHAPTER 16

Adair's Homestead

It was morning at the Adair's home and it had been a long evening and getting all the stock and supplies put where they belonged and then finding sleeping places for all the family members that were there, it had been a late night. Now it was just before 9:00 am and they were having breakfast for those who were awake.

Katasha came into the room and announced to them the events other news of last night.

"Well Martha did have her baby last night and it is indeed a pretty little girl. All were doing well considering the circumstances, sounds like they were going to keep her for a few days of observation for good measure before letting them come home."

"Well that's great news." Tarton said. Then he added. "At least some good has come from these last days of disaster. Aunt I am planning on going along for the search for Sariah and Levi as I feel it is partly my responsibility. I have not told my dad or mom yet. They are still sleeping. But I feel I need to go." Tarton stated rather matter of factly.

"Tarton, you're a young man, and can make your own choices now. I am grateful you wish to go. You and Ben will need each other from the way is sounds as you search for my children." Katasha replied sadly, she was missing her children terribly, but was trying her best to be strong for the others. She did cry herself to sleep most every night since they went missing. Now that she knew what had happened she was really stressed and worried about them, but at least they had a good direction to go on now towards finding them.

Natasha came into the room and sat down for some breakfast, she looked sad.

"What's the matter Natasha?" Katasha asked her.

"I asked dad and mom if I could go on the rescue mission and they both told me No! I really want to go help find them. Why won't they let me go?" Natasha blurted frusteratedly.

"So you woke them up and asked them did you, well you should have known better." Tarton said.

"Nat, you are too young to go, and you will be needed here. When your Aunt Martha comes home you will be needed to help us with your new baby cousin, it is a little girl." Kat tried to reassure her niece.

"But I still want to go. I think it's great she had a little girl, but I want to help find them." She stated still frustrated.

"Look Nat, you need to be here to help out here, I am older and will be going to help Ben and the others and it looks like it will be a dangerous trip. You'll be needed here and it will be safer." He said trying to appease his sister.

"Ok, ok but I don't like it one bit." She said unhappily.

Olaf then came into the room. "So I overheard that last part Tarton, you know I won't stand in your way. However let your mother know, she will be worried while you're gone and so shall we all. But then you know that." He stated as he looked at his two older children.

"Thanks Dad, I was planning on telling you both after you woke up. I heard the Sheriff talking they were planning to have a meeting around 10am today for those who showed an interest in going. Could you drive me into town then?" He asked.

"I will but you must know that James will be going as well. I will stay to watch over the families and Tom with his new baby he won't be going either. So you will represent our end of the family." Olaf stated.

"Then maybe I should just wait for Uncle James, and we can all go together to the meeting." He suggested.

"Well I would like to see what is going on as well. So I will go with you both."

Not long afterword, James entered the kitchen and saw the others eating quietly.

"Well good morning; you all seem quiet today, what's going on." James said as he sat down at the table.

"Well it seems like Tarton will be joining you on the search, Natasha really wants to go but we need her here, along with a long list of reasons why she can't go. I will remain to look after the rest of the family in your absence. So I hear there is a meeting in town in a little bit, so I suggest you eat some food then let's go see what the game plan is from here on out." Olaf commented.

"I see a lot of thinking has been going on, Tarton glad to have you." James mentioned as he started eating some breakfast quickly seeing that they would need to be leaving soon.

"Thanks, I feel the need to help and there is something else I just can't put a finger on it, but I feel the need to go despite the dangers that may occur."

"Then lets finish eating and we can talk more on the way into town. James I have some old friends I asked last night about helping in our search, they were in Salt Lake City last night working a business convention, they have agreed to come to the meeting this morning." Olaf said.

"Friends? Thanks, do you think they can offer some good help then?" James asked.

"They are from the old days and are very well skilled at finding people, we can use their help and am glad they will."

"Good look forward to meeting them then."

So they finished their breakfast then they loaded up and drove into Beaver for the meeting with the Sheriff, leaving Natasha on the porch still sulking about not going.

CHAPTER 17

Council of Spirit Owl

Far to the North East in the lands of the Dakota's we find Travis Walking Thunder walking to the council house of the Elders, Those who just last night he sat amongst speaking of the ancient times, about those who had long ago walked these lands, they had spoken of those times and of the current days. Of the many prophesies of the Great Waicomah, the Healer who had once walked amongst their peoples in the lands of the ancestor's.

Now he would seek their wisdom and council on this new matter at hand. As he approached the door a young man emerged from it.

"Travis how may I assist you this day?" The young man asked. Remembering him from last night's council.

"I seek to learn the wisdom of the Elders on an urgent matter that has come to me last night. I wish to address the council; I need to see Spirit Owl, for he will know what is to be done." He stated calmly.

"I see, come with me then for the council has gathered and are awaiting your visit." The young man stated. Then motioned him to follow.

They walked into the building and down the hall to the council chambers. All though the building was modern, the chambers themselves had the look and feel of the traditional council house of the ancient ones.

As they entered the room he noticed the elders were seated around the circle talking to one another. When he entered they all turned as one to look at him.

"As you know this is Travis, he has an issue to bring before you and seeks your wisdom."

"Come and be seated, I have asked the brethren to come together this morning to await your arrival, and your questions, Travis." He stated and motioned for him to be seated near him.

"Spirit Owl, if I may ask how did you come to know I would be here to ask you questions that would require the wisdom of the council this morning as it was only during the night I discovered the questions?" Travis asked politely.

"Ah yes that is a good question, however not the one I feel you came to ask, however I shall tell you this, I had a dream last night and the spirit of Waicomah came to me and said I should prepare for your visit as I have done, So tell us Travis what is it that troubles you this day? He inquired of him. As a slow and knowing smile slowly showed on his face.

A few quiet moments passed as Travis pondered the best way to explain his nephew's story to the council, but he found no simple way to address it, so he just said it blunt and strait forward.

"Members of the council, I ask you this day for my nephew Joe Running Deer who lives in Beaver Utah. He called me last night upon my return home from our meeting. He asked me a very unusual question and sent me some photos to look at. I have made copies of them to share with you if I may."

"That will be fine, speak with us as we look at your pictures." Spirit Owl commented as he extended his hand to receive the photos. He took the photos then slowly one at a time looked them over. To Travis' surprise he showed no immediate reaction except that of a hint of sadness.

"My Nephew contacted me last night about a search and rescue mission he has been involved in, there were several missing children and in the process of the search some members of the group where attacked by four men and this creature, one of their fellow searchers called it a Nemekans.

I believe the legends have a name for it as well; I seek your wisdom and guidance on how to proceed from here. They will be leaving to travel into its underworld home in search of the missing children soon, and my nephew wished your guidance so he could pass it along to the rest of the search team if you have any to share." He waited in silence for their responses.

As each of the Elders took the photos and looked upon them then past them to then next member, they sat and thought, no one said anything for quite some time, the silence became deafening. But Travis knew better than to speak until they choose to address the issue first.

Eventually Spirit Owl turned to one of the council members and spoke.

"Raven, you have seen this creature in your youth have you not?" He questioned.

"Yes long ago we did have several battles with these snake men demons; they are as serpents from ancient times and they have now returned to our world once more, today is indeed a sad day." He spoke thoughtfully with a sad tone in his voice.

"Continue then" Spirit Owl requested.

"We had a time when we had to fight these creatures, for they came in the night and would take the children and the old ones into their deep caves which lead to their underworld of darkness. Once they left our world we could no longer follow as it was too long a journey and our torches would go out long before we could find them. We had to fight them in our world it was the only way. They were great warriors and many of my brothers were taken to the world of the spirits during this time of battle. However we did realize they are of flesh and can be killed." He said then paused for a moment.

"If your nephew is to battle these serpents then he will need one who knows it's weakness and the legends about them. But tell him never to take these creatures lightly for when he does he shall leave this world and go join the world of the spirits. I will request a guide to go with him then. I have spoken." He finished and then waved for the young man at the door to come to him.

The young man did so, and leaned down to hear what Raven had to say.

"Billy, you will need to go find my grandson's and tell them they are needed here immediately."

"Yes I will do so." Billy answered and then he left the room in haste to make some phone calls.

In the mean time they sat and each member of the council gave his input and asked questions on the matter at hand. Travis answered from what Joe had told him. He was able to get a further understanding of the legends concerning the serpent beings. From the history of their Fathers came many stories, and this he wondered is why some Native American's had an affinity towards serpents some with a strong worship attitude towards them were the Natives who were related to the Aztec's and the regions around those lands, interesting that the Aztec's originally came from around the regions of what was now Utah prior to their moving to current day Mexico and taking over those lands in olden times. Now he understood more of all the histories he had learned of over the years from many lands, many tribes. Like a puzzle coming together the pieces of understanding where becoming more clear.

It was not 15 minutes before two young men entered the council room; they were both well-built strong solid young men in their early 20's by their looks Travis suspected.

"Grandfather you requested our presence, what is it you need." One of the young men asked reverently, honoring his Grandfather.

Raven held up his hand for silence, and there was a short pause as he turned to Travis and pointed at the young men.

"These are my grandson's, this is Tim Shadow Walker and this is James Little Beaver." Ravens said as he introduced them to Travis. Then he turned his focus on his grandson's.

"The stories I have shared with you over these many years there were some from my youth before my hair was grey and white with age. These you must remember now. In my youth there were battles and interactions with what we called serpent demons. Do you remember these stories I shared over so many years past?" He asked.

There was a long pause and silence the young men both looked at each other and wondered what was going on, They then look back upon their aged Grandfather, both nodded in the affirmative as they did remember the stories, each one thought they were but stories.

"Yes Grandfather we remember the words you shared of these stories. What is it you desire of us, and why do you speak of these stories now? Tim responded to his Grandfather.

"Ah yes Tim, I am glad you remember. Come here both of you and look here". Raven said and they both moved over to him. He then handed them the pictures.

The young men actually showed some shocked expressions on their faces. Then they turned to their Grandfather.

"With all respect Grandfather, I must ask if these are real photos or are they a hoax of some type, a test for your grandson's then?" James asked.

Their Grandfather never lost his seriousness; he looked from them to Travis and motioned his hand at him.

"Inquire of Travis your questions, for with him your answers are." Raven said as he folded his arms and awaited Travis's response.

They looked at Travis, and he responded.

"Yes they are real, and taken only yesterday by my nephew in the mountains of Utah." He said and then he explained who and how the information was gathered and why he was here once more to these grandsons of Raven.

"Grandfather, this is a marvelous story and the photos seem to bear them out. But how does this affect us, why have you asked us here then." Tim inquired.

"The Great spirit has a great future for you if you but desire to follow the path now set before you. His nephew is going on a mission to rescue those taken by these serpent beings, and their human helpers.

You have been chosen to assist in this path, to help your fellow human beings in this time of need. You will if you choose go and assist and fight these demon serpents when the time comes. Do you accept this honor?" He asked his grandson's already knowing their response.

After looking at each other they nodded to each knowing this was what they were to do.

"Grandfather Raven and Honorable Elders of this council. We do accept this honor in assisting Travis's nephew and those who will be on this mission to rescue these taken children. If it is to make war on these demons of the serpent race then let it be so, for they did start this with the taking of the children. We shall stand and fight, we shall gain victory or we shall join our ancestors in the spirit lands." James said as he bowed his head slightly to all present.

"Grandfather Raven and Honorable Elders of this council house, I do accept as James has said. We shall succeed or we shall join our honored ancestor's in the spirit lands. So shall it be done." Tim said.

"Very well then, Travis you must instruct these two on how to locate your nephew and do it in all haste as it is far to Utah from here." Spirit Owl requested of him.

"It will be done, I am grateful of your help." Travis said then he looked at the young warriors.

"Tell me again your names."

The taller of them said, "I am James Little Beaver and this is Tim Shadow Walker, we are brothers and we shall help your nephew, what is his name then."

"He is called Joe Running Deer."

"We shall be honored to help Joe in this task." James said.

"Now Grandfather, as speed of time is of importance will we be flying then to this place in Utah?" James asked.

"Yes you will fly; the council has agreed that you may be flown to your destination in one of our smaller planes. Arrangements will be made within the hour so go now and get your things together and remember pack for a long journey and take the tools and weapons for war you shall need at this time. Live well, live free, and help others in need my Grandson's may our Great Father above bless you both in this thing. For I have spoken."

"May you go and return in a good way, take the blessings of the Great Waicomah with you both, remember young warriors let the spirits of your ancestor's guide your journey, live well our son's. "Spirit Owl said in finality letting all know the meeting was now over.

They all nodded and then hurried out of the building and into their unknown future.

After they had left the old and wise Spirit Owl spoke to the remaining members of the council.

"So it begins as long ago we have passed the legends of the Serpent men and their evil ways, It has been said that in those days before Waicomah return's once again to our lands, that these evil ways and beings would also return to trodden upon the souls of men, causing much evil and darkness amongst the peoples of the Earth. Let us remember these young warrior's in our prayers and ask our ancestors to look after them that is all now, I have spoken." Spirit Owl said somberly. Upon ending his words there was a moment of silence and all the assembled council members slowly nodded and agreed with Spirit Owl's statement. Each arose and went to prepare for what was to eventually come, for the old legends and prophecy was indeed now before them, it was time and much had to be done.

CHAPTER 18

Searchers Assemble

Sheriff Thompson waited in his office for everyone to arrive. He had told everyone to meet by 10 am to discuss what had happened and the other matters as to what is needed next. To see if anyone was going to go and help the others in the search underground.

He was not sure what he was going to tell them, but there were normal protocols on keeping an ongoing investigation quiet at least until there was enough information to share with the public that would make sense to them. And this was a very unique situation, and the time for dealing with the media would come for sure.

He looked out his office window and watched as several trucks and cars began arriving one by one and taking up parking spots by the SAR building. The people began to gather and so does ones fate change in such a short amount of time he thought, it was not just a week ago that his own paradigm was different, normal or what he thought was normal reality at that time, now it was very different, it had been changed for him by the recent events. Enough of dwelling on this it was time to gather the crew together and see what the mornings choices by others would be and who if anyone was to go help Fairsong and Ben continue the search. After this was done he was going to have some words with the man now sitting in his jail, who showed a great lack of respect or willingness to talk about anything. That was going to be a hard nut to crack he felt. So he just might need to bring in a big nut cracker to do it.

He opened the door to the conference room and walked in.

He looked around at those gathered there, some he knew some he did not. Olaf, James, Tarton were there for the Adair family, and then several of the SAR team also had come. He saw Joe, Julio, and then the strangers. He walked to the front of the room and looked them over, all seemed to be in a very somber mood, that was good.

"Well I take it that this is to be our search group then, we had best introduce each other then I will get to the point of where we are at." Sheriff Thompson said.

"Well I am James Adair, the missing children are mine, they are Sariah 17 and Levi 14, Why I am going is obvious."

"I am Olaf Barrett, James is family thus I am here to support him and learn more of what is to happen, I will not be going as there are family matters that need my tending to while James is gone. I thank anyone who chooses to go and assist James in this search, so thank you."

"I'm Tarton, son of Olaf; I will go and help find my cousins, for it is what I feel I must do."

"Well Gentlemen, I would be next, I am David Ananiah, a friend of Gideon here, and was called to attend this meeting last night; it looks like I am going to help in the search for these lost ones."

"I would be Gideon Yahsef, Olaf is a long old friend of mine we have a long history together and I owe him much, for this reason and others I have chosen to go look for these missing children its my honor to do so. I am glad that Olaf invited me to do this thing for his family." Gideon stated as he looked James and Olaf in the eyes with a very stern resolved look.

"Well looks like I am next, I am Julio Ramierez I feel I must go being a member of the SAR team and I am seeking the children's return as well as to the answers to the mystery of their abduction. This is my mission in life now, I have never quit once a search has begun and I do not see fit to start now. So I must go with you."

"I am Joe Running Deer, I will go help find these kids, and Sheriff I have contacted my uncle and told him of these creatures the Nemekans for once long ago as a child he told me stories of such things in the legends of our people. I asked him for advice and in response he says that the councils has sent two young warriors to join us in this search, they will or are prepared to do what is needed to help us succeed, they should be here this afternoon, they are flying towards Beaver as we speak, we are honored to join you James, for this is the Creator's path for us, and we shall now journey down it with you."

"I am grateful to meet you all and for your desires to help my family. It would seem to be prudent then to await the friends of Joe before we leave for the mountain base camp then. In the meantime the Sheriff will fill us in on what is expected of us and what he can do from here in support of our search team, I remember to caution you all that this is going to be a dangerous mission based upon what has happened so far, so just be very aware is all I ask, thank you."

Sheriff Thompson again looked over those gathered before him.

"James thank you, we would not all be here if we were not ready to sacrifice for rescuing your children. Now what we need to find out a little about the backgrounds of each of you and what is useful to the team going. Skills etc. I will remain here to work on this end, I have to interview our guest to see if he will speak of what is going on and if we he will tell us where the kids are. I also need to find the identity of the dead soldiers as well. And try to keep on a lid on this. So each of you tell us some about your selves and as we await the two who are in route lets double check all the gear needed to make sure you have everything you think you might need, so gather the gear you have and meet me in the staging garage and you can talk there." Sheriff Thompson finished then motioned for them to follow him out to the staging garage.

CHAPTER 19

Warriors come to Beaver

Tim and James had plenty of time to think of their mission the Elders of the Council had sent them on during their flight to Utah. It was a curious thing that they were chosen to go out of the many others who had more experience in matters of like situations.

"Why do you think the Elders and Grandfather picked us to come on this journey?" James asked his older brother Tim.

"We should not question the why, but we must remember and learn from this journey, whatever happens we must always do honor to ourselves and the nation. The Great Spirit wishes us to grow and to learn by helping in this thing. So that is what we will do." He answered James with a knowing smile.

They were now almost to the Beaver Utah and they would be landing in a few minutes the pilot told them, so they each just looked out their windows and were lost in the rugged beauty of the landscape of the mountains and forests that lay before them.

After landing they gave Joe a call.

"Hey Joe this is Tim we are here at the airport so come and get us as soon as you can."

"Good I shall be over in a few minutes to get you, thanks for coming." Joe said and then he hung up.

Joe looked at the Sheriff and said, "That was our two volunteers from North Dakota, I need to go get them now and we will be back in a few." Joe said and turned to go to his truck.

"That is good news Joe, hurry back we have a lot to go over before we all head up to the base camp." Sheriff Thompson replied.

"Be back as soon as I can."

As Joe drove onto the air field where the plane had parked he noticed the two young men with their gear waiting for him standing near the plane. He drove up to them parked then got out and helped them load their gear into the back of the truck then they all climbed into the cab.

"Well you must be Joe, could you fill us in with some more details about what is going on here, what we know so far is a bit sketchy."

"Sure, but the Sheriff will give us all an up to date heads up when we get back there in a few minutes if it can wait."

"Then we can wait, by the way I am Tim and this is James, how long will it take us to get to your staging area then?"

"Like I said a few minutes from here, the base camp in the mountains it's an hour or so from here though. We will be leaving as soon as we can after the meeting."

Joe drove them back around to the staging garage where the other vehicles were already loaded for the return trip up the mountain. He parked and they all got out. Tim and James followed Joe into the inner building where everyone was waiting in the conference room. As they entered everyone turned to look at the new volunteers all a little curious about them.

Sheriff Thompson approached the men. "Well we are sure glad to have your help, I am Sheriff Thompson and we will have everyone quickly introduce themselves then we will get down to business. So tell everyone who you are and take a seat."

"I am Tim Shadow Walker and this is James Little Beaver we come from North Dakota we have been asked to help you at the request of our Elders and shall do what we can to find your lost ones. We are prepared to do what is required to make this happen." Tim said flatly with a strong calmness in his voice.

James nodded slightly acknowledging what Tim had said. Then they both took a seat.

"Well good to have you both. And thanks for coming to help find my children. I am James Adair their father."

Everyone then took a few moments to quickly introduce themselves to them, and then the Sheriff got down to business.

"Then now that we know each other, here is what we have been dealing with." He said. Then he laid out the current history of the events up to this time in heavy details as to what had occurred on the mountain, doing his best not to leave out any pertinent details. This took about 45 minutes. The Sheriff looked over those gathered before him.

"Look, everyone taking into account all that has happened so far, there is serious reason to worry and much to think on in a short time. Most of you are single with no family, however some of you do have family and you must consider that before you leave on this journey. We know it will be dangerous and some of you may not return. I know it is not what anyone would like to think about however that is the reality of this mission. I hope everyone has taken the time to settle your personal affairs as best you can, you shall be gone a good while I think so everyone should have a Will and a letter to your next of kin filled out and in my office before we leave today. Tell your family what your about to do and we shall seal them up and keep them safe in the case you do not return, I hope that none of them will need to be given to your next of kin."

This brought a somber reality to some of the younger members of the group. They did as requested then they went out to the garage and went over their gear and check lists again making sure they had what they would need.

Then they all loaded up in their vehicles and headed out in a caravan line heading once more up the mountain.

CHAPTER 20

Missing team and questions

Sargent Atherby and his team had arrived at sector 39 and were unable to locate any entrance. They had searched further than the spot where the tunnel entrance was supposed to have been however finding no evidence of it he had turned his team around and headed back to the base to report his findings or lack of it.

As they arrived back at command center he went to find Lieutenant Fred. The others stowed their gear then returned to the waiting room for some food and rest. He found Lt. Fred in the officer's mess having a meal; he walked up to his table.

"Sergeant Atherby reporting sir." He said.

"Well where did you find our lost team and what is their excuse this time for not reporting in as ordered." He demanded.

"Sir, we went to sector 39 as ordered, however we were unable to locate any entrance or opening or even a sign of any breach of security in that area. Where the old opening was supposed to be based on our map we could find nothing, either our maps are incorrect or it never existed. We saw no evidence of anyone having been in the tunnel system either. So if the other team went there then they have vanished without a trace, no foot prints in the dust, just nothing but clean undisturbed floor and the walls all looked solid. This is very strange sir."

As Lt. Fred listened he let the report settle in his mind for a moment. This was unusual we have not lost a team since the last quarrel with the Neme's some years ago. Maybe the Neme's were behind this; maybe they had taken the missing team for whatever their reasoning may be. One thing for sure all was not right, something unknown had happened to his men. He would pass on the report and see what the higher ups suggested. In the meantime he would restrict his men to local patrols until the cause of the team's disappearance became known.

"Sargent thanks for you report, return to your post until I contact you. Your efforts will be noted and I would agree this is most unusual."

"Yes sir." Sargent Atherby replied and he turned and left the room wondering in his own mind what could have happened to the missing team.

Lt. Fred finished his meal, then left to pass on the Sergeants report to the Major. He would let him sort out this problem, someone must have made a big mistake here and he could speculate all he wanted to however the brass seemed to know more about these issues than they did. He pushed the call button on Major Jones door preparing his mental report as he did so.

"Yes come in." Major Jones said.

He entered the Majors office and after he closed the door he went over and stood in front of the his desk. Looking down on him he gave his report as told him by the Sargent adding his own impute on the situation at the end.

"That's the report from the men, Major I must wonder if the Neme's did something to Sargent Smith and his team, with no sign of them not even a trace sir, this has to be some trick of theirs, you know we cannot trust those things, and they will do as they please when they want to. And well they are just not natural they are too strange. Only they could take our team and leave no sign of it happening I feel there has been foul play here sir."

"Well Lieutenant it's not up to you to think about what may have happened, however I would agree that something bad has taken place, Sgt. Smith and his team are missing. You're dismissed for now, and I shall deal with the Neme's and see what they know about it." He stated and waited for Lt. Fred to exit his office.

"Thank you sir, whatever happened if it was the Neme's we are ready to remind them how to respect humans again sir. Just give us the word." He stated then turned and left the office.

Major Jones sat for a moment in thought this was indeed a situation. He never did really trust the truce with these things, the Neme's were always getting away with walking the thin line that did exist and crossing it from time to time. What he knew for a fact was one of his teams was missing; the other went and returned safely however the team Sargent Smith took did have one Neme with them, that was the difference. No sign of foul play, but that did not mean much. However even though one Neme was capable of taking out his men if it wished, but the fight would have left evidence of its happening. Why or who would do such a thing he wondered there would be no rational reason for the disappearance of one of his teams, it just did not make sense.

This could have all been a ruse by the Neme's to capture his men then torture them for information about us, our defenses, our weakness's that could be it. They had lied about some kind of intruder alert in the first place, and then used it to abduct his team for their own purposes.

He had to keep that in mind, as they were a cunning and arrogant and deceitful race of creatures. Like a snake that would first distract you before it strikes, before it moves in for the final bite and the kill. Well they won't get away with it this time not on his watch.

He turned to the phone and dialed up the main command location near Dulce, New Mexico. He needed to speak to General Sills on this matter as he had dealt with these things for years. He would know how to proceed, and if needed payback was always in the back of his and everyone's mind. One of these days the Neme's will just push them too far and then a world of hurt will come down on them.

Finally after what seemed like forever the phone on the other end was answered.

"General Sills office how may I help you?" Staff Sargent Lilly Symrai politely said.

"Hello this is Major Jones I need to speak to the General immediately." He firmly requested.

"Major the General is in conference at the moment, can I take a message then and I shall pass it on to him when his meeting is over and he will get back with you as his time permits." She replied.

"No I am not able to leave a message, this is for him only. This is urgent go and interrupt his meeting if you must." He stated in a very firm and urgent tone, trying to impress upon her the importance of his call.

"As I said he is in a meeting, if you do not wish to leave a message then you will have to call back in 30 minutes." She said firmly, she had her protocol to follow and she did not like Soldiers who demanded things, everything was an emergency to them, even when it was not she had found out over the years, whatever this Major needed could wait.

"I don't have time for this, put me through immediately or we may just have a war with the Neme's, Is that understood, is that clear enough for you? Tell him green thunder." He was getting irritated with this secretary, again.

"I see, let me see if the General has a moment then to take your call, wait a moment." She told him and put him on hold, then pushed the button to the Generals phone in the conference room.

General Sills noticed the button on his phone light up that meant he had an urgent call. He picked up the receiver and said.

"What is the matter Lilly?" He said.

"Sir I have Major Jones on the other line, he claims a need to urgently speak with you I told him you were in a meeting and asked not to be disturbed, but he is insistent on speaking with you now. He told me to tell you, 'green thunder'. Do you wish for me to ask him to call back later?"

"No, go ahead and put him through." He responded.

"Just a moment, I must take this call before we can continue our briefing." He told those members of the Dulce Base council of representatives who were present in the conference room.

"Major Jones I will connect you with the General now." She told him and made the connections.

"General Sills? This is Major Jones."

"Speaking, Major what is so important you feel the need to interrupt my conference today?" He said in an emotionless but firm voice.

"General, it would seem that the Neme's have taken one of my teams sir, they have gone missing and were in the care of a Tessa Neme at the time." He said hoping the General would take the time to listen to the full report.

"I see continue Major with your report." He told him. The thought of such an event meant a lot; it had been some time since an incident had taken place such as this. However if the report turned out to be accurate then there would be some challenges needing to be dealt with and in a quick and very decisive manner as the Neme's could not think they could over step their boundaries once more without a strong retaliation for doing so.

The General listened as the Major reported the story mentioned to him by his teams from the beginning to the current time. He also listed his assumptions and his thoughts on the matter based on the information he had. As the General listened he realized this was a very serious accusation to be looked into. As he looked around the table at those sitting there he wondered what he would tell them of this new problem. As the representatives present were a mixed group of Nemekans and human science teams. This would have to be dealt with, but gently at first to discover who was to blame before punishment.

"Very well Major thank you for your report I shall take it from here then is that understood." General Sills responded as best he could since he was in mixed company.

"Yes sir, understood" He said and hung up the phone. It was obvious that the General was not able to speak freely at the time. He would have to wait till later for his orders.

"Good day then." Gen. Sills stated as he emotionlessly hung up the phone and turned his attention back to the group sitting around the table before him his eyes stopping on the lead science leader present who was a Nemekans.

"Sorry for the interruption, however I must say I have troubling news and you may be of help in uncovering the solution to the problem. We have had a team of four soldiers go missing; they were seen last in the company of a Nemekans Tessa warrior who was assisting them on a routine patrol. Now all are gone without any physical signs of any kind. Just disappeared." He said calmly, as he looked at the Neme.

"What do you have to say on this matter Garessaee Garsar?" The General said as he continued to stare into the snake like eyes of the Nemekans leader.

"It is indeed an unfortunate event that a group of your men have gone missing. It is most troubling news that a Nemekans Tessa clan warrior as well has then disappeared. I must say your tone of voice is accusatory however I shall forgive your paranoia as you're but only Human after all. I cannot respond at this time however as this is the first mention of it. If there be human treachery here there shall be conflict again between our warriors so we must learn of the truth of the matter before it goes that far. As our warriors both lust for battle where none here exists. Such is the way of the Warrior clans of our species. However General we of the educated must insist to focus a calm to our warriors and join together to find the reasoning behind why and where the missing have gone." Garessaee Garsar 3rd Head of Science of Level 7 stated as reasonable and politely as he could to the General.

This was indeed an interesting happening, He wondered if the Tessa were in fact troubling the weaker human counterparts once again. It would not be the 1st time for it to happen. The timing was unfortunate though. He would look into it. And if nothing was found he must then assume it could be an elaborate hoax on the human's side to abduct one of their Tessa warriors as well, for such things were expected from time to time. These humans would desire such, and use this as an excuse to take and turn a Tessa into one of their experiments to determine his weak points or other such things as humans do. Such a violent and immature race he thought.

"General, we shall both look into this disappearance from our individual sides and see where the truth of the matter is to be found. I suggest we terminate our current meeting and look into this immediately so we can see to this issue. The Tessa will not be pleased if they have a missing warrior, for they may feel the treachery is on the Humans side. They will seek satisfaction if this is so, you understand." Garessaee said as he stood.

"I agree, we both shall look into this matter at once, There is no treachery on our part I am sure, however if we find it be the Tessa Clan, then in like manner our warriors will demand their safe return, or their own satisfaction." He said with a thin smile on his face, he could not allow the Garsar Neme to think them weak.

He remembered the war back in the mid 1970's that took many lives of both races, all because a group of engineers while building additional tunnels happened upon a living space previously unknown to them while doing their work. At that time the Tessa attacked and killed most of the humans only a few survived, and then the war ensued until a balance was again retained and a new truce was agreed to once again.

If this were to escalate into another conflict many could die from it. The Neme's had their new weapons, but so did they, for his teams had developed some pretty good arms in which to defend themselves against the future wars that may occur while dealing with these backwards thinking Neme's.

Now he would have to activate the Anti-Neme teams and keep them on alert till this matter was in order.

All in the room arose and left each to their own investigations.

* * * * *

As Gareesaee walked down the corridor leading to the elevators that would take him back down to the deeper lower levels where humans were not allowed to go he pondered what the Human General Sills had told him. If in fact there was a missing team of humans, and a Nemekans was with them then he also was missing, that would be a problem, for the Tessa Clan did not take lightly when any of their clan disappeared for any reason, and when with a group of Humans they would only think the worse that these lower life forms had done something to their clan member. And they would seek vengeance upon the humans for their folly as a whirl wind so destroys a forest so shall the Tessa Warriors fall upon the humans.

However if the Tessa have taken these humans, then they would of course deny it, and use elaborate speech to hide their actions. They were Warriors and were a proud clan.

No matter this was a touchy matter to deal with, and he would know soon as he was about to report to them the matter.

Garessaee walked into the elevator and pushed the button for the lowest level of the base.

The elevator doors opened and Garessaee left it and walked to the office room where the leaders of the Tessa Clan were. He opened the door and bowed most graciously as tradition required then he righted himself to his full height again. As they looked at him with inquiring gazes for the reason of his uninvited intrusion upon their ground.

"Great leaders of the Tessa I bring news from the humans and it is not one of peace. There has been a great misadventure by an unknown party and we must discover the truth of the matter.

The humans sent a patrol of 4 with 1 of ours, of clan Tessa to advise and assist them. That Team has disappeared. General Sills has suggested by his behavior a lack of trust towards our race and clans once more and has accused us indirectly of abducting his men. I would encourage you as leaders to explore your clan and see if this is true or false. I do not think a warrior of Tessa would take prisoners of the humans without the knowledge of your leadership, thus you will discover if it be true or not.

However if you have done no mischief, then I can seek the General to show us then if they have in fact taken a Warrior of Tessa prisoner. This I must have proof of before we can seek his release, or find satisfaction in avenging his harm, if indeed harm has come to him."

Garessaee having thus spoken to them then remained silent for a response.

After a time a large and powerful Tessa warrior stood this was Eeeleesssoe 2nd leader of security of the Dulce facilities. He was in human terms 10 feet tall and 4 feet at the shoulders and of 654 lbs. of raw muscles. He spoke.

"I Eeeleesssoe will discover the truth of this, if the humans had done evil to our brother then many shall be punished for it, thus is the code. If one of ours has done evil to the humans then he shall be dealt with as well for breaking the truce and giving shame to our clan"

The others nodded and hissed their approval of his statement and his resolve to find the truth.

"Know this, if there is to be a war of revenge for your missing brother then we of the Tooashee do pledge our honor with you of the Tessa in this matter, these weak and pathetic humans need to learn their place and know they are of a lesser race and as such should be as our slaves. We shall once again have to teach them their place, if they in fact have harmed a member of our race." Gareesaee spoke in an icy coldness ending with his own guttural hiss.

"We of the Tessa accept your offer to join us as needed to punish these pathetic humans again. We shall be silent until we learn of the truth however if they did indeed do harm to a member of the clan then they have attacked the clan and so the clan shall live for retribution until satisfied." Eeeleesssoe spoke as thunder.

"Garessaee of the Garsar leaves you now to be about your mission as you join me in investigating the truth of this matter. Eeeleesssoe of Teesa may your journey bring forth the truth and if needed who is to be punished for this great evil. We shall be honored to assist as you need it." Garessaee spoke and bowed gently again as he slowly backed up and left the room closing the door.

As he walked down the tunnel to his own clans quarters a thin smile of sorts crossed his face, once again we shall slaughter you miserable humans for not long has gone by when we beat you down and put you in your place when you intruded into our private quarters and now we shall do it again if your guilty of this evil. If only the leaders of the Toomas Clan would give word we would in short order put all of you worthless humans into slavery even your whole race as it should be, as it was millennia ago back in the days of true honor.

Someday he thought maybe someday soon, time will tell. With these pleasant thoughts Gareesaee imagined to himself all the slaves and all the potential scientific projects he could do with an endless supply of fresh humans to work with. Yes that future day would be a great day indeed. As he walked into his quarters to meet with his own leaders and relate the story once again. Of course it would not hurt his dreams at all if he were to embellish it some, no not at all. For he was sure the human scum had done this deed. Even if some foolish Teesa warrior did the deed of the missing humans, so be it, there could be a way to turn this around and force blame on the humans for it. This could be the time he had been awaiting.

CHAPTER 21

Final Gathering Before Entering The Darkness

Ben and Fairsong had spent the last 24 hrs. of intense training. Fairsong had given Ben some time to get himself together and then taught him some more about the lands they might have to pass through in their search for his sister and brother.

It was evening when the Sheriff and the search team entered base camp.

Ben was looking out to the south west over the vast mountains taking in all the beauty of it all, the peace as he watched the sun dip closer to the rim of the western sky, they still had a few hours of light left but it would be a good sunset. His thoughts were disturbed as he heard the trucks of the search party enter the area; they had come up the old jeep trail on the south western slope of the area. Usually it was non-motorized, today however in this case there was an exception made.

Ben watched as the trucks and jeeps with their trailers and gear and a few old hummers all drove into the meadow area of the base camp and found places to park. It looked as if there were a few more people going on the journey and that thought made him feel a little better. He started walking back to the center of camp to meet all who had come.

The Sheriff was met by one of his SAR team members who had chosen to stay at the base camp.

"Well Al, how's it been since we left? I assume it's been pretty quiet up here." The Sheriff asked.

"It has been quiet, I have Fred and George up near the cave entrance with a radio observing just in case something new happens there. The rest of us have just been waiting and relieving them from time to time in shifts. Now that you all have finally come we can get this search started."

"Sounds good, now I need to speak with Ben and Fairsong then with the whole group to fill everyone in on what is going to take place. Go ahead and call your team back from the cave so they can be here for the meeting." He said.

Turning the Sheriff noticed Ben walking up to him, and then he saw Fairsong coming down the hill as well walking towards him, that is good will save him having to go look for them.

"Sheriff, so how many of these men will actually be joining us on the search party then?"

"There will be 8 who have come to help search, the others and I will help on this end and do whatever we can to support your search party."

"Good to hear, I was not sure if anyone would actually show up after Fairsong's last lecture." Ben stated.

"There are some who have come a long way to help your family, you have friends you did not even know you had, I will have everyone gather and we shall go over the introductions and what is to happen next. As late as its getting we won't be going anywhere till tomorrow."

"Sounds good."

"Now we need to get everyone organized." The Sheriff said and he walked off to tell everyone where to gather and to use the tents the SAR teams still had set up for the night. He was thinking it over and they should leave as soon as they could in the morning as that would give some of the team member's time for a good night's rest before their hard journey in the tunnels.

It took 30 minutes for everyone to get their stuff organized and for the men at the cave to get back to camp. The Sheriff had told everyone to meet at the camp fire pit so he could address the whole group at one time.

Once everyone was accounted for Sheriff Thompson motioned for James, Fairsong and Ben to come and stand with him before the group.

"It looks like everyone is finally here now. I would like everyone to introduce themselves briefly so we can know who everyone is. Then we will move on to the details of what needs to happen. James you start." The Sheriff said as he backed away to the side to give James some room.

"Most of you know me, for those who do not I am James Adair, the father of the missing children. I am grateful to all of you for your willingness to help us look for them. Thank you." James said getting a little emotional, but trying to hold himself together. He did not want to break down in front of these men.

"I am Ben Adair and James is my father. I know most of you however I am waiting to learn of the new men who have come to help our family find my brother and sister. Thank you for your willingness to help."

"I am Fairsong, I have known this family of Adair's a very long time and they are family to me. I also understand from my own people's history whom we may have to fight to obtain the return of the children to our family. My soul is filled with joy at seeing others here who also desire to go find these lost ones. I pray to our Creator to bless us all in this thing." He said then awaited everyone else to continue the introductions.

"I am Joe Running Deer; I go on this path to help find the Adair children for it is my destiny to do so. I will serve those who go to the best of my abilities I thank all for the opportunity to assist in this journey."

"I am Tarton Barrett, James is my Uncle and I go to represent my family as my father needs to remain to help the rest of the family in our absence. I go to find my cousins."

"Some here know who I am, my name is Julio Ramierez it would seem that my people come from the Aztec lines and our ancient fathers long ago came from these lands we now stand on before they journeyed to the southern lands. I go to help find these children for they are of innocent blood, and it is right for me to help, the rest of my reasons are my own."

"This is good to see who the Great Spirit has called upon and gathered us together this day to go venture and find these taken children. I am called Tim Shadow Walker, I come from the Dakota Sioux and we come to assist, Joe's Uncle who lives amongst our people did ask the council to help you. We shall fight to rescue the taken children from any foe who stands in the way. Including the evil demons of our fathers and olden times. We have come to do so, we have fought these demons in times past and now we are called to assist you in this journey. It is good to see a gathering of warriors who also seek to defend the weak from those who would harm them. May we journey together in honor." Tim said and he remained standing with his arms crossed across his chest. Awaiting for the others to speak.

"As Tim has spoken of where we come from and why we are hear I shall leave it at that. I am James Little Beaver and we shall succeed or we shall move into the realms of our spirit fathers and join them in the places of honor prepared for warriors who fight for honor and justice. For this is what true men do. I feel success in life is found in the stories of honor for ones service to all human kind told by those who follow him in the years to come. These innocent children were taken by men or the demons we know of who live in the deep caverns below, those who have helped the demons have dishonored themselves and their families in the taking of these children. There is no honor or valor in this thing. So I come to return those taken to their home, and to deal with the evil ones as the creator chose me to do. I am honored to serve the Adair family in this thing." James then also remained standing silently watching those who were to join him on this quest.

"It is good to have such men as have gathered for our mission. I am Gideon Yahsef and I am a very close friend to Olaf Barrett who is Brother in Law to the Adair's. It was good that David and I were in Salt Lake City at this time on business. So we are able to come here to help them find their children for it is my debt to repay Olaf for his help long ago. We shall bring justice to this family by returning their taken children. Knowing who or what has taken them as Olaf and the others informed me of these demons, I have chosen to bring with me some tools of my past trade to assist us as needed, speak with me when this is over and I shall make sure all who go have the proper tools of war as you need. For I have brought enough to share." Gideon stated bluntly and he also remained standing.

"Well it would seem my fellow country man has spoken well, I am David Ananiah a friend to Olaf as well. We have been invited by Olaf for our knowledge and skill that he feels may be needed for this journey to be a success, all you need to know of us at this time is that we have experience in this type of thing. We shall serve this group in a good way; I feel that the heavens have granted us the skills we have learned to date so as to assist in this rescue. So we shall. There will be much we can teach each other on this journey and much heart ache and blood may be spilt along the way. We will do our best and guided by the God of Israel we shall be victorious of that I am sure for it is known the righteous will overcome all evil, all darkness." David finished.

The group looked at each other taking each other in, and each thought about what had been spoken, then after a few moments Sheriff Thompson spoke.

"Well it would seem that the Creator or God has granted us a good group of men to search for the Adair children. I will be staying as I have work to do here on this side however I shall explain our situation. We seem to have some who have skills as warriors, some have never been in combat and some only recently have learned of it. I am appreciative of our new friends and for the tools they have offered, find those that you are comfortable with. As for us we will leave the SAR communications tent here at base and keep it manned, as well as have 24 hr. surveillance on the cave entrance in case you need help. You will be on your own, you must do whatever you must to survive and rescue the children. This will be very dangerous based on the experiences we have had so far. Some of you may be wounded, some may not come home. If you are prepared for this then make your piece with your God and ask for his help on your journey.

Make no mistake; you're going to fight military trained men, and these Nemekans Demons. Who look to be very formidable warriors as well. There is much that I cannot fully understand as it is all new to me, however Fairsong has some knowledge of these creatures and knows how to deal with them. Also he will be the leader of this mission; the rest of you will listen to him.

As you gear up tomorrow remember what you carry is what you will have to survive with. So take only what you can carry. My guess is where there are people there will be supplies to re-supply your needs.

Good luck men and go with God. Pray and ask him for guidance and for protection and he will bless you for I personally believe we all worship the same God of Heaven although we may call him by different names. He will listen to those who have the faith to hear."

As the Sheriff ended his comments the group spread out to prepare for the coming tomorrow, some went to check on the weapons cash that Gideon had spoken of and got advice on what would individually be best for each of them, for those who needed the tools of war.

Of all those present Fairsong chose not to use or take any modern weapons, he chose to keep his personal weapons of choice for battle as he felt guns and things were not as honorable a weapon as the ones of old, when fighting was more civilized, if one could think of war as civilized by any means. He did know how to use them, but he chose not to. Such was his way.

Ben chose the desert eagle as it made him feel a little safer as he knew how to work a hand gun and the .50 caliber should help in fighting the Nemekans, it came with a suppressor as well.

In fact most of the group took the Desert Eagle .50 caliber hand guns with suppressor's as they all felt that in fighting the Nemekans demons it would work better to have a more powerful weapon.

Some took the shorter versions of the Berrett .50 rifles that were available, and some of the other weapons of heavier caliber, since it was suggested due to the size and strength of the creatures it was always better to have heavy fire power.

Also in the mix were some hand grenades, flash grenades and other useful devices for war, it was as if Gideon and David had planned on outfitting a special opps team for such were the tools they brought. No one asked the men where they got the weapons, they were just glad to have some things to defend themselves along their journey if needed.

Tarton noticed that the two fellows from Dakota had bows and arrows, so he walked over and had to ask the question of why?

"Tim and James right? I don't want to be offensive but what good are bows and arrows going to be on these big creatures?"

"You are Tarton; these are very effective, and silent. Our grandfathers made these long ago when we once knew and understood the ways of metal working in the ancient days. An art long since forgotten as our brothers who once created such tools were long ago destroyed in a great battle. However they have been kept and taken care of for a long time. They are special the history of them is they were made from the metal of a falling star or meteorite. They are very strong and hard to pull; the power it contains is beyond any modern bows of today. They are very silent as well another reason to bring them, for there will be a need for silence. Only few of us can use these bows.

The arrows are of special design as well, be careful not to touch the heads, for we have covered them for a reason. As we have barrowed the ideas of those natives of other lands, we have brought with us the toxins of the tree frogs, very deadly and it acts very quickly, we have no antidote for it. It will come in handy as our grandfathers of old have once fought these demons from under the Earth, and these are the weapons they successfully used. And so shall we."

"Thanks for telling me, and I hope they do as you say. This is not going to be an easy task I feel and I am glad you both are with us." Tarton replied.

"You are most welcome; we shall each bring our own skills on this journey and will need to count upon each other to do their best with what they have. Each of us is different I see, and it is a blessing the Creator has brought such a good team together for our journey to rescue the children." James stated.

After a few more hours the evening turned to night, in that time everyone got to learn a little about each other and had taken some time to put their gear together and some asked the seasoned men who knew of military things advice on how to pack, what to take and would be needed.

Then each man was left to his own thoughts and his own reasons for his desire and need each felt to go on this mission. Each had made the choice to go, knowing that if needed or by chance they would each give their life in the cause of freeing the children from their captors. Even with these thoughts they all would do whatever they could to make sure if battle comes the enemies would more willingly give their lives before they would sacrifice their own.

Eventually each one turned to their sleeping bags and one by one fell into a sound sleep knowing that they were prepared and none really feared what was to come, it was just a knowledge of what fate would ask of them and what fate would take. They each new their God was with them for their mission was just.

Only Ben had a somewhat sleepless night full of dreams and night mares, which kept waking him up through the night until finally he gave up trying to sleep and sat in his blankets awaiting the morning sun since it was not long before it would arise over the eastern mountains and bring warmth to the camp once more. He wondered how cold the caverns would be without the Sun to warm it. His mind was full of many questions, some Fairsong had answered, some he just smiled and said 'You will learn of yourself along the way'. One thing Ben knew was his life was about to change, actually it had changed but where was it going to lead.

James was up early as he also had a hard time sleeping and he watched his son Ben as he sat by the edge of the camp waiting for the sun rise. He wondered at the dawning of a new day and a new time where a mixture of men from many different walks of life and backgrounds had joined together in a common goal to rescue two innocent children most did not even know, from the forces of darkness that lay somewhere in the caverns under these mountains. These are the men that songs and stories where written about, those who would never ask for anything just to have the opportunity to go and help others in need. James thought to himself and silently gave thanks to his God for those he has sent to help him look for his children, the fact that these men were actually present some with the skills and tools needed to make it possible now to free them was a miracle all in its self. He prayed for his children's safety and for those who were to go to find them, to rescue them that they would be safe as well. But he did feel a sense of dread of the possible coming of a doom upon some, it was vague and elusive but he felt it. And that worried him some.

Fairsong looked across the expanse of the Earth off to the east; Ben was by his side now taking in the warmth of the rising sun.

"Ben this is the last time we shall see your sun for some time. I shall miss these moments upon the face of this Earth for I have cherished the good times in your world and taken it for granted as well over these decades I have been here. But I have always had a longing for my home lands as well. It is good you will be with me; we shall find your sister and brother that I promise you. May they yet be alive and well. I fear there have been rumors for years of these beings doing bad things to our people in the name of science. I pray they have not been used as such, however if we find them in a poor way may God grant us victory and his vengeance upon those who have harmed them. I know that God in Heaven is the God of light and truth and justice and will defeat all darkness both upon the face of the Earth and beneath. That I know." Fairsong said in a determined voice.

"I too hope they are well, for I must feel so in order to move on today, I guess it is time to prepare for they are gathering now and we should join them. Shall we go?" Ben asked.

"Yes it is time, let us go." Fairsong said. And they both stood and walked over to where the group was gathered.

Everyone had gathered together all had eaten what would possibly be their last meal for a while consisting of a good cooked meal. All were packed up and ready to go as Sheriff Thompson and James stood in front of the group for one last word before they headed up the trail to the cave.

"Men I pray you shall go in peace and with success. If it is time for you to fight in battle then do so with honor and know that the God of Heaven and of Earth will be with each of you. I have asked James to grant us a final word before you go."

James looked down for a few moments thinking about what could be said that had not already been stated.

"Once again I thank you for coming to help, to risk your lives with mine as we go to find my kids. If you are willing I would like to offer a word of prayer to assist us before we leave this morning." James said this as he knelt down then upon the Earth and bowed his head in humble prayer.

Some joined James on their knee's others just waited in respect for as warriors they all knew their fate was in the hands of the Creator, their God in Heaven.

James prayed.

"Our Heavenly Father hear us now for we your humble children do go to seek and find my missing children who were taken by the dark forces of Earth. We do not seek to fight these men and creatures for glory or out of a thirst for bloodshed, but to rescue the children. We do not delight in the shedding of blood and death, but you have said if we are not guilty of the 1st or 2nd offense we can protect our family and loved ones, so grant us this day the power and wisdom to defend the lives of my children and those in the rescue team, Bless these men now gathered together that we can unite the knowledge, experience, wisdom, and the tools needed to succeed in this mission. Grant us success Father and let the warriors of light now gathered here this day be able to overcome all forces of darkness, we seek your guidance and wisdom and help. Let us go and return in a good way dear Father in Heaven as you can protect my children from harm and let us meet them soon. I do humbly ask for your help now, and do so in the name of your son Jesus Christ, Amen."

All agreed with his prayer by adding their Amen as well.

A sense of peace and understanding as well as an surge of energy some would say came from some unknown place that filled their hearts and minds of all present, they felt a sense of urgency and that all would be as it should. As the sun arose over Twin Lakes all the men put on their packs and gathered what gear they would carry. And with the warmth of the sun upon their faces and the slight mountain morning breeze upon their faces they turned and took a last look at the horizon, and some waved their goodbye's to those men staying behind in base camp. Then they all turned and headed up the trail and to the cave entrance that would lead each one to their future whatever that would be.

CHAPTER 22

The Search Begins

Once everyone had reached the clearing in front of the cave, Fairsong took the time to address the group one last time.

"I shall say this, Ben has a device that will guide us to the location of the children, he and I shall be on point most of the time. If we require a change or come upon a situation requiring your individual skills we shall use them as needed. If you have idea's based on your life experiences in dealing with whatever situations come about, let us know so we can as a team make the best with what we have.

We shall go quietly in this cave and tunnel system your breathing can sound very loud so do what you can to control it and think always of being as quiet as possible. Whisper to communicate or hand gestures are best. You men Gideon and David you have special operational skills so you will need to be on point or on rear guard as needed, help the others to understand what is needed as we go along. I suspect Tim and Joe have been trained by their fathers as woodsmen; this will be good as well. All who have experience help others who do not. When this comes into combat situations remember to act, do not freeze up. Take actions as needed to protect each other and think of it later if you wish. Let us be cold in battle and deal with those who stand in the way of success.

We shall begin with Ben and me on point, then Tim and Gideon after us. David and James you will be on rear guard and the others in the center."

"We are agreed it is a sound placement of our skills so let's move out then." Gideon commented.

Everyone took one last look at daylight and one by one they entered the cave door and moved in single file to the back wall.

"Fairsong what next, I don't see the tunnel." Tim asked him.

"Patients young warrior, for now you shall see some of the technology you're going to face for I used it here to hide the entrance to the lands you will journey much is different than what you know today. Watch and learn." Fairsong stated as a teacher to a student.

As he said this he took out his crystal tool and activated it once more revealing the tunnel opening.

"Now that is a sure curious thing to behold, we shall have to speak of this tech at a further time for I would like to learn more about it." Gideon commented as he smiled and wondered who this Fairsong was.

"If and when the time permits I shall show you the workings of these devices, it would be good for others to know them as well. Now one last thing that will assist you all as we walk in the darkness of these tunnels. From time to time they are illuminated by a unusual form of light that comes from cave walls a fungi type plant, but for now I will share this vile so pass it along and I would like everyone to put one drop in each of your eyes, this will last until we once again enter an area of bright light then it will dissipate. But it will give you a form of night vision of great clarity." Fairsong said and watched each one do as he asked.

The group all commented about their new ability to see in the blackest dark area's now, and were amazed by this knowledge Fairsong had shared with them.

"Ben are you ready then, bring out the Lev Antas Shuesa and let us begin our journey." Fairsong asked.

Ben took out the Lev Antas Shuesa and while holding it in his hands he focused on quieting his mind as Fairsong had taught him. Then he asked for Heavens guidance as well and sought with all his heart to know where to find his sister and brother.

The ball began to glow once more and the directors in the ball arranged themselves directing them to go down the right passage way in the tunnel.

"Well. Let go." Ben stated. As he led the way followed by Fairsong and the others.

"I find it amazing it is most magical how these tools work the tech involved would be most interesting to explore indeed." Tim mentioned to Gideon.

"Yes they are interesting devices; I look forward to the time when Fairsong can instruct us better in their functions as well." Gideon said to him. As they all followed Ben into the tunnel system.

Everyone else came and followed as Ben and Fairsong directed in a single file line they walked they had left one of the Sheriff team members at the door of the Cave who would notify the Sheriff that they had started the underground search. Soon they lost sight of the light that emanated from the tunnel entrance of the open cave door.

Now all was quiet and dark, with only the sounds of their breathing and their footsteps upon the tunnel floor.

The passing of time feels different once one is underground you lose all normal sense of time and minutes turn to hours and hours turn to days. However it did not take them very long to work their way down to where the tube transportation system was, the mode of travel the others had used. As they neared the soft lighted room before them Fairsong signaled the group to stop with a motion of his hand. And held his finger to his lips to remind all for silence.

He then took out his strange crystal tool again and pointed it toward the lighted room he then used it to scan the room for potential traps or alarms as well as for any signs of life. Finding none he took the lead position and motioned for the others to follow, and quiet as they could they moved towards the room.

As they all entered the open room Fairsong motioned them to follow him as he walked toward the transport tub area. He pointed at the tube car and motioned for them to all get in with him. Once everyone was aboard, he spoke to them just loud enough for all to hear.

"This is our transportation, it's a tube car and they go very fast based on a form of super magnetic rail system of sorts, it's quiet but fast. When we get to where we are going we must be prepared for conflict for one never can tell what may be at the next stop."

Then he manned the controls of the car and put it into motion as he spoke to Ben.

"This is important I shall not bring the car up to full speed until you can find us the correct stopping point, by that I mean use the Lev Antas Shuesa and focus on it to see where we go next. It should tell us how far the next stop should be in our search."

Ben focused on the ball and as the light glowed and the workings inside the device moved they seemed to not be able to agree on any single one direction but several of the pointers went in different ways, not like a left or right but more in a difference in distance, one closer one father away. He better ask if he was doing it right.

"I am not sure it is working right, take a look I seem to be getting mixed directions now." He asked as he stretched his hands out for Fairsong to take a look.

"Then let's look, see here." He said as he looked into the device. He did notice the confusion that seemed to be taking place and a thought came to him to help resolve it.

"Try focusing on only one of your siblings and see what happens then."

Ben did so he focused on Sariah and the arrows calmed down and maintained a one directional location but it seemed at a great distance from where they were now based on the other markings the ball contained that showed distance based on their current location.

Next he focused on Levi and they pointed in a different way, and in a closer location than Sariah's.

"I think we have two different locations as Sariah seems farther away than Levi, so they must have separated them. So based on that we should find Levi first then."

"Let me see then, based on the distance locater we should be there at the speed we will be traveling at in about 20 minutes so everyone be ready." Fairsong said to the whole group.

"Be ready for combat for when they stop the car we may only have moments to react before any guards at the area realize we are not friendly, they won't be expecting us that is for sure so there will be a few seconds of surprise in our favor that will be to our benefit, so be alert." Gideon told everyone.

They all prepared for armed conflict, some held their guns ready with the safeties turned off. Tim and James each notched an arrow and readied their bows. All took deep breaths and prepared themselves for quick combat.

As time went by Ben noticed they were close to the stopping area and he told them so.

"We are about 2 minutes out if I understand this thing right." Ben stated to the team.

"Can you tell if there are any guards waiting there for us or not?" Gideon asked

"No I don't think it can, so no help there." Ben replied.

Fairsong was ready; he knew he would need to use his tools to turn off any surveillance devices to hide their arrival. He was prepared to do this as soon as the car stopped. His tools would not work at the speed they were traveling to tell him if anyone was waiting for them, that was unfortunate.

"We are about there, I need your help let's try to do this as quietly as we can, and I need to try to locate and deal with any surveillance devices they may have in place the moment we stop. So be ready here we go, five, four, three, two, one" Fairsong said as he stopped the car.

Everyone looked out over the room they had stopped at. It was a very large slightly domed room there was evidence of people being there however none were present, that was good for them.

Fairsong found and disabled 3 surveillance devices in a matter of seconds. Then he motioned for all of them to exit the car.

They walked into the open room in a u shape formation from the car's location everyone's senses on total alert for any movement they stopped a moment, then Ben gave them the direction to follow. Fairsong and Gideon took the point and Ben and the others followed them down the left open corridor.

* * * * *

In the security control area for sector 18 - A Corporal Nolton noticed his cameras had gone out in the tube embankment area, they seemed to have all malfunctioned at the same time that was unusual, and they may have been disabled. He became alert and picked up his phone to contact Major Jones office.

"Major Jones, what's the problem?" He had been up all night preparing scenarios in case the Nemekans came and started trouble in his area. He had been put on caution alert since the team had vanished.

"Major, this is Corporal Nolton in security control; all cameras have gone out in the tube room sir. I do not think it's a malfunction; it would have to be deliberate. I do have a ground sensor that says we do have some moment in that area. None of our men are there that I am aware of at this time, are you expecting anyone?"

"I am expecting no one, act as if it could be a move against us by the Neme's, Alert your defenses to respond and hold whomever they find. Do not open fire, unless they do so first is that understood. If it is the Neme's they must make the first move before we can blame them for this intrusion. Is that understood Corporal?"

"Yes sir, understood." Corporal Nolton responded as he hung up the phone and dialed up the ready room.

"Ready room, Sgt. Atherby here." He said as he answered the alert phone.

"Sgt. we have intruders in our area in the tube room, they have disabled the visual monitors, however missed the floor motion detectors, they are now leaving the tube area and headed down the corridor close to your area. Major Jones said to engage, capture and hold whoever is there. If it's the Neme's you must fire in defense only. Is that understood?" Corporal Nolton told him.

"Understood." Sgt. Atherby responded and hung up the phone. It was just like those Neme's to pull off a stunt like this, and of course the brass idiots always say don't shoot till they shoot you dead 1st what a bunch of idiots. He did not care for the rules of engagement at all that they had to deal with. Once he entered the quarters of his men he started yelling commands to them and telling them a quicker version of the story. He had only a dozen men, as Lt. Fred had already earlier moved the rest of the men to another part of the zone and that left him undermanned. But it would have to do, he thought as they all readied for combat.

"Men let's move out. Quiet like looks like the Neme's are trying to mess with us again, so no shooting unless I shoot first, if they do attack then don't leave any of those lizards still breathing is that understood." Sgt. Atherby ordered. His men all acknowledged his orders with nods and followed him into the hall.

* * * * *

Fairsong and Gideon and the rest stopped in their tracks. Fairsong motioned to be ready.

"We have movement coming toward us, be ready." He whispered.

Ben put the Lev Antas Shuesa away, and drew his weapons and prepared for battle. Hoping he would not get himself or anyone else killed.

The rest of the team also prepared for the battle soon to commence. David and Gideon took up opposite sides of the corridor both on point, Tim and James also split each one near the front.

The others flattened out against the walls, or kneeling taking up positions and awaited the coming fight.

David motioned he could see them coming as he was using his corner shot weapon and it let him see what was around corners, and counted 12 soldiers, Suddenly Tim who was next to David lifted his bow and fired down the hall towards the men. Then David open fired at the coming men, Gideon using a corner shot weapon engaged the moment David did and then James also opened fired and in a moment it was over. The few shots the surprised soldiers got off went wild and missed the team.

* * * * *

As the Sargent moved down the corridor with his men spread out across the hall they moved quietly and were just coming to the next corner when out of nowhere the man next to him was hit by an arrow that went clear through him and into the next soldier behind him. He saw them both die in that quick moment, an arrow that momentarily puzzled him where did that come from, Neme's don't use arrows, who does. His shock froze him for a moment and in that moment he felt his own chest explode by the impact of a high energy round, as he fell to the floor he wondered what had just happened, he watched his men all get cut down in a matter of seconds, and just as he lay helplessly on the floor in a pool of his own blood he saw his last man fall, and as his own spirit felt the warmth of the next life embrace him calling for him to go with its comfortable feeling he thought, was it real? How strange, it looked to him to be an Indian bending down to remove the arrow's from his comrades, that's not possible an Indian? What was an Indian doing down here, he would never know for with those thoughts Sgt. Atherby left this world into the unknown realms.

* * * * *

Gideon motioned for the rest of the team to come and join them. It was amazing how quickly these four warriors had taken out the dozen soldiers, but surprise was on their side.

They gathered around as Tim and James retrieved their arrows. Gideon and David were searching the bodies for radios or anything that could be of use to the team.

Tarton noticed a door to a room not far from where they were and he pointed it out.

"This is a communications room, we should check it out." Tarton said.

David said "Agreed, let me see if this will open the door for us. James be ready."

David had taken a card from the dead soldier and tried it in the door. James was ready with an arrow drawn just in case. The light on the door went from yellow to green it had worked it began to open.

* * * * *

In the communication room Corporal Nolton was trying to contact the Sargent again to see what had happened, he heard some shots, but then it was all quiet. He heard the door as it made the entry click noise as it granted access to whoever was outside it. Normal protocol was to call him first before entering; something did not feel right about it. He grabbed the phone and hit the button to Major Jones office once again.

"This is Major Jones, Corporal Nolton tell me what's going on there." Major Jones asked.

"I am not sure, have lost contact with the Sgt. and his men, someone is trying my door Sir, wait its opening, Stop! No! Don't. Aaaaaggghhh..." the rest of whatever Corporal Nolton was about to say ended as his life ended at that moment.

"Corporal! Corporal what's going on, do you hear me! Hello?" Major Jones ordered into the phone, but soon realized that he would get no answer as he heard the phone click as it was hung up.

* * * * *

David nodded at James as he pushed open the door to the room, just as he swung the door open they saw a soldier on the phone speaking to someone, he was immediately silenced by James's arrow as it passed through him and the chair he was sitting in and into the concrete wall behind them, impaling both the man and the chair to the wall.

David held his hand up for silence then took the phone from the now dead man's hand and hung it up, he could hear someone yelling on the other end.

He then turned to James, "Well I guess bows and arrows do just fine, that's a mighty powerful weapon for what it is. Let's see if we can find anything useful in this room but be quick about it, I have a feeling whoever was on the other end will be sending someone quickly to see what's going on here." David finished and began his search.

After they had searched the bodies and the room, Fairsong told them to put the bodies in the office room, then he took out the black crystal tool, a Nemekans weapon he had taken from the dead Nemekans and used it on the bodies where ever there was a wound caused by their weapons he masked it with the energy of the Nemekans weapon burning all evidence of human weapons from the bodies. He hoped this would throw off the investigation team, and maybe starts a small conflict between these men and the Nemekans.

He then left the room shut the door and used the same device to melt the door closed, in order to give them a few more minutes. Fairsong turned to the group.

" Now make sure you all have your brass shells clean it up quickly it will help create added confusion, and buy us some time.

"I hope that will slow them down a little, and if my ruse works by hiding the death wounds we made it could cause issues between these men and their Nemekans allies. Let's be going." Fairsong stated.

"I found a map we can use from the office, let's see where we are, ok. Let's get out of this hall way we are far to expose and Ben can see about using his device to find where we need to go next, but we need to do it fast." David stated.

"Let's get moving then." James Adair stated and they all went down the hall away area and found a room they could use to get there bearings.

As they entered the room, it seemed to be a storage room they found a table and laid the map out on it. Ben took out the Lev Antas Shuesa and began again to search for Levi. The Ball glowed again and the pointers pointed across the room to where a wall of boxes were with many labels on them.

Ben hurried across the room and started looking through the boxes until he found one the ball designated.

It was labeled 'Intruder Sector 39 Boy'.

"Dad look at this, this must be about Levi." Ben called out.

Fairsong and James Adair quickly came over to see what Ben had found. They opened the box that Ben handed them, as he turned and noticed another box labeled 'Intruder Sector 39 Girl'. So he grabbed that one as well.

Tarton and Julio helped open it as Ben put away the Lev Antas Shuesa.

Inside the box that James was looking in he found his son Levi's clothing and personal belongings, even the pocket knife Ben had given him on his last birthday. He took the knife and put it in his pocket and hoped to return it to him soon.

"Ben these are Levi's things. They must have moved them somewhere else and put them in different clothes." James Adair stated is a sad voice.

"Right Dad, this box is Sariah's stuff and there is a note about where they took her as well.

This is what it says." Ben said as he started reading the note.

"Subject Girl has been move to Dulce Base for further evaluations that is all it says." He read.

"Yes Levi has a similar note in his box as well; it says he was moved to the same place." James Adair added.

"Folks, we need to speed this up, there is going to be a lot of upset soldier types heading this way soon, if not already on their way. Let's end this party, get back in that tube car thing and get moving we can figure out where once we get out of here." Gideon stated with a sense of urgency in his voice.

"He is correct, put the boxes back as you found them, and let's move to the tube car now." Fairsong stated as he looked out the door and prepared to leave.

It only took a minute and everyone was ready to leave. They all took their positions again and headed down the hallway the way they had come moving quickly towards the tube car.

Seeing no one had yet arrived in the area, they quickly got into the tube car and Fairsong started their journey deeper into the cavern systems at a high rate of speed.

"Ben, come here." Fairsong asked after they were underway once more.

Ben moved up besides Fairsong. Still a little stunned by the combat they had just endured, shaken but he knew that it would sadly not be the only time lives would need to be taken in order to find his missing family.

"Yes." Ben asked.

"Bring out the Lev Antas Shuesa once more, and try to quiet your mind enough to focus on where they may have been moved to. Think about each one individually, think of their face and see who is closest to us now and that is where we shall seek first to recover your family member."

Ben did as he was asked; he held the device in his hands then sat down on the seat. He did his best to put aside all the recent events, and to quiet his mind once again and focus on his lost brother and sister. As he did the ball glowed again, first dimly then in a flickering way from dim to light it grew steadily lighter and brighter. He saw the devices pointers begin to move again, as he focused on each ones faces, Sariah's and Levis he seemed to begin to feel the pointers as they moved inside the ball. It was as if each one was choosing one of the faces he was thinking on. Then he saw as it were a face, Sariah's face floating near one set of pointers, then Levi's near another.

He kept studying and doing his best to focus on the direction where each one maybe located at. As the pointers moved it seemed that Sariah was closer now than Levi, his pointer seemed to stretch out farther than Sariah's. So she must be closer. He then focused on her more intently and the pointers extended out, he figured out the direction to head in and the other seemed to be showing she was lower in depth than their current location, so they had to keep going and eventually go deeper down into the caverns. He was unsure about the distance and time it would take to get there, this was a strange device.

"It would seem that Sariah is closer than Levi, and this thing says she is far from here and lower in depth than we are now. I am not really sure how the distance figuring works on this thing."

"As you think on distance, look at the longer pointer with the runes on it, the spacing is in length of 1/4, 1/2, 3/4, and full days to the object at the end. In this case it should be Sariah if I am correct. So tell me count the lines, you will also notice that there are 12 smaller lines leading up to the 1/4 mark of the larger lines. This is what you term as hours above ground. Focus on these lines a moment and tell me what you see, and feel about the distance we need to travel." Fairsong said in a calm and teaching voice.

Ben did as he was asked and as he focused he noticed Sariah's face at the end of the longer pointer, then the lines began to move or shimmer, they seemed to glow in a greenish light to mark along the distance pointer thing. As it grew brighter green he could give a pretty good guess as to the distance or time it would take to get to that area.

"Based on what this is telling me, Sariah should be 2 hours from our current location. At the current speed of this tube car, then we will need to find a stopping point and continue in a downward direction,

I suppose we will find out how when we get to where we are going, right?" he asked Fairsong.

"Good, you're learning. And yet when we get there I am sure there will be several ways to continue our journey to where it will eventually meet with your sister."

CHAPTER 23

Missing Memories

Levi felt something poke his side, and a voice was talking to him. He was in the middle of a dream and was not sure what was real or what was part of the dream. He felt the poke again and the voice got louder.

"Hey Kid wake up." The voice told him.

Levi rolled over and about fell on the floor as he forgot where he was, as the bed was much smaller than the one he had back home. Catching himself before he rolled completely off the little bed he sat up rubbing his eyes and looked at the man who had awakened him. It was the guy who was here last time, great what did he want, he thought.

"So how are you feeling today? Any better?" The man asked him.

"Well you should know I keep falling asleep, so I guess I am sleepy. And my head hurts." He answered.

"Well that is all part of amnesia, it can really give one a head ache, and head trauma does that. Do you hurt anywhere else then?" The man asked.

"My neck hurts and my back but that's from sleeping on this hard bed, some hospital you run here, your beds are hard, no TV, radio, nothing like what a normal hospital room has." He responded.

"That is because you're in a special recovery room, we must keep it sterile and you're not allowed any outside stimulation for your brain, like TV as it could adversely affect your recovery. In other words the Dr's say it could actually harm your brain since it was hurt in the crash."

"The crash? I still don't remember any crash, and who are you, do you have a name?" Levi retorted he honestly did not believe in a crash at all. They had been in a cave he was sure of that.

"I am George, and a Nurse for this part of the Hospital recovery area dealing with brain injuries. I will be checking in on your progress as you recover." George said, he saw no harm in using his Base name, and this kid was not going to be around much longer anyway. Those Neme's had really made a mess of things breaking their machine. But soon they would try again, and succeed this time, they normally did. But if not then he had to keep up appearances and the crash and amnesia story was all he had to work with. Not that it was hard to keep that one up, this kid was so gullible.

"George, so when do I get to go for a walk and get some air, I am feeling kinda closed in here in this room." He asked to see what the George would say.

"Not until the Dr's give us the ok; you see with the brain trauma as you have suffered, the sun light can cause you severe headaches or worse. So as soon as they give us the ok I shall see about a walk around the hall's and then maybe outside if the weather is good." George told him thinking how easy it was to manipulate these kids.

"But I really don't remember being in a car wreck, I do remember being in a cave then I don't remember anything else until I woke up here."

"As I said before part of the trauma to your brain is creating false memories to help in the healing process, and as your family sadly all perished in the crash, and I am sorry for your loss, however your mind creates these false memories to help protect you from the reality of the bad events. Remembering a cave could be a way your mind is protecting you from the reality of what has happened to you, you see a cave is a safe and quiet place, also a place to hide, physically and mentally. I will have the councilor come and speak with you when he has some free time and he can do a better job of explaining how that works." George said putting a tone of sadness and remorse in his voice to help sell the 'sorry' for his loss of family. This kid was putty in his hands.

"I guess if you say so, but it seemed so real. I just don't know any more what is real maybe I should have a talk with your councilor." Levi said in a sad worn down voice. If he was wrong and this guy was right, then his family was all dead, that possible fact brought a sadness that brought tears to his eyes, and he began to cry.

"Now, you don't need to cry about it, you must move on in order to heal." George said as he moved forward and put his arm around the boy, giving him a slight hug that always worked to calm down the upset ones. And you had to have them in a good happy mood before they could do any harvesting otherwise it contaminated the potency of it, and that really upset the Neme's.

"Thanks, I'll try not to cry much, but if my family is all dead that's just not fare and I feel terrible." Levi said, he appreciated the little hug gesture; however something about this George did not make him feel too good, there was an uneasiness about him. He could not put his finger on it, but he felt like George could be lying to him about what was happening, but why would anyone lie about that.

"Well I need to go do some other visits but I will come back soon, you just calm down and try to relax, with all the stress of this it could cause you some harm. You will heal better as you learn to relax more." George suggested to him with as warm a grin as he could muster.

"Thanks, I do need to think about this, it is just hard to think they are all gone." Levi said very sadly.

"Well I will give you some time that is why we have you in a room all to yourself. So no one will bother you. See you later then." George said as he patted the kid on the head, then turned and left the room.

George thought to himself as the door closed behind him, these kids now days sure were good suckers, he was pleased with himself as it seemed the kid was buying the story even better. Pleased that he had not lost his touch. Soon the Neme's would get their machine fixed and he could be done with this little game and on to something more important.

CHAPTER 24

The Prisoner

Sheriff Thompson sat in his office, he had been thinking on how to question this soldier he had in custody. He had let him sit in his solitary confinement room to see if that would soften him up some more, He did not have the electronic weapon Fairsong had, and if he did he wondered if he would have been able to use it during his questioning. He decided it was probably good he did not have access to one.

Well nothing was going to get done just sitting and thinking on it. His finger prints like his dead friends did not register with any of the normal searches, and the FBI and military search came up blank as well, like these guy's never existed. Adding more mystery to this whole mess.

He arose walked out into the hall and down to the room where the prisoner was being kept.

"Sheriff you want some help questioning this one?" Deputy Gubler asked as he went to open the room for the Sheriff.

"No that won't be necessary, however I would like you to keep an eye on us, just in case I need your help, so don't go anywhere."

"Ok, no problem be right here if you need me." Deputy Gubler told him, he was disappointed at not being able to assist, he knew the Adair family really well, and he sure would like a crack at breaking this dude wide open literally. But the Sheriff was pretty good at this part. Be worth watching. He closed the door as the Sheriff entered the room.

The Soldier sat up as the Sheriff entered the room; he was not going to tell them anything more that was suicide. But then if the Neme's found him and blamed him for their buddies' death, oh well he would be killed as well as these fools.

"Well when do I get any food? I am hungry, and when do I get to make my phone call, I need my lawyer!" He demanded. This town Sheriff did not scare him one bit he was just a backward country idiot after all.

Sheriff Thompson just stared at his prisoner for a minute, then sat down on the metal bench and rested his arms on the metal table.

"Well it seems to me you missed breakfast already, sure was good had a big helping of fresh peach cobbler with a heaping stack of French Toast myself and about three eggs if I remember right. Should hold me till lunch I think." Sheriff Thompson replied smiling, it was a good breakfast he had this morning.

"So you're not going to feed me? That's wrong; I demand my lawyer, my phone call, and some food. You have to do those for me or you're gonna get it when my lawyer hears about your abusive treatment of me." The soldier threatened this idiot, he knew the rules of law they had to follow and the game he had to play with this idiot. He grinned as he made his demands, he knew once he got the phone call off, he would be out of here right quick. No questions asked.

"Well it seems that our phones aren't working very well this morning. Must of been an electrical storm last night, took out our phones, but don't worry I am sure the phone company will get here from Salt Lake City as soon as they can, of course we being way out here it could take a few days, maybe a week before those city folks make it down here to fix the problem, as for a phone call, guess you'll just have to wait until they get our phones working again. Sorry about that, but that's just how life is sometimes, never can tell when these thunder storms will just wreak havoc on our old phone system." Sheriff Thompson said trying to sound as sympathetic as he could.

"You know what I think; I think you're full of crap! There is nothing wrong with your phones you're just refusing to let me make my call, you're playing games here and I know it. So stop the crap and give me my call now!" The soldier demanded, he was not going to let this town Sheriff put one over on him.

"Just calm down there, soldier boy, not sure what to call you as you have not given us your name, and since your finger prints are a no show on any of our available records I guess you might not really exist right? And if you don't really exist, then I don't think you need a phone call as you're not really here, and since you're not really hear you won't be needing any lunch or dinner either, since you really don't exist after all."

"Even if you did have a legit name that we could verify, our phones are still out so you would have to wait anyway like I said. I had to send a Deputy out to the next county just to call the Phone Company to let them know of our problem.

"So Soldier boy, what do they call you? Since we seem to have plenty of time." Sheriff Thompson replied, not at all worried about this guy's threats.

"My name well it doesn't really matter now does it; I guess you can call me whatever you want, because I am not telling you any name. Now get me some food." The soldier demanded again, this guy was just trying to badger him. No way was he going to tell them anything else, he had said enough already when he was tortured by that dude on the mountain with the Neme wand, that really hurt and really sucked he still had some left over issues from that experience.

"So you want something to eat, well then you're just going to have to come up with a name, address, and who you're working with, then I might be able to find you something worth eating." Sheriff Thompson said with a thin smile as he sat back and just stared uncaringly at this prisoner.

"Well call me whatever you want, that's all I plan on telling you, so you can just get me some food or go jump off a cliff." The soldier responded flatly.

The Sheriff then just stood up and motioned for his Deputy he was ready to leave now.

"Well it seems soldier boy, that you are not very hungry at this time, you seem to have turned down a very promising lunch. We'll let me know when you want to be civil and tell us who you are, when you're ready just let the Deputy here know and he will get in touch with me." Sheriff Thompson said as he turned and left the room.

The Deputy shut the door, and watched as Sheriff Thompson walked down the hall not even looking back on the prisoner, who seemed a little puzzled and speechless as he watch the Sheriff ignore his requests. Deputy Gubler smiled at this, he knew no one could be pushy with the Sheriff; he was too smart and quite ornery and stubborn when it came to dealing with scum like this guy. He knew it would be quite a long time till the next meal ticket offer. He smiled served this scum right for what he had done.

Sheriff Thompson walked down to the desk to speak with his Deputies.

"Well our guest is not being cooperative at this time; make sure he has access to a little water, but no food until I say. He needs to do some serious thinking and remembering before he earns anything to eat. I think by morning he might start getting hungry enough to be civil to us. Is that understood?"

"Yes Sir, we understand completely", the Deputy on duty replied.

"Good then. Pass the word and let me know if our guest changes his mind. Oh and when it comes to meal times, just make sure you pipe in the smells of the cooking food into his cell, could you do that for me? And if you want to sit outside his room and slowly eat your meals that would be fine with me as well, I will leave that up to you." Sheriff Thompson said as he returned to his office to do some more planning and to see if he could dig up anything else on this guy, there must be a way to find something out about him.

* * * * *

Major Jones hung up his phone, Something had just happened in Sector 18, as Corporal Nolan had been silenced by something, or someone. This had to be the Neme's as they feared for he had heard what seemed to be a half plea from Corporal Nolan before the line went dead. It only took him a moment before he was dialing Gen. Sills' office once more.

"General Sills office how may I help you?" Staff Sargent Lilly Symrai politely said.

"I need to speak with the General immediately we have a situation here. This is Major Jones." Major Jones said in a very determined and urgent voice.

"One moment let me see if he has a moment." Staff Sargent Symrai responded and pushed the hold button, as she pushed the next button to the Generals Office phone.

"What is it Staff Sargent?" General Sills asked.

"I have Major Jones on the other line, he demands to speak with you again, do you want me to put him through?"

"Go ahead I have a few minutes."

Staff Sargent Symrai pushed the hold button and transferred the call to the Generals phone.

"This is General Sills, What is your update Major Jones on the earlier matter?"

"Sir, we have a situation down here communications with sector 18 just went dead, they seemed to be under attack by an unknown group, Corporal Noland was cut off during his warning to me, I must assume the worse that he is now dead by what I heard. Sir, based on what we know I think at least one group of Neme's has gotten out of control, request support."

"So you say communications went down, are you sure you think they were under attack? This is a very serious accusation and we must be sure with our next step, understood."

"Sir I fully understand, I heard the last plea and the death of Corporal Noland he was cut off as he pleaded for them to stop Sir. It must be the Neme's. Based on other recent events it all fits Sir."

"Then, put your sections on Full Alert, and I will send you A.N.T. 1 (Anti-Neme Team 1) to assist you in your situation, keep us informed as to the details of events as they happen. Understood Major?"

"Yes sir, I fully understand. Will let you know more as get more details on which Clan is out of control Sir."

"Good, now get to work." Gen. Sills said as he hung up the phone.

Then he picked up his other phone to connect him to the A.N.T. Section. He had always knew this day would repeat itself, these Neme's were a violent and obstinate race, always pushing their pride and ego's upon those in his command, now they had gone too far. That is why A.N.T. was developed.

"General Sir, how can we help you today?" Sargent Alvin said as he picked up and answered the Neme Alert hot phone.

"It seems Sargent we have some Neme's who are out of line, I need A.N.T. 1 to fully arm up and head immediately to sector 18, it seems they were under attack, and all communications and surveillance has been terminated in that area. Find out what is happening, if we have rogue Neme's prosecute with prejudice, Deadly Force is authorized. End this quickly do you understand Sargent." General Sills Ordered.

"Yes Sir, fully understand on the way immediately Sir." Sargent Alvin stated as he hung up the phone and started barking orders in the room for A.N.T. 1 to assemble in full Body armor and weaponry.

"This is not a drill, I repeat this is live, our men have already been killed, and more may be dead before we get down there, so let's move out!" Sargent Alvin Ordered his men.

In less than 10 minutes they were on a special tube racing at high velocity towards sector 18, they had trained for over a year for this, and knew what they needed to do. A whole world of pain was about to come down upon whatever Clan of Neme's were responsible for the attack on their men.

All 12 men sat quietly as they individually went over their training in their minds, knowing that a real fight with the Neme's meant some of them may not make it, however they had their new Body armor and weaponry and they really never felt they were going to lose. That was not what you thought, that kind of poor thinking got men killed. So they felt very confident in what they were about to do.

* * * * *

Major Jones was relieved that an A.N.T. team was on the way, now he needed to coordinate his own men, to recon and find out exactly who they were dealing with. Some of the Neme Clans were more psychotic than others, and larger and meaner as well.

He picked up his radio and dialed in the code for Lt. Fred.

"Lt. Fred do you copy" Major Jones called.

"Lt. Fred here, what can I do for you Major?"

"We have a Neme situation in sector 18, Corporal Noland was killed while warning me and General Sills is sending an A.N.T. to assist you. I need you to re*con* your area, and sector 18 to find out exactly what has occurred. I have no communications with anyone in that sector, and the surveillance is all out. You have a green light on deadly force as needed do you understand." Major Jones ordered.

"Yes sir, understand on our way. Over and out."

Lt. Fred instantly began barking orders to those men around him.

"We have a Neme Situation, they have attacked sector 18, there may not be any survivors, we are to go and recon that area, A.N.T. is on the way, let's go see if anyone is still alive. These are our guys, so let's make sure of your targets before you shoot. Let's Move out." Lt. Fred ordered as the men 17 in all, armed themselves and headed down the hall towards sector 18, they were the closest group to them, only about a 10 minute jog, so they moved out at a fast pace racing as quietly as they could down the corridor.

When they were a hundred yards away by his estimates Lt. Fred had his men slow down and they began their more quiet walk toward their target, slowing their breathing and heart beats as best they could, he knew the Neme's would be able to smell their sweat so he had to make sure they were cooled down before entering the target area.

Just a few minutes later they started going room to room in Sector 18, soon they got to the corridor outside the Communications room, and they noticed that there was indeed blood covering the corridor's floor, human blood. They also noted the bullet holes in the walls, so someone did get some shots off, hope they got a Neme at least.

"I don't see any bodies Lt. with all this blood there should be bodies, where do you think they are?" Private Dunlap asked.

"They will be here somewhere I hope, if not you know them Demons, they may have taken them back for dinner, I hope not though." Lt. Fred responded admitting what the others knew but did not want to express verbally. This could have been a rogue hunting party of the Neme's. It was a sickening thought.

"Lt, look here looks like the door has been melted." Private Mac Phearson noted, as he placed a small charge on the door to blow it open, so they could enter.

"Live charge, 3,2,1." Private Mac Phearson ignited the charge and the melted door handle disappeared, creating a 12 inch hole in the door. He carefully pushed open the door with his weapon ready for action.

"Lt. found them, those sons of demons, looks like there all dead for sure sir." Private Mac Phearson noted as he entered the room. Followed by Lt. Fred and a few others.

Lt. Fred looked at what was left of Corporal Noland, and it made him sick. It sure looked like the Neme's, as his friends chest was all but melted away, it was one of their beam weapons that was the only thing that could have done this type of damage, in fact all the bodies showed obvious signs of Neme weaponry as the cause of their deaths. He was becoming very enraged and his blood was boiling, there would be time for vengeance later, but now he had to report to Major Jones his findings.

He moved some of the bodies that had been tossed into a stack on and around the desk, and picked up the phone which still worked. Then he dialed up Major Jones office.

"Major, this is Lt. Fred I have a report for you." Lt. Fred said with a twinge of anger in his voice.

"Go, how bad is it then." Major Jones asked, knowing if Lt. Fred was worked up it must be bad.

"All are dead sir, 13 Bodies, Sargent Atherby and Corporal Noland and their men all dead sir, and piled up like trash in the Communications room, evidence is that Neme weaponry was used, and evidence of a small fire fight in the corridor outside the room Sir, I can definitely state it was Neme's that did this, And there is no sign of any Neme's injured or dead, looks like they surprised our guys and just slaughtered them Sir."

Major Jones paused, he knew that it would be bad but this was really bad, the Neme's had not tried this in a long time, to slaughter a whole sector team was not a normal thing, there must be some type of rogue military clan on the move.

"Lt. Fred, see to the dead, secure your position and stay put until A.N.T. 1 arrives, which should be shortly then notify me when they get there and I will give you your orders at that time how to proceed."

"Understood will do, and sir there must be payback for this."

"I understand, but do as I ordered, all in good time understood." Major Jones responded, he did not need his men out headhunting and out of control; he needed to have them thinking rationally before he made his next move. This would include some payback.

"Yes Sir, out." Lt. Fred said then ordered his men to secure their position and to start caring for the dead bodies of their fellow warriors.

Major Jones was on the phone immediately with Gen Sills.

"General, I have been informed that it was a Neme attack, all our team from sector 18 has been eliminated, that's 13 men Sir, and piled up in the communications room. No signs that any Neme's were wounded or killed. So it was a complete surprise, ambush Sir. My men are demanding some payback, when and how should we proceed Sir."

"Major, as soon as A.N.T. 1 gets to their position they will inform your men of their next action. I have given them full gloves off for this outrage. There will be payback as you say, however it will be done under their command, is that understood, Major." Gen. Sills told him sternly.

"Understood Sir. Will pass on the word. Out." Major Jones said and he hung up the phone, then he readied his gear for battle and headed out to join Lt. Fred and his team down in Sector 18. He was thinking, those were some good men, some friends of his, there would be some head collecting this time. These Neme's had crossed the wrong line with the wrong men this time.

* * * * *

Eeeleesssoe was moving swiftly, he had gathered his weapons and other tools he might need during his investigation of the disappearance of Seenswanee of Teesa, and he did not much care for the humans as they were a weak subspecies which must be ruled or eliminated eventually. If the Humans were at fault, and they had done evil to Seenswanee then there would be revenge upon them 10 fold. Until the blood lust of the Teesa was satisfied.

Eeeleesssoe did not much care for the tube system of transportation, yet it was needed to speed his arrival in the area of his search then he would use the many cavern tunnels he had grown up in, they had carved many of them, some were natural but all lead throughout the underworld. And now he enjoyed the run, for he did love to run while on the hunt, he could run for many hours without tiring, it quickened his blood, and made his senses fine-tuned for the hunt, for the battle. He was one with his ancestors and now he would do them and his Clan proud during this mission he was on.

It was not long until he entered the cavern just below the sector they called 18, where the team had been put together prior to their mission to sector 39. He would interrogate the human commanders at this place to see where the truth lay, if he sensed fear or deceit he would have to encourage their truth by physical means, with such a weak species, he would have to be careful not to kill them; however the game of interrogation would be quite entertaining for him at least. To kill them would only lead to a greater conflict and he was not allowed to start such a war that was up to the clan leadership for such an honor as declaring or starting war.

His job he must remain focused on was to find the truth, at any cost. So he would.

He knew where the secret entrances were on the various human habitats, they were well hidden but as 2nd Leader for security he knew the quick ways to get from one area to another, and where he could observe the humans without exposing himself to their view.

He stood quietly for some time looking over the corridor area of sector 18, he could smell the remnants of battle, he knew humans had died here he could smell their blood, and it quickened his heart and taste for battle as only the smell of prey could do. It was interesting that he saw no bodies, and no signs of Humans in the area. After a good while of waiting and observing he made the choice to search this area to see what the cause of the battle had been. Curious as he was, for if the humans had fought with the Neme's he would have known of it by now. However if they had chosen to turn on Seenswanee, then there would be reason for human blood, for he would not have gone quietly, he could easily have taken 10 humans to their deaths before they could overcome him at all. Could this be the betrayal then, the lie, saying they were lost to cover the treachery of murdering one of the Tessa. If this was so, then there would be war and these humans would surely die.

As he slowly and stealthily crept out from his hiding place he smelled the air for any signs of fear, and danger. Detecting none at that time he began his walk down the corridor area and shortly found the place of battle.

One of the communication rooms he noted had signs of battle; he could see the marks from the human's small weapons, their guns on the walls.

There had been battle here he knew death came to many humans, but he could not smell the blood of Seenswanee, no Nemekans had died here at least.

That was good. But the treachery was for sure, as he could see Seenswanee must have had to defend himself against some rogue foolish humans who thought they could murder a Nemekans Warrior. They found out they could not and it cost them their lives by the looks of it.

Suddenly the door to their communications room opened and he saw human soldiers carrying out their dead in those black bags they used for such purpose. He watched as he slowly backed away down to the corner of the corridor to watch and learn as he peered around the corner to see if he could hear any communications of the human's to see what had indeed taken place here, and if there were anything he could learn about where Seenswanee could have been taken.

What was that? A noise, from down the other corridor. Eeeleesssoe could now smell the foul smell of more humans there were more coming. It was time to go and report his findings to the Council so they can determine what is next to be done. Seenswanee must be found if they had him captured then they would do evil things to him as punishment for his defending himself from their evil human comrades.

He knew it was time to go, for this news must be told, he could not be taken now.

He slipped quietly back down the way he had come knowing the humans were behind him, he quickly ran towards his hidden entrance where he came in. He was just about to duck into the entrance to his tunnel when he heard the humans behind him shout at him. He turned to take a last look before he entered the safety of his dark tunnel. He saw a human in a new uniform to his eyes, black and white pattern of their camouflage he was raising a weapon he was not familiar with, how dare they do such a thing, then he felt the impact of heat and searing as the weapon was fired, he did not see any beam or did not hear any noise, but he felt his flesh tear in great pain as it hit his left shoulder leaving a huge slash of torn flesh, if he had not turned so quickly he could have easily been killed instead of just wounded. This was indeed an act of war by these lesser species for he had made no aggression towards them, they had attacked while his back was turned, such cowardly acts from these hairless monkeys.

He was able to hide the entrance with his tool so that they would not be able to follow him, then he ran a little ways before he stopped to tend to his wound. He was able to stop the bleeding with his medical kit, however he would need an expert healer to heal this wound, so he dressed it as well as he could, and realizing quickly that he could not run without reinjuring it, he would have to walk until he could find a tube vehicle to take him faster to the Counsel of Tessa, and once there he would relate the Treachery, and the unwarranted attack upon himself, and what he assumed must have happened to Seenswanee. The humans had crossed the line again, and this time all of the Nemekans would come to bear and punish them once and for all. They would be put in their place, and disarmed, and made slaves. For thus have they started the war against us. They have drawn first blood, however we of Clan Tessa shall bathe in their blood for thus it will be. War!

These were his thoughts as he planned his report for the council upon his arrival home.

* * * * *

Lt. Fred turned to Sargent Alvin of A.N.T. 1,"

The new sensor I put in the corridor by the communication room just went off, there was motion there. I think your plan worked, let's see what we have caught." Lt. Fred said.

"Agreed, they may of come back to gloat upon their kill, they may have come back to take the dead and fest upon them. Let's go see what we have." Sargent Alvin said as he took point and headed down the corridor.

As they rounded the corner they saw a Huge Neme, Green in color must have been over 10 feet tall, he was running towards a wall in the huge open cavern room.

"Stop!" Sargent Alvin ordered as he yelled at the Neme who was running from them.

The Neme did not stop, but ran quickly to the wall, then it seemed as if he were merging with it, he was getting away.

Sargent Alvin raised his weapon and took aim at the Neme's Head, then fired his weapon.

It was a beam style weapon like a laser but it was not visible light, it shot a heat wave that cut like a knife.

He saw the Neme turn suddenly as he hit him in the shoulder, visibly wounding the Neme, for he saw him stop and look at him with astonishment and anger in his eyes, then he was gone. He just vanished into the rock face.

He and his team crossed the area, coming to the wall they felt all over it and could find no opening. It was solid. Darn it, he thought.

"Well looks like he got away, however we know these new weapons work much better than the old guns we used to shoot these things with. It tore right into him. This means that next time we are on a more even footing, this one got away, but it proves he was here and could be the one who killed our men. He was large enough to take them all unawares. And they were not armed with these new weapons as we are. I think it was a Tessa by the color. Now we have proof and we need to tell the General and get everyone on board.

I think the Neme's want a war, and we will give it to them. They after all started it by murdering our men." Sargent Alvin stated with emotion rising in his voice, emotion of anger and one of revenge for the fallen soldiers.

"Yes indeed it will be time for some payback, we all need to arm ourselves with your new gun, and then we will teach them a lesson, finally." Lt. Fred stated.

CHAPTER 25

New Specie's

Sariah awoke with a sense of dread, she had been dreaming and in her dream she felt all freedom of movement gone like she was tied down. As she opened her eyes she realized she was once again in restraints on a table in a cold room. She was unable to move as her legs, arms, and body had leather straps holding her down, as well as one on her forehead and chin leaving her unable to even turn her head this time.

She was scared; this was not the first time since her meeting with the science team that had been tormenting her. Some days it felt like torture both physically and emotionally. The experiments they had done had left her physically worn down, then the mental tortures were too awful to want to think about, she had been water boarded, sleep deprivation, and other things to test her strengths and weaknesses and she wished it could all stop, if she could wish herself dead she would have done so days ago. Well not really but it felt like it was the only way to leave this place would be to just die. To accept her fate and fall into the peaceful sleep of death, at least then she would be free of this evil place.

But she was strong in spirit, and the thought that Levi could still be alive somewhere and needing her help. No one knew where they were she was definite on that issue. So if she could somehow survive maybe she could eventually find out what these evil men had done with Levi, and find a way to get them both free from this insanity. That one thought was keeping her going; she had to survive if only to help her brother.

She heard movement to her left, and moved her eyes to try and see what was there. She saw a shadow or was it shadows just outside the lighted area in the room, there was a light above the table she was on, but the edges of the room were dark and it was hard to see who was there and she was scared of what they were going to do to her today.

All her senses were alive the ones she normally took for granted, her ears, nose and eyes however she also had a sense like a sixth sense that had been growing stronger she could almost feel when others were in the room, feel their presence this was new and yet strange to her at the same time.

She felt there were men present however today she felt a new presence something different, something that made her skin crawl with fear, she was unsure of what it could be but she knew one thing, she felt a powerful darkness or evil somewhere in the room just outside of her view of sight. But now she was fully awake and her senses became fully aware she noticed a strange odor outside the normal smells of this place. She had become accustomed to the smells of the room, the men and women who came and went. But now she could not really place it, it was an unusual odor. She thought for a moment then a twinge of fear crept back into her again, it smelled like a snake or lizard or a dirty cage that had housed them, like one of her friends back home had some rattle snakes and a lizard as pets, this was similar only a stronger smell and it bothered her.

She had to get a hold of herself, she would go crazy if she let her mind run wild with all the what if's that were now popping into her mind. Where they going to poison her or torture her with snakes now? Why was there a smell of them, there must be some reptiles in the room now but what were they going to do with them, and to her? These people were evil that she knew, and now this. Her heart began to break in hopelessness again. Why me what did I ever do to deserve this.

Movement again in the shadows, then she heard a slow hissing sound like a lizard smelling the air or a deep breath with the exhale of a long slow hiss. That for some reason made the small hairs on her body stand up on end, as if she was in an electric storm. Some basic instinct some basic fear began to grow in her and she felt herself growing on the verge of panic. The figure in the shadows had moved and was now walking closer to her just outside the ring of light, and she could tell now it was a very tall figure, it seemed strange out of place she felt like she was in a dream again, she wished it was all just that a bad dream, she would awaken in her room any time now and it would be all over.

Then she heard them speak.

"Dr. Black it would seem our guest is now awake and fully aware of our presence shall we proceed." Tech Smith said. She knew this voice as he was the person who had become her guard and would bring her food and deal with her on a daily basis these last few days.

"Indeed it is time. Dr. White why don't you let our young volunteer know what you have finally chosen for her or shall I say her new gift." Dr. Black said with a glint of satisfaction in his voice.

At this time she noticed the three men step into the light around her on her right side, however the shadow to her left still stood just outside the light and she could not make out yet who it was, but something in her felt a great fear of what could be lurking in the shadows and she was not sure why she felt that way.

"Well Sariah, today we shall begin your preparations and the process to give you a gift we have been perfecting these last many years, you should feel honored and grateful, your help with our program is very much welcomed even if you do not agree with it, you will indeed be a new and fully developed evolution in the human species. Based on our tests you will be able to assimilate the process well, or you should. If your body accepts the process and I have no doubt of that, you will be able to in time mother a new breed of humans, just think of yourself as our new evolutionary Eve." Dr. White said with a arrogantly prideful smile of self-worth on his face. He was very much pleased with himself and his intelligence.

What were they going to do now, this White what he had said scared her, new species? What in the world where they going to do now? She was really scared now and a tear emerged from her eye and slowly rolled down her cheek.

"What are you going to do to me?" Sariah asked in a frightened scared sobbing voice.

"As I said you will have the honor of becoming part of the evolution of the human species, a hybrid being. No worry to fear the process for the outcomes does outweigh the discomfort, and I promise you this that won't last very long at all. You see we have finally perfected the process so your transformation should go very well as long as your body accepts the changes. And we see from our testing that you should do just fine." Dr. White said.

"Now we just need to give you something to help your journey be more, well I will say just a little less uncomfortable." With that Dr. Smith put a needle in her arm and injected something into her.

Sariah soon felt like she was floating in space and not soon after discovered herself in a type of dream state as she drifted off into a deep sleep.

"See how the subject is so compliant with our program, they never really complain from this point on, well as long as they survive the process." Dr. Black said smiling.

"You may now begin the transformation process." Dr. White said as he looked at the dark figure who was still standing in the shadows of the room.

Ssslaoosee of the Garsar, Head of the Human Experimentation Team stepped forward from the shadows, with a thin grin across his face, tongue flickering a few times.

He stood just over 9 feet tall by human standards, and his tail was a commanding 5 feet long as he was from good breading.

His many years of experimentations on humans and other species of the outer crust dwelling creatures had given him much challenge and pleasure for his goal of cross breeding them to see what would happen, To see his trial and errors finally come to a successful conclusion, or the beginning of a new species would bring him finally much honor to himself and his clan.

Finally these inept humans had found one among them that was physically and mentally qualified to survive the process, this young female would indeed someday give birth to a new species, His species for he was as the God's of old, he was now a creator of beings.

He relished in his self-importance and wisdom, yes the Clan would have the majority of the glory for that is how it was, but he knew that it was His training and work that paid off finally and would bring much glory to himself as well as to Clan Garsar, He hoped in the future it could lead to the reinstatement of their Clan to the seat of power as the ruling Clan once again.

Ssslaoosee approached the table, as he did so he spoke.

"Yes it is time at last to begin our journeys into the futures of your race, with our help we indeed have becomes the creators of new species..."

Ssslaoosee waved for his assistants to help him with the procedures that would take hours, but would be well worth it in the end. All gathered around, bringing the instruments and other needed items that would assist them in the transformation of this young female subject into the next phase in the evolution of the humans.

* * * * *

Sariah was not sure where she was anymore, she remembered vaguely a doctor speaking with her and then all went dark; she had fallen into an abyss of nothingness.

Now she felt strange and she ached all over. She was not sure if she dared move, or if in fact she could move. She turned her head and received for her efforts a blinding head ache that pierced her eyes with pain. She closed her eyes and a new fear began to creep into her.

What did they do to her, her arms, legs, actually her whole body hurt. But as she began to move a little here and there to see how things felt, she realized that her back and sides hurt the worst.

She seemed to be lying on a large bed of some kind, it did feel soft a lot better than the last bed she had found herself on in the past. But still she was not sure if she wanted to fully move so she just lay there becoming familiar with her surroundings by letting her eyes wander around her room and she only moved her head ever so slightly so as not to receive another head ache.

She was in a dimly lighted room, there was a closet it seemed in the corner, and then a bathroom with a large shower, toilet and sink was what she could see from her bed. She also noted there was what looked to be a miniature refrigerator with a sink and counter on the other side of the room. Interesting it would seem as if she was in an apartment now of some type. There was a window on the other wall however it was covered by curtain.

Her ceiling was plain with a light centered in the middle of it. Her floor still seemed to be a hard cold tile which was really an improvement over the plain concrete from her last prison cell.

Well after laying there for some time she felt she needed to get up and see what shape she was really in. She slowly sat up into a sitting position on the edge of her bed; her legs hung over the side her feet touching the cold tile floor that sent a shiver up her legs.

She was in some type of surgical gown, so they had done something to her, but what? That evil Dr. said something about transformation, a new type of human, sounded crazy. However she was worried they had done some evil thing to her.

She looked at her feet, legs and hands then her arms and found no changes. However there was an itching along her sides and her back area where her shoulder blades were, they seem to ache a lot and felt strange.

Well she hoped there was a mirror in the bathroom and she could see what damage they may have done to her. So she readied herself to stand up so she could walk to the bathroom.

As she stood her head ached again, and she was a bit dizzy and almost blacked out. She caught herself on the edge of the bed and stood there leaning on it a moment till her head cleared. It must be the drugs they had used on her she thought. Finally she was able to fully stand; she stood there a minute to make sure she would not lose her balance. Then she began to walk the short distance to the bathroom.

Again she leaned on the door way once she got there, and she took the moment to see that yes there was a mirror over the small sink. It was some type of polished metal not of glass. As she stood now before the mirror, she was horrified to see her face all bruised and swollen, in fact she realize that most of her body looked bruised and swollen. However there was her back, she wanted to look and see what they did to her, but it also frightened her to think about it as well. Her back did seem heavier than normal like she was wearing a day pack and it ached as well.

Slowly she began to turn sideways to the mirror so she could see what was wrong with her back.

What she saw was a large lump it rose a little above her shoulders and actually was lower than her butt she was amazed she did not realize this when she sat up on the bed, she was pretty numbed up still. However this lump on her back was starting to spook her and she started to get frightened, she could not tell fully what they had attached to her back, it was still covered and taped or strapped to conceal it, she realized the straps also crossed her chest and stomach area. She suddenly felt sick, really sick and she fell down over the toilet and began to vomit whatever was left in her stomach, then dry heaved for what seemed like 10 minutes or so.

Just as she finished her dry heaves, and was gathering herself and trying to come to grips with what had happened or what was happening to her it all seemed like some bad nightmare that she was not able to awaken from. That is when she heard the door to her room open, and she turned to see three men and one of the doctors enter the room.

"Well it looks like our little hybrid has awakened from her sleep finally." Dr. Black said as he stood and watched his men go and pick up the girl and help her back to her bed.

He watched her for a moment then spoke.

"Your operation was a success from the stand point of the physical, however now we must keep a watch on your mental status, Do you feel frightened in anyway, or panicky?" Dr. Black asked her.

Sariah just sat on her bed and looked at this Dr. If he was actually a real Dr. or not she did not care at this point.

"What did you do to me, she asked softly, for her voice was crackly and horse."

"Well as I said you should be honored for the privilege to be chosen for such a wonderful gift as you have received. You are weak, but that is normal. To explain the procedure would take too long and you would not understand it anyway, thus I shall be simple.

"You are the 1st human that was able to survive the process to this point, you should be honored. You are a special thing now, you see we have changed or begun the change in your DNA code print; we did several things that will become evident soon. Part of the process from our Allies who are Great Scientists and we could not have done this without their help. Now I shall tell you what we have begun. However I need you to remain calm and relaxed as best you can, try not to let your emotions overpower your being for this could damage the acceptance process that has begun.

Know this yours is a very special DNA code and unique and was very hard to find for it has accepted the new DNA coding that was necessary to complete this process of transformation.

You see we have changed your body; we have created a hybrid between you and another species known as the Nemekans. With their help we have given you some of their shall I say, superior qualities. In the hope that we can better the human race as a whole." Dr. Black stated rather proudly of his success.

"What are you talking about; you're not making any sense at all. What did you do?" Sariah said sadly.

Dr. Black motioned for the men standing beside her to undue the wrapping upon her back. As they began to reveal his creation he spoke calmly to her, to prevent he hoped any panic attack she would have.

"You see my dear, the Nemekans have some DNA that intrigues us, and some of their race have wings. The actual ability to fly. We felt that if we could create a human hybrid with the same type of wings we could transform the race to another level of existence. This could improve our race as a whole, for a lot of reasons." Dr. Black stated as the assistants finished removing the cover, and then they stood back.

"Now you're going to be sore for a while, and you may not be able to move them much at this time, you see your mind needs to accept then learn how to communicate with your new body parts, they must finish the neurological wiring process and then you must learn to use them as they grow stronger.

Like when you first learned to walk, or speak, it was not immediate. It took time and practice to be successful at it. "Dr. Black stated, then watched her for her response, if she were to panic. If she did begin to panic he would need to sedate her quickly, to prevent her from injuring herself both mentally and physically.

"But that's not possible, is it? How can you do that to me, or anyone? You are telling me I am just a guinea pig, a test rat in your lab. You have...."

Sariah said and her voice trailed off as she felt what must have been her new body parts wiggle, a twinge of discomfort but they actually moved some it was strange, yet as mad as she was, something inside her felt a little excitement about something new, and that scared her as well as gave her a sense of awe.

She stood back up, and the men standing on each side of her helped her keep her balanced this time. She walked back to the bathroom with their help, and looked into the mirror again and she turned once more to view her back, this time she noticed the bruises, scar's and incisions and stitches all over her back and sides, indeed there was a pair of wings on her back, however not what she would call wings, no feathers. They seemed closer to the pictures she had seen in books about dinosaurs; they had the look of the wings of a flying lizard, all skin and bones.

As she realized what they had done she felt overwhelmed again, and became very dizzy, then she felt herself falling into the abyss of darkness again.

She never felt the men catch her before she hit the floor, or that they carried her back to her bed and placing her in it.

"Thank you men for your assistance, that will be all for now." Dr. Black told them.

With that the men nodded and left the room.

"Well my darling little hybrid, this was expected. It is good that you seem to be able to accept the facts of your transformation, or it would seem you do. I shall return, and then we will make plans for your new beginning, your new life. You will if all goes well become the mother of a whole new version of the human race. So sleep you must for now." Dr. Black said, as he smiled to himself lost in his own thoughts, which were many, and most he had kept to himself.

Dr. Black turned and left the room the door behind him closed and self locked once again.

CHAPTER 26

Another Failure

Elasseear stood silent as he watched Lassoos and his helpers prepare the new harvester for use.

Soon they would erase their mistakes, and complete the harvest of this little human. Then he would regain good standing with Sosaeen who had made subtle and some obvious threats to him if they did not succeed this time.

So with his keen eyes he saw to this harvest personally so as to make sure nothing went wrong.

The boy lay sleeping and had been sufficiently prepared again although it seemed confused but calm and that is what they needed for success was a calm subject.

At last all was ready.

"Tech George be prepared to keep the boy calm during the process."

Lassoos told the human. He had done his work well enough last time, he was making sure for nothing to add to the possible repeat of the mistake, this must be a perfect harvest this time.

"I understand what I must do, these last few cycles I have been able to create a bond with the boy so it should be easier to keep him calm as he awakens for the harvest." George told him, these were arrogant overgrown lizards but they did have their purposes.

"That is well then, awaken the boy all is prepared." Lassoos ordered.

George who was now standing by the table where Levi lay, gently began to shake the boys shoulder to bring him out of his drug induced sleep once again, it was so easy to drug the food most never catch on to it. The boy began to stir, and then slowly opened his eyes.

"Where am I?" Levi asked groggily.

"You are fine, we are going to try and restore your lost memories, there is a new scientific process that has been working for those with amnesia. You should be honored to have the opportunity to have yours restored. It is harmless." George said.

"So it won't hurt then? Why am I tied down? I can't move." Levi asked becoming alarmed.

"The process is very delicate, you see if you move even your head it could do permanent damage to your brain, so we must strap your body down so that it cannot move for your protection and to be able to have the doctor's do their procedure in a correct and successful way. So don't worry about the straps." George said, he had been rehearsing all the possible questions over and over in his mind. This had to go right this time, the Neme's were very anxious now for success after their last failure. Or the harvesters melt down. He did not want any blame to come towards him if it failed again. He knew the Neme's leadership did not allow much failure before severe punishments were handed out.

"If you say so. It won't take long will it?" Levi asked.

"No not long at all, last time the machine had a malfunction so they had to get a new one. So it won't be long before you remember what you have forgotten in the accident. So just relax now, the more relaxed you are the better the machine works." George told him as he smiled down upon the boy in a very comfortable and hopeful tone of voice. All your troubles will be over very soon. And he could get back to more important matters.

Levi tried to relax as best he could; he was confused still and if this machine would fix his memory that would be great. But he did not like being tied down; it did not feel right at all. All he could do was move his eyes and the room was all dark, but around the table where he and George were.

He thought he could sense movement in the shadows like darker shadows moving inside the darkness but that could be his imagination. He could smell now a low snaky odor that was weird, he wondered if they had some pet snakes in cages close to this room. Oh well he would have to see about asking George about it when this was over.

"The boy is ready if you are." George told the others in the room that operated the Harvester.

"Very well we shall begin." Lassoos responded.

He lowered the machine once again over the boy, targeting the forehead once more this would all be over soon and he would regain some lost respect from his leader. He pressed the buttons that would begin the harvest.

Levi looked up at the lighted machine as it focused on his forehead, it was like being X-rayed like after the horse had kicked him in the head a few years ago he had learned the hard way not to sneak up on a horse from behind.

He felt a sudden electrical feeling like the last time they tried to do this. A warm and calming feeling his whole body seemed electrified the hairs standing on end it was strange. He felt like he was floating and about ready to go into a deep sleep again. Then he heard that strange melodious voice as if in a dream again.

"Lassoos it is happening once more, look at the screen." Elasseear said alarmingly.

All in the room watched in amazement and alarm as the harvester once more had problems with this subject. The essence grew once again and changed into unusual colors before the brilliant light of white once again filled the whole of the monitors then the machine failed to function just as the last one did.

George watched as he saw an alarm or panic in the eyes of the Neme's working the harvester something was wrong again, and then he looked down on the boy and took several steps back away from the table in amazement and a little fear.

"Look, look at the boy!" George said alarmingly to all in the room.

All had been so busy looking at the harvester screens they had failed to see what was taking place with the boy on the table.

The boy seemed to be floating, the straps had failed as well, and the boy was emanating a white glow as he floated about 2 feet above the table.

All in the room were speechless for none had ever witnessed anything of this nature before.

Moments later Elasseear knew what must be done. He contacted Sosaeen.

"Sosaeen, the harvester has failed again same as before, there is some strange magic at play here, you must see the visual record of this last attempt to witness for yourself the strangeness of the matter." Elasseear humbly reported to his leader.

"You say magic? I am not to be made a fool of Elasseear, so beware if I see nothing but ineptness on your part on these visual records You will be severely punished for your failures on such an easy matter. Is that understood now send the visuals to me and I shall see the truth of your problems." Sosaeen reported bluntly to him.

"It will be done; even now they are being transmitted to your location." Elasseear replied and shut off the communication device.

He looked over at the boy; Lassoos was now standing there by him with George and a few others in the room, slowly the boy floated down upon the table gently and the white glow that surrounded his form disappeared.

There was something very strange about this subject; he was more than a mere human boy. Of that he was sure of now for something, or someone was protecting the boy from their harvesting of his essence. He would let Sosaeen view and make the choice of the day's events however he would need to speak to one of the old wise one's, who may now of such magic. He would need to speak to Groomasssee of the Etosa.

Sosaeen stood watching the visual of events in the harvester room many times his tail twitching in greater amazement, he realized that indeed this was a special human subject; his essence indeed was powerful to have achieved the destruction of two harvesters. He would send these visual records and a report to Ssslaoosee he would know how to precede with this unexpected and very unusual finding. He may even be rewarded for such a rare find as this one.

CHAPTER 27

Searchers Discovered

They had left the tube car a while ago, for traffic seemed to have increased on the tub system and it was now better and stealthier to go on foot, through the caverns and tunnel systems.

Gideon and David were ahead walking point they had been switching off with Tim and James as they maneuvered through the passageways.

Fairsong, Ben, James, then Tarton followed not far behind in the rear at this time was Joe and Julio making sure they were not followed or noticed.

Gideon held up his hand for all to stop. And then he signaled for Fairsong to come forward.

"What is it" Fairsong spoke quietly for noise traveled easily here.

"We are at a cross roads it seems, notice this is a large cavern with multiple avenues in many directions we can take from here. Have Ben see if he can divine which is the best way to continue, as he does so it would be good to rest a moment and have some food before we continue." Gideon stated. He had almost lost track of time he just had to keep up on the hours with his watch, it was unusual how time seems to be lost as one travels underground with no natural sun and night to be your companions.

"It is good, pass the word to the others and we shall do as you advise." Fairsong stated.

Then he went over to Ben.

"Ben we are at a junction here as you can see, let's see where the Lev Antas Shuesa guides us from here."

Ben nodded and brought forth the Lev Antas Shuesa from its resting place, and proceeded to activate it, this was becoming easier now to use as he became more familiar with its workings.

He focused first on Sariah; he was confused that he could not immediately find her as easy as he did the last time. Her marker was a lot fainter in the device. (He had discovered that he could use a marker color a little glowing particle for both Sariah and Levi each a different color, Sariah was Gold and Levi Silver. The closer they got to them the stronger the glow of each marker.)

"I seem to be having problems finding Sariah now; she is not very strong see here its fluctuating in strength, what could it mean?"

James who was standing over Ben and watching with interest as he searched for his children's locations again, this was an amazing gift or product of science that kept him wondering about other such tools he had read about, that seem to be magic, but in reality they were just tools that ran on principals of nature or science that current humanity did not understand so they would call it miraculous or magic. Thus have many things over the generations since the days of Father Adam and Mother Eve that have been sent or created to assist humanity in its journey here on Earth have been deemed by some magic or gifts of heaven. He remembered the journey of the Jadeites and the use of their clear stones that God had touched and turned into glowing lights so they would not cross the great oceans to the Ancient Northern lands of America so long ago, then the compass the Liahona that by description was not much different than this tool Ben now used. That led other ancients to the North America's from the ancient lands of the Middle East so long ago. Yes tools like these and others spoken of have been prepared for the usefulness of humanity in their times of need.

Now James wondered why Ben was having a more difficult time locating Sariah, since it was growing stronger the last few times he had looked for her.

"What is it, why would you have a weakened signal? Is she alright, is she hurt? Would that affect the signal strength?" James asked Fairsong.

"Let me see then, (Fairsong bends down to Ben who was kneeling on the floor and looks into the device) Yes she is there and it is weaker, James if she has been injured it could affect the strength, for if her spirit was weaker, or if she has been moved, or maybe if ...(he paused with the thought of what he would say next, for it had been a fear in the back of his mind)...maybe if her being has been changed it would affect the signal."

"What do you mean changed?" James asked.

"It has long been a practice of those taken by the Nemekans and their human comrades to use some as experiments, thus changing their physical body in some strange way, always trying to create hybrids that would do their bidding, it is an evil practice my people have always sought out to find and destroy such labs over the generations, such are the abominations of these creatures. However do not Fear such at this time, she may only have been moved deeper into the underworld for many reasons. Ben you're searching for her as she last appeared in your memory, try searching now for her heart and mind search for her spirit thus if any physical harm has occurred it seldom affects the heart, mind, spirit of a person. This may help." Fairsong stated.

"They use us for experiments like rats then?" Tarton who had joined the little gathering had heard what Fairsong had said.

"Yes if it seems there is a need, and worse things they can do, however we shall focus on the positive and hope for the best. We must put our trust in the Creator of all to bless and protect them until we join with them and are able to rescue them from their captor's." Fairsong told Tarton giving him a warning glance in the hope he would not focus on the negative possibilities or outcomes.

"I see." Tarton replied, he noticed the message Fairsong had given and he was right we must focus on the being positive for Ben and James and the rest of us.

Ben now focusing as Fairsong suggested noticed her glow a little stronger but not by much.

"Where is Levi? Are we any closer to him yet?" James asked.

"I will see." Ben replied and he focused all his energy on searching for Levi. The little silver glow did seem stronger than Sariah's, as he was focusing on direction something really different happened.

Suddenly the little silver glow of Levi became a pulsating dot, then it grew larger and larger and become white and all but encompassed the whole of the Lev Antas Shuesa, it was a powerful and strong glow it lasted for about 30 seconds then returned to only twice the size of the original silver glowing marker that was Levi's. Then the words written in silver appeared under Levi's marker, they read. 'Make Haste Levi', Ben shocked at the sudden happening, looked at Fairsong.

"What do you make of that?" Ben asked Fairsong.

Fairsong who had witnessed the remarkable event with the rest present took a moment of thought on this matter before he spoke.

"Someone else is watching over Levi until we can obtain him. I have heard of events like this but they are of older times, what I think just occurred is that the spirits have chosen to protect Levi from some evil that was taking place, the Nemekans tried to harm him, and the energy spike could only have been a form of protection for him. This is unusual, this is also worrisome. Levi is in danger and this will draw unexpected attention on him from the leaderships of the clans of the Nemekans for they are drawn to that which is unusual or different. I suggest we now focus on Levi's rescue first, and soon." Fairsong said in a worried and urgent tone in his voice.

"I think I have it, There that is the next tunnel we shall use to lead us to Levi." Ben said as he pointed to the 3rd opening to the right of their current position.

"Very well then, 1st let us rest and eat for we will need our strength once we find Levi." Fairsong stated.

As they ate, they spoke quietly to each other of the journey, and learned some more of each other along the way. They learned that David and Gideon had been in Utah for an educational meeting on weapons and tactics that the I.D.F. (Israel Defense Forces) had been using to successfully route out terrorists and other bad guys. They represented certain companies who supplied training and materials to American agency's both government or private who needed their advice to protect those who concerned them. So they had been in Salt Lake when Olaf had contacted them for help. Gideon owed Olaf a debt; he would say a life debt, as Olaf had saved his life in a past conflict. So he came and his good friend David chose to assist. That is how they found themselves now on the rescue mission.

Joe, Tim, James shared a little about themselves they preferred not to share much about their personal lives, however they let the group know that their nation had been in conflicts with these creatures Fairsong called Nemekans, but that it was not spoken of in public.

The rest just shared as they went not a lot but enough to familiarize each other and the capabilities or the lack thereof. So Fairsong and Gideon made sure that all were spread out in line based on experience or lack of evenly to the benefit of the whole group.

"It is time, the ball has spoken we must make haste, so we shall. I will walk point now as we move out." Tim said and with that he seeing all were ready, he slowly and cautiously moved to the next tunnel opening that Ben had pointed out and began the next phase of their journey.

The rest followed quietly and each now lost in his own thoughts about the mission.

As the last one vanished into the darkness none had noticed that a lone set of eyes had watched their passing. The eyes of a faded orange colored Nemekans one's who has seen many more years than most, he had felt the presence of these humans and had come to see who or what they were about, He had seen the device the boy carried, he had witnessed the glowing and heard their words to each other. As he thought what to do, he knew what had to be done. He would send word to find this boy they called Levi, who must be with the Garsar's now, this must be the boy spoken of by the whispers of words, who did destroy a harvester not long past, if these are his clan who search for him, he is special no doubt, then he would see how he could assist them, for he had no kindness towards the Garsar's and their ways of darkness.

It may just be the time, and yet a few more things must occur to be in complete fulfillment, but this could be the moment his clan and others have awaited for a very long time.

He stealthily waited until he could no longer hear those who searched for their clan members, and then he stood and began his journey as well but by another route. He would go to the corridor where the Garsar's did their harvesting and find this human and see what the boy was about for himself.

Who am I one might ask, one who long ago was a leader, a guide, one who knew the spiritual and wisdom one who knew the dangerous truth of who truly ruled the clans, that darkness that overtook his race long ago, he was one who sought for freedom, not of himself but for all those yet unborn. He was once in the great councils of old, now banished. He was Zsaaleessao of the Etosa.

As he walked he puzzled about the one called Fairsong, he had a familiarity about him he was unsure of, like the old mists of time there was a slight twinge of something and yet he could not quite grasp it as it played upon his old memories, teasing them but without conclusion. Interesting he thought, or rather felt.

CHAPTER 28

Mistrust and Assumptions

Sariah was awakened by a young woman she had never met before who entered her room while she was asleep, she had gently shaken her shoulder until she awoke.

"Hello Sariah, my name is Samantha, I work with Dr. Black and he has asked that I come and see how you're doing. I am a recovery Nurse and physical therapist Dr. Black would like us to see how your body is responding to its new tissues."

"I am very sore, I feel bruised all over and it hurts to move much." She told Samantha sadly.

"That is to be expected, I have some medicine that should help with the pain and discomfort since the operation. We do need to get you on your feet and moving around now; it will help in the healing process. Later we will see if your nervous system will be able to control your new wings, we will start a little at a time and go slowly during the learning process for your body to come to an understanding with your wings and how they will function. It's a lot like learning to walk all over again." Samantha said.

"I feel like I need a bath or shower, do you think it would be ok to do that?" Sariah said, she had come to grips with the fact her body was now different and changed for good, so she may as well learn to deal with it.

"Yes you can, that's another reason I am here and not any of the males, I can help you with those things and make sure your healing in a good way and you have no infections, but we will need to have only a mildly warm shower to start with, if it's too hot it could adversely affect your healing right now. So before we have breakfast then, let's get you cleaned up and some new clothes on you. It will help you feel much better." Samantha said smiling at the poor girl, she was glad that she had lived through her ordeal many others in the past had not. This was a special and strong gal and she would do what she could under the circumstances to help her recover well.

Samantha left her by the bed and went to the shower and started the warm water flowing at a nice soothing rate, not too hard of a stream as that would only hurt the girl. Then she went back to the bed, and helped Sariah stand up and walk to the bathroom shower.

There she helped her into the shower and checked her for any signs of infections as she helped wash her back and other area's she was too sore to wash herself.

When the shower was done, she helped her dry off then handed her some clothing.

"Here this is specially designed to accommodate your new wings; I will help you put them on until you can do it yourself. If you do not mind that is."

"I don't mind, and thanks for the help the shower did help me feel much better, I think I will need to rely on you for a few days or until I can figure out how to do things on my own again. Thanks for the clothing I hope it fits."

"Do you have any feeling in them yet? Have you tried to move any part of them?" Samantha asked.

"Outside of the pain, aches and stuff, no. I have been afraid to try to do anything with them; I think it would hurt too much right now. It kinda feels like a broken arm that is healing, I am not sure if I want to try to move them."

"Well for now then let's get used to walking and sitting, then lying down without hurting yourself. Maybe tomorrow we will see if your mind and body can make them move just a little wiggle to see if the nervous system is alright." Samantha said, she knew this was going to be a long process, and if all worked out well Sariah would soon come to learn how wonderful this was going to be for her, it would open up a whole new world, now if the DNA transfers also where complete and successful in time she would be a mother to a whole new race or version of humanity. This was a future goal, but to her a worthy one.

Samantha would spend the whole day with Sariah helping her learn the basics of living with her new body parts, as well as helping her emotionally just being there talking with her. It had seemed forever since she was able to just spend time with anyone just talking.

Samantha made her some meals from the refrigerator in her room, and then she had to go but promised she would return latter in the day.

* * * * *

"General Sills office Staff Sergeant. Symrai what can I do for you?" Lt. Fred heard as he phoned up the Generals office.

"Staff Sergeant. I need to speak with the General immediately."

"I'll put you through." Staff Sergeant. Symrai said. She knew something bad was happening But was not fully sure what.

"General Sills, what's going on down there?" General Sills asked Lt. Fred.

"General, It's the Neme's we were in the final stages of removing the last of the murdered men when the a sensor I had placed in the area alerted us, We went to see who set it off, A.N.T. 1 was just getting here and Sargent Alvin ordered the Neme to stop and it refused then he shot and wounded the Neme before it disappeared into a wall. Sir, it was a very large Green Tessa Sir, A.N.T.1 must have spooked it from its hiding place so it ran. That is my update Sir."

"Sounds like you did what was needed, I am going to alert the base and put them into a level 1 lock down until we can see if this is only an isolated incident, a rogue Neme or if it is something bigger. This could have something to do with our missing team. Now we have more deaths, and it looks like it could be a group of Neme's out to cause problems. So lock down your area you are now on level 1 and Sargent Alvin will share with you what will need to happen there. Do you understand?" Gen. Sills said.

"Yes Sir, I understand, will update you if anything more happens here." Then he heard the phone hang up on the Generals end.

"Well men we are now on a level 1 lock down finish what you're doing as fast as you can, then we will go from there." Lt. Fred told his men.

"Sargent. Alvin, we will need to talk and you can update us on your new weapon you wounded that Neme with." As he led the Sargent away from the group so they could talk.

* * * * *

General Sills put his phone down, and then pushed the button for his Staff Sargent Symrai to come into his office. She came quickly.

"Symrai, order level 1 lock down, all humans are to immediately go to a secure area, and to separate themselves from all Neme's immediately until further notice is that understood."

"Yes Sir." Staff Sergeant. Symrai said and she left the office and began the process to comply with the Generals orders. This is serious she thought.

* * * * *

Sariah heard the door begin to open to her room the sound of it had awaken her from her sleep. As she turned her head to look to see who was coming in she saw it was Samantha. She was sore all over and felt like one big bruise. She slowly sat up on her bed and as she did so her head exploded with a big migraine once again and she winced with the pain.

"Good afternoon, looks like you're having some discomfort, I brought you something for the pain so here take a few of these and it will help." Samantha told Sariah as she handed her some pills and a cup full of water.

"Thanks, I think. Have they done this to anyone else?"

"I really am not to talk about that, but there have been similar things done in the past, I am just here to help you recover, and to see if we can get you to return to a more normal balance of life with your knew body.

"In a little while we will try some movements of your wings to see if the nerves have joined properly, it is too early to do much else but some exercises to get you used to commanding the wings and to get them stronger over time.

"It's like learning to walk, only in the future when you are strong enough you should be able to fly to some extent, but that is up to you when you feel stronger."

"Do you really think I will fly then?"

"You should, the size of the wings is not the issue, and the design and strength are. There are other beings in the world that can that are larger than us, so it should work fine for you."

"Other beings, what do you mean." Sariah asked curiously. If she was to have to live with this new body, she may as well face that as a fact and learn as much as she could about what was really going on here; she still had to find a way to escape and find Levi and get him home, If she could. So for now she had to recover and then figure out the rest along the way.

"You're going to find out soon enough, you see there is a race called Nemekans they are large and reptilian, and some do have wings the larger ones. They can get as tall as 15 feet and they are very powerful and fly very well. The doctors of both races have been trying to create a hybrid of our races for some time to better join our races together so they might get along better. It will improve the human race they say, but we will see.

"You Sariah are the first who's DNA has been able to adapt to the foreign DNA mix of the Neme's. Yours alone, there have been many attempts but none as successful as yours. You are very special in this way and if you continue with no rejections then you will make history amongst both races."

"So where then is my brother, Levi? Have you done some experimentation on him as well then? What have you done to him?" Sariah asked she was truly worried about Levi and what these evil people could have done to him.

"I did not know you had a brother, if he is here I have not been told of it, and actually would not be for there are many different groups here. I can ask around and see if I can find anything out about him, but I really doubt I will learn anything. Security here is very tight." Samantha said she was worried now she had said too much to this girl about the workings of the base; however she did need to gain her trust and friendship if she was to recover and become fully functional. And this she felt was the best way to help that happen. She would ask but she knew if there were family members in this place they were always kept separate.

"Thanks, any news about him would be nice.

"So what do I have to do now then?" Sariah asked her.

"Well let's focus on trying to move your wings, just small motions nothing large as I do not want you to hurt yourself." Samantha said encouragingly. She had to get her to focus on her recovery now.

"I will try." Sariah said. She thought for a minute, since she did not have to consciously ask her arms, legs, hands etc. to move, she knew she must focus on the wings. So she thought about fingers and told them to wiggle in her mind.

That worked she thought now let me do the same thing only thinking wings. She thought wiggle and as she did she felt some pain in her shoulders.

"Well you made them move a little bit, try it again." Samantha told her with a grin.

"But it hurts to do it." Sariah answered.

"That is normal, but we need to do it anyway, keep any motion small for now we do not want you to fully open them as I don't think you're ready yet."

"Ok" Sariah replied worried about the pain. But knowing once she learned how to use them and was fully recovered she would then and only then be able to help Levi.

She thought wiggle wings again and they did move a few inches they raised then she let them fall back into place. She would have to practice this a lot she felt.

"Very good, now what I need for you to do is every 5 to 10 minutes repeat what you just did, as the pain grows less each time, then raise or move them farther and slowly we will be able to have you working them in no time."

Suddenly another person dressed like a guard opened the door.

"Mam we have problems we are on a level 1 lock down, you will need to leave your patient and come with me to a secure area until the emergency is over." The Security Team member told Samantha as he motioned her to leave the room.

"What's going on?" Sariah asked her puzzled.

"You just don't worry, just a normal test procedure they do every now and then. I will be back later, just remember to do your practicing." Samantha responded then she turned and left with the security team member.

"See you later then." Sariah said as they left her room and shut the door.

She could tell something was wrong, for whatever a level 1 was she noticed that Samantha's face turned a shade whiter than normal and saw it worried her, whatever it was she hoped she and Levi would be safe.

* * * * *

"What is happening?" Samantha asked the security team member as they hurried down the hall way to the security room.

"I am not fully aware, however it would seem the Neme's have started a fight somewhere in the system or else we would not be on a level 1. They should fill us in soon, but all humans are to head to the security rooms, and to break off all contact with the Neme's until given permission to have contact with them again from the brass." The security member replied. As he opened the security room door for her.

"Ok, then." Was all she said, she knew it was bad then. Just when they were making progress with the combined Neme - Human teams. That could set us back some time.

As she entered the room she saw all the staff that was located on her floor had already been moved there. And the Security Teams who were there to protect them all with a mixture of anger and fear across their faces. All were armed. This was bad she could tell. Whatever this was she would hope that the Neme's would not harm the experiments in progress. It would be terrible to have to start all over again. She took her seat and waited to see what would happen.

"She the last one then?" Floor Security Chief asked the other officer.

"Yes the last on this floor."

"Good then lock down the door, we open it for no one until we get the ok." Floor Security Chief ordered. And it was done. The locking bars had a hollow sound as they slid into place with a clang and the door was now secure.

CHAPTER 29

Eeeleesssoe Speaks

Eeeleesssoe realized whatever the new weapon the humans had created was giving him more problems than he wanted to admit to himself.

His shoulder seemed to becoming infected, it was a strange burn as it had cleanly sliced through his shoulder had he not turned he may have been killed, as it was his arm may be in danger of removal if he did not arrive at the healers station soon.

The unprovoked attack on him created a darkened anger that swelled deep within his large chest, war it was these weak humans desired it, so he would grant them their wishes in their deaths.

He had been able to locate a tube car and was soon on his way thinking as he traveled; soon he would invite all of the Nemekans to WAR.

After some time Eeeleesssoe arrived at his location deep under the humans base, as he exited the vehicle he noticed the other Nemekans as they stared at his shoulder, and the blood that covered his body. He knew they had questions but his answers would be for the council.

He stood tall and walked proudly down the corridor that led to the council chambers.

There had been guards placed at the door, so they must have sensed some form of treachery that was good.

"I will speak with the council and report my findings on the human treachery, allow me to pass." Eeeleesssoe spoke in a solid tone of demand.

"You are wounded, should you not seek the healers and clean up prior to speaking with the council" The guard spoke.

"They will see me now, the wound can wait." Eeeleesssoe said, and with his good arm pushed the door open walking passed the guard and into the council chambers.

The council had been gathered together to determine what the humans were up to, they had gone on a lock down, separating themselves from all Nemekans. This could only mean they wanted to protect their people, but why? What were they planning, this had been the discussion for some time when the door burst open and in came Eeeleesssoe covered in his own blood he stood now in the center of the council room.

Garessaee of the Garsar spoke first. "Eeeleesssoe you must speak, you are wounded tell us how this took place and what you have learned."

Eeeleesssoe slightly bowed his head as was the custom then began.

"Great council, I have traveled to the area where Seenswanee was last known to be. This is what I have discovered. There was sign of a battle many of the humans were killed, however I did not sense any death of Nemekans, as I was going to search further a new group of human warriors in clothing I am not familiar with, they were in white and black uniforms, they came forth against me so I retreated to my entrance in order to bring my report to this council. As I was entering the wall entrance they attacked me without warning, a new weapon has been designed to kill us, I show you my open wound as proof of my story.

"These humans did try to kill me; the weapon made not a sound, and easily injured me as you can see. I must assume Seenswanee has been taken prisoner or killed by these humans.

"I must demand that the council enter the war chambers and call all of Nemekans to unite against the outrage and unprovoked attack upon us. The humans have drawn 1st blood, we must not allow this outrage go unpunished. We must exterminate these lower forms of life before they can harm any more of our clan. I demand justice." Eeeleesssoe stated then remained standing defiant in the circle awaiting their answer.

Garessaee stood as he spoke.

"These humans have once more broken their oaths to us, now they have deliberately attacked our clans again, this outrage must not go unpunished. What say the council, I agree with Eeeleesssoe we must claim our rights of defense we must have blood for blood, we must call for WAR!"

The council erupted in anger and emotions ran strong. They spoke amongst themselves about the need to send a message, to defend themselves against this new attack upon them by these humans.

In the darkness there sat one quietly the head of all chieftains and the head of the council. He watched and listened then he lifted the stone ball in his hand and struck it upon the flat stone creating a large and understandable crash that boomed throughout the council chambers. This was the stone of judgment. The room fell silent.

Akishtoas of the Grey Toomas watched as all fell silent then he spoke.

"Eeeleesssoe has spoken, the evidence is before us and true, for it is written in the bonds of blood as all can see. We shall declare War upon those who have chosen to attack our clans without reason; this cowardice shall not go unpunished. Buy this testimony we must assume Seenswanee also befallen ill from these humans, however he went out as a warrior for it has been spoken there were many dead humans where he met his fate.

By the throne of Jeeauusshua above we shall find justice as we bathe in their blood, for it is written we are not guilty of any offence, they have offended us twice and we shall answer as allowed us as Jeeauusshua taught our ancestors of old, I demand the council order the Warriors to assemble and we shall decide were the doom of the humans in this place shall be. As I have spoken so shall it be!" Akishtoas had spoken; he knew none would counter his word for it was sound.

All in the council room roared with approval, standing brandishing their anger openly drawing their weapons and swearing before the Throne of Jeeauusshua they would avenge the wrongs done before them.

The messengers were sent to all the clans for the justice of blood vengeance and war was sent with them, they were to call the Nemekans to war.

Eeeleesssoe had turned and left to visit the healer for his wound would need to be treated and healed before he could join his clan in the coming combat, and he desired justice he would be there and avenge himself the wound he had received by 100 fold. They would cry peace before he was done, and as they begged for peace kneeling before him he would remove their heads with pleasure. There would be no peace now until the humans were put in their proper place, slaves or worse.

CHAPTER 30

Master Keronkenken

Sosaeen had gathered the documents and visuals of both events with this human boy named Levi and the destruction of both harvesters'. He had spoken with Ibwaaa of the Toomas who had granted him audience with Master Keronkenken of the Garsar who had developed the Essence Harvesters and who would possibly understand the problem they were having, if not he would want to be made aware of the new difficulties with this one subject. There must be a rational reason for it.

As he entered the outer room to Master Keronkenken room he was met by Ibwaaa.

"Master Keronkenken is awaiting you in his room, I did inform him of the problems you have had with the harvester, and he is not pleased that you have destroyed two of them, he is awaiting your excuses. Beware you walk on thin stone, if you are found at fault he may very well punish you. You may go in." Ibwaaa stated to Sosaeen as he opened the door to the Masters room, and after Sosaeen had entered he closed the door behind him.

Master Keronkenken was not pleased, he waited whatever excuses Sosaeen would make up as to why the harvesters had failed, but he had created the devices long ago and to date had never had any issues with them. So it must be this fools mistakes and when proven so he would be made an example of.

"Sosaeen of the Garsar tell me your reasoning's then and be quick about it, I am not pleased to see you." Master Keronkenken spoke very unpleasantly and with the hiss of warning.

"Master, for this long time I have but served you and done so well in the harvesting of the human essence, but we are unsure as to what the problem is at this time for two harvesters you have entrusted us with having failed, the only common connection in their failure is this human subject we call Levi. He is a boy and yet each time we have gone to harvest his essence for your benefit we have failed, the machines have failed.

I have brought the visual records and data of the events for you to compare and study so as to find a way to overcome whatever issue is preventing us from a successful harvest of this subject.

We know his essence is strong, but do not understand how that could affect the machines you have created that have worked so well these many cycles.

I shall leave it to you." Sosaeen bowed for he knew he was in danger here. If the Master found it his fault he knew his punishment would be great. But he knew it was not due to any fault of his or his team.

"Leave them then, I shall study what you have brought and then make my conclusions as to what has happened. You may leave now." Master Keronkenken said, then glared warningly at Sosaeen and added the slight warning hiss until he had left the room and closed the door.

Master Keronkenken took the items left and started to study them, he watched the visuals several times and it puzzled him how the machines would short out it would seem just prior to being able to harvest this boys essence. There was indeed some strange issue here. The rest of the data showed that the machines had been in good working order, the key was this human known as Levi, who was he and how had he come into their hands. Once he had these details he would have to share these findings with Semiazas of the Toomas who would then speak to the Grand Master of all Nemekans Nukpana Ahriman who would know how to deal with such strange things.

He pushed the call button on his desk and spoke.

"Ibwaaa come here."

Ibwaaa entered the office immediately.

"Yes Master." he said.

"You will find all information about this human boy named Levi, then bring it to me and I shall take it and these visuals that Sosaeen had brought and visit Semiazas for this is a very unique and strange occurrence." Master Keronkenken spoke in a calm tone.

"Yes Master it shall be done." Ibwaaa said. Then he hurried back out the door, closing it.

Sosaeen had just left the office so Ibwaaa hurried down the corridor and found him before he got on a lift.

"Master wishes all your information on the human boy in question, he will need it immediately is that understood." Ibwaaa spoke urgently his tail twitching nervously side to side.

"I shall provide it upon my return to my office I shall send all the details to your desk then." Sosaeen replied his own tail beginning to twitch some, there was a mystery here and it needed to be discovered.

Sosaeen pushed the button on the lift and began his return to his lab where he would do just as he was asked by Ibwaaa.

Ibwaaa returned to his desk to await the information he would need to pass on to his master.

This was a mystery and it was puzzling and exciting at the same time.

* * * * *

Once Sosaeen returned to his lab office he called Ssslaoosee.

"Ssslaoosee I need all the data and history on this subject called Levi, and have the human Tech George report to me as well, we must have any learning he has gained from interacting with the boy for I must send it to Ibwaaa for Master Keronkenken to study. Is that understood?" Sosaeen said flatly.

"Yes it is, however Human tech George will be a problem, in your absence the humans have gone to another one of their practice alert events, and all humans have been removed from our presence. We have not been told when they will lift the alert. So he will not be available for questioning at this time."

"Have one of our techs meet with the boy then and befriend him so we can learn more about his past. Gather what you can then and it will have to be enough." Sosaeen said then turned off the com device.

Ssslaoosee thought a moment, he was unsure what the humans were up to and it bothered him, normally they were informed when such a practice was to take place, however it would not get in his way. He thought about whom he could send to befriend the boy, there was one Elasher a Tessa he was good with humans it seemed he did not mind spending time with the lower life forms, so he would work. Once that was in motion he would be able to gather the information that was now required, should not take much time he thought.

He left the room and made his way to the corridor where Elasher would be.

He entered the Tessa's great hall room of rest and started looking for Elasher, after several inquiries he located him.

"Elasher I have work for you to do, you will come with me and I shall speak of your new assignment along the way." Ssslaoosee spoke in a blunt commanding manner expecting him to agree and follow without question as was the way.

"Let us go then." Elasher said as he then left the great hall and entered the corridor with Ssslaoosee close behind him, he knew the Garsar would tell him his duties as soon as they were in a more quiet area so that he would fully understand what was needed of him.

After they had walked to where the corridor was quiet again, Ssslaoosee stopped and looked at Elasher.

"The humans are having a practice drill again, and we are unsure of the length as is the case with these inept beings. We have a young human in the essence harvesting room 3 that will need some special care. You will need to befriend him; you are open to tell him who and what you are and whatever is needed to befriend him. He is a unique specimen as he has not been harvested yet; however two of the harvester machines have failed when attempting to do so.

"Take care and keep him safe until I return.

"Your job is to keep him calm, as he is yet unfamiliar with our species he will need some time to adjust to that reality. Are there any questions?" Ssslaoosee asked him.

"I understand what is to be done; I will attend to this human until you return. I will do what is needed. For in my time here I have learned much about how their weak minds work, it will be done as you ask, Ssslaoosee." Elasher replied. He was much pleased as this would be a very interesting assignment and he did like testing his skills with this immature species.

"Very well then be on your way, I shall be about my task then." Ssslaoosee stated then walked away to go about his own tasks. Satisfied that Elasher would be up to the task required of him.

Elasher watch Ssslaoosee walk away, he thought about the task at hand, this was interesting for the harvesters have never failed, and yet this human or something about him would not allow his essence to be harvested it would seem, and since Ssslaoosee was unable to complete the task it would be up to him, this was a great opportunity to show his skills to his leadership and to move up in the clan upon his successful conclusion of this thing. He allowed a thin grin upon his face, and his tail twitched with anticipation of what was to come, this was very pleasing to himself. He continued towards the harvesting room where the human was, thinking of all the ways he could fulfill his mission.

Elasher knew what he had to do, normally when the humans first saw those of his race they were put into a state of fear immediately with the flight mechanism on automatic. In the past when first introductions were made by himself to any human he had learned from experience that a more subtle approach was most effective.

He stood outside the holding room near harvester room 3. He touched the panels on the wall near the door and dimed the light in the room to the point that it would cause shadowed darkness in the corners. He also looked at the monitor to see where the human was located in the room. It was pleasing to see him lying on the bed facing away from the door, if he was resting or sleeping it would make it much easier for them both, since he had not moved when he dimmed the lights he must be asleep he thought.

He left a light on the wall by the door entrance thus with the room being dark and the light would be in the humans face it would allow him the needed time for a proper and less fearful meeting.

With all in place he opened the door and quickly entered. As the door closed the human turned to look at the door. However by that moment he was well to the side and in the blackness.

"Is there someone there?" Levi asked softly, he was dozing in and out when he heard the door open but when he turned to look he could not see anyone, and the rooms lights were all off except the one on the wall.

"George is that you?" He asked again.

"It is not George; he is about other duties at this time. I have been sent to look in on you." Elasher spoke as evenly as he could doing his best to mimic the human way of speech.

"Who are you?" Levi asked the unknown person, he sounded like a foreigner his voice was strange but he could not figure out why exactly.

"And why are my lights off?" He added.

"Well I understand you are called Levi that is a good name as I understand your human history. I am called Elasher, the lights are off so that I can introduce myself properly to you, for I have a different look and do not want to scare you, so I find it better to speak a moment before you see me." He spoke calmly.

Levi thought, that sounds really strange, he wondered if this guy was crazy or playing some type of game with him. He did notice now the strange snaky smell he noticed in the x-ray room, and now he began to worry about what this Elasher had said, he was starting to get spooked some.

"What do you mean? Are you scary looking?" Levi asked.

"Well Levi, let me speak this, I am different looking, you are not prepared yet to see me, your history does not speak about us much, or at least they have forgotten my race for a very long time.

You see some who I have met think we are Alien, but we are not just a different race. We have lived on this world as long as your race has since the beginning. I am not to be feared, I am here to help you as I can.

You see I can sense your fear beginning to rise, so remain calm. You must prepare your mind for the adjustment to see me. I am of a race known as Nemekans; we live in the Earth in caverns and large open pockets of space within the Earth. We have had contact with you humans for a very long time. You see we study each other to learn more about each other and learn how to become better friends. I have seen some of your T.V. and movies; I am what some have called in your culture Reptilian. We are of all sizes large and small. I am tall and large compared to humans, but not of unusual size in my own race." Elasher spoke doing his best to sound friendly and in the calm voice he had practiced for so long.

Levi thought a moment; this was a very bad joke, or a real bad dream. This could not be happening He would soon wake up and find himself in the cave with Sariah and none of this had happened, it was all a dream he was sure of it. This was really weird.

"Ok let me see who you are, I bet your just some guy George sent in here in a costume to play a joke on me. So turn the lights on and let's get it over with."

Interesting this human was a little different than most he had dealt with in the past, so it may not turn into a fear event with this one. However he knew there would be a shock value that was normal.

"Very well as you said, I will turn on the lights, just no loud noise is that understood no matter how you feel about my appearance." Elasher said.

"Just turn on the lights." Levi said. Bracing himself for whatever the joke was. Then the lights came on, and he about jumped, he did however feel himself very nervous for if what he saw was a costume it was one of the best he had ever seen, even in the movies.

"You see, I am of a reptile look to your eyes, no it is not a trick it is who I am and I shall not hurt you. You are one of the very few humans of your time to have an introduction to our race and you should be honored for this. I am like an ambassador, a go between for both our races. I am honored to meet you Levi of the human race." Elasher did his best to calm the boy; he could tell he was somewhat shocked, however not as fearful as others in the past. This was a very unusual boy that was good.

"So you're like a snake then that would be the smell I have smelled some of the time I have been here. So what about George, he said I am in a hospital, am I? I have never seen your kind in a hospital, where am I and where is my sister? And my family?" Levi said, getting a bit braver he was in trouble now he was sure, where was he, and Sariah and his family he felt very uneasy like he had been lied to since he got here, where ever here was. He wanted answers.

"I will tell you. George is a helper with us, I am not fully aware of where you actually came from nor how you came to our hospital. I am told there was an accident of your family, and you were brought here. I must think that the humans we work with found you and we had the closest hospital for your needs to save your life. You are the only one I am aware of. I am sad it seems you have lost the other members of your clan or family. This is all I am aware of at this time, I can take your questions and ask them to others if you desire it." Elasher spoke.

"Yes I need to know the truth; I feel I am being lied to about what ever took place." Levi said honestly.

"What do you remember about your accident then maybe I can assist you in your memories." Elasher suggested.

"The last I remember we were exploring a cave and then everything went dark and I woke up here." Levi said.

"We?" Elasher questioned.

"Yes me and my sister Sariah, we were together looking at this old cave and then I don't remember much else, we had found a tunnel but then I blacked out or something. I am not sure what happened. That guy George said we were in a car wreck and the family all died, I don't remember being in a car at all." Levi said truthfully.

"Where do you come from then?" Elasher asked, it would be good to know as this sounds like these human children found an entrance to the tunnels and a security team was sent to investigate thus they ended up here. Just by chance or fate.

That was not his concern here. But to befriend the boy, and since it would not matter in the end it would be good to learn more about how they got here.

And if the boy was of no use he would discover where they had taken the girl, maybe there was a link to the effects of their bloodline and the harvester, it could be an interesting experiment to attempt the harvester on this girl as well, to see if they had an immunity of some irregularity that prevented the success of the harvester. It was an interesting puzzle to be sure, and if he was able to find the answer, he would be rewarded for his efforts and rise among the known ones of his clan.

"I am from Beaver, Utah. We were camping when this all happened." Levi said. He was not sure he wanted to fully trust this big lizard, he did not feel safe, something deep within him wanted him to just run as far and fast as he could from this overgrown lizard man.

However that was not possible, but if he could find a way to get outside this room just maybe he could get away and find Sariah.

He had to think and the more he talked to this thing, the more he was accepting the fact he was in trouble, everyone had lied to him at this place, so this lizard was probably lying to him as well.

What did they want from him, and where was his sister. He knew he had no one to rely on but himself right now. So he had to find a way to trick this lizard and get away somehow.

"So where do you come from, I have never heard anything about you." Levi asked hoping he could learn more about what he was facing.

"I am from Terra, what you call Earth. However we live mainly in the cave and tunnel systems of our ancestors, they did build them long ago." Elasher told him.

"No I mean where on Earth do you come from, where were you born, your family and stuff." Levi asked him.

"I see, we have a city under the mountains, it is under your Rocky Mountains of Colorado and Utah. We travel not unlike you do on the outer crust, we call you crust dwellers. I started my life in this city, I grew in my clan and was educated in the sciences thus I am here to assist with their work."

"As for what you call family, we have the Clan, our group or family as you humans call it. The Clan is our purpose in our life to do honor to the ancestors." Elasher told him.

"You said you live under the ground in cities? Are we under the ground then? "Levi asked he hoped to find out more about where exactly he was so he could escape some time.

"We are under the ground, we have built this base with the help of your government it keeps our work and needs hidden from those who would fear us and do us harm." Elasher told him the basics he was not about to give this human any good information.

"So why am I here then? Why don't you just let me and my sister go home?" Levi asked.

"It seems you came upon our tunnel by accident and the guards over reacted. Once we have changed your memories of this place and your adventures here you will be able to return home. You see the device they were going to use to erase your experiences here has broken down, so we need to repair it then you will be prepared to return home, and you will find yourself outside of the place you trespassed upon." Elasher told him, he chose to let the boy know or feel he would be released eventually, thus it should calm him down some.

Make him more relaxed in this situation which was new to him, and as always a fearful moment for humans. They were so simple minded in their youth, it was easy to bend their minds as he saw fit.

"So you're going to erase part of my memory then, so why can't I see my sister, and where is she I know she should be here somewhere because we were together, if your guys took us together she should be here right." Levi said, they should know where Sariah was, and he wondered what they were doing to her, was she locked up in a room like he was, and worried about him?

This was not fare at all, and he wished he could get out of there, and keep his memories. People had to know about these lizards, and the humans working with them, he did not feel right at all about this place.

"As I have said, I know not of your sister. I can make questions for my leaders to see if they know of her or her location. The humans who found you may have separated you thus we will need to locate her, that could take some time. I will go and search if you remain and await my return." Elasher said, he was ready to go, and wanted to give the boy some hope.

And it looked like he had done just that by how the boy reacted.

Levi's face showed his excitement as he felt he would finally get some truth about what has happening to them, and this monster thing was going to go find his sister that would be a good thing as they could be together and Sariah would know what to do to help them get out of this place.

"Thanks Elasher come back as soon as you find my sister."

"I shall, upon gaining word of her I will return. I must go now." Elasher told the boy, and then he proceeded to open the door and leave the room. The door closed behind him and as he walked down the corridor he smiled within himself, these humans were so easily controllable; their weak minds were no match for him. This was a good start the boy was beginning to trust him and so on his next visit he could ask more in-depth questions about him.

He was curious as to where the other human, the female had been taken for they had no knowledge of this as yet in his group. What could they be doing with her; this was a good thing to discover so he would seek out this other human to see how it could benefit his Clan.

* * * * *

In the communications room that monitored all traffic both in and out of the base one of the computer monitors flashed a red warning bringing the tech that was next to it to full attention, upon reading what it was about, he called over his supervisor.

"Lt. Alston Sir I have a situation here you need to be aware of." Corporal Jonston said.

"What is it" Lt. Alston said as he came across the room to see for himself. He noted the Corporal just pointed at the screen so he read what was there.

"I will notify the General of this, keep an eye on this in case any more new developments are noticed." Lt. Alston told him, as he was heading for the phone.

"Gen Sills office." Staff Sergeant. Symrai said.

"I need to speak with the General immediately, this is Lt. Alston." He said in an urgent tone.

"I will see if he can speak with you, one moment." Staff Sergeant Symrai said has she put the call through to the Generals desk.

The phone lit up as it rang; he wondered what's next these last few days were getting too interesting for his taste. He picked up the phone.

"Gen. Sills what can I do for you." He said firmly.

"General, this is Lt. Alston in communications; we have had a flag hit on the missing men from the recon team that disappeared Sir. It would seem that their fingerprints were sent through normal FBI and law enforcement channels searching for their identities. Of course they found nothing but we do have a location of those who were looking for their ID."

"And were would that be?" Gen. Sills asked. Alston should have told him already, this was important, if there was a survivor or more then maybe they can figure out exactly what happened.

"The Sheriff Office in Beaver City, Beaver County that's in Utah Sir." Lt. Alston told him.

"Thank you, Keep me informed if any other traffic occurs." Gen Sills said and hung up the phone.

He would have to send an extraction team to recon the situation and then bring back his men.

He touched the intercom button for Symrai's desk.

"Symrai send in Colonel Sheato ASAP."

It was less than 10 minutes when Staff Sargent Symrai escorted Colonel Sheato into the office, then turned and closed the door.

"Colonel, we have a situation, your aware that we have had a team go missing, and presumed dead, we have had a hit on the FBI ID files lists, and you're going to go investigate it with your team. The hit came from Beaver City, Beaver County Sheriff's office in Utah.

You will take a flying machine; make sure you do this quietly and without notice if you can. You know what to do. If we do in fact have survivors then bring them back, but check their morgue as well just in case, we need all evidence collected or destroyed you know the drill, and do your best not to harm civilians as that just adds to more questions, we want to put a lid on this and keep it closed. Understood!" General Sills ordered.

"Yes Sir, you know we will do you proud as always. Be good to get some fresh air. Will be on our way as soon as we are loaded up Sir." Colonel Sheato replied, then saluted the General and hurried out the door.

It was good to be getting out of this place and if he remembered right Beaver Utah was near the mountains so fresh air was a great idea. They would retrieve and fulfill the mission as normal. His team was very good at that.

He gathered his team together and they loaded up in what most civilians would deem a U.F.O., it was actually a newer flying machine developed over the years with the Neme's for missions such as this.

They were quiet, stealthy, rarely showed up on radars and they could hover over the location for a quick in and out job like this one.

It would not take them long to get there as these flying crafts were very fast.

After they had all loaded up, he told the pilot to take off. And they did so headed to see what they could learn.

CHAPTER 31

The Watcher

Niberio had been observing the activities and communica-tions of the Dulce Base over that last few cycles, he had noticed the out of normal behavior of the military men as well as listening to their communications.

He also noted that the Nemekans had unusual activity as well; however it was unfortunate that he was unable to put listening devices in their secret chambers as they were inaccessible to humans.

He felt he had waited long enough to obtain a basis of information in which to alert the High Guard back home on the situation.

He had moved to a secured area in the older tunnels that would give him the privacy he would need to make his report.

He pulled out a device not unlike the human's version of a computerized tablet but much more advanced. He sent his request for contact with the needed security codes.

After a few moments the tablet lit up and before him stood the hologram apparition of a member of his monitoring team back in Jehu.

"Niberio it is a pleasure to see you, it has been some time since your last report what are the humans and the Nemekans about this day?" Samuel Hectea a member of the High Guard monitoring team spoke to him as if he were standing before him.

This technology was very interesting; it projected the visual of the person communicating in real time and life size or approximate version of them. It was a truly interesting device the School of Science had come up with.

"Samuel, There is a strong undercurrent between the Nemekans and the Humans here, I am not 100% sure of the nature or details at this time.

However from what I can gather based on my over watch Intel, A group of human soldiers has disappeared, and with them one Nemekans. Until recently there had been no word of what took place or why.

However a new message came in that gave the General Sills hope of locating his missing men and he has dispatched a team to do just that.

However the Nemekans and the Soldiers have come into conflict in a more isolated part of their base, several soldiers were found dead, and they are preparing a defense against the Nemekans as they feel it could have been them who killed their men.

The Nemekans as always are showing signs of distrust with these humans here at the base, they also seem to be moving to a defensive / aggressive posture.

This maybe a conflict not unlike that back in the mid 1970's when there was a short war here.

I will do what I can to learn more and update you as I am able to.

This could upset the balance of peace between these two groups.

That is all I can say for now." He gave his report and bowed slightly as was their custom and sign of respect to one another.

"Thank you for your report, I shall inform those who need to be made aware at this time, It would seem there is something afoot in your area. Keep us updated as soon as you learn more of the nature of things there. Until then, be safe. Yod Hey Vav be with you brother." Samuel responded and bowed as well as was customary.

"And all be well with you, Samuel till I contact you again, Yod Hey Vav be with you as well." Niberio responded. Then he smiled and turned off the communication device.

Looking around to make sure no one or thing had overheard his report and seeing no one, he began his journey back to his post of observation.

* * * * *

Zsaaleessao had been moving at a good speed, based on the conversations of the humans they were looking for a young human boy and girl, however with his contacts he had only heard of a new boy that had been an unusual conversation topic recently, as those who had attempted to take his essence had been unsuccessful, and reports that strange things were happening around this human.

He knew where those who were taken to have their essences removed would be held.

This was his object of desire, if he could take the boy from his captors, and then befriend the boy he may learn what power he had in preventing the essence harvesters from doing their tasks.

And what had caused the other rumors surrounding him.

Possibly he might be the one spoken of in the fore telling's of the old ones, but one truly never knows for prophesy and history and pure mythology over time can and does become mixed together.

Be it human or Nemekans or others history such has always been the case.

He would arrive before the searchers would, for even though they had some magical device guiding them, they would have to take extra time to avoid all the security along the way.

That he knew would not be easy for strangers.

Yes, he felt he was correct for at the thought his chest did warm from within, a gift to know truth of things from the creator of all life. Thus he must indeed be doing a service for the creator.

He would free the boy, and if his thoughts were correct he would need to find a way to bring him to his most ancient master of wisdom so as to direct him best on how to walk this new path and possibly where it could lead. That would take some doing for he would need the right vessel for such a journey, one he had not taken since his arrival long ago into these cavern cities.

And yet he felt the journey was the right thing, as he felt now he was being guided by his creator to help this human, why he could not understand, but to do as guided that he must.

He entered the long corridor that led to the secured rooms or holding cells. He noticed the human warrior guards were not at their posts; in fact he noted that it was all quiet no one was moving as they normally would. This was also unusual.

Suddenly he heard someone ahead of him, he felt or smelt it was a Nemekans.

Then he crouched in a hall intersection and peered around the corner, he did see a member of the Tessa clan with a tray of food stuffs on it, he was close enough to know it was human food.

Just maybe the creator had allowed him a guide to find this boy; he would follow this Tessa and see what developed. If his guess was correct the creator was blessing him this cycle.

He did not have to follow this Tessa very far before he stopped at the cell door, placed his hand on the sensor and entered.

This was his moment, the door would only be open for a short moment so he raced the short distance to the door way, and before it had a chance to close he placed his hand and held it open.

There inside was the Tessa, and also there was a human boy on the bed.

The boy had a shocked expression upon seeing him, Zsaaleessao behind the Tessa, yet he said nothing at the moment.

Then the Tessa spoke.

"Levi, I have not been able to find your sister at this time, however those of my clan have chosen to search until they do so. Here is some nourishment for you while you await further information about her." Elasher told the boy. He noted a surprised expression upon the boy's face if he read it correctly.

Levi that was the name those who were searching had used, this was the missing boy. The creator did have his hand in this thing. Zsaaleessao thought to himself.

Now he must do what normally would have greatly displeased him yet the Creator had put him here for this reason.

He moved quickly and suddenly, his move made the boy back up to the wall upon his bed, then the Tessa sensing a change turned to look behind him, and saw Zsaaleessao of the Etosa.

It would be the last thing he would see in this realm of existence.

For with a look of shock, he opened his mouth to speak as Zsaaleessao drove his blade deep into his heart, and then covered his mouth so he could not speak.

"I am truly sorry my young Tessa, however this is the judgment of the Creator, and now you shall go see your ancestor's. Go in peace young warrior." Zsaaleessao spoke softly to him as he gently laid the Tessa's body upon the floor, for his spirit had by then left for the journey to his ancestor's.

He wiped the blood on the Tessa's clothing. Then he looked upon the shocked and very scared human boy.

He stood and softly spoke.

"Child, do not be alarmed. I am Zsaaleessao of Clan Etosa, I mean you no harm. I would help you escape your prison at this time, for the Creator of life has sent me here to do so.

"It is unfortunate that the young Tessa had to leave us as he did however there was no other way. Now let us go, we must go quickly for others will soon notice. We must be gone when they get here or I shall myself be taking the journey to see my ancestor's, and I would prefer to make that journey in the long future from now."

Levi sat stunned, and then he quietly spoke.

"I have never seen anyone die before, and you scare me. Even though I did not trust Elasher, I don't see how this helps anything, why should I trust you?" Levi said in a shaky voice.

"Ah little one, this I understand. What you do not know is that you are in this room which they call the waiting room for those who are to be harvested. You see they desire to take your essence from you; these Tessa and others use it as what in your world would be called a narcotic, a drug. You perish in the process. They take your spirit of soul this is the essence. I have been sent by our creator to assist in your avoidance of this thing, as there is another path you shall walk if you're willing, however we must leave or neither of us will walk any future path but that of death." Zsaaleessao spoke evenly and yet with the sound of urgency.

"I must trust you then, if what you say is true. Let's go I would like to be free of this room. So where are we going then?" Levi said as he stood up to follow the one called Zsaaleessao.

"Take of the food he brought, you will need it. I shall take you to a place where we can find transportation then we shall journey to an old wise teacher of mine who can assist us in helping you. Let's go we can speak along the way when it is safe, for now you must be quiet until I tell you it is safe to make noise." Zsaaleessao spoke.

He then lead the boy and they hurried down the corridor and into the roughhewn walls that led to the inner caverns of which he knew there would not be any surveillance devices.

After some time of running and walking through the caverns, hiding when others came near, avoiding them. For to be found out would mean instant death to the boy, for no humans were allowed at these depths in the home lands of the Nemekans.

Suddenly Zsaaleessao stooped and motioned for Levi to remain silent and still. They crouched along the wall, and then slowly Zsaaleessao peered around the edge of his hiding place, and he knew he had arrived at their destination.

He saw the hanger of flying craft that they had used for so many generations. This is what he would use to fly to see his old teacher.

Now he had but to wait for the right moment so they could slip into the closest craft that would work for his journey.

"Boy, this is where we find our craft, when I say you will follow fast and quietly understood? And do as I do. We shall have only a few moments to avoid detection, and there is no room for error." Zsaaleessao had spoken in a very serious tone.

"I understand." Levi whispered in response, he hoped he would not mess this up, he was scared. He was not sure what was happening, but this creature seemed to want him to go with him, they were escaping from this place, and that was good enough for him. At least for now.

He thought a small honest prayer, asking God to protect them and allow them to get out of this place safely.

He nodded that he was ready to the creature before him. And then waited for his signal.

After what seemed like hours, which actually may have only been minutes, Levi suddenly saw this Zsaaleessao make his motion to follow and he moved, Levi followed.

They made their way to a strange shiny disk shaped craft, Levi thought great we are going into a UFO now, what next.

Zsaaleessao placed his hand upon the right wall, on a small rectangle mark, and then a door opened and they both went in.

Again he put his hand on the wall as before and the door closed without any noise.

They hurried around the small hall in the craft and came to what Levi thought must be the pilots area. There were several seats and control panels.

"You boy will seat yourself here and put these straps on, make sure they are snug so you do not move. I shall sit at the controls and we shall soon be leaving this place."

"You may call me Levi. So you can fly this thing then?"

"Yes it has been some time, but I should do just fine. It may be a little bumpy on the way out as I do not have permission to leave, and they may disapprove of me taking their craft." Zsaaleessao said as he smiled as best he could.

Levi was not sure he was ready for this or not, but anyway he looked at it he was along for an interesting ride. He wondered where on Earth they would be flying as he had never heard of these lizard type creatures before, he wondered if they lived in some remote city in a jungle hidden somewhere. He guessed he would know soon enough.

So he nodded his head and got ready then he waited.

Zsaaleessao did his overlook of the craft, and all was as it should be, he started the craft and slowly it hovered a moment, then he took the flight control stick and pushed them back and they moved faster, as he sped up he looked for the entrance to the launch tube that would guide him up out of the caverns into the sky above and to freedom.

There it was he was aware that the security flight office had not challenged him as yet, this was good.

He entered the launch tube and pulled the stick all the way back, keeping it from touching the walls and they shot forth at an exceeding rate of speed and soon into the air of the Earth.

A few moments later he was over what was called Washington State by the humans, and then headed towards the north, ever flying higher and higher.

He looked back at his passenger, this boy, Levi. He seemed to be doing very well for a human's first flight.

Then back at his controls as he looked at the screen before him. They had just passed through the last layers of high clouds and he could see the stars before him, slowly come into view, and then as he cleared the last vestige of the Earth's atmosphere he felt Free, more free than he had in many cycles.

It was good to be back in flight above the Earth, heading home once again.

Levi was watching as they flew higher and higher, then he too saw the stars. This frightened him some. It was unexpected.

"Hey where are we going, did we just go into outer space?" Levi said nervously.

"Yes Levi, we are in what you call outer space, we are on a journey to see one who can help you." Zsaaleessao said calmly.

"But you never said anything about this! Why don't you take me home to my family? They will be worried about me. Just turn this around and take me home will you please."

"It is sad that I am unable to do so, you see there is a special thing about you boy, I am not sure of yet, but if I am wrong I shall return you to your home, unharmed. It is why we must go to my home so I can seek counsel of my master for he will know what is needed.

Do not fear, just relax and be calm the journey will not be as long as one would think. However it will take a day's journey as you human's recognize time." Zsaaleesao said. Then he turned back to his monitoring of the flight.

There was no one following that was good. He was unsure why no one stopped or questioned him that was highly unusual, however he would count it as the Creator was once again assisting him in their journey, for that was the answer he felt.

Soon he would be home. Many memories there mostly good, some not. But that was how life was in the Etosa Clan. He only hoped they would welcome him home upon his return. Only time would tell.

Levi was a little scared; however there was some excitement about being in a space ship, a UFO, none of his family or friends would believe this.

As he watched out the viewing screen before the one called Zsaaleessao, he saw to his right the moon, they were passing the moon. This was going to be one crazy adventure and yet he was happy to be out of the prison cell. At least now they were going somewhere. But where?

"Ah, exactly where are we going then Mr. Zsaaleessao? Where is your home?" Levi asked.

"Yes that is a very good question, We are going to my home, I lived on the red planet in our solar system, the planet your ancestor's termed the planet of War, for such it is a good name for from it came many good warriors. We are going to what you humans call Mars. It is a good place." Zsaaleessao spoke with pride, and upon seeing the reaction of the boy he was amused by it.

Mars? wow, I was going to Mars. Levi thought to himself. This was crazy, he felt like he was in a dream and yet he knew it was not.

How would he ever get home? What about his family when would he ever get to see them again, what about Sariah?

He was beginning to feel all alone and a very gloomy feeling was beginning to overpower him, he was wishing he had never ever seen that darn cave, it sure was cursed.

What was he going to do, what was this monster Zsaaleessao really going to do with him?

He did not trust anyone anymore how could he, he would just have to wait and see what would happen.

As he dwelt on all these and more worries, he once again felt a warmth overcome his whole body it was a warmth like he felt when his mother gave him a hug when he was sad only way better.

Then as he vaguely remembered like before a small voice seemed to be speaking in his head again.

"All will be as it should be Levi, your family will endure and so shall you for your growth and learning have only just begun be at peace all will be well, for we are not far from helping you if you but ask Levi. Zsaaleessao is but helping you along your way he is a good spirit all shall be well."

Wow it was kinda spooky it was a soft yet nice voice, he just wished he knew if it was his own mind or if it was someone or something else for sure.

He pondered on this new message as he again looked out the window and viewed the stars and in the distant he could see the planet he was now destined by fate to go to.

CHAPTER 32

Getting Close

Ben had been following Fairsong and with the others right behind them, each would take a turn on point and would rotate through to rear guard.

The search since the first days fight had been for the most part uneventful, from time to time they had to hide from patrols; however they did their best to stay off the main tub transportation systems.

They had been following Ben's directions through some more unimproved caverns.

And it seemed they found fewer patrols in doing this.

"Ben, take a look once more and see if there is yet any change of where Levi is." Fairsong asked Ben.

They all took a short break as Ben brought out the device the Lev Antas Shuesa once more; with continued use Ben had found it easier to focus and better follow the directions on the device.

As he watched it glowed again, and he saw the pointer he used for Levi that it had not moved, and that they were close, very close now. That was good, soon they would be able to rescue Levi, and He hoped Levi would then know where to find Sariah in this maze.

"We are almost there by the looks of this."

The message was whispered down the line and all were glad to hear it, they had been wandering around down here for some time, all nodded and they grouped up for the run down on what would take place.

"We are close to Levi, I must assume we will enter newer tunnels and corridors not unlike those of our first battle, so be aware, I will need to scan for security devices and destroy them before we continue, this could slow us down but it is needed. As yet they do not know we are here.

So let us be cautious, I will need James, Joe, Gideon and David close to me in case we have to fight again as they are the most experienced in such matters, James you and Ben hang back with the others. When we have to fight it will be quick.

All must make sure we are not followed. Tim you take the rear.

If we are discovered here by the military we have seen it will be a hard fight to get free of this place; however if the Nemekans discover us it will go much harder on us, so be alert, be quiet, is that understood." Fairsong stated to the group.

All silently agreed and moved into the new positions for the journey forward.

"Ben is Levi still in the same spot now?" James Adair asked his son.

"Yes dad he is."

"Can you see Sariah? Can you find her anywhere on that thing?" James Adair asked again of his son. He was worried about both his children, he had been going over and over in his mind why did God let this happen to his family, and he was becoming very concerned about what could be happening to them in this place. But he knew that whatever happened, God had his hand in it, he just did not understand himself all the why's about this.

"Let me focus on Sariah, there I think that's her, she is closer but her signal is very faint, I do not understand how this all works, but I think that's her, but something has changed about her marker. Let's get Levi as he is the closer still then we should be able to find Sariah soon and get on our way home." Ben said to his dad and those close enough to listen.

"Ok." James Adair replied.

"Well if all are rested up now, let's make sure everyone is loaded, with a round chambered I don't need any noise if we come into contact, and if we need to fight every second will count. So let's be on the ready." Gideon mentioned to the group.

Everyone did a quick check on their weapons, and then Fairsong motioned for them to lead out.

It was less than one hour later when they had come to the actual corridors of a base, Ben looked at the Lev Antas Shuesa once more to get a new direction to go as they were at an intersection of hallways.

"There, let's go to the right, and... what? Hey wait something's happening... It looks like Levi is being moved, his marker is moving." Ben said worried.

Fairsong looked at the Lev Antas Shuesa and yes indeed the boy was in motion now. Away from them and moving at a good pace.

"We need to hurry, I will go first to look for surveillance items, the rest follow close." Fairsong said as he headed out not waiting for a response.

Soon the team came up on a room with the door open, Fairsong held up his hand and all stopped.

Joe, James, Gideon and David took up positions around the door, and David was the first to take a look inside with his corner shot weapon, He motioned all clear. Then stepped inside.

The others followed, and then they waved the rest of the group into the room.

They all looked down on the dead body of another creature a dead Nemekans, and there was no Levi.

"Ben, give me a heads up on Levi." Gideon asked.

"He was here, I can tell by the strength of the marker, however he is still moving away from us now, He must have found a way to escape. He will need our help."

"Yes we need to hurry." James Adair said as he went outside the door of the room and started moving down the hall to where he should find his son.

Everyone followed James, as he was like a shark smelling blood in the water; he was on a fast track to where ever Levi was. Everyone was racing to catch up to James.

In their haste some forgot the one thing, to look behind them to make sure they were not being followed.

* * * * *

Sheersconn had been sent to follow Elasher to make sure all was well with the human subject, and to make sure that Elasher would get the details he had forgotten the last time he interview the boy.

He had entered the corridor to his left where at the end the boy's cell was, and he noticed the door open, that should not be open, He ran cautiously to the door and as he looked in he noticed Elasher dead upon the floor lying in his own blood.

This cannot be what outrage! His blood boiled and his heart raced and his warrior's spirit became fully alive.

Someone will pay for this crime! He swore out loud.

He noticed the room was empty, so the boy was gone, then he noticed some tracks, a human boot had walked through Elasher's blood, well your enemy will be shown to me Elasher by your last drops of blood this will go well with you, I can avenge your death quickly then.

Sheersconn looked down upon his fallen clan member, "Go with the ancestor's Elasher, I go to avenge your blood." With that he left and quickly followed the direction the boot print was headed in.

He quickened his pace, and soon he heard some movement, he raised his beam weapon and prepared for battle, the lust of blood vengeance almost blinding him in rage.

He turned a corner and saw some human's fleeing in the distant, these did the deed. He had heard already that the War council had been called, that Eeeleesssoe had been wounded by these humans without warning and in a cowardly way from behind.

So too would he avenge both of his clan in like manner not of the coward as the humans but as a warrior.

With that he raised his weapon and fired it down the corridor and with a pleased expression and the lust for battle he saw the first human cut down by him.

He quickened his pace to find and target his next human, he ran fast into the heat of battle.

Julio had been taking up rear guard, and actually running to catch up to the rest of the group who were some yards ahead of him.

He did not see the Warrior who had run up behind him, he did not see him lift the weapon and discharge it, but he did feel the heat of the impact as it turned him sideways and through him against the wall.

He tried to raise his weapon to return fire at the Nemekans he saw running towards him, but his arms would not respond nor would they.

For just before he passed out into oblivion he realized he had been torn in half and his right arm was missing, his weapon lay on the floor, then he saw the Nemekans run by him then all was black and he was lost in the abyss of his lost mortality.

With a shock, Fairsong new that they were in trouble. He stopped and everyone else did as well.

"That was the sound of a Nemekans weapon, where is Julio? Everyone on guard we are going to have company, now."

Everyone turned to where Julio should have been, and was not in view as they had gone around a curve in corridor.

They could hear the sounds of heavy breathing and hear the foot falls of a large and heavy creature.

All raised their weapons; soon a Nemekans came into view with a weapon raised at them all.

"Fire!" Gideon ordered, at that moment all fired and the creature was stopped dead in its tracks by a wall of high powered lead.

The creature had the look of rage then anger as it fell to the floor, then struggled to sit up and once again raised its weapon, only to find Fairsong now standing over him, and with a stroke of his sword the Nemekans lost his head, and so he also followed the others into the spirit realms now to visit his ancestor's.

"I have to know." Joe said as he ran around the curve to see what had become of Julio.

Soon he found what was left of him; he knelt down and said his goodbyes quickly then stood to find the others next to him.

"This is a great loss; we must remember we are always in danger here. We do not have time to mourn him now, let us do him justice by finding Levi and Sariah, so he will not have died in vain." Tim told everyone.

Sadly they knew he was right; there was no way they could take Julio with them he would have to be left behind.

They all sadly continued their search for Levi.

About 20 minutes later Ben stopped to look again at a junction of tunnels. They were being led farther downward into a more natural tunnel system.

"Dad I don't see, wait, there he is we still are behind him but we are closer now. Wait... No! That can't be, Fairsong take a look, what do you think?" Ben said excitedly and worried.

Fairsong looked at the marker for Levi, he saw it move but not in any linear way or fashion. It moved up towards the top of the ball, then as those gathered closest witnessed the marker as it left the Lev Antas Shuesa and like a spark leaves the fire in the wind, it floated up towards the ceiling then disappeared into nothingness.

"What happened?" James Adair said.

"Where did he go?" Ben asked Fairsong.

Fairsong stood there in shock a moment; he had not planned for this, for how could he have known this would occur.

There was only one reason why the marker for Levi would act in such a way; he put his head down a moment in thought. Then slowly lifted his eyes to James Adair and Ben and the others who had all gathered close around now.

"I fear Levi is no longer within our reach of rescue." Fairsong said sadly.

"What do you mean? Is he dead? What ... tell me!" James Adair demanded to know what this meant

"Levi is not dead, however the only thing this could mean is that Levi is no longer in this base area, nay he is no longer in America. I fear now by the behavior of the marker he has been taken on a journey off planet."

Everyone stood in stunned silence.

"Off Planet!?" "What do you mean?" Ben asked. Seeing his dad was becoming distraught.

"There are means of flight that these creatures have, and some other races, even my own that are above those of your surface races.

You know them as UFO's those unidentified flying objects are these ships. They have the ability to fly in space as well. I fear someone has taken Levi off world at the moment." Fairsong stated somberly.

"Can you follow them then?" James Adair asked.

"No not at this time, I would need to speak with those of my old city for assistance. However let us focus on Sariah, Ben where is she?, Levi is a loss for the moment and our presence will soon be known, we must hurry to save Sariah before we are in a constant fight for survival."

"I understand, let me focus on her, as I said earlier she is below us we need to get down to the lower tunnels of this place and find her." Ben stated.

Even though all were in a state of shock awareness of the unexpected, they knew their mission and started looking for the corridor or an elevator that would take them to the lower levels of this place and bring them closer to Sariah before her weak marker signal was also lost.

CHAPTER 33

Prisoner Rescue

Colonel Sheato gathered his team together in their operations room; once all were seated he commenced his briefing.

"We will be going on an extraction mission in a populated civilian area, we will focus on bringing out a member of a missing search team who has been caught and put in the local Sheriff's jail.

We will avoid hostilities at all costs; we must go in and out like a whisper. We do not need any exposure or press on this one. I know you will do your best as always.

The location is Beaver Utah. Estimated population 3200 souls. The Sheriff's department is a normal small town one. We will go in at night as usual and we will subdue all in the building by using type 1-X sleeping agent, they should not remember much. This should prevent any un-needed confrontation.

Our sources and last satellite images of the area show that after midnight will be our best time.

The Sheriff leaves only a few on staff in his office and their small jail."

Colonel Sheato pointed to the screens on the wall behind him showing his men the location of the buildings and their layout in a 3D hologram to be searched as he spoke.

"Here is where our target is located you will enter here, and leave the same way. We shall land or hover based on the need at the time, so be quick about it. Team A you will focus on the Sheriff's office and our missing man, Team B you will need to do a recon on the local morgue which is here, we will be looking for any bodies of the missing team, also there was a Neme sent along with them so it is also missing.

We do have a confirmed ID hit on the known living member at the jail. The others we are not sure of. If you do locate the bodies we shall bring them home as well. If you find anyone at the morgue use your 1-X as well and make sure you take any data you find about our men, leave nothing for the locals. This will keep the situation under containment." Colonel Sheato finished his brief.

"Any questions?" Colonel Sheato asked,

"Sir what if we encounter any civilians outside the buildings how would you like us to handle them?" A-Team member Rock asked.

(A-Team had chosen earth name designations for their ID's. Rock, Stone, Flint, Boulder. B-Team had chosen Water, River, Lake, Stream. These were their call signs for the mission at hand)

"Everyone should be asleep by the time we arrive; it is a small farming town most go to bed early. If however someone see's you by chance just stun them and leave it at that." Col. Sheato told them.

"If no other questions grab your gear and meet me on the flight deck a.s.a.p. get moving." Col. Sheato said, and everyone responded as usual, all left to do as ordered.

Once all had arrived on the flight deck they loaded up in a strange cigar looking ship about 40 feet long by 20 wide with no markings what so ever on it, it was smooth on the surface, and they boarded from underneath on the platform that had lowered from its belly for entry. This is what most civilians would deem a U.F.O. it was actually one of the newer flying machines developed over the years with help from the Neme's for missions such as this.

They were quiet, stealthy, rarely showed up on radar and they could hover over the location for a quick in and out job like this one.

After all had taken their seats, they silently rose up towards the opening in the caverns ceiling and soon were high above the clouds and speeding towards their destination.

* * * * *

Deputy Gubler had just left the prisoners cell after giving him his evening meal. He wondered who this soldier was and all the why's of the whole situation surrounding him and the Adair's missing children. He had attempted to get the man to speak with him but he refused to say anything of substance.

Deputy Gubler walked out of the main door leading to the holding cells, and stopped at the main desk, as he noticed the Sheriff was still there discussing some other matters with Deputy Jones who was just preparing for the evening shift.

Seeing Deputy Gubler the Sheriff turned to him.

"So how is our prisoner tonight, any change yet is he wanting to talk or make a call to anyone yet?"

"No, no changes there, just as stubborn and clamed up as normal. He does give me the creeps though, he is definitely some type of military or black ops group he just has that air about him. But he won't speak; just something about him bothers me, and I can't place a finger on it." Deputy Gubler replied.

"Well there you go, he looks at us like a bunch of redneck cops I am sure, no respect for those outside his circle I am sure, typical of his type. So you won't have any problems with this prisoner tonight, however old George is back in the drunk tank again, poor guy just can't get off the bottle, so make sure he is tucked in tonight as well and see if you can get him to eat something for dinner, I am sure he has not had much real food for a while, it's normal for him when he gets into these bad stages. But we will dry him out again, so he might get a little noisy not having any of his medicine as he calls it tonight."

"Sounds like a quiet night then, unless ole George gets sick or something. You guys get going I will be just fine, Oh Sheriff, Jorgensen called in and will be late getting on shift tonight, had some issues to deal with before he can get here, but he should be here in about an hour. We can handle these 2 just fine."

"All yours then, Karolynn is making her shepherd's pie for dinner, and some of her good ole homemade pies, so I will just leave you now to go have a nice dinner, have a great shift, Jones, and tell Jorgensen he needs to be on time, this getting to work late is becoming a habit, so give him the usual warning, if he needs any help with whatever his issues are have him talk to me tomorrow morning before he leaves."

"Sure thing Sheriff, so when are you going to bring some of Karolynn's pie over again, that sure does help us on the night shift, just a hint." Jones said with a smile, the Sheriff's wife was known for her cooking, and one could not get to Arshel's all the time for their homemade pies. That and when they bring some of their homemade ice cream just makes it all the better.

"Don't you worry, maybe if your good I will see about her sending you some later in the week, after all she's not your cook keep that in mind Jones, now what about you and the Torgerson gal, aren't you two an item now? Give her some hints and maybe she will make you some of your own pie." The Sheriff said with a wink and a smile.

"Now don't go there, we're just getting to know each other, and with me working the night shifts and her working days at the hospital, well we don't get a lot of time together." Deputy Jones commented back.

"You know she likes you when she starts baking you pies, kind of a tradition in their family you know. Then she'll set the hook and you're caught, and become a respectable married citizen like the rest of us." Sheriff Thompson smiling at Jones knowing eventually these two just might tie the knot; he liked his deputies in a family way calmed them down and made them more mature in many ways than the single men, but all in due course.

"Night Sheriff, now you and Gubler get going so I can go to work."

"Have a great night then." Sheriff Thompson replied.

"Night, Jones, but keep in mind my aunt runs the theater I could set you up for a quiet personal movie show when you and the pretty Sarah Torgerson could spend some time together, maybe dinner and a movie, just give me the word." Deputy Gubler said jokingly.

"I don't need any help from either of you two, now get going before I throttle you." Jones replied he really liked to keep his personal life to himself; he didn't need any help from these two.

The Sheriff and Deputy both laughed and left the office, smiling. They did like to tease Jones about his dating. Both headed off to their homes, leaving Deputy Jones on his own.

It was a little over an hour when Deputy Jorgensen finally arrived for his shift.

"So Jones, how goes it tonight." he said as he walked into the office.

"Well just fine, Ole George is in the drunk tank again, other than that our mystery guest is still here that's about it, Oh and the Sheriff needs to talk with you about being late again, so make sure you speak with him before you leave in the morning."

"Ok will do. I take it my turn for rounds then?"

"Yep it is, and take George a sandwich an maybe an apple or banana see if you can get him to eat something you know the routine make sure the mystery man is still locked in his hole, and since your late, if ole George has made a mess your turn to clean it up, remember a clean cell is a happy cell."

"Will do." Jorgensen said and began his shift.

"5 minutes out, everyone gear check." Rock said leader of team A.

Everyone did as told and double checked all their gear.

Team A would secure the Sheriff's office, find their comrade and be gone before anyone knew it, should be less than 10 minutes on sight.

"Water, you will have 10 minutes to secure any evidence from the morgue, do you understand, be quick and silent. Now everyone, its 2 am so all should be quiet, remember we were never here be as ghosts, any encounters with the public just stun them. Understood." Rock ordered.

All nodded in agreement, they understood just fine.

"Team B do it by the book, in an out if we find any bodies we will extract them so be quick about it notify the pilot as soon as you can, we will use the back dock area for the extractions. I will see to the computer files or notes if any on our men and the Neme." Water team B leader reminded them.

"Here we are, Team A, we are above the sheriff's office, and we will use the gas in the vent system then enter through the roof access understood." Rock team A leader reminded them.

Again they just nodded, they knew their mission and knew it would go off just as planned.

The Pilot gave the thumbs up and lowered the access ramp; it lowered to about a foot above the roof top never touching. Then A team was out and on the roof in seconds. The craft moved over to the mortuary building and performed the same maneuver only in the back of the building at ground level as there was no roof access there, team B was out and moving also in seconds. Then the craft rose up to 500 feet and waited.

A team was moving, Stone popped the safety off the gas canister and let it empty into the air duck system, it took but moments before they knew it would start affecting anyone in the building.

All donned their breathing masks, and then Rock motioned for them to move into the building.

Flint was first inside down the ladder into the storage room, followed by Boulder, Stone and Rock. Once all were inside they waited one minute then opened the door and went about their mission.

Rock went to the security desk and found the Deputy sleeping just fine as expected, he would wake with a tremendous head ache. He took out his tech devices and began scanning their records, there it was what he was looking for and then purged the computer system of all records of their man being there.

Flint and Boulder moved down to the holding cells and stepped over a Deputy who had fallen to the floor, they found only two cells occupied some old guy sleeping well, and their man.

Using their tools they opened the cell, and picked up their man and began to move back to the roof.

Stone had found the security recording room, and destroyed all evidence of their man being there as well as disabling the cameras so they would have no record of their nights visit. Moments later he left for the roof, meeting Rock in the room gave him the thumbs up and they climbed to the roof.

"Team A ready for extraction." Rock contacted the hovering craft.

Silently the craft appeared and they all entered it, then it returned to its station 500 feet above the mortuary and waited.

Team B had gained access easily through the garage door, they moved quickly through the mortuary finding the cold room where the bodies would be stored.

Water went to the office area and began his job of scrubbing all evidences that related to their mission.

River and Lake began going through the storage wall units checking each one for what they were looking for. River gave thumbs up, he had found one of their men, and then Lake found another in all they found 3 bodies but nothing of the Nemekans.

"Water, this is River we found our guys, but no Neme, you have any idea where else they may have put it?" River said into his communications device.

"Wait one." Water replied.

"Nothing found, the Neme must be in another place no records here."

"Lake, Stream get these bodies ready to move, meet me in the garage." River told them, they gave him the thumbs up. And he left the room.

"Done here everyone meet in the garage." Water said.

"Team B Ready for pick up." Water called to the waiting craft.

The craft descended quickly and quietly, and floated just above the ground, the ramp was lowered and members from team A ran out and assisted team B with loading the bodies of their 3 team members. Once all was done, the pilot of the craft closed the ramp door and ascended to 500 feet in a matter of moments.

"Rock we found no remains of the Neme, must be somewhere else, maybe back at the Sheriffs buildings, we need to look there." Water reported.

Rock nodded and thought, where would he put such a body, in a freezer for sure, he looked at his map of the area, the buildings, yes there that large one by the Sheriff office could have one.

"Lower us back down to the Sheriff's office pilot; we need to recon the building next to it for the Neme body." Rock ordered.

"Confirmed." The Pilot replied and did as ordered in only moments he was next to the large garage building, he hovered again only feet above the ground and lowered the ramp.

Both teams A and B ran to the door, gained entry and began their search of the building; it was a garage style storage building.

Not too long they noticed a large walk in freezer in one corner that must be the place.

Water and Flint were the first ones there, and cut a lock off the door; inside they found the body of the Neme, strange it was in two halves.

They gathered up the body and then all moved to the waiting craft.

Once aboard the pilot getting the thumbs up lets go home sign did just that he ascended to 30,000 feet and headed back to base. Another successful mission under his belt.

* * * * *

Deputy Dalton was a little early for shift change that morning he wanted to give Jones some time to leave a little early in order to meet up with his sweet heart before she started her day shift.

As he entered the building he though it unusually quiet, something seemed out of place.

He did not see Jones sitting at the front desk until he got close enough to look over the counter and there he was. A sleep his head laying on the desktop out cold.

"Hey wake up sleepy head; you know the Sheriff will be upset if he caught you sleeping."

No response. Interesting, so he shook him gently at first then firmly several times before he got Jones to begin to wake up.

"Hey Jones wake up! He about yelled in his ear, what's the deal man, if Sheriff Thompson finds you like this you're gonna get in trouble, so wake up!" Dalton said loudly.

Jones moved then raised his head, and quietly said.

"That you Dalton? not so loud man my head is killing me, feels like I got kicked by a horse, what happened? Why are you here this early?" Jones seemed very out of it, he was trying to clear his mind he was sleepy but why and what happened he could not remember, he did realize that the sun was up so it must be morning, what in the world was going on. His head really hurt.

"Jones, your sleeping on the job that isn't cool man, hey where's Jorgensen at? I'm gonna yell at him for not keeping you awake he shouldn't let you sleep on duty. Now where is he?" Dalton asked him. Half serious half-jokingly as he thought this was funny to a point catching Jones of all people asleep on duty.

"He was last checking on the prisoners, last I remember then you yelling in my ear and shoving me, dude I have no idea what's going on, I feel awful seriously." Jones stammered. He sat up and the world went in circles so he laid his head back on the desk, he was a bit dizzy.

"I'll go find your partner." Dalton said and left Jones to his issues. Man they were gonna get a lecture for this the Sheriff did not put up with this behavior at all. As he walked to the cell area he found Jorgensen on the floor of all places asleep. This was not good.

He bent over and shook Jorgensen until he also woke up.

"What am I doing on the floor, what is going on?" Jorgensen asked groggily.

"I am not sure now; I found you and Jones asleep." Dalton replied worried now.

"I am going to check our prisoners. Something is not right." Dalton said. He stood and went to the cells, he found old George sleeping like a baby, then he went to check the mystery guest and found his cell empty, the door open. He turned and ran for the front desk jumping over Jorgensen who was still trying to sit up against the wall holding his head.

He picked up the phone and dialed the sheriff's phone.

The Sheriff was just sitting down for some cold cereal when his phone range. He noticed it was the office calling.

"This is the Sheriff, everything ok there Jones?" He asked.

"This is Dalton, no we have problems Sheriff you need to get here a.s.a.p.! I found Jones and Jorgensen both sleeping out cold, and the mystery prisoner is gone." Deputy Dalton responded urgently.

"Be right there." Sheriff Thompson replied and hung up.

He grabbed his stuff and was out the door in less than a minute and drove to the Sheriff's office in record time.

He ran into the front desk and saw Jones and Jorgensen both leaning on the counter looking sickly.

Dalton met him.

"Sheriff it seems neither of them remember anything, I found Jones at the desk asleep and Jorgensen down the hall way by the cells on the floor asleep as well, I had to really shake them to get them to wake up, and George is still sleeping. And your prisoner is gone. I have tried to view the security cameras but they have been erased."

Amazing just amazing since the kidnapping this whole deal was getting stranger by the minute, the mystery prisoner gone, what about...

"Dalton I need you to get Bill over at the mortuary to let you in, go see if the bodies we brought off the mountain are still on ice, I need to check our freezer to see if the lizard is still there as well, this is not looking good if what I think happened has happened."

"On my way to Bill's" Dalton said as he darted out the door.

The Sheriff hurried down the hall out the door to the Search and Rescue garage and found the door open; as he entered his fears were realized as he saw the freezer door opened as well. Upon looking inside he found the lizard creature's body gone, missing as well.

What was going on here? How did anyone know they were here... oh darn, I should have thought of that, we ran his fingerprints if anyone was looking for them if they were government related it would tell them exactly where they were, he should have known better, but then how would he have known this would be the result. He walked out and went back to check on his deputies.

Dalton drove up to the mortuary and found Bill outside just about to walk into the building.

"Bill, I need to go in with you wait a second." Dalton said as he got out of his truck.

"What's up Deputy?" Bill asked.

"I just need to check on those bodies we brought off the mountain the other day, make sure they are still here is all."

"Well they are on ice, unless they turned into zombies or something and walked out of here on their own." Bill said comically.

"Fine, just let's go look, we had a break in at the Sheriff's office and our mystery man is missing, gone. Someone broke him out last night."

"Follow me then." Bill said now a little concerned this type of thing did not happen in Beaver Utah.

As they entered the cold room his new fears were realized.

"Yep they took the bodies; see here these were the three drawers they were in. They are definitely gone."

"Let's check the security camera's to see who did the taking" Bill added. And headed to his office.

As Bill entered his office he noted things had been disturbed.

"Well Deputy who ever it was went through my office, and yep they did turn off the security cameras, and it looks like the history for the last few weeks has been erased. I will check my records on the computer but as they are digital I bet they are gone as well." Bill said sadly.

"I am going to go tell the Sheriff, if you find anything relating to this call us, thanks." Dalton said and hurried out the door. This was a professional job that was for sure, they knew what they were doing and got it done.

Dalton met the Sheriff in his office.

"The bodies are gone, and Bill's cameras are like ours no evidence of who did what. These guys were real pro's it seems."

"Same here, the lizard creature is gone as well. Seems they were very thorough indeed. Thanks I have some thinking to do, I doubt there will be any finger prints left by these guys." Sheriff Thompson replied.

"I am going to have Jones and Jorgensen go get checked out at the hospital to see if there are any side effects it would seem who ever visited used something to put these guys to sleep, so better safe than sorry."

"Yes good idea, have them report to me after their checkups." Sheriff Thompson said.

It would seem they have entered a new realm of reality now, some type of secret ops group prowling his mountains, now his town taking his people, alien creatures, this is like a bad sci-fi movie only its true and he is living it. God help the Adair children and all of us. I wish I knew what was really going on here it would help I am sure. Only time will tell.

CHAPTER 34

Rumblings of War

"So calm down Specialist Alpin and tell me again who killed your team mates and the Neme Seenswanee and be clearer this time." General Sills asked the only survivor of Sargent Smiths team.

"Sir, as I said we went to see the entry point 39, when we got there and entered the room we were ambushed, someone was waiting we had no warning until it began and was over in a matter of seconds." Specialist Alpin said and took a breath. He was both glad he had survived and yet found himself feeling guilty that his friends had died and he had not. This is what they must call survivors remorse. What he did know was he wanted some pay back and soon.

"There was a strange man there who killed the Neme, later when they tried to question me he seemed different than the others, he had a strange way about him, and Sir, he knew what the Nemekans were by name, and the use of their weapons and tools, which he removed from the body of Seenswanee. I do not know how he knew I never heard but he knew about the Neme's at least."

Specialist Alpin paused again to reflect and started once more.

"I was almost beaten by the mother of the kids who were taken for intruding in the area; she was really upset I guess that's expected. They did take me down to the county jail were your team found me and the bodies. I did not tell them anything, as soon as they ran my prints I knew I would be on your radar and you could send a rescue team for me, thank you sir. That is my report at least the main part." Specialist Alpin reported and waited for the Generals next round of questions if he had any more.

"Well that seems to sum it up then. Did you hear about them mounting their own rescue attempt of the children?" General Sills asked.

"They seemed to be planning to search the cave system, so yes I would say they were going to go look for the kids, and they went armed as well. I do not know how many were to go but I would not doubt those people trying to find them, have you had any contact with them since that time?" Specialist Alpin replied.

"As a matter of fact yes, not long after your disappearance we had an attack on your sector 18 everyone there was killed, at the time it seemed like the Neme's were the cause, however now I am not sure, the weapon signs looked like the Neme's had attacked us, we are now on full lock down, the Neme's also are riled up with their missing Seenswanee. We have had another intrusion or attack inside the area since.

It would seem we could be on the verge of another large conflict with the Nemekans." General Sills told the Specialist to bring him up to speed as to what was currently happening at the base.

"Do you think the town people took out sector 18, how can a group of hill Billie's from Utah do that, our teams are trained so well, and if they did then they would have had to stage it to look like the Neme's did it, to cause a problem with us and them, wow I wonder if that one guy who knew the Neme's could have done this." Specialist Alpin said to the General and himself as he realizes the gravity of the possible set up by the strange man.

"I have been thinking the same, I think their team is trying to stir up the Neme's and us and then sneak on through as we fight it out blaming each other, not a bad plan at all, get some rest and food in you, then join the security team here with us and arm up. This will most likely get messy before it's all over." General Sills said as he stood up and turned to leave the room.

"Sir will do. When will we start looking for the Utah hill Billie's sir, I would like some pay back." Specialist Alpin asked.

"As soon as we can calm down the Neme's, then we shall have them join us in the search for these trouble makers, and they better pray we find them before the Neme's do." General Sills answered.

General Sills opened the door to the room they were in to see his security team running down the corridor towards him.

"What is the matter?" General Sills asked him when he was close enough.

"General the Neme's are on the attack they have just taken levels 6 and 5 they are about to our location and will have all of level 4 soon, we do not seem to be able to stop them." The Security team member said quickly and in a scared voice.

"Where is the A.N.T. team?" General Sills asked.

"I do not know they could still be over in sector 18's area they are too far away to help us right now that's for sure. We need to move sir, they will be here soon." The security team member said.

Specialist Alpin had overheard and was standing by the two men now.

"Let's move then and figure out where everyone is later." Specialist Alpin said.

"You're right let's move, once we are in a safer area we can ...." General Sills was not able to finish as the hall door in front of him disintegrated before him, once the smoke cleared he saw a host of Neme's coming at them. It was too late to do anything but stand and fight.

The General pointed his side arm an Israeli Desert Eagle .50 cal. with special ammunition that would explode on contact he had made for such an occasion. He open fired at the closet 2 Neme's watching with satisfaction as they both fell mortally wounded, then he rapid fired at the wall of Neme's behind them hitting many.

The Security Team member also was firing into the mass of Neme's still closing on their location, it seemed as soon as 2 or 3 fell more would just step over the bodies and they just kept coming.

Specialist Alpin had taken the full force of several Neme weapons and was mortally wounded on the floor.

Soon the Security team member followed lying dead in his gore.

Only the General seemed un harmed, they did not seem intent on his death but wanted him alive, This was an un nerving thought for the General as he knew what the Neme's were capable of doing to live prisoners, and he would prefer death to that. So he kept firing, kept hitting his targets until he was out of ammunition, then as he went to reload the next clip he was over whelmed by force of numbers and hit in the head for all was now dark and he slipped into the abyss of unconsciousness.

The Council chamber was filled to capacity; standing room only was left so they made a circle around the human leader known as General Sills, who was chained to a post in the center of the room before the council seats.

Garessaee of the Garsar on the council of Nemekans spoke.

"Make sure he is awake we have questions and he must answer fully aware of his situation here."

Agars of the Tooashee a council guard reached down and picked up a bucket of water and threw the water on the General's face and upper body, it was very cold water, he did so with great pleasure he did not like working with these weak humans.

With a gasp of breath the cold had indeed brought the General to full awareness of his area. He looked around and saw many Neme's, he noticed he was before what must be their great council seated in chairs before him. All glaring with hatred at him.

"Garessaee, what is the meaning of this, why have your people broken the treaty and attacked my people?" General Sills spoke firmly.

A gasp of incredibility filled the room with hisses and then followed by murmurs and calls to kill the human.

Garessaee raised his arm for silence.

"Silence we will hear what this leader of the humans has to say, before we pronounce justice upon him."

The room became as quiet and silent as death itself.

"General Sills, it was not us but your warriors who did break the treaty, in the disappearance of our Warrior Seenswanee, and with the unprovoked attack upon Eeeleesssoe who went to search for Seenswanee. Your warriors did attack without warning with your new weapons that were designed to murder us. Your warriors did start this and we shall no longer allow such actions to go unpunished. Justice shall be given. What have you to say General?" Garessaee spoke with a tone of hissing disgust for such treachery that had taken place.

"I know of no such orders to attack your Eeeleesssoe, as for your missing Seenswanee I had just gotten word as to the truth of his disappearance as well as 4 of our own warriors who went with him to inspect sector 39, will you listen to what I must share then?" General Sills said firmly and yet calmly as well he knew they respected courage and honor, and they should hear him out at least.

"I would hear what this human has to say, be it truth or treachery I shall know of it." Eeeleesssoe said as he stood before the man,

General Sills looked at this powerful Etosa before him and saw the great wound he had taken, that must have been the A.N.T. team's new weapon it was effective. He wondered if they were able to escape the takeover of the base with their new weapons, they would be needed to retake the base and put things on an even level once more with the Neme's.

"Who is this that stands before me then?" General Sills asked

"I am Eeeleesssoe who was attacked in your sector 18 by your warriors. It is I who went to see what befell our missing warrior, so tell me then human what became of him." Eeeleesssoe said firmly as he leaned in close to the Generals face snarling and hissing to make his point clear.

"We had gotten word that there was a survivor of the team that was lost, we did find and rescue him from his captivity amongst some outer world law enforcement. They were investigating the loss of several of their children, who had been taken into your science labs from that area. When the lost team was sent to investigate and make sure the outer opening of section 39 was sealed, they were ambushed by a group of humans who did slay our men and your kin Seenswanee.

It was reported that one in their party knew who and what your race is by name and he knew how to use your weapons and tools. I was unable to learn more for your attack did end the life of the only survivor. I am all that is left of who knows the truth, it would seem this outer town sent a rescue mission into the caverns to find their kin, and in the process sought to create a war between the Nemekans and Humans in order to go undetected as we fought each other.

They have used our natural animosity for each other to their betterment; they started the war that we now each suffer for. As we fight each other they walk freely amongst us. This is tactful but not honorable. We must stop our fighting and seek out this number of outer dwellers and when we find them you will find the true killer of Seenswanee amongst them." General Sills responded as strongly as he could.

"The human lies to save his own self." Came a voice from the shadows. Followed by a large Grey Nemekans stepping into the light of the council.

"I say he lies, as they all do to save their own self; he has no honor nor respect for our kind." Akishtoas of the Toomas and a War Chieftain of great renown had spoken.

"General do you speak lies? Or is this truth then, how do you answer Akishtoas." Garessaee said firmly and without emotion.

"I do not lie great Garessaee, I speak truth. I have nothing to gain in lies. I may have nothing to gain by truth either, for by your mood I am surely dead soon enough, no matter what I say." General Sills said as firmly and strong as he could.

"You say these humans of the lost children have entered the underworld to rescue, fight for their kin, this is sensible. For would not anyone one of us do the same, in fact we have now done this for those slain already." Garessaee spoke.

"How is it we have not found them, if this was true no one could go undetected with our patrols, and the humans and our surveillance tools, it is not possible to go undetected?" Akishtoas spoke.

"Maybe so, but did not Eeeleesssoe himself find ways to go undetected by the humans during his own travels, yes it is possible." Garessaee said.

"The evidence of the rescue is still in our computer files if they have not been destroyed. You will see the video of the rescue and recovery of your kin. Who now lies in our own depository for the dead until we were to contact you to return his body for your burial. Send your tech teams and they will find this to be true." General Sills said. He wanted the war to end here at the base; they must see to reason and punish those who have angered them, not his men.

"We shall send the team to do as suggested, if you lie then you have made fools of us, and you General are on trial and shall be greatly punished if you lie, you will suffer death in a very slow and creative way." Akishtoas spoke sneering at the human before him.

"Agars take some techs and see to it, bring us the information here once it is found." Garessaee said.

"It shall be done as you require." Agars spoke with respect and bowed then left to do as ordered.

* * * * *

After what seemed to be hours Agars and his team returned with their findings.

"See here Great Council of the Nemekans, here is the truth, the General is accurate in his statement." Agars spoke and he directed the techs with him to present the video files of the recording from the helmets of the rescue teams they found on the computers of the humans.

All in the council room watched, and they found it was as the General said.

"General it seems you have spoken well, we shall now choose what to do with you, and the humans that have caused us so much trouble." Garessaee spoke evenly.

"One more thing great council, we have discovered more that you need to see." Agar spoke urgently but respectfully.

"So be it show us all your findings so we can let justice be done." Akishtoas said somewhat impatiently.

"See here I will show you that it was the human's mistakes and weakness that did cause the murder of our great warrior Seenswanee. Yes it was the outer crust humans who did kill him, but it was the mistakes of the Generals warriors that did cause it. We found in their reports that the 1st team sent did not hide the opening well, and then had to return to do it the correct way. This leading to the trap where Seenswanee was murdered. It was due to the incompetence of the Generals warriors that originaly caused the problems leading to the war we now have. The Generals in ability to train honorable and good warriors has led to this war, and the deaths of many of our kin. And the General did take many lives as we sought to capture him for questioning did he not, they have created special weapons to murder us, and in our findings they have plans for ruling over the whole of the base of operations here. There was a plan for them to eventually attack and put us into submission to them. This is what we have found Great Council, we find behind the humans open hand of friendship is the other with a knife to cut our throats, it is only time. That is my report." Agars spoke with firm resolve.

The council was very quiet at this time, no one spoke for what seemed a long time.

"So General, it would seem you have been building weapons of war against us is this so?" Akishtoas asked, with a thin grin upon his face.

"We only build weapons to defend ourselves against your warriors if the time were to ever happen and we needed to do so." General Sills responded.

"But I see many designs for new offensive weapons in the report Agars has brought us, it would seem your warriors plan to attempt to enslave or control us, this is what I see." Akishtoas spoke glaring at the General, as he began to pace back and forth before the council.

"You see here a General a Warrior leader of the humans, one who knew they were planning to overpower us in the near future, regardless of the deeds done to Seenswanee the greater crime here is that they were planning to attack us all. This General must stand for this crime against all Nemekans. I demand Justice for such treachery." Akishtoas spoke most eloquently and with the power of the mood and feeling he was in, as a War Chieftain he knew how to stir the blood of his kin, and he was doing it now. These humans, needed to learn a great lesson this day. That forever they will be subject to their superiors the Nemekans.

"General Sills, these are very strong charges against you, how do you respond." Garessaee spoke carefully; he knew where Akishtoas wanted to go with this.

"I shall not deny we created weapons to defend ourselves against you. But I know of no plan to conquer your race, that is a creation of Akishtoas own twisted mind." General Sills responded.

"Enough, we shall suspend these new accusations until we shall deal with these trespassers who did kill Seenswanee, and we shall deal with them now. The Generals intrigue or that of his leaders can be dealt with once this is finished. Put him in a prison cell and keep him alive he will be questioned fully. We have the location of the outer crust town who did murder our kin, and who did openly set our two races against each other to cause death amongst ourselves as they sneak into our world as thieves.

Let us punish first our known enemies then we shall deal with the rest at a future time." Gleenas of the Toomas had spoken, he was a large grey of the ruling clan and he was respected and was the true head of this council.

"So let it be, so the Great Gleenas of the Toomas has shared his wisdom with us, so shall it be done as he has said." Akishtoas spoke reverently as he bowed to Gleenas.

"General Sills, tell us what is the number of humans that do infest this town who has caused as you say this terrible crime?" Akishtoas asked.

"I shall not, they should be left alone, only those involved need to be punished not the whole of the town." General Sills replied.

"We shall discover for ourselves then, Remove him from our presence." Akishtoas said with satisfaction.

"Summon all the great war chieftain's, we shall send an army against this small human town, and they will become an example to all the Earth what will happen when you choose to openly rebel and use lies and deceit to murder our kin. We shall stop the war here and hold our current lines of battle, but we shall regroup and plan the extermination of these outer humans. Gleenas has spoken in his wisdom." Garessaee spoke with a sense of finality and urgency.

"Agars go and see the human's computers and find us the number of humans living there and any other useful knowledge that will assist us in their punishment." Akishtoas requested.

The General was removed from the room as ordered, and the war chieftain's came one by one until all the clans were present.

Agar returned and shared the information he has been requested to find. He stood before the Great War Chieftains.

"There is an estimate of less than 4,000 human's including the adults and children. There are very few of the Sheriff's men to defend the area, it should be easy for your warriors to deal justice to them." Agar told them.

It was then planned that only 300 Nemekans warriors would be needed to exterminate such a small group of humans, this also would set an example of how powerful they were compared to the small and weaker humans. This would send a message that all must submit or be destroyed. They would be awakened to the facts that the Nemekans have indeed been on Earth a very long time, and were the dominate species on the planet. They would finally be out in the open, no longer needing to hide in the caverns any more. It was time, the world was theirs, and now they would let the humans realize this.

"Let it begin, gather your warriors and travel to the field of battle, this Beaver, Utah and let no warrior return until the town is no more. As for any survivors you may take prisoners as you like, bring as many of the young ones for some will become servants others we shall have a wonderful harvest of their essence." Gleenas had spoken and was pleased at the thought of both punishing and refreshing their human slaves, as well as a fresh harvest.

All bowed in agreement and left to fulfill Gleenas's commands as they prepared to finally treat these humans as nature had intended, the blood lust of battle began to swell in their chests as they went to gather their warriors.

* * * * *

About 1 hour after the great council meeting, Akishtoas opened the cell room door where General Sills was being held. It was now time for him to discover what other treachery the humans had planned.

"So general, shall we be plain one with another, you will answer my questions or you will suffer and in the end answer them anyway. So what shall it be? The easy path or the hard one?" Akishtoas asked. He hoped the General would be stubborn he would enjoy the questioning better if he choose the hard path.

"I shall not allow you to question me Akishtoas, your heart is black and I shall not respond, nor shall I allow myself to tell you anything more that will help your insane new war you desire to wage against humanity." General Sills spoke in a strong and determined voice.

"You will tell me what I desire, you know you will, you are aware of some of our methods that are very effective however listen well. I must keep you alive for the moment and I shall, however we shall begin with removing your legs one at a time, then seal the wound thus keeping you quite alive. Then little General you will watch as I feast upon your flesh one leg at a time, then I shall beat you with your own bones, and you will speak, you will tell me what I desire to know. If not then I shall continue to your arms. By then you will cry and tell all, for such all have been broken in the past, none have needed any further methods.

"All break and so shall you. Then you will be kept alive as long as the council desires as an example of your treachery and evil designs upon our clans. You will be put on display before our clans so all can see how weak your race of beings really is. That General is what we shall do as our warriors exterminate your people one town at a time." Akishtoas said in an evil slithering voice. Very well pleased with himself for it looked as if the General had turned a few shades whiter than usual. He motioned for the guards in the room who were standing on either side of him to take the human and strap him down to the metal table that would be used during the questioning.

The guards grabbed the General lifted him off the ground and placed him forcefully upon the table, he tried to fight them but it was useless as they were so much stronger than him. Soon they had him strapped down and unable to move. They both then stood off a few feet and waited for the questioning to begin.

"Do whatever your evil heart wants, I will not speak! Not a word, I know you will just kill me later eventually." General Sills said defiantly. He knew his life was about to end, he knew how irrational these Neme's thought and also how evil they could be to humans. He did have one last move available to him and he was determined not to suffer for the twisted pleasure of this Neme.

"Well then since you have chosen the path of most resistance let us begin then, I am pleased you have made this choice easy for me as

I have not had a good meal yet this day." Akishtoas said pleased with himself. He reached into a drawer under the table and pulled out a large knife he would use this to slowly saw off one of the legs. He then pulled out another device that would be used to cauterize the wound.

General Sills knew what he had to do, and with that knowledge he almost grinned as he knew it would take away the power from this Neme. He moved his tongue to the back of his mouth and with the tip flipped the last molar on the bottom left, it moved more easily than he thought, once completed he moved the now loose tooth to the right side of his mouth and bit down hard, breaking the capsule and with that he swallowed. He felt himself slipping into darkness, into death and moments later he knew nothing but darkness.

Akishtoas looked over at the Generals face so he could watch with pleasure as he began his fun, he noticed the General smile at him then he heard a cracking sound, he had bitten on something. He knew it must be a poison of some kind. He reached for the human's mouth in an effort to prevent his death so soon. And as he did he knew as well it was too late. Whatever the General knew or had planned was now left to the other dimensions as he was now quite dead.

"So the human has chosen a warriors death then, so be it. You two stay with the body, stand outside the door and let no one else in, until I return or send you word. I shall go and tell Gleenas what has taken place." Akishtoas said, a little disappointed but then humans were unpredictable at times.

There would be plenty of others soon to entertain himself with, he was sure the warriors would bring a plentiful catch from their battle that will soon take place. With that he walked down the corridor to give his report to Gleenas.

End Book # 1 of the series

Thanks for buying my story on E-book media or physical print
I hope you enjoyed the journey thus far.
Book #2 is in process.

Contact information
Author / Pre publishing cover Art Idea, Stephen T. Huls

Editing & Proof Reading
Stephen T. Huls
Laura A. Frick, Huls & Kalecia L. Huls

Email: pureheartguide@hotmail.com

http://levantasshuesa.blogspot.com
This is the official web site for the books

If you liked this story let us know here and all your friends.

Like us on FaceBook:
"Pure Heart Guide Book Series"

© 2014 All rights reserved by Stephen T. Huls